"Elizabeth English stakes her claim [...] [Sc]ot-
tish Borders with a story rich in love and hist[...]"
—Miran[...] [Ja]rrett

"Full of intrigue, action, and Scottish folklore." —*Booklist*

"Will delight historical romance readers . . . with a feel for
the intrigue of the fourteenth century through a strong cast,
especially the heroine. Energetic Elizabeth English demon-
strates to her audience that if her debut is any indication,
she has quite a long career ahead of her."
—*Midwest Book Review*

"An enjoyable and fast-paced romance . . . It kept me turning pages right through to the very end . . . with it's twisting plot and strong characters." —*All About Romance*

"Interesting twists and turns . . . well-crafted."
—*The Best Reviews*

"Impressive . . . [Ms. English's] talent is evident in her
ability to weave a remarkable story . . . beautifully rendered with vivid imagery. She captures the very spirit of
the Scottish people, depicting them very true to the time."
—*Love Romances*

"[A] stimulating setting, compelling characters, pleasing
plot, air of mystery, and sense of hope. [It] opened my eyes
to the talent of Elizabeth English."
—*Crescent Blues Book Reviews*

Titles by Elizabeth English

THE  Linnet

Elizabeth English

BERKLEY SENSATION, NEW YORK

This is a work of fiction. Names, characters, places, and incidents either are the product of the author's imagination or are used fictitiously, and any resemblance to actual persons, living or dead, business establishments, events, or locales is entirely coincidental.

THE LINNET

A Berkley Sensation Book / published by arrangement with the author

PRINTING HISTORY
Berkley Sensation edition / January 2004

ISBN: 0-425-19388-8

BERKLEY SENSATION™
Berkley Sensation Books are published by The Berkley Publishing Group, a division of Penguin Group (USA) Inc., 375 Hudson Street, New York, New York 10014. BERKLEY SENSATION and the "B" design are trademarks belonging to Penguin Group (USA) Inc.

PRINTED IN THE UNITED STATES OF AMERICA

10 9 8 7 6 5 4 3 2

For my sister Katie
who always believed in me

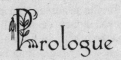

Prologue

Between one day and the next, spring came to the borderlands. It arrived without warning after a week of rain, transforming the gray brown winter moor to a brilliant tapestry of green and gold and purple beneath an azure sky. The air was mild, rich with the heady scents of thyme and heather as the earth woke from its long sleep.

Three riders moved across the springtime landscape: two men, one old, one young, and a golden-haired lass who was singing as she rode between them. It was a pretty sound, for her voice was bright and clear, and the song was a merry little ballad, one she had composed over the long, cold days when it seemed that spring would never come.

Now it was here, all around her, and she was glad to be outdoors, away from smoky fires and dull responsibility. For this one day she had abandoned her newfound maturity, tucked it away with the long skirts that tripped her when she ran. She was just herself, clad in her old kirtle, a bit too short but far more comfortable than velvet. More practical, as well, for walking round the village. Today she meant to visit every cottage, just as her mother used to do.

She glanced back at the laden donkey following behind. The villagers would be pleased by the gifts she brought: manchet bread and red wine for the sick, a good joint of mutton for the headman and his wife, candles, currants, flour—even honey cakes, still warm from the oven when she packed them an hour ago.

"Mmm," she said, drawing a long breath. "Cowslips! Can ye smell them?"

She looked up, one hand shading her eyes against the sun. A kestrel swept in slow circles above the moor, wings outstretched to catch the wind, its high, keening call both beautiful and plaintive. *Ah,* she thought, *if I could but get that sound into a song . . .* And she was off again, busy trying words and melody together, a pastime that constantly enchanted.

After a moment, though, she fell silent, frowning as a new scent drifted across the bracken, one that did not belong out here at all.

The smell of smoke.

Dawn was just breaking when Fergus McInnes walked across the moor, headed for the village of Mallow. From his cave, perched high up in the Chevron Hills, he had seen the smoke the day before and started out as soon as he was able.

The raiding was a fact of life, though it was not one Fergus could accept. The gain of a few sheep or cows was not worth the price in human suffering. But a man could only do what he could do, and at least he could bring help and comfort to the victims.

He stooped and picked up a thick wax candle from the ground, turning it in his hand. Beyond it lay another, and a woolen shawl. The bracken was blanched, the vivid hues of heather, thyme, and pansy dusted with a fine white coating. Flour, Fergus realized, taking a few steps forward, blowing from a sack that had split open. Frowning, he followed the trail . . . and then he saw the lass.

He knew her only by the ring on her finger and the bright hair tangled in the bracken. But for them, she could have been any lass, her clothing torn and her face so battered that her own mother could not have named her. Yet still she breathed.

Once Fergus had made certain no bones were broken, he lifted her in his arms. For all his seventy years, he was still able to carry her, for she was very slight, and anger lent him strength. In the event, he did not have far to go. Less than a mile from the spot, her father found them.

He had come alone, no doubt fearing what had happened. A prideful man he was, too proud to let any other eyes look upon the ruin of his daughter. He was off his destrier in a flash, running forward, but a few paces from them, he stopped, as though fearing to come closer.

"Is she . . . ?"

"Nay, my lord," Fergus said.

Lord John Darnley had done his share of raiding across the border, leaving many a village in the same condition as the one still spilling acrid smoke into the fresh spring air. Fergus cared no more for him than he did for Laird Kirallen, Darnley's ancient enemy. Both were brutal men, implacable in their hatred for one another. Even so, he could not help but pity Darnley now.

Down on his knees, tears pouring down his face, he reached a shaking hand to touch one strand of his daughter's hair.

"Will she—*can* she live?"

"There is some hope. But we need to get her home."

"Home?" Darnley drew a shaking breath and wiped his eyes. "Nay, not home . . ." He looked about, eyes narrowed, and came to his decision. "The White Sisters," he said. "We'll take her there."

"But why? She should be—"

"One look at her, and they'll ken—the news will be all over the border by sunset."

"Ye canna hope to hide this."

"I can. I shall. No one will ever know." He raised his head, and his eyes burned into Fergus's. "Swear to me," he said. "Swear ye will not tell of this."

"My lord, that is hardly—"

Darnley leaped to his feet, sword flashing in his hand. "Do it, *taibhsear,*" he snarled, "or I will kill ye here and now. A binding oath."

Tight-lipped, Fergus swore, shifting the weight of the unconscious lass in his arms. Darnley kept his blade at the healer's throat.

"Ye will make her well again."

"I will do my best," Fergus said. "But I fear 'tis not so simple. Even if she lives . . . oh, my lord, do not expect her to ever be the same."

Darnley's face twisted. "Maude," he cried, "I swear— by all that's holy I swear I will avenge ye. I will kill them all, every one of the bastards—"

"My lord," Fergus said sharply, "that will not help her."

"There is no help for her. Not now. There is only vengeance."

The Chevron Hills, 1379

Fergus groaned and stirred upon his pallet, his mind rising from the depths of sleep to skim the surface of consciousness.

It was a dream, he told himself. Just a memory of a tragedy that happened long ago. Yet Darnley's words still echoed through his mind.

Only vengeance. How many men had died, how many lives had been destroyed as Darnley sought his vengeance? Lady Maude had lived, though it had been a near thing. She was a strong lass, though, far stronger than she looked. Over the next months—first at the convent and then, when the worst of the bruises had healed, at Aylsford Keep—Fergus had come to love her as his own.

"A name." Darnley had demanded, pleaded, cajoled her for the information. "Just name them. Surely, Maude, ye can do that." But she could not. At some time during the wasting fever that had so nearly claimed her life, she had put the memories of that day aside, locked them away until even she could not find them. A young man, brown-haired, with several others. That was all that she could say.

And so the slaughter went on, Darnley striking out blindly in the madness of his grief. But nothing could ever bring back the daughter he had loved so well. Once time had drawn its healing mantle over the worst shock, Fergus hoped to help her find herself again. But he never had the chance.

It had wrenched Fergus's heart to part from her, though he agreed that a change of scene could only help. Get her straight away from this place, most of all away from Lord Darnley and his endless vows of vengeance. So she was bundled off to London to stay with her uncle for a time. The parting had been hard, for she clung to Fergus, weeping, and it took all his strength to send her off with a smile.

Three years later, he heard of her return. He listened without comment to the tales of Lady Maude, who made enemies wherever she might go. Cold, she was, and haughty, with a temper so sharp that even bold Lord Darnley was said to walk in terror of his daughter.

It was rumored that when the chance came for Darnley to make peace with his ancient enemy, Laird Kirallen, Lady Maude refused to make the marriage. It was for her sake—most likely at her order—that Darnley attempted to deceive the Kirallens by sending his baseborn daughter in Maude's place. It was said, as well, that Lady Maude had nothing but contempt for her half sister, and had sent that poor girl off to what could have been her death with no more than a shrug.

My child, Fergus thought when he heard the tales, *my poor, sweet, gallant lass, what has become of ye? Why, why do you not send?*

It was no thanks to Lady Maude that the peace had at last been made between the families. Too proud to accept marriage to a Kirallen herself, she'd had no qualms about sacrificing her young brother as a hostage. No sooner was the bargain struck than she was off again to London. Fergus had never heard the tale told that it did not end, "And good riddance to her."

It seemed that only Fergus mourned her. Still he kept her in his prayers, always hoping that one day he might receive the summons he had awaited for so long. But it never came.

Fergus sighed at the memory, then turned over and drifted back to sleep. And dreamed that he was walking across the moor, headed for the village of Mallow . . .

One

In the hour before dawn, Ronan Fitzgerald bolted out of sleep. He was halfway across the cave before his eyes were open.

His master, Fergus, was gasping, struggling to sit upright, one hand pressed hard against his chest. Ronan knelt swiftly by his side.

"Fergus, what is it? Can you speak?"

Fergus shook his head mutely, and Ronan grasped his free hand in a comforting grip while feeling for his pulse. Too fast, too thin, but steady.

"Do you have pain?"

Fergus shook his head again. There was no pain, not this time, just the heartbeat galloping like a runaway horse and a terrible tightness in his chest.

"Good, then, that's very good," Ronan murmured, his voice low and soothing, "just be calm, take it slowly, one breath at a time . . ."

Beneath Fergus's palm, his heartbeat began to slow, and the iron band about his chest relaxed its hold. He drew a shuddering breath and fell back against the sheepskin.

"Better, then?" Ronan wiped the beads of perspiration from Fergus's brow with a cloth. "Rest now, and I'll get you a warm drink."

Fergus drew a long breath, relief washing over him. Not tonight, then. Soon, but not tonight. It was only the dream that had startled him from sleep, not the hand of death. He lay staring at the roof of the cave and tried to weave the wispy fragments of the dream into a pattern.

All at once it came to him, sharp and clear, etched in vivid strokes across his mind. God help them all, it had not only been a dream of a tragedy long past. There had been more. What he had just seen had not yet happened . . . but it would.

The peace was nearly over. What had seemed an end was no more than a pause in the long history of hatred between the Darnleys and Kirallens. *I should have gone to Lady Maude four years ago,* Fergus thought. *I was a fool to wait for her to send.*

Poor lass, he thought, *poor lass, such a burden to bear all alone. It is no wonder she has nearly reached the end of her endurance. She will die,* he thought with blinding certainty, *before the summer's end, and then the carnage will begin again.*

She must be saved, he thought. *I must do something.* He half rose from his pallet, then fell back with a gasping sob. He could not possibly survive a journey to London, where the lady dwelt while her father fought in France. They would return to Aylsford Keep, for he had seen it with the sight that never lied. But the same inner certainty told him that he would not meet Lady Maude again.

Why show this to me now? he cried in silent protest. *Now, when it is too late for me to go to her as I should have done four years ago?*

"How are you doing, Fergus?" Ronan called. "Are you still with me?"

"I'm well enough. Just resting."

Fergus's eyes narrowed as he studied his apprentice.

Aye, it was too late for him to go to Lady Maude. But it was not too late for Ronan.

He watched as Ronan blew the fire into life and pushed the heavy iron pot over the flame. With swift, sure hands he selected various herbs and bottles from the shelves and laid them on the table. Foxglove, Fergus saw, nodding to himself, to spur a failing heart. Herbe yve, as well, he noted with approval, a sovereign remedy for a disturbance of the nerves.

Ronan was intent upon his work, one hand impatiently brushing the dark hair from his eyes as the other moved from table to pot, crumbling herbs into the heating wine. Fergus wasn't sure what was going into the mixture now, but that did not worry him. It had been months since he felt the need to oversee this part of his apprentice's training.

It is not enough, a voice said sternly in Fergus's mind, *a* taibhsear *must be more than a healer.*

He is still young, Fergus comforted himself, *scarce five and twenty, and but halfway through his training. A dangerous time for a man like Ronan, cleverer than anyone around him but without the wisdom to see how much he does not ken. Time will teach him better; it always does. . . .*

Time. The one thing Ronan needed most . . . the one thing he would not have. Not if Fergus's vision had been true. The time was coming—was nearly here—when Ronan would hold the fate of many in his hands.

"Here you are," Ronan said, handing him the cup. "Drink it all, now, while 'tis warm."

"When I am gone—" Fergus began.

"Whisht, now, don't be talking like that. Once the weather breaks, you'll be feeling stronger."

"No lies, lad. Did I no tell ye from the start that there would be no room for lies between us?"

Ronan bowed his head, silently acknowledging Fergus's words. For the truth was that Fergus was dying. He was dying easily, as such things went, and no man could ask for better care. But he was dying just the same.

"I'm sorry," he said gently. "I ken this isna easy for ye. I didna expect to be leaving ye so soon."

"And you shouldn't be," Ronan burst out. "You say I have this great gift for healing, but what good is it if I can do no more than sit and watch you die?"

"Stop that," Fergus said sharply. "Ye know better—and if ye do not, then I have wasted all my time!"

"I'm sorry," Ronan said at once. "You're right, of course, I do know better, but . . . it's only . . ."

Slowly, carefully, Fergus reached out to touch Ronan's hand. "I will miss ye, too."

He sighed as Ronan looked away, unwilling—or unable—to acknowledge his own grief. Either way, it was not good. A *taibhsear* must face his feelings squarely, not sweep them out of sight as though they were some shameful weakness.

"You rest now," Ronan murmured, tucking the coverlet more closely about Fergus's throat. "I will be fine. Don't fear for me."

But Fergus *did* fear for him. Ronan was not ready for this challenge. He was a gifted healer, to be sure, with an uncanny knack of grasping every fact that came his way. Astronomy, anatomy, herb lore—oh, he knew them all and more. But the deeper mysteries were still just that to Ronan.

The lad had his share of gifts, to be sure, if only he would use them. Soon into his apprenticeship, Ronan had taken up Fergus's own dagger and recounted the circumstances of Fergus's receiving it. He had described Fergus's uncle, a man dead these fifty years, with unerring accuracy, repeated the exact words he had said when handing it to Fergus, described the thrill of astonished pride Fergus had felt when his fingers closed around the hilt. A knack, Ronan had said with a shrug, a trick that served no purpose. And as far as he was concerned, that was the end of it. He had refused to ever attempt it again, just as he refused to use the scrying bowl or rune stones.

Even in ritual he maintained a wary distance, viewing the experience with cool detachment. But unless he could break through that detachment, he would never make a *taibhsear*. For that, he would need his entire being, heart and mind and soul. But to Ronan, the heart was but a lump of flesh, the mind a tool for grasping facts, and the soul . . .

Oh, Ronan could go on about the soul for hours. He could quote entire passages of Plato, Aristotle, Aquinas, and Avicenna on the subject without glancing at his notes. It wasn't only their wisdom Ronan admired, but their manner of expressing it. Step by step, idea by idea, they supported their arguments with flawless logic, each principle building on the one before and marching in a straight line to the next. To Fergus, it seemed they would take the mysteries of the universe and divide them into pieces, each one easily digested by the mind.

But the *taibhsear*'s path led in the opposite direction, and it did not go in a straight line at all. It wound round and round, a spiral leading ever inward. The only way to understand existence was to experience it with mind and body, soul and heart and spirit, not breaking it to pieces but ever striving to embrace the whole.

"Ronan," he said urgently, laying a hand on the younger man's arm. "Listen to me. Ye canna divide the world—or the people in it—and label them as good or evil. 'Tis not so simple."

"I know, I know," Ronan murmured, "rest now, and—"

" 'Tis the brightest light that casts the darkest shadow, but shadow is in the pattern, too. Light and dark," Fergus insisted, lacing his fingers. "Together."

Ronan nodded, stifling a yawn. He had heard this all before, for such discussions had made up the earliest part of his training. But Fergus was sick—

Dying, he is dying, at least admit it to yourself.
—very sick, and sick men were prone to rambling.
"I hear you," he said clearly. "I understand."
"Ye do not understand at all," Fergus snapped, sounding like his old self. "And I canna change what must be, though I wish . . . well, 'tis no matter what I wish."
"It's all right," Ronan said, "I understand about the shadows. They may seem frightening, but they only have the power that we give them. The light will always prevail."
He believed what he was saying, Fergus had no doubt of that, but the words were as empty as a lesson learned by rote.
How can I do this to him? he thought, his heart aching with a different pain. *He isn't ready; this could break him—and yet I must send him in my place. I must. And I must send him all but blind, for I have sworn a binding oath to Darnley.*
"Ronan, there is something ye must do for me."
"More wine? Or are you chilled? I could—"
"No, nothing like that. Sit down, ye make me nervous hovering about. This is something else entirely. Something only ye can do."
"Name it," Ronan said at once. "Whatever it is, you have my word it will be done."

Two

When Lady Maude Darnley entered the solar, eight women rose to their feet as though pulled upright by invisible strings. "Good day, my lady," they murmured in unison as they dropped into their curtsies. They straightened as one and stood motionless, awaiting her response.

Maude let the moment spin out. Yesterday it had taken six repetitions before she was satisfied with their performance; the day before, it had been nine, and they had yet to perform the simple ritual correctly. And today . . .

She nodded. "Good afternoon."

An audible sigh of relief rippled through the chamber. The women sat down again and took up their work as Maude seated herself before her tapestry frame.

They had not been perfect. That chit Elena had not smiled with her greeting, and her mother, Lady Cullin, never *would* learn to curtsy with any grace. But they had come a long way in the fortnight since Maude had returned to Ayslford with her father. Then, not one of them had understood the proper way to greet their lady.

Glancing around, Maude saw that the solar was in good order, each woman's work folded neatly by her seat. Aromatic rushes covered the floor, and the candles burned evenly in freshly polished stands. A small brazier stood in one corner to warm the chamber.

Maude's bower had been built to face southwest, with a number of windows set into the slightly rounded walls. Every shutter was closed tight, but late afternoon sunlight sent questing fingers through the chinks, tiny shafts of brightness that held bits of chaff and dust suspended in their depths.

All was as it should be, as Maude needed it to be. The pattern was maintained. This morning she had seen Father to inquire what he would like for supper. He had said he did not care, just as he always did, but he was pleased that Maude had asked. Then down to the kitchens for the daily row with Cook, and after that a visit to the steward. Every chamber was spotless, the linen fresh. Now it was time for sewing.

Next was supper in the hall, perhaps a game of tables by the fire. Only then would she be free to retire to her chamber, shut the door, and wait for the next day to begin.

And the next. And the one after that. Each day following the other in an unchanging round, every one perfectly predictable.

She touched the keys hanging from her girdle and settled the golden circlet more firmly about her brow. She was well gowned, her hair looped in shining braids over her ears, the lady of Aylsford Keep going about her daily rounds. There would be no more sleeping the day away, rising only to eat, not bothering to comb her hair or change her shift. The last few weeks in London had been very bad, but that was all behind her now. She was home, and everything would be different.

She would be different. She was certain of it. So long as she maintained the pattern.

"How goes the tapestry, lady?" Lady Cullin asked politely.

"It goes very well."

There was a faintly audible sniff from Lady Nixon. She and the others had offered several times to take a corner of the tapestry and speed the work along. Sulks had resulted when Maude refused, but she had no intention of letting any of these ham-handed women touch her creation. This would be her work, made to her design and stitched by her alone.

A handspan of the tapestry was finished, not enough to show the pattern. Only the tip of a bloody claw and a streak of crimson flame shone bright against gray silk.

Maude had started one much like it years ago, only to give it away in a burst of misplaced confidence. How eager she had been to cast off all the trappings of her former life and start afresh in London, how certain she would never see this place again!

Ah, well, she thought, plunging the needle through the linen, she had been wrong about that, just as she had been wrong about so many things back then.

" 'Tis a fine day, Lady Maude," one of the women said, breaking into Maude's reverie. A frown creased Maude's brow as the woman rose, throwing open the shutters.

"Oh, aye, it is! Please, lady, can we no go to the garden?"

Maude glanced up from her work. A spear of sunlight invaded the cool dimness of the solar, and a cool, sweet-scented breeze rushed in, catching the pile of silks beside her seat to send them drifting to the floor.

"I do not care to sit outdoors."

The girl turned from the window. "Oh, but lady, if ye would only come and see! The sun is out and the day is—"

"Please take your seat."

Elena Cullin flopped onto her stool with a gusty sigh and took up her sewing.

"Elena."

The girl looked up, lower lip pushed out, the very picture of injured innocence. Maude caught her eye and held it as the seconds ticked slowly by, until Elena's face was poppy red, and her lips began to tremble.

"Have I not said before that I prefer to sit indoors? Perhaps if you spent the evening in your chamber, reflecting on the instruction I have given you, your memory will improve."

The girl bent her head. "Aye, my lady."

There was no talk after that, just the sound of scissors clacking and the occasional rustle as the younger women shifted in their seats. The silence was not right, Maude thought, a faint stir of fear fluttering in her belly. This was the time for the women to talk among themselves, sharing their tedious little tales of suitors and husbands and children.

"You are almost finished with your gown, Lady Cullin?" Maude asked.

"Aye," Lady Cullin answered, holding up a shapeless swath of blue wool. "I don't doubt it will be ready for Maisry's churching. I saw her yestere'en and she's out to here—" She measured an improbable distance from her belly. "—and her ankles are that swollen she can scarce set foot to ground. I told her . . ."

Maude stopped listening. She had done her duty; the pattern was restored. As though her question had broken some spell, the others all began to chatter.

Maude's seat faced the open window, giving her a clear view of blue sky and rolling moor. She considered ordering the shutters closed or turning her chair so her back was to the window, but to do either would provoke a host of questions and complaints she was not prepared to deal with.

Keep your mind on your work, she told herself. *Build*

*the slope stitch by stitch, a darker shade here to bring
out the sharpness of the rocks, perhaps a bit of green
just there. . . .*

The breeze blew against her face, carrying the scents
of springtime; wet earth drying beneath the sun, the sharp
tang of the moors, the smell of cowslips . . .

No. Not cowslips. Surely it was too early for them
yet. The needle began to shake in her hand, and her next
stitch went awry. *Don't stop,* she told herself. *Keep going. You can pick it all out later.* She sewed feverishly,
stabbing the needle blindly into the fabric with fingers
grown slippery with sweat.

It was too hot in here, too close. Surely the others
must feel it! She raised her head to look at them, but they
were dim and insubstantial.

"No," she whispered. "No, not now—"

All at once there was no chamber, no women, no tapestry before her. There was only blinding sunlight, the
rolling moor, and the endless sky above. The scent of
cowslips was all around her, and from above came the
high keening of a hawk.

Then she was choking, coughing, turning her head
from the acrid scent of burning feathers.

"There, she's coming round," Lady Cullin was saying,
waving the feathers more vigorously beneath her nose.
"Lady Maude, can ye hear me?"

Maude pushed her hand away and sat up. "What happened?" she asked, pretending puzzlement.

"Ye swooned. Do ye have a pain?"

"No, I feel well enough." Maude forced herself to
smile wryly. "Just foolish. Father Aidan warned me
against fasting overlong."

They looked at one another, brows raised. Maude
could hardly blame them; it was a clumsy lie. This was
not Windsor Castle, it was Aylsford Keep, where nothing
was kept private. Pattern or no pattern, Maude refused to

set foot into the chapel, a lapse that had been noticed long ere now.

"You may all go," she said. " 'Tis nearly time for supper."

A mistake, she realized at once, another rent in the pattern. The women began to cluck at her like so many chickens in a barnyard. "Are ye certain ye are well?" they asked. "Should we stay with ye—call Dame Becta— bring ye bread and honey?"

No, she answered, no and no again. She would be fine now, everything was fine. She hardly knew what she was saying, but it must have been convincing, because they all began to leave. Lady Cullin stopped at the window.

"There, ye see, foolish lass," she scolded her daughter, "our lady was wise to keep us in. Spring weather is always chancy."

Looking past her, Maude saw a flash of lightning split the darkening sky before Lady Cullin pulled the shutters closed.

Alone, Maude stood, feeling slightly dizzy, and opened them again. A gust of air rushed past her, extinguishing the candles in their holders. Rain blew in sheets across the moor, and the mist rolled in from the north, shrouding everything in gray until the landscape vanished into blankness.

It seemed that Aylsford Keep stood alone in some enchanted land, cut off from the ordinary world where people hurried about, caught up in their small concerns. Once Maude had thought to take her place in that busy world, but now she knew she could not escape her fate. Here she belonged, and here she would remain, like a spirit bound to one place forevermore.

I am my own ghost.

The thought rose unbidden in her mind, and all at once she began to shake with fear.

"God help me," she whispered. "God help me, please help me, send Fergus back again—" Over and over she repeated it, until the words ran together in a senseless stream of sound, inaudible against the wind.

A mocking voice spoke clearly in her mind: *"God? Help you? How ridiculous!"*

It *was* ridiculous, and she was an utter fool. She began to laugh and found she could not stop, until the sound was lost in the shrieking of the wind, and she could not tell if the moisture streaming down her cheeks was rain or tears.

She forced the shutters closed again and leaned her brow against the wood. "Chin *up,*" she ordered herself fiercely. "You are a Darnley."

She groped her way across the darkened bower and stopped inside the door to wipe her face, pat her hair, touch the keys hanging on her belt. She was all right now. She was fine.

But for how long? she wondered wearily. A week? An hour? Where would she be the next time it happened? How long before it all began again, just as it had in London: the stares and pointing fingers, whispered conversations quickly silenced when she walked into a room. How long until the folk of Aylsford knew their lady was a madwoman?

She pushed the thought aside, for there were no answers to her questions—or none that she dared think about. It was far safer not to think at all, but just maintain the pattern. Now it was time for supper, followed by a game of tables by the fire. Then she could go to her chamber. . . .

Shoulders straight, head high, she opened the door and stepped out into the corridor.

hree

This is a *cold place*, Ronan thought, standing outside Lord John Darnley's chamber and waiting for the servant to announce him. Every nerve was alive, sending an unmistakable message to his brain: *Leave, get out of here right now.*

I hope you knew what you were doing, Fergus. I'm trusting you had good reason to send me here. Because I'd rather be anywhere but where I am right now.

Lord John Darnley might make a good subject for a song, but he was not a man Ronan particularly wanted to meet in person, let alone be bound to in any way at all. If his instincts hadn't told him that much, there was the matter of Ronan's friendship for Laird Kirallen, who had—quite understandably—been most unhappy when they had parted this morning.

Four years ago Darnley had ambushed Laird Kirallen's elder brother and stabbed him in the back. No matter what hostilities had existed between the families at the time, there was no word for it but murder. And that was neither the beginning nor the end of Darnley's treachery.

No, Jemmy Kirallen had not been happy. He had been coolly distant when he said that Ronan must of course do as he pleased. His lady, Alyson, had been more worried than angry at Ronan's defection. Ronan did not want to hurt either of them, but how could he explain what he did not understand himself?

Even young Haddon Darnley had looked on him with surprise when he learned that Ronan was off to Aylsford to offer his services to Haddon's father, newly returned from a lengthy sojourn in France. Haddon, who was now being fostered by the Kirallens—a polite way of saying Haddon was a hostage to the peace—was devoted to his foster family.

Christ's wounds, what a muddle it all is, Ronan thought, pacing the chamber and peering out the window. *And here I am, an Irishman, blundering into the midst of some ancient quarrel that has naught to do with me.*

But not for long, he reminded himself. *Just do as Fergus asked, and I am free.* He imagined himself riding down the road stretched before him, headed toward some place he'd never seen. It didn't matter where, it never had; he'd pick a ship for its name as he'd done sometimes before and let it carry him where it would. . . .

"He'll see ye now," the squire said, gesturing Ronan into the inner chamber.

Ronan shivered as he crossed the threshold. Though outside the sun warmed the earth to springtime, a winter chill clung to the stone walls, seeping through the thick, rich hangings. A stand of half a dozen candles stood close to the hearth, yet the room was sunk in gloom.

Ronan wasn't sure what he had been expecting in Lord Darnley, but it was not the man who sat before the hearth, one bandaged leg resting on a stool. Darnley's hair was heavily streaked with gray, his shoulders stooped, his face scored with heavy lines. His scarlet robe, though fine, hung loose upon his frame, as though it had been made for a larger man. *He's so old,* Ronan thought. *I wonder what's the trouble with that leg?*

"So ye come to me from Fergus?" Darnley said amiably enough, gesturing Ronan to a seat.

"Fergus was my teacher and my master," Ronan said, "and now that he has passed, I have come to you as he asked."

Darnley's brows shot up. "Fergus is dead?"

"Aye."

"And ye are *taibhsear* now, are ye?" Darnley leaned forward and studied Ronan closely. "Ye look a bit young."

Ronan wondered whether to explain that he had served but half the traditional seven years of his apprenticeship, but in the end he only shrugged. "No younger than Fergus was when he began."

"He always seemed an old man to me." Darnley shook his head and drank deeply from his mug, then refilled it from the pitcher before continuing. "Well, then, *taibhsear,* what brings ye here? What messages do ye bring me from Fergus?"

"My lord, he spoke of you before the end. He asked that when you returned to Aylsford, I come to you and offer you my services."

"What services?"

"That is for you to say."

Darnley leaned back in his seat. "That's Fergus for ye, still riddling beyond the grave. God rest him," he added, signing himself with the cross. "There's no denying he kent things that others did not, and if he sent ye here, he had his reasons. Fergus stayed with us some years ago," Darnley added, reaching for his mug again. "Did he say aught of that to ye?"

The question was put very casually, but Ronan noted the sudden tension in the nobleman's shoulders.

"No, my lord," he answered, surprised. "He never mentioned anything about it."

Darnley visibly relaxed. "Well, 'twas no great matter. How did ye come to know him, then?"

"Lady Deirdre Kirallen is my foster sister. When her first husband, Brodie Maxwell, died, I came to her to offer my assistance. She has since wed one of Kirallen's knights, and I stayed to take service with Fergus."

Let Darnley make what he would of that! Fergus only said I had to offer, Ronan thought. He never said Darnley would accept.

"Laird Kirallen and his lady have been good to me," Ronan added for good measure. "I count them as my friends."

"And if it came to choosing sides?" Darnley asked, leaning back in his seat and regarding Ronan narrowly.

"I could not," Ronan admitted. " 'Tis not the place of a _taibhsear_ to take sides, only to render what services he can to those in need."

"Yet ye have fought before?" Darnley asked, his gaze straying down to the livid scar on Ronan's hand. "It seems I remember hearing something of an Irishman—a minstrel—who was there when Maxwell went against Kirallen some years ago."

"Yes, I was there, before I ever heard of Fergus or agreed to serve him. I took up arms in defense of the Kirallens, but the Kirallens in question were Lady Alyson and the child she carried at the time. Your granddaughter, my lord," he added pointedly.

Darnley's eyes sparked with anger, but after a moment he threw back his head and laughed. "My granddaughter! Whelp of that kitchen slut who calls herself a lady! Are ye thinking I shall thank ye for it?"

"Blood is blood."

"And a Kirallen is a Kirallen, no matter what she might have been at birth." Darnley shook his head, still laughing. "Either ye are verra brave or verra stupid, _taibhsear_. Which is it?"

"I cannot say, my lord."

"Weel, I daresay we'll find out."

Ronan's heart sank a little further, for it did not sound as though Darnley meant to dismiss him out of hand. "In fact, I have just come from Ravenspur," he said. "I bring you greetings from your son."

"Haddon," Darnley said flatly. "Christ's blood, my father must be turning in his grave. If he ever knew his grandson would be living among Kirallens . . ."

"Perhaps," Ronan suggested, "your father would be glad to know you had succeeded in bringing peace."

"Now, that I wholly doubt. My father was a warrior, and he made damn sure I was one as well. By the time I was Haddon's age, I'd fought in many battles. I killed my first man when I was but fourteen."

Ronan raised a brow. "A Kirallen?"

"That's right. And," Darnley added, shooting Ronan a wry look, "had I not killed him, he would surely have killed me."

"Killed you? Who, my lord?"

A woman stepped from the inner chamber, clad in a flowing robe that revealed a glimpse of rounded shoulder. A good deal of butter yellow hair tumbled about her face, which was blurred with sleep. Her eyes were heavy lidded, drowsy, but they held a sharp intelligence as they ran over Ronan in a quick, assessing glance.

Ronan imagined she had just woken from a well-earned rest. He could imagine all too well how she had earned that rest, along with the velvet robe, the costly scent that enveloped her like a wave, and the ring that flashed on her finger as she ran a familiar hand over Lord Darnley's graying locks.

His face lit and he grabbed her hand, pulling her down on his lap and nuzzling her neck.

"Good morning, Celia."

"And to you, m'lord," she answered pertly, dropping a light kiss on his nose as she nimbly extracted herself from his embrace. "Now, what's all this about someone trying to kill ye?"

"Ancient history." Darnley waved a hand. "I was speaking of the Kirallens."

"Were ye? And who were ye speaking *with?*"

This time her gaze was bold, and Ronan was certain she'd been listening to every word they spoke.

"Celia, this is old Fergus's apprentice, Ronan Fitzgerald. Fiztgerald, this is Celia."

"Charmed," Ronan murmured.

"I'm certain ye are. What brings ye to Aylsford?"

"He came to see if I had need of him," Darnley said.

"Why does he come here for that, my lord?" Celia asked lightly, pouring herself a cup of ale. "Seems to me he could be sitting up in his cave and staring into the flames, conjuring up the past and future and God alone kens what. Is that no how old Fergus used to do it?"

"Oh, I've done a bit of that, as well," Ronan answered pleasantly. "You'd be surprised at what I've learned."

Celia stiffened. "And what d'ye mean by that?"

Ronan had not meant anything at all; he'd been annoyed at her tone and spoken the first words that came into his head. But now he frowned and adopted a forbidding, distant air. "I mean what I said, mistress."

Darnley settled back in his seat, grunting as he shifted his leg. "There *is* something ye might do for me," he said cautiously.

"Yes?" Ronan said. After a moment, he added, "Is it your leg?"

"Nay, that's well enough. It is . . . well,'tis my daughter." Having said that much, Darnley fell silent, frowning. There was an audible sniff from Celia as she sank down on the settle.

"Lady Maude?" Ronan said.

"Aye."

Ronan waited, but when Darnley did not speak again, he ventured, "Is she ill?"

"Nay, not ill. Only . . ."

"Only? My lord, it would be a help if you'd just tell me what the trouble is."

" 'Tis a bit difficult to put my finger on. She's pale, and lately her appetite isn't what it should be. Her maid tells me she suffers from nightmares. Yesterday she swooned."

"Does she complain of any pain?"

"She doesna complain of anything at all. I doubt there's much the matter with her," he added uncertainly.

Ronan doubted it, as well. He had heard much of Lady Maude, and would wager he could name her trouble without rising from his seat. She had, he knew, gone to London in search of a grand marriage, yet she must be a full twenty-one and home again unwed, a curious circumstance considering her father's wealth. Disappointed in her hopes and with the first blush of youth behind her, the lady's legendary temper had likely soured even further.

"What a pother over nothing!" Celia said irritably. "There's naught amiss with Lady Maude that canna be cured by a husband in her bed."

"Maude will wed when she is ready."

"And when will that be? When ye force her to it, and not a moment sooner. Ye do your daughter no service by this shilly-shallying about, my lord."

"That will do, Celia. Now go fetch me bread and cheese. And this is empty again," he added irritably, holding out the pitcher. "I want it straight from the well, mind ye."

When she was gone, Darnley slumped in his seat. "She's right. I've let Maude have her head too long. She must have received two dozen offers in London and not one would suit. I dinna ken what to do with her the now."

Ronan sighed, looking toward the door. Of all the ridiculous coils! Surely Fergus had sent him here for some higher purpose than to help Lord Darnley marry off his daughter.

"I am certain Lady Maude is—" he began, but Darnley cut him off.

"*I* want to be certain. Ye are a healer, are ye no?"

"I am."

"Then go see to her. Come to me after."

Ronan turned in the doorway. "My lord, Haddon does well at Ravenspur. They care for him as one of their own."

Darnley looked up sharply, and for the first time Ronan saw the man who had struck terror along the border for thirty years.

"I have welcomed ye into my home, *taibhsear,* but do not seek to meddle in things beyond your ken. My son is a Darnley, stolen from me by treachery. God help them—and him—if he has forgotten that."

Four

Ronan knew from long experience that the best time for a minstrel was toward the end of winter. By then, the inhabitants of any keep or castle were so starved for diversion that any entertainer would be assured a welcome. And if the entertainer was a harper who happened to be young and presentable, the ladies would seize upon him like so many birds of prey, making him the focus of their petty jealousies and quarrels.

Ronan had first been flattered by the attention, until he realized he was no more than a new possession for the ladies to flaunt before their rivals. What looked like a game could soon turn ugly if he accepted—or rejected—the wrong poem or flower. It could turn deadly if the lady intended to flaunt him before a husband grown overly complacent.

All in all, minstrelry was a far more dangerous occupation than most people understood. He sighed, resigned but not surprised when the ladies in Lady Maude's bower crowded round him, eyeing him with avid interest.

"A harper!" one of the younger ones exclaimed, clasping her hands together.

"Yes," Ronan answered pleasantly, "I would like to—"

"Have ye come to play for us?"

"Not just now. Lord Darnley has asked that I—"

An older woman interrupted. "Are ye Irish? Oh, they say that Irish harpers are the finest in the world!"

"Thank you, we try. I was told that Lady Maude is here. Would you please tell her that—"

"Och, go on, lad, give us a tune."

"—Lord Darnley has asked me to attend her, and—"

" 'Tis so dull here, we *never* have any music," the youngest of the ladies said, pouting prettily.

"Another time, demoiselle, I would be happy to oblige you. But just now Lord Darnley has sent me to speak with Lady Maude."

"Then of course you must speak with me."

Ronan turned sharply. He had prepared himself for an assault upon his ear; shrill tones that demanded attention, made even less appealing by the querulous tone that so often accompanied imaginary ailments. But the speaker had a low, rather husky voice, unexpectedly attractive, and her words were tinged with dry amusement.

"Ladies, would you please stand back?"

They obeyed, and Ronan found himself facing a young woman seated before a tapestry frame. She was dressed in a gown of ivory samite, embroidered with tiny pink blossoms, and hair of spun gold waved softly about her face. Her skin was pale as new cream, her features so perfectly regular they might almost have been boring, save for the wide set of her eyes, slightly tilted at the edges, and the lush curves of her lips.

This is Lady Maude? Ronan thought, entirely bewildered. *There must be some mistake.* From all he had heard of her, he'd been expecting an ogress at the least. This lass looked as sweetly innocent as any maiden in a ballad; he would hardly have been surprised if a unicorn wandered into the chamber to lay its head down on her lap.

Looking more closely, he could see the resemblance to her half sister, Lady Alyson. It was there in the long, slender neck, the tilt and color of the eyes . . . though where Lady Alyson glowed like sunlight, her half sister shone as softly as the moon.

A harper? Maude wondered, studying him through downcast lashes. That was a kindly thought of father's. No matter how poorly he played, she would keep him for a time. He could hardly do worse than the last one, that filthy old piper with his shrieking, wailing dirges. At least this one looked as though he had bathed in recent memory.

He was young, not above five and twenty, quite tall and broad of shoulder, his dark brown hair drawn back and neatly clubbed. He faced her squarely, shoulders thrown back, chin tilted upward, his gaze coolly distant and utterly remote. Perhaps the ladies had been mistaken, she thought uneasily. Despite the harp slung over his shoulder, he had more of the air of a cleric than a minstrel, though his clothing gave no sign of any religious affiliation.

His cloak had once been fine, with traces of delicate embroidery about the neck and hem, but it had seen long years of heavy use. The robe beneath was plain gray wool. A noble's cloak, a peasant's robe, a fine harp on his shoulder . . . and the face of an angel on a chapel window. Who *was* he? *What* was he? And whatever was he doing in her bower?

"Father has engaged you to play for us?" she ventured. "Let us hear, then, what you can do."

"Lady Maude, it would be my pleasure to play for you another time, but today I am on other business. Ronan Fitzgerald at your service," he said, sweeping her a very graceful bow. "I am a *taibhsear*—"

"A *taibhsear?*" she interrupted sharply.

"Aye, lady. I was apprenticed to Fergus McInnes."

In an instant, before Maude had even understood his words, fear sank deep talons into her heart.

"You—you *were*—? What do you mean? Where is Fergus?" she demanded, hearing the rising panic in her voice.

"He died at Candlemas."

Maude drew a sharp breath. "Dead? Oh, no, he can't be dead." Recovering herself, she added, "I am sorry to hear it."

"I can see that."

Could he? What else could he see? She chanced a look and found brilliant green eyes fixed on her in a penetrating gaze. She quickly looked away, desperately grasping at the shreds of her composure. Fergus had promised—had *sworn* that if she needed him, he would return. How could he abandon her like this?

Or had he?

"Did Fergus send you here?" she asked, not daring to breathe as she waited for the answer.

"He did."

Maude felt herself begin to tremble with mingled terror and relief. Fergus had not forgotten, then. He could not come himself, but he had sent his apprentice in his place.

"Ladies," she said, raising her voice. "You are dismissed."

When they were alone, she sat silent for a moment. How much did he know? What exactly had Fergus told him? Hot color flooded her cheeks, and she could only sit helpless, shaking hands clenched in her lap, waiting for him to speak.

"Forgive me," he said, "I am sorry to bring you such ill news. I did not realize you knew Fergus well."

She looked at him then, seeing he was indeed sorry— and that he was surprised by her grief. And that made no sense. Surely he must understand what Fergus meant to her.

"Well?" she repeated, stalling for time. "No, I cannot say I knew him well. He was always something of a mystery."

The young *taibhsear* inclined his head. His hair was black, she saw, not brown at all, black and shining as a raven's wing.

"Aye, he was that. I hear he visited at Aylsford some time ago."

Here it was, then. Maude swallowed hard and looked down at her hands. "He did."

"What brought him here?"

Maude's head snapped up. "He did not tell you?"

"No, lady, 'twas your father who mentioned Fergus had stayed here. Fergus never spoke of it."

Never spoke of it? Then why is this man here at all? She did not understand; the whole thing made no sense. Unless Fergus had sent him on some other errand altogether.

Of course, that must be it. Fergus had not been thinking of her at all. He had forgotten her. She forced herself to laugh, though it wasn't easy, not with grief digging iron fingers into her throat.

"No, of course he didn't speak of it. Why would he? It was all so long ago, and no great matter. He cured me of a fever when I was—was just a child."

Her heart was beating so quick and loud that surely he must hear it. But no, he didn't seem to. He merely nodded. "Fergus was a gifted healer."

Maude stood. "Thank you for bringing me the news yourself." She looked toward the door in polite dismissal, but Fitzgerald did not move.

"When I spoke with your father earlier," he said, "Lord Darnley said he is concerned about your health."

Damn Father, Maude thought, *why can he not leave*

*well enough alone? How many times must I prove to him
that I am fine?*

"My health?" she said, adopting a puzzled air. "Oh,
there's naught amiss with me. You may tell him—"

"Lord Darnley said you had a fainting spell," Fitzgerald interrupted.

"Hardly anything so serious as that. I fasted overlong
and grew a little dizzy. Poor Father," she added with an
affectionate shake of her head. "He worries over nothing."

"He also mentioned something about upsetting
dreams."

"Even the most fearsome dream is cured by waking,"
she said reasonably. "I seek no other remedy."

"Are your dreams fearsome, then?"

Maude's hands clenched on her skirts as her pulse
pounded in her throat, but she forced herself to hold his
gaze until she was certain of her voice.

"At times," she replied with a smile and a shrug. "I
imagine most people could say the same."

He did not return her smile. If anything, his expression
grew a little graver as he continued to regard her steadily.
The muscles of Maude's face began to ache with the
effort of keeping her smile in place.

"I *am* sorry Father put you to all this trouble," she
said, taking a few steps toward the door.

"Sure and 'tis no trouble at all," Fitzgerald answered
pleasantly, but with a hint of steel in his voice. "If you
would just take your seat again . . ."

"But there is no *need*. Oh, I *was* ill—an attack of ague
that lingered—but I am quite well now. I am sure you
have many pressing matters to attend to, so I will not
keep you any longer."

"Sit down, Lady Maude."

He removed the harp from his shoulder and laid it
carefully on the window seat, then unfastened his cloak
and hung it on the peg behind the door.

"You are dismissed," she said, allowing a hint of annoyance to creep into her voice. "Speak to the steward on your way out, and he shall see that you are paid."

"I am not here for payment, but at your father's bidding. Please, my lady," he added, softening his tone, "I shan't be long."

Maude considered arguing further, but one look at the determined set of his mouth convinced her the argument would be a long one. It was time for a change of tactics.

She sat down. He drew pen, ink, and parchment from his bag and laid them neatly on the table as he asked a number of shrewd questions regarding her diet, the exercise she was accustomed to taking, and other more personal matters, noting her responses carefully. He wrote a good hand, fair and flowing. She added *educated* to the list of things she knew of him.

"If I may . . ."

He took her hand without waiting for permission. His skin was cool to the touch, his grip impersonal as it closed around her wrist. He is a *taibhsear,* Maude reminded herself, Fergus's apprentice. Maude knew how Fergus had longed for an apprentice, for he had told her so himself. Strange, she thought she had forgotten, but now she remembered every word. *"A taibhsear must be born,"* he used to say, *"I'll ken him when I see him."*

But anyone less like Fergus was impossible to imagine. Fergus had been old and wise and comfortable. This Fitzgerald was too young, too hard, and his every word and gesture were tinged with a subtle arrogance that Maude distrusted.

"Come over to the window, please."

She obeyed silently, keeping her gaze averted as he threw open the shutter. He lifted her face to the light and pressed her neck. He had extraordinarily long fingers, she noticed. Harper's fingers, very deft and gentle. A twisted scar ran over his left wrist and cut across the soft skin of his palm.

"Hmm. Turn this way."

When he bent to peer into her eyes, she froze. For a moment, just the briefest flash of time, it seemed those strange green eyes were looking past the body that was failing her, beyond the words that were her last defense, that he could see her, really *see* her. . . .

"Help me!" she cried desperately. *"Please help me, I'm so frightened—"*

Oh, God, what had she done? She nearly fainted with shame and terror. Then he straightened and stared at her, faintly puzzled but not at all alarmed, and she realized she had not spoken the words aloud.

She tore her gaze from him and set her jaw to still her trembling. He had seen nothing. It had all been an illusion, that strange moment of connection. He could not help her. She had been a fool to think he might.

Oh, why must Father interfere? He meant well, Maude knew that, but he had no idea what was happening. And he mustn't know, she thought with a sharp stab of fear. Not ever. It would only upset him. And when Father was upset, he was apt to do terrible things.

The first step was to be rid of Fergus's apprentice. She must send him off at once and in such a manner that he would not return.

He sat down at the table, his dark head bent as he wrote something on his parchment.

"You are Irish?" she asked.

"I am."

"My uncle was in Ireland some years ago," she ventured. "With Prince Lionel." The words lay between them like a lure upon fast water. She held her breath, waiting to see if he would take the bait.

"I remember when the prince visited."

His voice was expressionless, but his brows contracted in an almost invisible frown as he continued writing.

"Uncle Robert used to say the peasants were thick as fleas upon the road whenever the prince rode out, gawping at his finery," Maude went on smoothly. "Were you among them?"

He looked up at her then, a flash of emerald between dark lashes. "There was no need for that. The prince came to *us.*"

Us? And who might that be? Maude wondered. She did not doubt he spoke the truth; his voice and bearing were unmistakably those of a nobleman, and the Fitzgeralds were a family of some consequence. Was he some noble's by-blow, then, or the younger son of a minor branch? Even if he could hardly pluck out a tune upon that harp, his looks alone would assure him a place at any court. What ever was he doing here in the very back of beyond?

Well, whatever he was doing, he wouldn't be doing it at Aylsford for much longer. She would make sure of that.

"That must have been quite an honor for *you.*"

"An honor?" An amused, slightly scornful expression passed across his face.

"Prince Lionel was a great man," she said, though actually she'd always heard King Edward's second son was a bit of a fool. "He was the queen's favorite," she added more truthfully. "They say her Majesty never got over mourning him when he died."

"Well, I'm thinking Her Majesty never saw him kick an old man in the face who'd done no worse than present himself as ordered. But there, I mustn't be too hard upon the prince. Wasn't he too drunk to know what he was doing half the time?"

Most likely true, Maude thought, but hardly relevant just now. She sniffed. "Nobles cannot be held to the same standards as other men."

"How convenient for them. Now, were you born here at Aylsford Keep? What day was that?"

She plucked a date and time from the air, watching with satisfaction as he noted them in his flowing hand.

"If you had ever been to a real court—" she began.

"What do you consider real?" He put down the pen and leaned back in his seat. "Spain, Portugal, England, France?"

"Don't tell me you've seen any of them!"

"And a few more, besides. A good harper always finds a welcome."

"I suppose you are that good."

"There was none better."

He spoke calmly; not boasting, simply stating a fact, with a smugness that set her teeth on edge.

"I think you lie," she said, switching rapidly to French. "You've never been to any of those places, and you have no idea what I'm saying, do you?"

"I do not lie, and I know exactly what you are saying," he shot back swiftly in the same tongue. "Though your accent is abominable."

"You *are* clever, aren't you? Impertinent, as well."

"Right on both counts," he answered evenly. "I think I've finished here."

"Good. You've wasted enough of my time, Master— what was it?—Rommel?"

He stood abruptly. "The name is Ronan Fitzgerald."

There was no graceful bow or "at your service" this time. He wanted only to escape. But Maude was used to people leaving her presence in a hurry. *My one talent,* she thought, a rush of laughter—or was it tears?—catching at her throat.

"So you've traded your place at court for a cave up in the hills?" she said, her mocking tone hiding the tremor in her voice. "Bit of a comedown for you."

"I consider it a step up. Good day, my lady."

He turned with a swirl of his patched green cloak. Maude stood stiffly, hands clenched at her sides, not daring to relax until the door slammed shut behind him.

ive

Ronan strode from the chamber, down the winding stairway, and barely stopped himself from continuing out the door. He wanted to be away from this place right now, this very moment, but his promise to Fergus held him fast.

He stood in Darnley's antechamber and willed himself to calm, summoning the remnants of his detachment about him like a shredded cloak. He was surprised to find his hands were shaking with the effort as he knocked upon the door of Darnley's chamber.

"Come in, come in," Darnley called. "What did ye find?"

Ronan stepped inside and moved closer to the fire. *This is a bad place,* he thought. *A dark place.* Again he had to fight the urge to run.

"Lady Maude insists her health is fine," he began. "I saw nothing to make me believe otherwise."

Darnley brightened. "Is it so? Well, perhaps 'twas nothing much. She has always been of a delicate disposition."

Ronan repressed a smile. He could think of many descriptions of Lady Maude's disposition, but delicate was not one of them.

"She thinks you worry overmuch," he said.

"Did ye think to *bleed* her?"

Ronan whirled and for the first time noticed Celia sitting in the shadows, a bit of sewing in her hands. Her butter yellow hair shone in the dim room, and her candid blue gaze was guileless as a child's.

"I've heard there's naught like a good bloodletting to let out the evil humors," she added, widening her eyes.

"In some cases, that may be true," Ronan said. "But not in this one. In fact, a *good* bloodletting often does more harm than good."

Celia cast her eyes down, meekly accepting his rebuke, but not before he'd seen the flash of rage in their cornflower depths.

" 'Tis only that she does seem a bit . . . odd . . . lately," Celia murmured. "What with the dreams and all."

Have I missed something? Ronan wondered, going back over his examination. Lady Maude's pulse had been quick, but she was admittedly upset by the news of Fergus's death. Her skin was cool and dry, her breathing normal, her hair lustrous with health. Perhaps she was a bit pale, but no more than was fashionable these days, and her eyes . . . Ronan frowned. Hadn't there been a moment, when he looked into her eyes . . . nothing he could put a name to, just a feeling that there was something she wanted to say to him?

He shrugged off the impression. Lady Maude's eyes were clear and bright—*quite beautiful in fact,* a small voice whispered in his mind—and that was all that need concern him. If she had wanted to say something, she would have said it. Reticence was *not* one of her problems.

"The dreams, the nervousness . . . perhaps a surfeit of

black bile," Ronan said thoughtfully. "What you might call a melancholic humor."

Celia shot him a keen glance. "A melancholic humor, eh? Is that your way of saying the lady is a bit . . ." She tapped her brow.

Darnley paled. "Is that what ye mean to say?"

"Of course not, my lord," Ronan said. "Oh, melancholy can lead to madness, just as choler can lead to apoplexy, but such an outcome is by no means inevitable. I do not think there is anything amiss with Lady Maude."

Darnley nodded, looking relieved, but Celia only muttered, "Save for her temper."

"My lord, is there any other way in which I might serve?" Ronan asked, hoping against hope that Darnley would say no.

"I'm not quite certain yet," the nobleman replied. "I'll have to give it some thought. Can ye play that thing?" he added, nodding toward Ronan's harp.

"After a fashion."

"Then ye may play for us after we have supped. Maude has a liking for music, though she's somewhat difficult to please."

What a surprise! Ronan thought, but he only nodded. "It would be my pleasure."

He was a bit alarmed at how smoothly the lie slipped past his lips. It would not be a pleasure at all, but a penance. *One I probably deserve for something,* he thought grimly. *Or why would Fergus have sent me to this wretched place?*

The chamber Ronan was given was small but comfortable, a step up from the servant's quarters he had expected. He unpacked his bag, arranging the pots and bottles neatly on an empty shelf, adding the book and parchments he had brought along. The hangings about the bed were undyed wool, though finely woven and obviously new, and the feather mattress was thick and soft. At the foot of the bed was a roughly carved chest that smelled faintly of lavender and tansy.

Darnley showed far more respect for Fergus's memory than any of the Kirallens ever had. To them—with the exception of Sir Alistair, Deirdre's husband—Fergus was simply an old man with a gift for healing and some eccentric ways that were best ignored. But to Darnley, Fergus was something more. Ronan was clearly reaping the benefits of a relationship he hadn't known existed. Strange that Fergus had never thought to mention it.

Or was it? Even at the best of times, Fergus had always kept his own counsel. Darnley had obviously been fond of him, though—and so had Darnley's daughter. Though in her case the respect she'd felt for Fergus did not extend to his apprentice.

Well, he hadn't liked her much, either. But that did not matter. Lady Maude was not important; she had naught to do with him or his errand, and he would put her from his mind. No matter how the image of her face might linger.

Why is it, he thought irritably, *that ladies are never what they seem? Why go to such great pains to appear so sweet and biddable, only to destroy their careful work just by opening their mouths?*

"He used to say the peasants were thick as fleas upon the roads. . . . Were you among them?"

A peasant. Ronan smiled wryly, remembering. He had been called many things in his time, but Maude Darnley was the first to insult him in that particular manner. There was nothing wrong with the lady's wit, he'd have to give her that much. Damn it, he thought, flinging a tunic into the trunk, there was nothing wrong with her at all.

But what had he seen when he looked into her eyes?

Nothing. He had seen nothing, because there was nothing there to see. She had played him for a fool, taking him in with her sorrow over Fergus, looking so bereft that he wanted to take her in his arms and tell her she mustn't worry, he was here now, and everything would be all right.

And then, while he was still reeling with the shock of *that,* she turned on him quickly as an adder. Prince Lionel indeed! It was quite clever, really, the way Lady Maude had used the one name guaranteed to rouse fury in any decent Irishman. She had summed him up quickly enough, he thought ruefully, and he had fallen straight into her trap.

With a sigh, he abandoned his unpacking and sank down to his knees. It took a long time to frame his mind into the proper state of receptive stillness, but when at last he managed to order his thoughts through the ritual of prayer, he felt calmer, though he was still far from understanding what had happened between him and Lady Maude.

The one thing he did know was that he had handled the situation badly. And even to say that was putting it with too much charity.

"Be still," Fergus used to say. "Listen." And had Ronan listened? No, he had run his mouth like the greenest of apprentices, reacting to every insult she had flung at him.

But *why* had she flung them? He frowned, sitting back on his heels. What *had* he seen when he looked into her eyes?

The truth—shameful as it was—was that he'd been too busy admiring their brilliance to notice much of anything. But something had happened in that moment, and whatever it was, it had frightened the lady badly.

Why else would she have tried so hard to drive him off for good and all? For that was what she had done, and he must admit she had succeeded . . . for the moment. But if she thought he would give up as easily as that, she would soon realize her mistake.

He began to dress for his appearance in the hall, then

stopped and stared down at the tunic in his hands, emerald velvet worked about the hem and neck with gold. The last time he had worn this was at the Castilian court. He remembered the silence that hung over the hall when he finished singing, the flush of pleasure he had felt when King Pedro stood to thank him for his song.

Now he ran his fingers over the prickly soft velvet, smiling faintly, remembering how much he had paid for this tunic, enough to feed a village family for a year. Yet it was no dearer than those he had worn as a child. Then, Ronan had gone as finely clad as any prince, and the Fitzgeralds of Desmond bowed to no man.

After a moment he shook his head, bundled the tunic into the trunk, and shut the lid with a bang.

"Do whatever Darnley asks of ye," Fergus had said, "so long as it does not interfere with your conscience or your vows."

Darnley had asked him to play in the hall tonight. So he would play. In his own clothes, not the cast-off finery that belonged to another life. He was no courtier, but a *taibhsear* and a minstrel, and needed no outward show to prove his worth to any man.

Or to any lady. Particularly one who had named him a peasant and a liar.

Six

Maude sat down before her dressing table and ran a finger over the shining wood surface. Alabaster, crystal, gold, and silver reflected back at her from the mirror hanging on the wall. She watched her own hand reach out to rearrange the shining jars and bottles, ordering them by size.

"Ye look weary," her tiring woman, Becta, observed.

"I didn't sleep well with you away."

"I'm sorry for that, lady, but my niece had need of me. 'Tis a fine strong boy she had, and I couldna leave until the two of them were settled."

Maude began to line the bottles up again, this time grouping them by contents.

"I'm glad *they* rested well."

She spoke without heat, for she was starting to relax. It was good to be here, safe in her chamber, with soft rain pattering against the windows and a fire burning in the tiled hearth. Becta moved about, adding wood to the fire, laying out a gown for her to wear. The green, Maude noticed, watching her in the mirror, and how did she know that was the very gown Maude had meant to choose herself? It was not as if she wore it often, for though the color was good, it was simply cut, not nearly as fine as the gowns she had brought from London.

She frowned, sniffing at a bottle filled with a heavy, musky scent that was all the fashion at court. The gowns had been a bit of an extravagance. There were so very many of them and they all had been scandalously expensive, made in the latest fashion and trimmed lavishly with pearls and fur and jewels.

But that's how it was at court. There was nothing much to do but order a new gown, a different headdress, and wear them to another feast or tournament, one very like the other and all of them a dismal disappointment.

"Becta," she said. "Do you remember Fergus?"

Becta, who was bent over the bed, turned her head and met Maude's eyes in the mirror. "What put him in your mind today?"

"He's dead, you know."

Becta crossed herself. "God rest him. But he was very old, lady. Even he had to die sometime."

"I suppose so. Had you heard he took an apprentice? An Irishman named Fitzgerald."

"Did he, then?" Becta sat down on the bed. "And what has that to do with us?"

Maude turned on the stool. "He's here."

"Here? Why?"

"I don't know," Maude said. "Father asked him to stay."

"Fergus's apprentice," Becta said thoughtfully. "What manner of man is he?"

"Young. A stranger to these parts."

Becta nodded. "I see."

Aye, Becta saw. There was no need to explain further. Maude turned back to the dressing table and opened her jewel box. *There is magic in his voice,* she thought; *his hands are wondrous gentle. And his eyes* . . . She held up an emerald necklace, letting the heavy gold chain slide through her fingers, the links chill against her skin.

Glancing up, she frowned at her reflection.

"He is very arrogant."

"So was Fergus," Becta commented dryly. "Will ye be wearing that tonight?"

"What? Oh, no, I won't." Maude dropped the necklace back into the box and shut the lid with a snap. "In fact, I don't think I'll go down after all."

Becta turned, her eyes sharp with apprehension. "Oh, lady, are ye certain ye want to do that?"

Keep to the pattern, Maude reminded herself, then dropped her head into her hands. The pattern was unraveling around her; Fergus dead, his apprentice here at Aylsford . . .

"I'm too tired," she whispered. "Becta, I'm too tired to weave it all together. . . ."

"Aye, lamb, all right. Get into bed and I'll bring ye a posset."

Yes, Maude thought, bed was the place for her, safe beneath the coverlet drawn up to her chin.

But sleep was long in coming. Becta returned from the hall and sat down by the fire with her spinning while Maude lay watching her. Up and down the spindle went, round and round, until Maude grew so dizzy that she had to close her eyes.

When she opened them again, the fire had burned low, and Becta's seat was empty. Maude lay very still, watching the shadows flickering on the wall. Her entire body clenched with dread as they took form.

"I am dreaming," she said aloud, and the sound of her own voice frightened her. If she could hear herself speaking, she must be awake. Yet the shadows were still there, growing more solid with every passing moment. And they were moving closer to the bed.

"Becta!" she cried. "Becta, are you there?"

"What is it, lamb? I'm right here, dinna fear—"

The shadows wavered at the sound of Becta's voice. A moment later the fire sprang suddenly to life. When Becta straightened, a candle in her hand, the shadows fled into the corners.

"A nightmare?" Becta asked gently, setting the candle on the table and touching Maude's brow.

"I saw—" Maude bit her lip. "Aye. A nightmare."

"I'll just leave the candle burning, then."

Becta settled down to sleep, and Maude lay unmoving, her eyes fixed on the corners. They weren't gone. They were only biding their time. She watched them, afraid to close her eyes until dawn slipped through the windows. Only then did she relax enough to sleep.

But even as she succumbed to exhaustion, she knew they would be back as soon as darkness fell again.

It was midmorning when she rose, her eyes scratching and a dull throbbing in her temples.

"Leave off!" she cried, wrenching the comb from Becta's hand and flinging it against the wall. "Ye are pulling it out by the roots! Just let be!"

"Aye, my lady."

Becta placed a gauzy veil on Maude's head, then set a thin golden circlet about the high white brow. Maude seized the circlet and threw it across the room, then pressed her fingers to her temples.

"Does your head ache? Mayhap if ye went back to bed . . ."

"What would be the point? I never sleep well in the morning. You *know* that."

"Nor do ye sleep at night," Becta pointed out. "If ye would take the posset—"

"I don't need any posset."

"Mayhap, if ye would try it, the dreams would not—"

"I need a good bed. Is that so much to ask? The mattress wasn't aired—"

"It was."

"—and there's something about this chamber—'tis musty."

"Lady, ye are haverin'. The mattress was fresh picked and aired, and if ye can find one speck o' mold or dust in here, then I'm the queen of England."

Maude glared at her. "So you say."

"I do. Now, if ye will not go back to bed, then go to the garden for a time."

"I don't want to go to the garden," Maude said stubbornly. " 'Tis far too bright out there."

"A bit o' sunlight will not hurt ye," Becta said inflexibly. "Have that *taibhsear* come and play for ye. He can chase away your headache."

Maude looked at her suspiciously. "What makes you say that?"

"I heard him last night in the hall. And saw him." Becta shot her mistress a shrewd look. "Ye never mentioned he was so fine to look upon."

"Is he? I hadn't noticed."

Maude stood and walked to the window. The garden was bathed in sunlight, last night's rain sparkling upon fresh greenery. The scene rippled behind the heavy glass until it was merely a collection of shapes, dry and barren, bleached of color.

"Did he play well?"

"Oh, aye, and when he started in to singing, half the lasses swooned upon the spot. I hear," she added confidentially, "that Lady Mortimer sent him a ring."

"You gossip too much," Maude said severely.

"Aye, lady."

Maude traced a finger along the glass. "Did he accept it?" When there was no answer, she said sharply, "Becta!"

"Did ye call me?" Becta asked from behind her.

"Did he accept it? Lady Mortimer's ring."

"Nay. He sent it back again, saying he served the lady

of the manor and had no need of any gift not from her hand."

"Damned impertinent of him," Maude remarked.

"Oh, aye."

"It isn't as though—it wasn't I who asked him here! And I *never* promised him any gifts."

"Of course not, lady."

Maude leaned her brow against the glass. "I do not play these sorts of games."

"Aye, hinny, I ken ye don't." Becta's voice was suddenly gentle. "But it means naught. 'Twas canny on his part, a pretty way of turning her off with no offense on either side. Who would want to do wi' that jade?"

Of course. He hadn't meant anything by it. It was only courtier's talk, the sort of empty nonsense Maude despised.

"Now be off wi' ye," Becta scolded. "Get ye to the garden and sit awhile. And if ye have need of music . . ."

Maude seized her lute from the window seat. "I am well able to make my own."

Seven

The first lady of Aylsford Manor began with half a dozen rose bushes, wrapped in sacking and carried from her home. With these, a handful of bulbs, and a willow sapling, she created a pretty little garden where she could escape the smoky hall.

The next lady came there in springtime, to weep for the home and family she had left behind. By the time summer came, she had begun to plant—a small shrub here, a new flower bed there, and when the leaves fell, she sang as she cleared them from the garden. The next spring, she sat with her lord on the stone bench he had ordered and they watched their child sleep beneath the willow.

The child grew to manhood and took a wife. Her contribution was the flowering border of larkspur, and her lord's was a small fountain to cheer her while she worked. And so her child was born, and he, too, took a wife, who planted the first rows of hedges.

Now the garden stretched over acres and was filled with a profusion of soft scents and bright colors, with

winding paths leading to tiny alcoves set within tall
hedges. Maude was drawn to the original pleasaunce, set
deep within the garden, and it was there her steps led her
this morning.

She turned the corner and stopped short, gazing with
surprise on a long figure stretched out on soft grass in a
patch of sunlight. Arms folded beneath his head, the
young *taibhsear* lay at his ease, a smile on his lips and
ridiculously long lashes fanned against his cheeks. His
harp rested beside him on his folded cloak, as if he had
just this moment put it down.

"So this is how you abuse my father's hospitality?"

"This is how I enjoy it." He rose without haste and
bowed. "And by my faith, lady, I am enjoying it right
well, for 'tis a fine morning altogether, and this is the
prettiest garden I've seen in many a year. Have you come
to play for me?"

She blinked, momentarily at a loss for words. Was
there something gone amiss with her memory? Surely
this was the same man who had stalked out of the bower
and slammed the door behind him only yesterday. And
now he was asking if she had come here for the purpose
of amusing him!

"Indeed not," she said coldly. "This is my private garden."

"You have excellent taste, my lady. Won't you sit
down?"

"But I—you—"

"The name is Ronan Fitzgerald," he said helpfully. It
was the same thing he had said the day before, but now
he smiled as if the words were a private joke between
them. As if, she thought, he was quite certain she remembered his name. Which, of course, she did.

She turned and began to walk away.

"Did I tell you yesterday that I came here from Ravenspur?" he said behind her. "No, of course I didn't; it

slipped my mind altogether when we spoke. Your brother sends you greetings."

Maude stopped. He had seen Haddon? Spoken with him? A thousand questions crowded her mind, but she only said, not turning, "How does my brother, then?"

"Merry as a trivet, grown half a foot this past twelve-month."

Did he really send me greetings? she wanted to ask, but she did not quite dare to do so.

"He and Malcolm Kirallen are the best of friends," Ronan went on, "and the laird and lady have taken him straight into their family."

"Well, he is family, isn't he?" Maude said, turning back to face him. "I'm sure Alyson is keen to draw attention to the connection. Did you know she is my father's by-blow?"

He nodded, unsurprised. "I did. In fact, she told me the whole tale of how she came there."

He was watching her closely, as though expecting some reaction. What did he think she would do? Scream? Fall down in a faint? If so, he was bound for disappointment. Maude was not the least ashamed of anything she'd done. And it wasn't as though Alyson had suffered. Little Alyson Bowden from the Aylsford kitchens was *Lady* Alyson now, wed to one of the most powerful men on the borderlands, wealthy, respected, with a child, or perhaps two by this time.

"She's quite a clever little thing, isn't she?" Maude remarked. "For a kitchen slut."

"Did you know Lady Alyson's mother?"

Maude glanced at him, brows raised. "I may have seen her about. I do not acquaint myself with serving girls."

"Ah, but she was no ordinary serving girl. She was the daughter of a Highland chieftan. Did you not know?"

"No," Maude said shortly. "And—"

"Her name was Clare McLaran," Ronan began, his voice taking on the rhythmic cadence of a storyteller.

"She was betrothed to one of the Kirallens. Stephen was his name, uncle to the present laird. She was taken in a raid, captured as she rode to her own wedding."

Why was he telling her this? What made him think she could possibly be interested in things that had happened so long ago, before she was even born? She wanted to turn and leave, but the power of his voice held her to her place as she waited for the ending of the story.

"They say," Ronan went on, "that once Clare had been given up for lost, her betrothed defied his laird and set out all alone to find her. No one knows exactly what happened to him here, but his body was returned some time later, marked with your father's crest."

The man must have been a fool, Maude thought, *to come all this way for a woman who was ruined. What would be the point? He could not have wanted her, not after* . . . Maude knew that men sometimes killed their women in such cases, counting it a kindness; more often they sent them to a nunnery and mourned them as forever lost.

"Poor Clare knew none of this. She waited for Stephen, certain he would come for her. But he did not. When she quickened with your father's child, he gave her to his man Bowden as a bride. Bowden was a cruel man, a brute who gave her no chance to get a message to her family. She died believing herself entirely forgotten, abandoned by her lover. And there was her lover in his grave and her kin up in the Highlands, thinking she was dead. . . . I always thought it would make a good ballad," Ronan said thoughtfully, "though I don't imagine anyone in these parts would care to hear it."

"No, we wouldn't. We've heard enough of their lies already. But I suppose they had to come up with *something* to explain Alyson." Maude managed a laugh. "It has all the right touches—the noble background, the tragic air—and the Darnleys as the villains of the piece."

Ronan grinned. "It *is* a bit neat, isn't it? I was hoping

you could tell me what really became of Stephen Kirallen."

"I doubt he existed."

"Oh, he was real enough, but as for the rest . . ." He shrugged.

"You could always ask my father."

"Aye, I could. But will I?"

"What, don't tell me you're afraid of him!" Maude said, mocking.

"Afraid? Why should I be? But perhaps it is not wise to meddle too much with legends. The truth has a way of being so much less interesting . . . speaking as a troubadour, that is."

"Is that all we are to you, then? Material for a new ballad?"

"Why not? Songs have to come from somewhere, don't they? Aye, this will be my finest piece, and for a change we'll have a happy ending of a sort, what with Clare's daughter marrying into the Kirallen family after all."

"Oh, very happy, I'm sure. They must be thrilled to have that little drab as their lady."

"They are, indeed," Ronan replied at once. "For isn't Lady Alyson a fine woman altogether, so generous and beautiful and kind?"

"You sound quite besotted," Maude snapped. "Are you her lover?"

His laughter filled the garden, a pleasant sound, very free and easy. "Now, what sort of question is that? If I was, I'd hardly be admitting it to you! But as it happens, Lady Alyson is my friend, as is the laird. I am godfather to their daughter, Isobel—your niece, that would be."

Maude drew herself up and looked down her nose. "My *what?*" she asked in freezing tones.

"Your niece," he repeated, raising his voice a bit, as though perhaps she hadn't heard him the first time. "Isobel, named for the laird's mother, and isn't she the image of her father? She's quite fond of her Uncle Haddon, you know."

Maude shuddered. *"Uncle* Haddon? Surely he does not allow her to call him by that name."

"He welcomes it. And 'tis only natural, as he calls Lady Alyson his sister."

That was a lie. It must be. Haddon would never . . . *She* was Haddon's sister, not Alyson. *Her* name was the first word Haddon had spoken; *she* was the one who had held his hand when he took his first steps, told him stories, sung him songs.

And she was the one who had turned her back on her brother four years ago, abandoning him to their enemies.

She sank down on the bench. "I'm surprised to hear he sent me greeting," she said carefully, twisting the lute in her hands. "He was very angry with me when we parted last."

"So he still is. And to hear him tell the tale, he has every right to be. Of course, every tale has two sides, and I've heard but the one. . . ."

He lay down at her feet and propped himself on his elbows, tipping his face up to the sun.

"Do you think my brother lied to you?"

"Oh, no. Haddon's not a lad given to deception. But he knows only what he knows. As for your reasons for leaving him behind . . . only you can say."

And I am not about to, Maude thought, *no matter how sweetly you invite me to confide in you.*

"Thank you for the message," she said coolly. "And good day."

"What, I'm not to hear you play at all?"

She opened her mouth to refuse but instead heard herself say, "It has been so long. I wouldn't know where to begin."

"Start by listening, then. There is music in this place already."

Maude frowned at him, but his eyes were closed, his

face peaceful and relaxed. Cautiously, she shut her eyes, and slowly became aware of the splashing of the fountain. It was rather pretty, she thought, bright yet peaceful, too, and she drew a deep, lilac-scented breath. Above, the leaves of the ancient willow rustled in the breeze. A family of larks went back and forth among the branches, calling to one another, their liquid notes a bright counterpoint to the fountain's song.

After a time, Maude sighed with pleasure and opened her eyes to find Ronan watching her, a smile on his lips.

"Would that I could make such music," he said softly.

His eyes were as green as the grass beneath him, clear and dangerous as a mountain tarn. With an effort she wrested her gaze away.

"You do well enough."

"And how would you be knowing that? You were not in the hall last night."

So he had noticed. That was no reason for her heart to beat more quickly, for what he noticed or did not notice was no concern of hers.

"I heard—" She remembered Becta saying that half the lasses had swooned, but that she would not tell him. "—that you played passably."

"Why, thank you—I think. Now let me hear what you can do."

"With this?" She gazed ruefully at her lute. " 'Tis sadly out of tune."

She began the painstaking business of trying each string, her fingers clumsy and unpracticed.

"What are you really about here?" she asked at last, plucking a few chords to test her handiwork. "Why did you come to Aylsford?"

"Oh, I thought I'd drink some good wine, catch up on the latest news, try out a new song or two—"

"The truth," she said severely.

"Fergus asked me to come."

Maude's hands faltered on the strings, but she recovered herself quickly. "Why?"

"I'm not quite certain. He seemed unsettled in his mind about your family and the Kirallens."

Maude looked at him beneath her lashes. "What did he say?"

Ronan shrugged. "Hints and riddles, mostly. The only solid bit of information he gave me was that I should come here and offer my services to your father."

"But why? What possible good could *you* do?"

"None that I can tell," he admitted cheerfully. "But here I am."

Maude was quiet for a time, remembering Fergus's patience, his kindness, the long stories he used to tell her through all the endless nights.

"How did you come to meet him?" she asked.

"I could say 'twas chance, but the truth of it is that I was sent there."

"Sent there? But who—oh, I see, you mean *sent* there. By *God.*"

"So I believe."

Aye, he did believe that. There was no mistaking the ring of sincerity in his voice. And perhaps it was the truth. He had the same look she had often marked in Fergus, as though he was always looking a bit beyond, seeing things invisible to Maude. But where she had admired that quality in Fergus, for some reason it annoyed her unbearably in his apprentice.

"I've always heard the Irish are fanatical about their gods," she said. "Tell me, do you still practice human sacrifice?"

"Oh, that went out some time ago, if it ever existed at all. But one day," he added, leaning close and lowering his voice, "if you behave, I'll tell you all about our pagan rites."

Maude's lips twitched in a smile, instantly suppressed.

"I can think of nothing more tedious than listening to a fanatic drone on about religion."

"You've been subjected to that before?"

He was quick, she thought, a bit too quick for her liking. Before she could think of an answer, he went on, "There, I'm doing it again! Fergus always said there was no need for my every thought to fly out of my mouth."

Maude shrugged, signaling that the subject was of no interest, and her fingers moved upon the lute into a melancholy air. "How did he die?"

"Very easily. 'Twas his years that took him off, lady, and he was not loath to go. I miss him."

He added the last in a lower voice, his face averted, and she knew his grief was as real as her own. After a moment he turned back to her. "What is that you're playing? I don't know it."

"This?" She stopped, confused. "Nothing."

"No, go on . . ." He reached for his harp. "Is it French?"

"I don't remember."

He began to pick out the melody. "Aye, it has a French air to it, but this part—do you hear it? 'Tis very odd. I've never heard anything quite like it. Yet it fits. . . ."

He sat beside her on the bench. "Do it once again, would you? I didn't catch this change. . . ."

Maude began to play, and halfway through he joined her, at first staying with the melody, then breaking off into a string of notes that was so perfect, so completely right, that the simple tune was transformed into something rich and strange. Yet it was not strange at all, Maude thought, not really; it was exactly what she would have done if only she had thought of it.

Not bad, Ronan thought. *Not bad at all.* Her skill was nowhere near to her ambition, but that was unimportant, a thing that could be cured by practice. But the ambition was definitely there.

"Here, do you know this one?" he said very casually, careful not to betray the extent of his interest as he began again. She listened, head cocked to one side, and after a moment took up her lute and followed. When he came to the verse, he began to sing, and with a jerk of his chin invited her to join him.

Dame de meintieng joli,
Plaisant, nette et pure,
Souvent me fait dire "ai mi!"
Li maus que j'endure
Pur vous servir loyaument.

He closed his eyes and listened, not wanting to be distracted by the picture of her sitting on the bench, with her hair loose and shining like new-minted copper against the bright green of the willow. What he heard made him sit up very straight.

Her voice was true. Untrained, aye, but again, that didn't matter. She hit each note roundly; not, God be thanked, singing through her nose—which for some reason he'd never understood was considered seemly for young maidens—but straight up from her heart. And that was only the smallest part of it.

Ronan had heard many ladies sing before, some of them quite beautifully, but not one had ever conjured disturbing images of raw silk and honey in his mind. *That* could not be taught. It was simply there, a gift from all the gods. With just a bit of guidance, she could be even better. She could be brilliant.

"You," Ronan said, "are very good. But you must practice more."

She bent her head, a shimmering wave of golden curls hiding her expression. "I used to, when I was younger...."

"Sure, 'tis a sin you ever stopped. How could you? Why?"

"This," she said, holding up her lute, "is no more than an invitation to flirtation. Ladies are not expected to do more than pluck out a pleasant little tune that no one really wants to hear."

"And that bored you."

"Aye."

"I don't wonder. The first song we played—you made it, didn't you?"

She looked up at him, eyes wide and startled. "What makes you think—"

"I don't think, I know." He shook his head, puzzled. "It is a good song, Lady Maude, one you should be proud of."

Her cheeks grew pink as she smiled with the first genuine expression of pleasure he had seen her show. All at once she was heartbreakingly young and terribly vulnerable. Despite the smile curving her lips, her eyes were filled with shadows that twisted his heart strangely in his breast. The urge to take her in his arms and comfort her swept over him again, more strongly than it had the day before. He actually lifted his hand when a voice spoke, shattering the moment.

"That was verra nice, Maude."

Ronan turned sharply to see Lord Darnley standing at the edge of the path.

"It has been years since I heard ye sing, hinny," he added, his voice unexpectedly gentle.

"Oh, it was nothing—only that I had an hour to spare—but I should see Cook now—" Maude stood quickly and made a brief reverence to her father. "If you will excuse me . . ."

"Go on then," Darnley said genially, "dinna let us keep ye from your work."

When she was gone, he lowered himself slowly to the bench where she had sat, his bad leg stretched out straight before him. "Well, *taibhsear.*"

"My lord?"

Ronan met his gaze squarely. He had done nothing wrong; there was no reason to flinch from the nobleman's sharp eyes.

"I kent Fergus half my life," Darnley said at last. "Even when he was twice your age, the lasses had an eye for him. And he for them."

"Did he?" Ronan couldn't help but smile at the thought.

Darnley snorted. "That's the young for ye. Can't ever imagine that old dogs were once pups themselves. Aye, Fergus had a way with him, but he never had your looks. In fact, ye are the sort of man who makes a father wonder."

"Wonder what?" Ronan asked, though he knew quite well what Darnley was saying. He would have been insulted if he weren't uncomfortably aware that had Darnley not arrived when he did, the nobleman might have good cause for his suspicions.

"What ye are after here. My daughter is a bonny lass herself—and a wealthy one. Who are your people?"

"My mother was an O'Donnell, from the Inishowen Peninsula," Ronan said. "My father was Richard Fitzgerald."

Darnley nodded. "I kent a Fitzgerald once—a good friend to King Edward, he was, and a braw knight. If I remember aright, his name was John. Is he kin to ye?"

Ronan sighed. "Yes."

Darnley looked at him, brows raised.

"My grandfather," Ronan admitted grudgingly.

"Is it so?" Darnley mused, shredding the new leaves from a slender willow branch. "Are ye certain of that?"

"I think I know my own grandfather."

"I have friends at court who can tell me."

"Then ask them."

Darnley smiled suddenly, a surprisingly charming smile that reminded Ronan of young Haddon, Darnley's son. "As I said, it has been years since I heard my daughter sing. It is something I would hear more often. So do ye meet her on the morrow and have her play some more."

Ronan was a bit alarmed by the sudden lifting of his heart. "My lord," he said carefully, "I hardly think that Fergus meant—"

"I dinna care what Fergus meant, nor what he wanted. Ye are under my orders, are ye no?"

"I am."

"Then tomorrow ye shall give my daughter a second lesson—but not alone. I am no such a great fool as that! She shall bring her woman with her. It will give ye something to do until I find a better use for ye."

"As you will, my lord."

"Quite right," Darnley said mildly. "As *I* will. Mind that ye remember that. For I have many eyes, *taibhsear*, and many tongues to tell me tales."

"I don't doubt it for a moment."

"And I *shall* write to my friends at court."

"I don't doubt that, either."

"John Fitzgerald was a prideful man, as I remember. His brother is the Earl o' Desmond, is he no?"

"Yes."

"And his grandson was apprenticed to Fergus Mc-Innes, living in a cave!" Darnley laughed. "What does Sir John think of that?"

Ronan stood. "I wouldn't know," he said shortly. "I haven't asked him."

Eight

The last time Celia had visited Cranston Keep five years before, it had been a poor and dismal place. Now the small hall had an air of quiet affluence, with hangings adorning the fresh-scrubbed walls and aromatic rushes covering the floor.

She had heard the Maxwells were prospering, and now she saw that it was true. Head bent respectfully, she followed the page into the new laird's presence chamber. She had met Kinnon Maxwell once before just a fortnight ago, when he had come to greet Lord Darnley upon Darnley's return from France. Now he greeted Celia courteously, pouring wine for her with his own hand and pushing a dish of oatcakes across the table.

"I have heard, Laird Maxwell," Celia began cautiously, "that ye have had your troubles with the Kirallens."

Kinnon Maxwell lifted the heavy goblet before him. "What gave ye that idea? Why, the Kirallens are my trusted friends and allies."

His eyes met hers over the goblet's rim. Very clear

eyes, they were, very penetrating, so dark a gray as to seem almost black. A spark of amusement and curiosity lit them from within.

"Aye," Celia said. "And so your brother, Brodie—God rest him—was acting without your knowledge three years ago when he attacked them?"

Kinnon nodded. "That's right."

"Of course," Celia murmured, "now that Brodie's gone, there is no one to say otherwise."

"My brother's death was a great tragedy for our clan, but I've done what I can to ease the loss."

Celia barely kept herself from laughing at this pious declaration. Brodie had been a greedy, stupid ox, and his death was the best thing that had ever happened to the Maxwells. Celia doubted he was mourned by anyone, particularly Kinnon, whose hand had almost surely wielded the dagger that finished his elder brother off.

"I'm sure ye have, Laird," she murmured, helping herself to an oatcake. "And from what I hear, the Maxwells prosper from the change."

Kinnon smiled modestly.

"And now that ye are settled in," Celia went on, "is it not time ye wed and got yourself an heir?"

Kinnon's brows rose, and a smile quirked the corner of his mouth. "Are ye making me an offer?"

"Would that I were in a position to do so," she answered, looking at him from beneath her lashes. "But alas, my affections are . . . otherwise engaged. No, 'tis a lady I had in mind, one who is in need of a husband. Her father's mind would be much eased if a suitable match could be arranged."

Kinnon rested his chin in his palm. "Then why is he not here himself?"

"Oh, he has some strange notion that the lady should have some say in the matter, but she is proving . . . difficult to please. I happen to ken that his patience is wearing thin."

"Interesting. But I am not quite sure. The lady—if indeed we are speaking of the same lady—is rumored to be a bit more than difficult. A man must be careful when choosing his life's companion, mistress."

"She's verra rich."

Kinnon sat up a little straighter. "I have heard something of the sort. Her dowry is . . . ?"

Celia was ready with her answer. Her voice tinged with bitterness, she recounted each coin and jewel and manor Darnley had promised to his precious Maude. When she finished, Kinnon whistled softly.

"I had no idea Darnley was so wealthy."

He wasn't. What Darnley was offering was hardly short of madness, far more than he could ever pay. But there was no need for Kinnon to know that.

"Weel," he said thoughtfully, "that does put a different complexion on the matter. Still, I'm hardly a pauper myself. While I won't pretend the gold would not be welcome, I put a high price on my peace of mind."

"I think the right man could gentle the lass. Get an heir on her, and she'll be a different woman." She paused, then added very casually, "If she survives childbirth, that is."

"Aye." Kinnon's eyes narrowed. "There is always that."

"If you were to press your suit, I think I could promise it would be well received."

"Could ye? But—pardon me for asking—why would ye do so? Apart from concern about my unmarried state, that is."

When he smiled, Celia could not help but smile in return. "May I speak plainly?"

Kinnon inclined his head. "Please do."

"Time has taken its toll upon Lord Darnley; he grows old, Laird, his resolve wavers, and I would not see the honor of his house destroyed. He needs a son, and the one he has is worse than useless."

"Darnley could still marry again," Kinnon pointed out. "He grows old, but I don't doubt he could still get himself another lad. In fact," he added slowly, raising one brow, "a clever woman would make sure he did."

Celia nodded. "He may. In fact," she said, looking at him straightly, "I am quite certain that he will soon be a father. But Haddon *is* his heir. Unless . . ."

Kinnon pursed his lips. "Bare is the back that has no brother."

"Exactly so," Celia said, pleased that they understood each other. "But it will be years until *my* son is grown to manhood, and his father will be in his dotage long before that time. Meanwhile, the Kirallens will continue to flourish. 'Tis certain that *Haddon* willna lift a hand against them."

Kinnon sat up straight and folded his hands before him on the table. "Let us have this plain between us, mistress. Ye want my help in this matter of the Kirallens, and in return ye are prepared to offer me Lady Maude—"

"And her dowry," Celia reminded him.

"Why?"

"The honor of the Darnleys—" Celia began.

Kinnon waved a hand. "—is no concern of yours. I am not a fool, mistress, and I have no time for lies. Speak plainly, or this interview is over."

"Very well, then," Celia said. "I would see Jemmy Kirallen dead."

Kinnon blinked. "Well, that is plain enough. May I inquire . . . ?"

"No."

He sat back in his seat, his eyes hooded. "What help could I count upon from Darnley?"

"Well," Celia said, "things being as they are, he canna move openly . . ."

"What *will* he do?"

When Celia did not answer, Kinnon laughed. "Well, this is a fine offer you're making me, when I am to bear all the risk and trouble! Darnley has no idea ye are here today, does he?"

"Well, no, but given time, I am certain I could convince him—"

Kinnon stood. "Good day, mistress. I'm afraid ye will have to find some other means of killing Jemmy Kirallen off."

"But I thought—three years ago—"

"Three years is a long time. Much has changed since then. I have exactly what I want, and I'm not about to risk it all on some bootless venture. Besides," he added, "I'm rather fond of Jemmy. *And* his lady."

He grinned, and Celia felt herself begin to flush. "Then I see I was mistaken in you," she said stiffly. "Pray forgive me."

"Willingly. For ye have given me something to think about. The clan needs a lady and I an heir. Thank ye for the advice."

Celia gritted her teeth. "You're very welcome."

Putting a finger beneath her chin, he tipped her face to his. "Will ye take some in return?"

"What?"

"Forget the Kirallens. They're stronger than ye ken."

"So you're afraid of them!" she cried contemptuously.

Kinnon smiled and stroked her cheek. "Perhaps," he said, "or perhaps I learned something three years ago."

"And what might that be?"

"When the game begins to turn, a wise man cuts his losses and moves on." He chucked her beneath the chin. "There's a bit o' wisdom for ye, lass, and ye may have it free of charge."

Celia jerked her head away. "It sounds more like cowardice to me."

"Hard words, mistress!" Laughing, he held out his hand. "Let me see if I can make amends. Perhaps ye would care to join me for a bit of supper in my chamber?"

He was a rogue, Celia thought, and a fool, as well, if he thought he could have her for the price of a smile.

"Even if I canna help ye, I can listen," he said. "I confess I'd like to know what poor Jemmy did to earn your ire. And I don't deny I could use your help should I decide to go a-courting at Aylsford Keep."

When she hesitated, he smiled. "Oh, come, mistress, you've had a long journey on a wet day with naught but disappointment at the end of it. The least I can give ye is a meal—and perhaps a bit more, if ye will have it."

He winked, and Celia could not help but laugh. At least he was an honest rogue. And the way he was looking at her brought a rush of heat to her cheeks.

Oh, why not, she thought. He was young and not bad looking, and God knew he would make a pleasant change from Darnley. These days, the old man could do no more than pant and fumble. If she meant to get a son, she would have to do it elsewhere, and she could do far worse than Kinnon Maxwell.

He watched her, smiling, sharp-eyed, and she had the feeling he could read her thoughts as easily as if she'd shouted them aloud. She was surprised to find she did not mind at all.

"A warm meal would be welcome," she said primly.

"Warm?" He tucked her hand into the crook of his elbow, sending a shiver up her arm. "Oh, I think I can promise ye at least that much."

Later, with a thin rain pattering on the hood of her cloak and hours of riding before her, Celia reflected glumly that she had met her match in Kinnon Maxwell. He was too canny to be manipulated, too clever to make a single move without an eye fixed firmly on his own advantage.

Yet, she thought, a reluctant smile playing across her lips, perhaps the journey had not been entirely wasted. Kinnon might have proved a disappointing ally, but at least she could say this much for him: when the man made a promise, he knew how to keep it.

Nine

Rain lashed against the windows of the hall at Aylsford, running in rivulets down the glass. Three hounds were sprawled before the fire, twitching in their sleep, and Dame Becta nodded over her spinning. Ronan yawned, leaning back against the cushioned settle as Maude began her lesson for the day.

The lessons had become part of the pattern, fitting neatly between her daily row with Cook and her inspection of the linen. One hour out of the day was not much to give, not if Father asked it. He asked so little, after all, and considering all that he had done for her, it would be churlish to refuse.

Though she wished he had asked something else. *Anything* else.

These hours were a form of torture, and their sweetness only added to the pain. Had it been her choice, she would not have sat in the same room with Ronan Fitzgerald for a single moment. She did not trust him—not his humor, which matched too well with hers, or that smile, contagious as the plague. His voice she liked least of all, for when he sang, her mind would drift off into strange thoughts and foolish fancies that made her distrust herself as much as him.

He was nothing like the knights considered handsome by the ladies of the court. They tended to be fair and florid, with necks so thick their heads seemed to grow straight from massive shoulders. Simple men, given to loud laughter and coarse jests that Maude never found amusing. Their chivalry was but a thin veneer, for they lived to fight, their thoughts as narrow as the bit of life they could glimpse through the visors of their helms.

Ronan was quite different. Nothing was beneath his notice, from the type of rushes used in the hall to the scent Maude happened to be wearing or the proper time to plant a field. He'd spent an entire morning watching the dredging of the moat, a noisesome job that seemed to interest him profoundly.

And she had spent far too much of that morning sitting by her window, watching him. By this time she should be weary of his face, for she knew it as well—or better—than her own.

His brow was high and very fair against his coal black hair, his mouth set always in a humorous cant, as though he were amused by everything he saw. Eyes the color of new grass slanted over high cheekbones, cut sharp enough to carve deep hollows beneath, reaching to a fine-drawn jaw that was an intriguing blend of strength and delicacy.

God help her, she was doing it again, watching him half-dreaming on the settle with the firelight gilding his features while she should be tending to her lesson.

It did not seem fair or right that her heart should so betray her. This was not the sweet pain of poetry and song but a savage ache, striking with all the power of a blow unlooked for on the one part of herself she had still believed her own.

She could not like Ronan for it. Indeed, during the

past week she had come close to hating him. Yet still she counted the hours until they met again and found herself remembering every word he spoke and each expression that passed across his face as she lay wakeful through the night.

Ronan watched the fire playing on the hearth through half-closed eyes as he listened with approval to Maude's lesson. Much to his surprise, he was quite enjoying the role of teacher, one he had steadfastly avoided in the past, no matter how tempting the student might be. Flirtation was one thing, but when it came to music, he had no patience for the slovenly and no sympathy with idleness.

But Maude was neither slovenly nor idle. She must have been practicing for hours every day, to judge by the results. There was no doubt she had talent, but apart from that, Ronan was drawn to her in a way he understood no better than he did the lady herself. Even as he went about his work each day, fitting up the old stillroom as a surgery and tending to the illnesses and injuries of the manor folk, he was always aware of the time. No matter was so pressing that it could not wait the hour that belonged to Lady Maude.

He suspected she did not approach their lessons with the same enthusiasm. Though always prepared, she clearly took no pleasure in their meetings. Indeed, since the day they had sat together in the garden, she avoided looking at him at all, and the few words she spoke were confined strictly to the task at hand.

Today she was clad in a simple woolen gown of blue, her hair caught back with a ribbon. The perfect curve of her high white brow, the delicate skin of her eyelids, the auburn lashes tipped with gold all reminded Ronan of certain paintings he had seen in Rome. But any resemblance she bore to the Madonna ended when he reached her mouth.

A Madonna painted with such a mouth would surely be banished by a compassionate church, for she would drive any male, no matter how devout, straight to the confessional.

Maude had taken his lesson for the day and, as she sometimes did, added something more. As always, it was a melancholy tune, but today her invention was passing strange, harsh and dissonant, almost painful to the ear.

Ronan moved restlessly in his seat, anticipating the moment when the melody would resolve, until the anticipation became a need, a hunger for the chaos to end and order be restored. From those small white hands, too delicate for even the simplest of work, the music continued to flow, strange and dark and as much of a mystery as the lady was herself.

Just as the tension grew unbearable, she struck a single chord of such power that the hair stirred on his neck. And then she stopped.

Ronan stared at her, astonished. How could she have ended in such wise? Nothing had been completed, nothing resolved. The last chord simply hung there with terrible finality, heartbreaking in its emptiness. And somehow perfect. He knew that he would dream of it. He suspected the dreams would be nightmares.

Outside the circle cast by firelight and candle, the hall was dark and cold. *She does not belong here,* Ronan thought. *She should never have come back. For all her hard words and haughty looks, she is too fine to live in such a place.* One only had to hear her play to know she was no simple maid but a woman unlike any other he had known.

Her head was bent, her face in shadow, the fire drawing sparks of gold and crimson from her hair.

"Lady Maude, that was brilliant."

She slanted him a quick look, her expression one of deep suspicion.

"Truly," he added softly. "There is nothing I can say except to thank you."

She sighed, and a hint of a smile touched her lips.

"Now, for tomorrow's lesson," he went on. "We will explore a new concept, something so startling I doubt you've ever heard of it." He ran his fingers across the strings of his harp, sending a ripple of bright sound dancing through the air. "I call it major chords."

She glanced up at him, tense and wary, and he held his breath. But then she laughed, a pretty sound, and he was laughing, too, even as he wondered that she was capable of laughter with such dark music in her heart.

"Oh, I have heard of them," she said, and she played a bit of a popular ballad. "Nasty little things, all bright sunshine and false promises."

"Not all promises are false," he answered, picking up the tune. "And sunlight does exist, you know."

"Aye, and so do pretty ribbons and apple blossoms and deathless love. So does cow dung, for that matter, but I don't have to sing about it, do I?"

"Sing of anything you like, so long as it is the truth."

"Truth? What is that? No, don't answer—I forbid you to answer! For, in *truth*, I don't care to hear what you have to say."

"Without giving me a chance? Oh, fie, lady, that is hard."

She smiled wickedly. "But I *am* hard. Did you not know? Ah, yes, you do know, I can see it in your face, you know all about me, don't you? My brother and the Kirallens have told you all my secrets."

Ronan's hands stilled. "How could they? You alone are mistress of your secrets, and I do not think you give them lightly."

A blue green flash showed beneath her lashes, then was veiled as she dropped her gaze. "Quite right. But I always did say you were clever. What will you do when you leave here?" she added suddenly. "Go back to your cave?"

He blinked, taken aback by the question. "No, I will not be going back there. That part of my life is over."

"Where will you go?"

"I've been thinking of Constantinople. Perhaps Jerusalem."

She caught her breath, looking up at him with wide-open eyes. "Jerusalem? Truly?"

"I'd thought of it. First I might stop in Paris for a time. There are many learned men in the university there."

Maude's lip curled in a delicate sneer. "Oh, aye. Very learned. 'If a pig is tied with a string and led to market, is it the man who leads it or the string?' Now there's a fine question, and since I heard it, I have not slept a night for wondering."

"That question is actually quite interesting. You see—"

"What I see is the waste of a good pig. Why not slaughter the porker and have done with it? Then use the rope to hang all the poor fools who waste their time debating such a pointless question."

"Who has been telling you about the university?"

She shot him a scornful glance. "I can read, and I do."

Ronan looked at her with new interest. Most ladies he had known were barely literate, their time being occupied by other matters. Those who could read seldom did—at least not for the pleasure of the pastime. "What do you read?"

She shrugged. "Boethius—I rather liked him and his wheel—and Augustine, though he hasn't a kind word to toss to a woman. Aquinas," she added carelessly, "for I'd heard the man came up with proof of God's existence, and I wanted to see how he had managed *that*. But they were only words," she added in a lower voice. "They proved nothing."

"What proof did you need, lady?" he asked, even more intrigued. "And why did you want it at all?"

She bit her lip, frowning, as though regretting having spoken. Then her face went blank, and she shrugged again.

"Why not? Is it only men who can ask that sort of question?"

"No. No, I don't suppose it is. But—"

Maude stood abruptly. "I must away. I've much to do this afternoon. In fact, I am far too busy to waste my time with music. If I want you again, I will send." She waved her hand, dismissing him.

Ronan felt as though he had been slapped. "If you do, I shall be pleased to answer . . . if I can find the time."

Her eyes narrowed. "You may go. Now. At once."

"With the greatest pleasure, lady."

Ronan was halfway across the hall when he heard swift footsteps behind him. He turned, thinking Maude had repented of her rudeness. But she went past him, her face transformed by a smile of delighted surprise, and ran lightly to the door.

"Uncle Robert!" she called, and the man who had just entered lifted a hand in greeting.

"Hello, Maude. And—" he turned to Ronan, who stood back a bit, watching them. "Why, it's Fizgerald, isn't it?"

Ronan bowed. "Good day, Sir Robert."

Sir Robert Allshouse, Lord Darnley's half brother, was a man of about thirty years with a sharp eye and an even sharper wit. Ronan had quite liked him when they met at Ravenspur the year before. Despite his relationship with Darnley, Sir Robert was a welcome guest at Ravenspur and often visited the Kirallens and his nephew Haddon. As always, Sir Robert was clad in the latest fashion, though the feather in his cap was draggled with the rain. He grimaced at the cap and tossed it onto the nearest table, running a slender hand through thick, chestnut hair.

"I must thank you for your help with that ballad," he said to Ronan. "It went down very well at court."

Ronan imagined that it had. Sir Robert had a good ear

for a rhyme, coupled with an acid humor. Once the melody was complete, it had been a wryly amusing little ditty.

"So, what do you here, Fitzgerald?" Sir Robert continued. "I thought you would be at Ravenspur."

"I was until but lately."

"How is Alyson?" the knight asked eagerly. "I trust you left her well?"

"Quite well." Ronan glanced at Maude, who stood forgotten by the door. He had marked the glow that lit her face when she first saw her uncle. Now it was quite gone, vanished so abruptly he could scarce believe it had been there at all.

"And were you there, too?" Sir Robert smiled warmly, turning to Maude. "How splendid! I always knew that once you gave Alyson a chance, the two of you would be fast friends."

Maude raised her chin. "No, I was not there."

"I thought you might have ridden over to see Haddon by this time. He must think he's been forgotten."

Maude shrugged.

"I'm sure Alyson is taking great care of him," the knight said after a moment. "She is so good with young things. I daresay he's very happy there with her. The only trouble will be convincing him to come home when his time is up."

Maude's hands shone white-knuckled on her lute. "Won't you come inside, Uncle, and tell me all the news of court?"

Sir Robert grimaced. "I came her to escape all that! I'm afraid I've no time for gossip, anyway. My visit is a short one. I just wanted to give my greetings to John, and then I'm off to Ravenspur."

"I see." Maude's voice was flat, her expression one of utter scorn. "I shall tell my father that you are here."

She spun on her heel and walked away.

Sir Robert handed his cloak to Becta, who spread it before the fire and tipped a cup of spiced ale from the warming pan. She gave it to him without a word, her face stony.

"Thank you, Becta," he said, shooting her a winning smile as he sank down on the settle. Becta nodded without comment, gathered up her wool, and walked off.

"Like mistress, like maid," the knight said, lifting his cup to her departing back. He stretched his legs toward the fire with a contented sigh and sipped his ale, clearly in no hurry to meet Lord Darnley.

"You seemed a bit . . . short with your niece," Ronan said.

"Do you think so? Well, you don't know her as I do. Trust me, Fitzgerald, Maude doesn't listen to a word I say."

Ronan rather doubted that, but before he could make up his mind to pursue the subject, Sir Robert smiled.

"Sit down for a moment, won't you? What are you working on these days? I remember you told me of the ballad you were planning, the one about Stephen Kirallen and Clare McLaran. How does it go on?"

"It does not go on at all," Ronan answered, resuming his seat and taking up his ale.

"You could always ask John for the details," Sir Robert suggested with a grin.

"Oh, I've done that."

Sir Robert's brows rose sharply. "You *never* did."

"Why not? I wanted to know, and he seemed the one to ask. But I ended no wiser than I began. Lord Darnley did not even remember the name at first, then he shrugged and said one of his men must have come upon Stephen wandering the moor."

Robert grimaced. "Well, at least Stephen tried. That's what matters, isn't it?"

"Is it? The man's betrothed is stolen on her wedding day, and the groom sets off to rescue her single-handed . . .

only to bungle the attempt. 'Tis a bit difficult to make a hero out of *that.*"

"Except, perhaps, a comic one," Robert agreed, "though I don't suppose that's what you're after."

Ronan laughed. "Oh, I've thought of it. For I'm sick to death of the other sort of songs. All those heroes tossing life away for love's sake—why, you'd think it happened every day! And here it took me years to find just one, only to discover that the poor fool blundered his way to his own death. I am sorely tempted to tell the simple truth."

"But people do not want to hear the truth. Particularly not in ballads."

"No, Laird Jemmy would hardly thank me for a comic rendering of his favorite uncle's death, nor would Lady Alyson. Best to leave the whole thing alone."

Robert grinned. "You are a wiser man than I. That little song we put together made me quite a few enemies."

"I did warn you. . . ."

"Aye, you did, but, oh, you should have seen Lord Latimer's face! It was well worth his anger. Here, give me a bit more of that ale, would you? I'm not quite up to seeing John yet. Tell me what brings you to Aylsford."

"An errand from Fergus."

Robert nodded politely.

Ronan knew the knight had always regarded Fergus as a figure out of folklore, quaint but not particularly interesting.

"And how do you find it here?"

"Well enough," Ronan answered. "Your brother is not in the best of health."

"Oh, John will go on forever! He's indestructible, you know. I think he's kept alive by sheer malice. And what of Maude? Are you surviving her? Or has she shredded you with her tongue?"

Ronan bit back a sharp reply. Lady Maude was Sir

Robert's niece, and to judge from her expression when he'd first arrived, quite fond of him, a fondness that was clearly not returned. Still, no matter what quarrel they had, it was wrong to speak of her like this, particularly to Ronan, who was all but a stranger to the knight.

"I find her conversation . . . refreshing," he said. "She has quite a gift for music."

Sir Robert grimaced. "She plays well enough, or at least she used to, though her songs are damned odd."

The knight sipped his ale and tipped his head back, staring up into the rafters. "You'd scarce believe it, but she was an enchanting child. Very sweet and always laughing . . ."

Ronan looked at him with interest. "So what happened?" he asked, lightening his voice to take any insult from his words.

Robert shook his head. "I was quite looking forward to bringing her to court, but when she arrived, she was so altered I scarcely knew her. Well, fourteen is a captious age, and I hoped she would improve with time. But she never did."

He frowned, then shrugged again. "I would almost think she was a changeling, but the fairy folk only take infants, don't they?"

"So I've heard," Ronan answered absently.

"What, you do not know? And here I thought your grandfather was a lordling of the Sidhe!"

The knight's russet eyes were sparkling with amusement, and Ronan couldn't help but laugh. "I'd forgotten that. Sure, my imagination ran away with my tongue on that one."

"Alyson said she half-believes it after hearing you play."

"Lady Alyson is kind."

"Aye, she is," Robert said, suddenly grave. "I'm very proud of her, you know. What she went through—well, no ordinary lass could have survived it. 'Tis a pity Maude isn't more like her." He heaved himself up with a groan. "I suppose I have to see John now if I hope to reach Ravenspur today. If we don't meet again, farewell."

He walked away, whistling, and Ronan sat awhile longer, remembering bits of conversation. What had Haddon said of his sister? He had liked Maude well enough before she went to London, but she had come back a different person. But Sir Robert said that by the time she arrived in London, she was so altered he scarcely knew her.

An enchanting child. A sweet lass, always laughing. A heartless young woman who had sent her half sister off to almost certain death.

Who is *she?* he wondered, sitting back and watching the fire on the hearth. He doubted the answer to that question had anything to do with the reason Fergus had sent him here, but still, he wondered. He wondered very much.

Ten

When Ronan had told Sir Robert that his brother was not a well man, he had spoken only truth. But until the night of Sir Robert's visit, Ronan had not known the extent of Darnley's failing health. The nobleman let out a hissing breath between clenched teeth as Ronan laid a steaming poultice on his leg. The wound Darnley had taken in the wars in France had never really healed, and from time to time it would break open again, an angry ulcer that caused him agonizing pain.

"That should ease you," Ronan said, straightening. "And I'll send you something to help you sleep. Would you like a cup of wine?"

He suspected that Darnley had not slept for several nights, though the nobleman refused to answer any questions on the subject. It was Celia who sent for Ronan soon after Sir Robert departed, and Darnley had only grudgingly accepted his ministrations, though it was clear the older man was suffering.

"I have some brandywine in that cupboard," Darnley said. "The key's over there." He gestured toward the mantel.

Ronan picked up a small iron key. "This one?"

"No, the silver—"

But Ronan didn't hear him. His entire body had gone rigid when his fingers closed around cold iron, and—

The chamber was in shadow as he moved silently, stealthily across the floor, the key clutched in his hand. From time to time he cast a quick look over his shoulder to make sure the man in the bed still slept. Oh, God, let it be the right key, it must be, I haven't time to search again. *His heart pounded, and sweat dripped down his face as he moved carefully toward the door.*

Clare was up there. She was alive. Nothing else mattered. So long as he could get to her it would be well, everything would be all right if only he could find her, hold her in his arms, see her smiling again.

I'm coming, lass, don't give up, it's been a long journey, but I'm almost there. *He knelt before the door, trying to fit the key into the lock with hands so slick with sweat that he could barely keep his grasp on it. It slid between his fingers, and he cursed steadily beneath his breath, but then it fit, God be thanked, it fit, it was the right key—*

"You!" a voice called from behind him. "What are ye doing over there?"

His heart leapt into his throat, and he turned, managed to straighten, tried to twist his face into a smile as Lord Darnley lifted himself on one elbow.

"My lord," he said, and no, that shaking whisper wouldn't do, so he cleared his throat and tried again. "My lord, I didna want to wake ye. I've brought a tray from the kitchens."

"I gave no order."

Darnley was sitting up, frowning, trying to make out who he was. The livery was not a perfect fit—too tight across the shoulders, too short at the wrists—but it was so dim in here, it should be all right. . . .

Only it wasn't. Darnley's expression changed and,

Oh, God, he's recognized me somehow, but that's impossible, he's never seen me, he cannot know.

Say something! *he ordered himself.* It's not too late, you can still get out of this, if you can only find the words.

"Cook asked me to see to it," he managed, one hand still touching the key, the other moving toward his dagger. *He'd have to kill him. That hadn't been in the plan, but plans changed, and little as he liked the idea, he'd kill Darnley if he must. But it was too late.*

"You?" Darnley whispered. *"How did you—Guards! Guards, to me!"*

The key turned, and he threw open the door, wrenched it from the lock, slammed the door behind him, and wasted precious seconds searching for some way to secure it from within. But this was a prison door, Darnley's prison where he kept sweet Clare caged for his own pleasure, and it locked only from the outside.

He abandoned the door and raced up the narrow stairway. He'd never live through this, he knew it now, but he'd accepted that possibility before he'd ever started out. Death didn't matter. Nothing mattered but that he see her face once more and tell her he would wait for her, forever if he had to, that a thing as small as death could never part them.

"Clare!" he cried. *"Clare, 'tis I—"*

Hands seized him from behind, dragged him back, away from her. He twisted, lashed out with the dagger, and one guard fell with a cry of pain. But it was not enough. There were too many guards, too many hands on him, and all the breath went out of him as a fist connected with his stomach. He fell gasping to his knees and, as the door slammed shut, he could not believe that this was happening, could not accept that he had come this close, only to fail.

Pain exploded in his skull, and the floor rose up to meet him. A hand was in his hair, dragging his head up.

He was looking into Darnley's face, and Darnley was smiling; he was laughing, saying, "Ye stupid bastard, you're too late. Do ye no ken I've had her already?"

As if that mattered. As if anything this man had done could make the slightest difference to what he felt for Clare. "Oh, love, I'm sorry, I'm so sorry," he tried to say, but the room was fading, the world dissolving; the key fell from nerveless fingers to clatter on the flagstone, and—

Ronan was himself again, his head hammering, his face streaked with tears.

"What's the matter with ye?"

Ronan looked up, and it was Darnley, staring down at him, but a different Darnley than he'd seen in his vision. That man had been young, with ruddy hair and a florid countenance. This Darnley was an old man and was watching him, not with triumph, but concern.

"What ails ye, lad? Come, sit down, I'll have Celia bring some—"

Ronan shook his head. "Stephen Kirallen," he said. "That's who it was, Stephen Kirallen. He was in here, wasn't he? *Wasn't he?*"

Darnley rocked back as though he had been struck. "Aye," he said. "But how did ye—"

"He was dressed in your livery. And he made it as far as the door. Oh, God," Ronan cried, his voice shaking, "he made it to the door, and then you caught him, you stopped him, you murdered him—he was *nineteen years old!* He only wanted to see her once—that's all he hoped for at the end, just to see her face!"

"What are ye talking about?" Darnley demanded. "How do ye ken this?"

Ronan stood and dropped the key on the table. "Does it matter how I know? It is the truth."

Darnley took a second key from the mantel and limped over to the cupboard. He returned to his seat with a bottle. "Aye, 'tis the truth," he said, splashing liquid into his mug. He sipped, grimaced, then tossed back the brandywine. "Stephen Kirallen crept in here like a thief in the night. He tried to steal what was mine by right of conquest."

"Are you referring to his betrothed?"

"They said he was a coward, the laird's youngest brother," Darnley went on, his eyes distant as he gazed into the past. "I wasna expecting anything from him. Yet he got in here—right into my own chamber. 'Twas a brave deed," he admitted grudgingly. "I was . . . impressed. I might even have let him live."

"You might have—? Oh, no," Ronan whispered. "He didn't die then, he was still alive—"

"I was sleeping, but he walked right past me," Darnley said as though Ronan hadn't spoken. "Right past me and never struck. Why do ye think that was?"

"Did you not ask him?"

"I never did," Darnley said heavily. "At the time I dismissed him as a fool, but after . . . I wondered. In his place, what would ye have done?"

Ronan sat down. His head was still pounding, though not so badly as it had been, and his mouth was dry with remembered terror and despair. What *would* he have done in Stephen's place?

"To kill a man while he is sleeping . . ." He shuddered. "And yet . . ."

"And yet. Aye. He should have done it. I would have—and so, I think, would you. I thought at first that I might let him go. 'Tis God's own truth," Darnley said, putting a hand on his heart. "I told him he only had to ask. *Properly.* But he would not. God *damn* him," he added in savage whisper, "he would *not.*"

"And so you killed him."

"I killed him and I took his woman and fathered a bairn on her. He is long dead, and yet . . . sometimes I lie awake and wonder, why? Why did he not strike?"

"I think, my lord, that the answer is a simple one. Stephen Kirallen was a man of honor."

Darnley looked at him, his expression unreadable. "A man of honor. Whatever *that* means. 'Tis more likely he was a coward and a fool."

"That could be. But a coward would have begged for life. And a fool would have never made it past your guards. You know this," he added, surprised to hear his voice come out so gently. "Or you would not lie awake and wonder."

Darnley rose, pressing one fist to the small of his back with a little grunt. All at once he was just an old man, bent and worn, with faded eyes and a face scored with lines of pain.

"There are other reasons for that," he said. "I dinna sleep much these days."

"And her?" Ronan insisted. "What of Clare McLaran? Do you think of her?"

"I did all right by her," Darnley said with a shrug. "I gave her a strong bairn, didn't I? And I found her a husband, as well, to look after the both of them."

"And that made everything all right?"

" 'Twas more than I had to do, considering the circumstances. More than any of them would have done."

"The Kirallens do not make war on women," Ronan said stiffly.

"Aye, they're all wee saints over there," Darnley sneered. "They never raided, never stole, never—" He broke off and turned toward the window, bracing his hands on the deep sill as he stared out into the darkness.

"How it must gall you that Clare's daughter is Lady Alyson now, wed to Stephen's nephew!"

"Do ye think I care what became of the brat? Let Kirallen have her, 'tis naught to me. Oh, leave me, get out, I am too weary for this blether. Send me one of your potions so I might sleep tonight."

It was on the tip of Ronan's tongue to refuse. Why

should he make this man's wretched life more bearable? Darnley *should* suffer; he deserved more than a sleepless night in payment for the damage he had done.

It is not your place to judge.

That's what Fergus always said, and it had seemed just and right when he had said it. Now, though, it seemed wrong for Ronan to blind himself to the truth he had just learned. But he had promised. He had vowed to help anyone who came to him in need, and in all truth, he must admit that Darnley needed rest.

"Very well, my lord," he said, his voice grudging.

Darnley turned his head and smiled faintly. "Not so easy, is it, lad? Well, that's all right, ye dinna have to like your duty so long as ye don't shirk it."

Ronan choked out a good night that was barely civil. To be lectured on his duty by Lord John Darnley was almost more than he could bear.

Nor did it help matters that the words Darnley had spoken were almost certainly the same ones Fergus would have used.

Eleven

The air was warm and still in the gardens. The daffodils and lilacs were gone, and now it was the season of the rose. Ronan paced over the gravel path from one end to the other, winding through the shrubbery, past the flowering hedges, deep into the heart of the pleasaunce.

The small bench was empty today, surrounded by a sea of roses. Red and pink, white and yellow, and every combination of the colors spilled their scent into the air.

Ronan walked over to the fountain and dipped his hand into the water, then splashed his face. *Now I know,* he thought. Stephen Kirallen was a hero indeed, a man of dauntless honor and high courage. He deserved to have his name immortalized in song. But Ronan would not be the one to make that song.

What had all Stephen's heroism gained him? A cruel death at nineteen, his life cut short before it ever properly began. And Clare—poor Clare, who had never known how close her lover came to her, who had gone to her grave believing he abandoned her. Only Darnley had survived. And prospered. Where was the justice in that? Where was the meaning?

The same questions had been running through his mind all night, but he was no closer to the answers. His wits were thick today; the headache that had plagued him since last night had retreated, but it was still there, hovering in the background, both a warning and a punishment.

God's blood, he knew better than to leave himself so open. Six months into his apprenticeship with Fergus, he'd had more control than that! But he had shirked his prayers lately, cut short his meditation, found a hundred excuses to skip the exercises Fergus had set him. It had been all too easy to allow himself to be distracted by Lord Darnley's daughter.

I should leave this place, he thought with sudden clarity, *go back to the cave and mend the damage that's been done. In a few days—or weeks—I can return. Perhaps then I can forget Lady Maude and concentrate on the task Fergus sent me here to do.*

He strode back down the path, his headache gone. As he turned the corner he was feeling better, a man in control of his own destiny.

And then he saw Lady Maude seated on a bench.

Go on, he told himself, *walk by her with a nod. Don't stop, keep moving.*

He meant to. He actually took one step forward, then another. She glanced up at him. "Oh, it's you. Good. I have a question on those major chords."

"I am sorry, lady, but I cannot stop."

He spoke the words with confidence, but then she smiled up at him. Her smiles were infrequent, all the more to be valued for their rarity, and this one was particularly sweet.

It was all the apology she meant to offer. It was enough.

Before Ronan quite knew what he was about, he was seated next to her, and she was asking him her question, though he hardly knew what she was saying or what he answered. He thought he could listen to her voice forever and never grow weary of the sound.

"I have something new for you today," she was saying now. The very thought of leaving seemed absurd as she began to play.

Lady Maude was more than a talented amateur. She was a true musician, though her vision was so very odd that he doubted most people could begin to comprehend it. He didn't understand it himself.

No, he thought, don't lie to yourself. You understand it well enough. You just don't like it. In fact, he hated the despair in every passage. He rejected it with all his being, even as it drew him with a force he was helpless to resist.

"Lady, I have nothing left to teach you," Ronan said when she was done.

She glanced up at him shyly, and his throat went dry as dust. "Do you really think . . . or no, you are just being kind."

"I am never kind, not in the way you mean. What I said is precisely what I meant."

"But I cannot sing as you do."

"I have trained for years, with some of the best masters to be found. 'Tis more a matter of breathing than anything. I could show you—"

"What would be the point?"

Her face, which had been alive with pleasure, now fell into lines of sullen discontent. But no, that was too pat, too simple. The woman who made such music was incapable of such petty emotions.

"For your own satisfaction," he suggested. "You seem like a lady who likes to do well what she has undertaken."

She shrugged. "I sing well enough to please myself."

"Then for amusement."

"Amusement? Is that all you think there is to life? It seems rather pointless."

"What point is there to anything?" he asked, keeping his voice light, giving no sign that this very question had tormented him all night.

Maude looked up at him, surprised, for he had put her own thought into words. He reached over his head to pluck a rose, which he offered to her with a smile. The deep red of the rose glowed against the white skin of his hand, and when Maude met his eyes above the blossom, she could not force herself to look away. Confused, she reached out and took the flower, turning it between her fingers as he went on.

"Look at this, lady," he said earnestly. "One of God's creations. See how beautiful it is, how perfect, more perfect than anything man could ever hope to make. Would it not be a great sin to cut if off in bud, trample it on the ground, saying that it serves no purpose?"

"But it lasts such a short time," she said, the words slipping out before she could stop to think.

"Now there you're wrong. It lives, it blooms, it dies— but sure as spring comes after winter, it will bloom again."

Maude stared into the vivid red heart of the petals through a shimmer of tears as the flower's scent enveloped her. "People are not flowers."

"No, but we are all children of the earth, all of us, the trees and flowers and each soul born, all known, all beloved, all part of God's great plan. Everything happens for a purpose, lady. Life is a great gift, but it is for you to choose how you shall use it."

His voice was passionate; almost, she thought, as though he spoke to convince himself as much as her.

Her fingers tightened on the stem and sharp pain stung her palm. "Life is a curse. We are born to suffer and die. This life is but a shadow and the flesh is an illusion."

Ronan's dark brows rose. "And I thought you never went to chapel! You must have a wee bird whispering Father Aidan's sermons in your ear."

"I have heard them all my life."

"Much as I hate to disagree with the good father, he is a fool. We are born to *live,* and if suffering is a part of life . . . well, then, so is pleasure. Just look around you," he said, waving one hand to encompass the garden. "Sure, the world is full of flowers."

"And thorns," Maude pointed out.

"Well, you could have one of these. . . ." He plucked a lily from the flower bed and laid it on her lap. It looked pale, insipid, beside the vibrant rose.

"I—I don't like them," she said with a shudder. "They remind me of funerals."

"Whose funeral?"

"My mother's," she said, pushing the lily aside and raising the rose to her mouth. She brushed the soft petals across her lips as she spoke again, her voice almost a whisper. "The chapel was filled with them that day, and the smell . . . I've never cared for lilies since."

"No more do I. I much prefer the rose. Thorns and all."

Their eyes held for a long moment, while a lark sang from the branches of the willow and the bees buzzed among the flowers. Maude's heartbeat quickened; she wanted to run, but for some reason she could not seem to move. She could only wait, for what she did not know, suspended in a breathless space between hope and terror. Ronan took her hand in his, slowly raised it to his lips, and kissed the small scratch on her palm.

Her fingertips brushed his cheek, every nerve alive to the feel of him, smooth and rough, his skin warm to the touch. Her hand began to shake, and when he encircled her in his arm, she leaned against him, not daring to think about what she was doing, for she knew that if she stopped to think, she would be up and gone.

Maude gazed up at him, a little frightened, a little curious, her cheeks flushed a brilliant red. Even as his lips touched hers, a small warning voice urged him to

draw back and consider what exactly he was doing. Lady
Maude Darnley was well-born, unattached—the sort of
woman he usually avoided at all costs.

Yet the woman in his arms was not just any noblewoman. She was Lady Maude, the one who made that
music, the music that was driving him insane. *Avoid* her?
He had been looking for her all his life without dreaming
she existed.

But who was she?

She cannot be like her father, he thought. *She isn't
part of all this evil; it hasn't really touched her. I won't
believe it. If only I could understand her . . .*

Her lips were softly parted, her face turned up to his
as she gazed at him with shy anticipation.

"Lady," he said softly, "I have wondered something. . . ."

"Yes?" It was hardly a word at all, but an exhalation,
soft and trembling on her lips.

"You are not what quite you seem, are you? Won't
you trust me with the truth?"

"The truth?"

She straightened abruptly. The color fled from her
cheeks, and her fingers were icy in his grip. He covered
them with his other hand.

"About—well, about Lady Alyson. I've heard the tale,
of course, but now that I've come to know you, I can't
believe 'tis as I heard. What really happened between
you?"

"I do not know what you mean."

"Your father forced you to it, didn't he?"

Maude looked down at their joined hands. "No," she
said quietly. "He did not force me."

"Then what—?"

"My father had promised me to the Kirallens, though
it was done against his will. He saw no reason to honor
such a vow. Nor did I. He thought of the plan, and I

agreed it was a good one. I trained Alyson—with Uncle Robert's help—and sent her in my place."

"But how did you really feel about it?" he insisted. "About Lady Alyson?"

She removed her hand from his and sat up very straight. "I felt nothing. Or no, in *truth*, I did feel something. I was glad to see her go."

Ronan stared at her in shock. "But there must be more to it than that!"

"Why must there? Because you *want* there to be more? Well, I am sorry to disappoint you, but that is how it was."

"But how could you—your own half sister—she could have died! What harm had she ever done you?"

Maude shrugged. "I disliked her then, and I like her no better now. I was not sorry to send her, and I cared naught for what happened once she got to Ravenspur."

"I don't believe you. You are not like that, not really—"

"I am as I am," she cried with sudden passion, "not as you would have me. And you know nothing—*nothing* about me!"

She jumped to her feet and ran down the path and through the garden, vanishing through the gate before Ronan had gotten to his feet.

Twelve

"Ah, Maude," Lord Darnley said as she hurried through the hall. "I want to speak with ye."

"Not now."

"Aye, now," Darnley ordered, and there was a note in his voice Maude had heard many times before, but never directed at herself.

"What is it?" she demanded, arms folded across her middle, each hand clutching the opposite elbow. She was shaking with cold, her head pounded, and she wanted nothing but to shut herself inside her chamber.

Darnley sat down before the empty hearth and patted the settle beside him. "Sit down, lass."

Maude wanted to refuse. She was not in command of herself just now, and Father mustn't know that. It made him so angry when she was upset, so miserable that there was only one remedy to be found.

The hunt.

Not the sort with hawks and hounds and pages winding horns. Father's hunts were swift and silent, and his prey ran on two legs. Maude could not bear another such prize to be laid proudly at her feet.

So she composed her face into a smile and sat down beside him. "Yes, Father?"

"I have been thinking that 'tis time ye . . . well, time ye thought about a husband."

"A—a what?"

"Ye are one and twenty, Maude. 'Tis past time ye wed."

This could not be real. It was just another nightmare, not happening, not to her. She squeezed her eyes shut, but when she opened them again, she was still sitting in the quiet hall, the scents of stale ale, hounds, and old rushes surrounding her.

"You said—" Her voice was high, cracking with hysteria. She swallowed hard. "You said," she went on more calmly, "you would not force me."

"Aye, I did, but that was when—well, 'twas long ago. I shouldna have to force ye, for ye are old enough to understand your duty."

"Duty? To whom? To what?"

"To your family and yourself. 'Tis not as though ye lacked for offers! But perhaps 'tis well that ye did not accept any of those men in London. I wouldn't want ye to bide so far from home."

Oh, why did he have to speak of this today, when her wits were scrambled and she was too terribly close to tears? She wanted no husband, she wanted no man at all . . . save one, and he did not want her. She blinked hard against the sudden stinging of her eyes. One moment she had been in Ronan's arms, his lips just touching hers, and the next he was pulling back to stare into her eyes as though he would read her very soul.

What had he seen? Not the whole truth, but a part of it, enough for him to know that she was not what she seemed.

"There's one who's been asking after ye," Darnley went on, startling her from her thoughts. "Kinnon Maxwell came by just the other day, and—"

"Kinnon Maxwell? Father, surely you are jesting!"

"Aye, he's a Scot," Darnley said, as though that could be the only reason for her objection. "But for all that he's a canny man. He would take good care of ye."

Maude pressed her hands to her temples. "No."

"Don't be saying no right off, lass, not without—"

"You promised!"

Darnley sighed heavily. "And I fear now that such a promise did ye a disservice. 'Tis time—past time—ye got over your reluctance."

Maude shook her head, too stunned to stop the tears rising to her eyes. Darnley coughed and looked away.

"I only thought 'twould be best for ye—never mind, then, we won't speak of it now. Just promise me ye will think it over. Will ye do that?"

Maude stared at him dumbly.

"There, that's fine," Darnley said, patting her shoulder. "Ye think it over and then . . . then . . ."

His words trailed off and he stood, giving her shoulder a final pat. "I'm glad we had this talk."

When he was gone, Maude sat as he had left her, every limb cold and lifeless. It was only when the servants came into the hall that she managed to rouse herself. Slowly, moving as stiffly as an old woman, she made her way up the stairway to her chamber.

Thirteen

"Becta," Maude called, and the tiring woman hurried from the inner chamber.

"What is it, lamb? What's happened?"

"Becta, I—Father said—"

"Whisht," Becta interrupted, glancing over her shoulder. "Celia is here. She's been waiting to see ye."

"Celia?"

"Aye, lady."

Celia reclined on the window seat, nor did she trouble to stand as Maude approached.

"Get out," Maude said.

"Nay, lady, ye sit down." Celia patted the cushioned window seat. " 'Tis time we had a little talk."

"I've naught to say to you."

"Weel, I've plenty to say to you, and I'll not leave until it has been said."

Becta moved to stand behind her mistress.

"Be off wi' ye, Celia," she commanded sharply, but Celia only laughed.

"I'll no be takin' orders from ye, Mistress Becta. Now,

Maude, I've come to speak wi' ye about your wedding to Kinnon Maxwell."

"Get out," Maude repeated, her voice shaking. "How dare you—"

"Your father wants the match, and for good reasons. Ye shall wed the man, and I'll have none of your tempers."

"You'll not . . . ?" Maude could barely choke the words past her rage.

At last Celia rose to her feet. "No need to be skittish," she said playfully. "Kinnon need not ken he's getting . . . less . . . than he bargained for."

The sharp answer Maude was about to make died upon her lips. She could only stare in frozen horror as Celia continued.

"I ken what ye must be thinking, that he'll surely know on your wedding night. But even then, there are ways . . ." She winked.

Even if Maude could have spoken, words had deserted her entirely. The betrayal was too sharp, too sudden to comprehend.

No one will ever know. That's what Father had promised. And now he had told Celia, who was watching her, contempt and triumph mingled in her eyes.

Maude swayed, but Becta was there behind her, her hands firm on Maude's shoulders.

"But we'll talk of that another time," Celia said. "For now 'tis enough that all is plain between us—just as it should be in a family. Did your father no tell ye I bear his child? Just think, a wee sister for ye . . . or a brother."

"I *have* a brother."

"Haddon?" Celia shrugged, dismissing him. "He's one of *them* now, isn't he? But that's none of your concern. 'Tis time—past time—ye had your own family to worry for, your own husband and bairns. You're lucky your father did not put you away—God knows why he did not—but now ye *will* wed Kinnon Maxwell. Get used to the idea."

With that she left them, head held high, one hand laid proudly on her belly.

Fourteen

Ronan went from the garden to the records chamber, a musty cell belowstairs where he sometimes helped Niall, Darnley's clerk. As always, Niall was pleased to see him, for he was an educated man half starved for conversation.

But today Ronan went straight to the back shelves. He began to pull down parchments with such energy that dust flew through the air and spiders scurried about in panic.

What the devil had just happened? But no, he would not waste his time thinking about Maude. Here he had been believing she was everything he wanted, and she turned out to be just as cold and scheming as her father.

His jaw tight with anger, he flipped through the records, wondering why anyone had bothered to keep this trash. Laziness, no doubt; just stack it on a shelf and save the bother of going through it. Who cared how many sheep had been brought down from the pasture fifty years before? Or that some long-dead Darnley's bull had taken a ribbon at a market fair? Lists of foodstuffs and wine

long consumed, cloth that had moldered into dust . . .
Damn it all, he thought, flinging the pile on the floor in
a choking cloud of dust. What was he doing here?

"Master Fitzgerald?"

A page hovered at the corner of the shelving, eyeing
Ronan warily.

"What?" Ronan snapped.

The boy took a step back. "Lord Darnley has asked
that ye play for him tonight. In the hall."

"Not tonight. Say I am unwell."

"He—" The page swallowed nervously. "He com-
mands it."

Ronan slammed a book down on the table. *Do whatever he asks of ye, so long as it does not interfere with
your conscience or your vows.*

All the years and all the miles he had traveled, and
where had he ended? Trapped by a thoughtless promise,
doomed to dance attendance on some conniving nobleman. Surely there was a jest here somewhere, but just
now he was in no mood to find it.

Ronan played. Not well, for his heart was seething
with resentment, but still he played. It was not so easy
here to forget what had happened earlier, not with Lady
Maude sitting up there on the dais. His mind kept running
over their conversation in the garden, every time coming
to the conclusion that he was a fool.

Damn Fergus! Damn him for not telling Ronan about
Lady Maude! If Fergus had been so clever, why had he
not foreseen that they would meet? And if he had foreseen
it, why had he not spoken? *But why blame him?* Ronan
asked himself bitterly. *A wise man would never have
made the promise you made without at least asking for
the details.*

But then, a wise man wouldn't have been trying to

kiss Lady Maude in the garden today. A *wise* man would have known that if everyone who'd ever met the lady agreed she was a heartless jade, the probability was that they were right.

And yet she made such music! Even now, Ronan could hear its echo in the piece he was playing, and there was no denying the song was richer for it.

So be content, he told himself. *You've learned something new and gained more than you lost. Only a fool would ask for more.*

He looked at Maude, sitting up at the high table beside her father. She wore an ugly, high-necked gown of saffron, so stiff with jeweled embroidery that it would probably stand on its own. It was far too heavy for her slender frame, and beneath an ornate headdress, her features were obscured by a pearl-encrusted veil. The only word for the entire ensemble was hideous.

When she moved, he caught a glimpse of her face— rosy, bright-eyed—completely untroubled by what had happened earlier. But what had he expected? She had no heart. Just look at her up there, chatting brightly with her father, smiling at the squire who filled her cup, laughing at the witticisms of some elderly knight who sat at her left hand.

False, he thought, clenching his jaw until it ached. *None of it is real. She doesn't care a whit for the jests that old man is pouring in her ear.* Her laughter, when it came to him, was shrill and forced. Looking more closely, it seemed her eyes were feverishly bright, her color hectic, and he wondered with a spurt of fear if she was ill.

And then he knew he was a fool indeed, for he did want more, wanted it so much it left an aching hollow in his center.

Oh, Fergus, he thought, despairing, *what have you done to me? Why did you send me to this place? And why, why did you not tell me what I would find?*

"Because," Fergus's voice said clearly in his mind, so clearly that he could hear the asperity in the old man's words, *"ye were not meant to know."*

Fifteen

When the chart began to blur, Ronan set down his pen and rubbed his eyes. He must have made some mistake. But he'd been over this twice now, and the answer kept coming out the same.

There was nothing, absolutely nothing here to give him any insight into Lady Maude. Had he read her natal chart before meeting her, Ronan would have predicted she was well married with several living children and no serious impediments to happiness. Moreover, he would have guessed she was a merry soul, perhaps a little giddy, with two or three amusing love affairs behind her before she settled on her life's companion.

In short, the woman whose chart he was reading was born under exceptionally propitious stars, destined for a long life filled with joy and laughter.

He consulted the notes he had taken during his first meeting with Maude, then checked the chart. It was all in order. Yet there must be some mistake. With a muttered curse, he turned over the sheet of parchment and began again.

His eyes were growing heavy when he heard voices in the passageway, hurrying feet moving past his door. Curious, he flung his cloak around him and stepped outside. It was Dame Becta he had heard, Maude's tiring woman, hair loose about her shoulders and a candle in her hand.

"What is it?" he asked. "Is someone ill?"

"Nay, 'tis naught. Go back to sleep."

Lord Darnley strode around the corner. "No sign of her in the garden. I'll try—"

He broke off when he saw Ronan. "What are ye doing up?"

"I thought I might be of some help."

"Help? Nay—"

"Now, my lord," Celia said, appearing from nowhere to stand by Darnley's shoulder. "He may ken something. Lady Maude has gone missing," she added with a sigh.

"Missing? But she was in the hall tonight—" Ronan began.

"Aye, and she went to bed," Darnley said impatiently. " 'Tis likely she's wandering in her sleep."

"Again," Celia said, casting her eyes up to the ceiling.

"I'll find her," Becta said, her mouth tightening. "All of ye go back to bed."

"Aye, lass, ye need your rest," Darnley said, turning to Celia with a proprietary concern. "I'll take care of this."

Ronan glanced at Becta. The tiring woman was staring at Celia with distaste—and something else, Ronan thought, something that looked very much like fear.

"Nay, my lord, I want to be sure she is well," Celia said sweetly. "Where *could* she be?"

"On the battlements," Becta said. Darnley looked suddenly old and weary beyond measure.

"Aye. That must be it."

Ronan followed Becta's candle down the passageway, up the narrow staircase that led onto the battlements. A cool wind fanned his cheeks as he stepped outside and closed his eyes for the space of ten heartbeats to allow them to adjust.

When he opened them again, he saw Maude at once, standing between the parapets, her nightshift fluttering in the breeze.

"There she is," Celia said briskly. "Lady! What are ye doing? Come down from there at once!"

She started forward, but Ronan took her by the arm. "Nay, Celia. Don't," he whispered, "she could go over."

And wondered suddenly if Celia had already known that.

"Maude," he said quietly, moving to stand behind her. "Maude." He was careful to say her name, for it was dangerous to wake a sleepwalker too suddenly, lest their spirit be severed from their body.

"Maude," he said again, and this time he touched her hand.

She whirled, startled, and he caught her from behind to lift her down. Gentle as he was, she still struck out at him and tore herself from his grasp.

"Lady," Becta said softly, " 'tis naught to fear, ye were wandering, that's all. Come, lamb, we'll get ye back to bed."

Maude's eyes cleared as she pressed her back against the stone wall. "No. Leave me. All of you."

"Oh dear, my lady, ye must come down. The night is chill."

"Go," Maude said harshly. "Just go!"

"Come, my lord," Celia said with an impatient sigh. "If she wants to stay, there's naught that we can do about it. And 'tis late for ye to be up."

"Go along," Ronan said. "All of you. I shall see no harm comes to her."

"You had better see to that," Darnley growled, but he allowed Celia to lead him inside, Becta following reluctantly.

When they were gone, Ronan removed his cloak and draped it over Maude's shoulders. She clutched it about herself and sank down against the wall, knees drawn up and arms clasped around them. After a moment, Ronan sat as well.

"I haven't done that for years," she said at last.

" 'Tis not a pleasant thing," Ronan said. "Waking in a strange place with no memory of how you came there. It used to happen to me often, after my father died and my grandfather took me to live with him."

He leaned his head back against the cold stone and stared up at the frosty stars, rising high above the mist.

"I started when I was fourteen," Maude said. "After I'd been . . . ill."

"When Fergus was here?"

"Aye. When Fergus was here."

Ronan opened his mouth to speak, but guided by some deeper instinct, he shut it without uttering a word. A sudden breeze swirled the mist about them.

Do it, Maude ordered herself. *Tell him now. There will never be a better time than this, when you won't have to see the shock and horror in his eyes. Let him go back into the world where the memory will fade until he has forgotten me completely.*

"It was spring," she began. "One of those days you sometimes get, all sunshine and blooming flowers, the earth waking again and everything all new and green. I decided to ride to the village of Mallow—an hour's ride or so, and my palfrey was in need of exercise. I packed food and other stuff to bring to them. We were nearly to the village . . ."

The scent of cowslips. The sharp keening of a kestrel.

". . . and I smelled smoke. The village was aflame."

A cock crowed in the distance, its strident voice cutting through the mist-laden air. Maude chanced a look at Ronan, relieved to find he wasn't watching her. His profile was just visible against the predawn light, as clear and clean as if he had been carved of stone.

She drew a long breath and steeled herself to continue.

"We were soon overtaken by the raiders. Kirallens, they were, a small band broken off from the main party in the village. They pulled me from my horse and demanded my name, but I could not tell them. I couldn't speak at all. It was all too strange—too sudden. They were arguing, I think, but I couldn't make out what they were saying—and I couldn't seem to catch my breath."

She was having the same trouble now, but she would not weep, she *would* not. One word of sympathy would undo her altogether.

"What happened then?" Ronan asked, his voice as casual as if they were discussing what dish to have for supper.

"What ye would expect," she answered in the same tone. "Only I wasn't expecting it at all. I kent nothing then, naught of men or what they could do to—"

She stopped abruptly, her throat working as she swallowed hard.

"I see. How did you escape them? Did they let you go?"

"I dinna remember. Sometimes bits come back to me—like a nightmare where nothing makes any sense. I remember being on the moor at dawn, alone, and wishing I was dead—and then I was in a strange bed in the dark and everything hurt. . . . Someone lit a candle, and a voice spoke to me so kindly, and Fergus held my hand and talked to me until I fell asleep."

The parapets were black against the gathering light. From the fields below drifted the sounds of lowing cattle and the high bleating of the lambs. The church bell rang out, deep and musical. Maude eased around and looked at Ronan fully.

"That is how I came to know your master."

He nodded, his expression thoughtful, his gaze fixed on the hills. She wasn't certain what she had expected, but it was surely not this calm, almost indifferent acceptance of her story. But she was grateful for it. His leaving would be far easier this way.

"I've never told anyone before. My father swore—and made me swear—that none would ever know."

He turned to her then, looking at her directly. His eyes were very bright against the pallor of his skin. "Why do you tell me now?"

"Celia knows; my father's doing. So his oath is broken and I am free of mine." She held his gaze with desperate courage, for now that she had started, she must see this through. "And I—I thought that you should know."

A shudder passed through her and she drew her knees against her chest, clasping her arms about her shins. It was finished. Whatever had shimmered between them was now dead, and all that remained was the bitter satisfaction of knowing she had killed it with her own hand.

Deliberately, Ronan loosened the muscles of his jaw, clenched so hard that sharp pain speared his temples. *I have been a fool,* he thought, *letting myself forget that Fergus never did anything without a reason. He was under oath, no doubt, but he trusted me to find the truth, and not to fall to pieces once I'd found it.*

Ruthlessly, he thrust his feelings back, for they had no place here now. He was a *taibhsear,* not some green boy to be thinking of himself and moaning over things that might have been. Whatever reasons Maude had given herself for telling him did not matter now. Surely she had been guided to confide in him.

He stood and held out his hands to her. "Show me," he said. "Show me where it happened."

"What? No. I won't."

His voice rang out, sharp, commanding. "Show me."

Maude took his outstretched hands and allowed him to pull her to her feet. Their eyes met and held in a silent battle. In the end, it was Maude who looked away.

"I haven't been there since . . . Aye," she said slowly. "Very well. I'll show you."

Sixteen

"It was here."

Ronan heard the panic in her voice and reined in beside Maude's coal black stallion. Such a strange mount for a maid, he'd always thought, but now it was not strange at all.

"We can go back," he said, and her frozen form relaxed slightly in the saddle. "If you are afraid, I will not force you."

"Of course I am afraid, d'ye take me for a fool? But I said I would do this and I shall."

He smiled slightly. "Then lead on."

"There is the village," she said, pointing to a neat row of thatched roofs, almost invisible against the rolling moor. "And it was here—or close to it—that I first smelled the smoke."

Step by step they retraced Maude's journey, and finally she dismounted. "There were two men with me that day," she said. "One they shot down as we fled. The other—Gavin was his name, he was just a lad—stayed by me. Here is where they caught us," she said. She stepped back a pace, hands covering her face. "I canna do this," she said, the words muffled. "I thought I could, but—"

"Wait. Stop. Look at me."

She shook her head blindly.

Ronan took her by the wrists and pulled her hands from her face. "You are not there, it is seven years past, and you are safe with me. No harm will come to you, I swear it—no, *look* at me. Listen. You are seven years away from that, and you can look at it. Like a pageant, something you can watch, but you are not a part of it. Do you hear me? Can you understand what I am saying?"

Some of the blind terror faded from her eyes, and after a moment she nodded briefly.

"Then do you understand that you can look? Nothing you see can touch you; it is all very far away. Now tell me what happened next."

"They pulled us down," she said. "And there was one, a great brute, who was shouting at me. He hit me—" She touched her cheek. "There was the most awful sound— he'd broken my nose, but I didna ken that then. I only knew I couldn't breathe. Gavin began to cry, and I remember wondering why he would weep when they had not hurt him. . . ."

Ronan looked at the moor, stretching endlessly in all directions. He looked up at the sky, so wide, so vast. Then, at last, he looked at Maude. Her eyes were open, but she was staring past him.

"What did he do next?"

He was braced against her answer, but when it came, her words sliced through his defenses.

"He knocked me to the ground and dropped down on his knees beside me. Gavin began to scream, but one of the men clouted him and knocked him down, stopping his cries. The others were laughing, shouting out, 'Go to it, laddie!' And then," she stared down at the ground, her eyes wide, "then he shoved my skirt up and—and fell on me—"

Ronan closed his eyes. He didn't want to hear this, he didn't want to know.

"I screamed for help—I screamed and screamed . . . but no one came. No one came," she added in a desolate whisper.

"And then? What did he do?" Despising his own cowardice, he added quickly, "After. What happened after?"

"After?" Maude spoke the word slowly, as if it was one she'd never heard before. "Why, after, he rolled off me and cursed. And then," she frowned, concentrating, "someone said they should be gone before the others came back. And someone else said, no, not until he'd had a—a taste. The man—he said, 'Sod off. I'm the one who found her, wasn't I? There's plenty of time, and she's barely broken in.' "

Ronan could not catch his breath. Sweat trickled coldly between his shoulder blades. "You were awake."

"Oh, yes," Maude said, and she gave him a twisted smile. "I've met ladies who could swoon at an insult. Can ye imagine that? I was awake. I saw it all. But not with my own eyes. 'Tis strange, but it seems that I was up above, watching myself and him, seeing it all happening below me."

He had to get hold of himself. He cleared his throat and said, "How long did he—did it go on?"

"It was just after noon when I set out, and when it grew dark, they built a fire. It made shadows—huge shadows—on the ground. They were quite drunk by then," she added in a cool, dispassionate voice. "And then others came, riding back from the village. There was a great deal of shouting, and then . . ." She shook her head. "Nothing more."

It was enough for one day. More than enough, more than Ronan had ever wanted to know.

"I wonder what happened to them," he said, not realizing he'd spoken aloud until she turned to him.

"I canna say. My father tried—he swore he'd kill them all, and then . . . then . . ."

"Then what?"

"My honor would be avenged."

"*Your* honor? Oh, lady, no! They were the ones who were dishonored, not you. Never you."

"Weel, now that you put it that way, 'tis all well," she snapped, color flooding her cheeks. "They were dishonored, not me. Now, why did I not think of that myself? I'm certain their dishonor has been a terrible burden to all of them."

She began to walk away, the wind snapping at the edges of her cloak.

"Lady Maude, wait!" Ronan hurried after her. "I didn't mean—"

"What?" she flung over her shoulder.

"I didn't mean you were not the one to suffer. But they were the ones at fault. You did nothing to deserve—"

"If I did nothing to deserve it, why did it happen?" she demanded, not slowing her pace.

"It doesn't matter why; that isn't important now—"

She whirled to face him. "But everything happens for a purpose, Ronan. Everything! That is what you told me, isn't it? So you tell me what purpose there was to this, how it was all part of God's great plan. Go ahead, I'm listening. *Tell* me, damn you, explain it all to me!"

Ronan could not speak. He could only stare at her as he glimpsed a world that made no sense, where God stood by uncaring, helpless, as innocent people suffered and evil triumphed. *Fergus,* he thought, *help me, tell me what to say. You always had the answers.*

But there was only silence.

"I don't know," he said at last.

"You don't know," Maude said, her voice contemptuous. "Well, there's a first."

And with that she walked away.

Ronan sank to the ground and watched her go. There was nothing he could say to her, no comfort he could give. What kind of God let such things happen to children? he wondered with sudden fury. What excuse was there for any God to countenance such suffering?

He drew a shaking breath. "Pull yourself together. At once."

He remembered his grandfather saying that long ago, the first time Ronan realized how unjust the world could be. But no, this wasn't the same at all. Ronan wasn't a child now, he was a man. No man could comprehend the will of God, but that didn't mean God wasn't there; it didn't mean God didn't love all his creation; it only meant that Ronan was human and didn't understand.

"Asleep, are ye?"

Maude stood over him. Her eyes were dry, but she was fearfully pale.

"Not quite," he answered, astonished to hear his voice come out so normally. "Though I am tired," he added, running a hand across his neck. "Aren't you?"

She nodded shortly.

"Shall we go back, then?"

Instead, she sat down beside him and ran one hand lightly across a patch of small white flowers. "Why did you make me come here today?"

"To show you that the past is past," he said carefully.

"You *are* a *taibhsear*," she said, sounding faintly surprised.

"Did I not tell you so?"

"You did. But I didn't think—Fergus was so old . . ."

"I am getting older quickly. Why, just today I've aged ten years."

She smiled faintly. "Aye."

If he wanted to help her, he must come up with some answers. He could not let her questions—her very good, very important questions—pass without more than "I don't know." So he had to think, and quickly, of some comforting platitude that wouldn't sound too false.

"Lady Maude, what I said before—" he started, groping for the words.

"What you said—" she began at the same moment, and they both stopped.

"Go on," he said.

"I thought—I was certain you would have some answer ready," she began haltingly. "I thought you would say what others have said, that I must have faith—or all would be well if I could forgive—or that vengeance is the answer and killing all of them will somehow make things right. But you didn't. You didn't say any of those things."

"And if I had?"

She looked at him with eyes that seemed at once very young and terribly old, filled with all the world's sorrow. "I would have known you for a liar."

"I won't lie to you. Not ever."

Her eyes filled with tears, and he gathered her close. He held her without speaking as sobs racked her body until all her tears were spent.

"It will be all right now," he murmured against her hair. "I'm here, don't worry, all will be well. . . ."

She leaned against him with a little sigh, her body soft and trusting in his arms. Terrible as her story had been, he was glad that it was out and all was plain between them. Everything was very simple now, very clear in his mind.

She was his. He had known it almost from the first, but only now, understanding her, could he accept it. Whatever she was, whatever she had suffered, she belonged to him as surely as he belonged to her. While he lived, no one would ever hurt her. Not again.

Fierce protectiveness swept through him and his arms tightened in a convulsive grip.

She moved restlessly against him and he held her

closer, his heart aching with wild tenderness. "It's all right," he said again. "Maude, I promise—"

"No, no—let me go—don't!" Her hands were on his chest, pushing him away, and he released her instantly.

But it was still too late.

She drew back, shaking, breathing in short gasps. "I'm sorry, Ronan, I—I can't—no, don't!" she cried as he reached for her again.

"I only meant—"

"I know what you meant. Dear God, do you think I blame *you?* But I cannot bear it—even you, even now—" Her eyes were wild with anguish as she turned from him; she turned away, and there was nothing he could do to stop her.

"It isn't something that happened long ago," she said, her voice shaking. "It is still with me, still happening, even after all these years. God, I'm such a coward! I know you want to help me, but it's no use. It is too late."

Had he really thought that it could be so simple? That he could vanquish all her pain with an embrace? Selfish, arrogant, that's what he had been, thinking only of what *he* wanted, what *he* needed.

But now the time had come to think of her.

She does not need a lover, Ronan thought, *and I cannot be that to her. Not now. Perhaps . . . but no, I cannot hope for that. I must not even think of it. And if I cannot put my feelings to one side and give her what she needs, I will be no use to her at all.*

"Of course it's not too late," he said. "Never think it, lady."

Kind words, bracing, spoken almost cheerfully, as though nothing of importance had just passed between them. *He meant to comfort me, no more,* Maude thought, and she knew she should be grateful for even that. For of course there could be nothing more between them, not now that he knew.

And even if there could be, she thought bitterly, what

good would it do her? She, who could not accept what she had spent hours dreaming might one day come to pass, could never hope to know what love might be. But while it lasted it had been sweet, far sweeter than her most vivid dream to be held like that, close and secret in his arms, his breath against her hair and the scent of him around her. It had been the one perfect moment of her life. Until she spoiled everything.

He means well, she thought, *but he is wrong. It is too late.* She sought the words to tell him, to make him understand that now she knew what she must do . . . what should have been done long years ago. But then he smiled, and she could not bring herself to speak a word.

Oh, she was a coward, but that was something she had known for seven years. The fierce blood of the Darnleys ran thin and sluggish in her veins. Else she would have fought—she would have died before she ever allowed herself to be so basely used that day.

She *should* have died. Instead, she had clung to life, and in all the years since, she had been too weak to put right what had gone wrong.

But not now. There was nothing left, no hope that things might one day be different, no sweet dream to sustain her. She had seen her dreams come true when Ronan held her, only to watch them slip away like water from her hands. There was no hope for her, no comfort.

And that was only right, for she deserved neither.

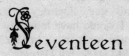

Seventeen

By the time they rode into the Aylsford courtyard, bars of late afternoon sunshine lay heavy on the cobbles. Ronan dismounted stiffly, feeling as though his jesting words were true; he was indeed far older than he had been just yesterday and too weary to even walk across the courtyard.

Maude looked no better than he felt. She was deathly pale, with dark purple patches encircling her eyes, and her steps were slow and heavy. They did not speak but walked together to the entrance.

"You should rest," Ronan said, and she smiled faintly as he broke off to stifle a yawn. Before she could answer, her father's voice forestalled her.

"Maude, where have ye been? I've been looking everywhere for ye—" He broke off, frowning, his gaze moving between his daughter and Ronan.

"I was out riding," she answered, running a hand over her tangled hair.

"I see that." Darnley's voice was hard, and he scowled as a small leaf drifted to the ground.

Maude raised her brows. "Is there something amiss, Father? You," she nodded briefly toward Ronan, "may go."

But her attempt to spare Ronan his share of Darnley's anger was quickly quelled.

"Nay, he shall stay," Darnley ordered curtly. "We have guests and I would have him play for them."

"About that, you must speak to him."

Maude turned to leave, but Darnley's voice halted her. "And I will have ye in the hall, as well, Maude. Now."

"Like this?" She held out her travel-stained cloak.

"Ye may change."

"Thank you." Her voice was cool, and she dropped her father a curtsy that was both faultlessly correct and somehow faintly mocking.

"What have ye been about, *taibhsear?*" Darnley growled when Maude was gone. "Where have ye been with my daughter all this time?"

"Riding on the moor, my lord, just as Lady Maude said."

Ronan lifted his chin and looked Darnley in the eye, challenging the nobleman to contradict him.

"Riding, eh? Is that how she got the leaves and twigs in her hair? And her cloak all stained with the heather?"

"We rested for a time. Surely you are not suggesting— no, of course you are not. You would not dare."

"Oh, I would dare many things," Darnley said softly. "Do not try me."

"Then do not try *me,* my lord. Lady Maude has no interest in dalliance with me or any man—as you well know. Why do you insult the both of us by pretending that she might?"

The light of battle faded from Darnley's eyes. "She told ye."

"Yes, she told me. Do not fear; like Fergus, I can hold my tongue. Now, if you will excuse me, I shall prepare to play for you and your guests after you have supped."

Ronan bowed and walked quickly to his chamber. He changed his robe for his green tunic, splashed cold water on his face, and combed his hair. Feeling somewhat calmer, he walked into the hall and took his place at the harp. Once he had finished the first song, he was feeling calmer still.

Until he looked up at the dais.

Maude was in her accustomed seat, dressed in an ugly crimson gown with a matching headdress. She looked pale but quite composed as she spoke to the man beside her. He was of about thirty years, with sandy hair and a swathe of Maxwell plaid over his shoulder.

As though aware he was being watched, the man looked down the hall and lifted his goblet with a grin that Ronan did not return.

The last time Ronan had seen Kinnon Maxwell had been three years ago, at Ravenspur. Soon after had come a time Ronan did not like to think about, beginning with the death of the old Laird Kirallen, followed by the murder of Brodie Maxwell, Kinnon's elder brother. There had been other deaths, as well, attempted murders—including that of Ronan himself—culminating in an attack on Jemmy Kirallen and his family.

Ronan clenched his left hand, so nearly lost defending the Kirallens, as Kinnon shrugged and grinned again, turning back to Maude.

Kinnon had vowed to avenge his murdered brother, but they were only words. Everyone knew that Kinnon had done the deed himself. Kinnon also denied any involvement with the Maxwells who had sought to overthrow Jemmy Kirallen. He blamed his dead brother for the deed and expressed great shock and sorrow.

But Ronan knew damned well that Kinnon had been behind the whole plot from the beginning. The man sitting beside Maude had coldly planned the murder of his elder brother, along with that of Jemmy Kirallen and his entire family—including Jemmy's unborn child.

Three years ago, Kinnon had been a diffident fellow with a dozen nervous mannerisms, all of which had magically disappeared. This new Kinnon held himself easily and smiled often. His wispy fringe of a beard was gone, revealing a surprisingly strong jaw, and the thinning hair that once hung about his eyes was cut short about his brow. He looked, Ronan thought, relaxed and prosperous, the sort of man any father might consider a fine match for his daughter.

And there was Maude, sharing her cup and trencher with him. And there was Darnley, beaming at the pair of them.

The meal was nearly over when Maude looked down the hall toward Ronan. Standing, she called, "Master Fitzgerald, do you play 'Glenkindie' for us." When he hesitated, she added brightly, "There isn't a harper born who doesn't know *that* tune! Come, let us hear what you can do with it."

She picked up her wine and drank deeply, then gestured the page over to refill her goblet as Ronan began to sing.

> *Glenkindie was a harper good,*
> *He harped for the king,*
> *Glenkindie was the best harper*
> *That ever harped on string.*
> *He could harp a fish out of salt water*
> *or water from a stone;*
> *He could harp the milk from a maiden's breast*
> *Though baby she had none.*
> *He's harped in the king's castle,*
> *He's harped them all asleep;*
> *All but the bonnie young countess*
> *Who for love did waking keep.*

Maude was right; every harper who could pluck a few notes was keen to perform "Glenkindie," though most were far from equal to the task. It had always been a favorite of Ronan's. With it, he had reduced royalty to tears.

He began the next verses, in which the young countess invited Glenkindie to her chamber later that night. But Glenkindie made the fatal mistake of confiding in his serving lad, bidding the boy to wake him before dawn.

The serving lad, Jock, had other things in mind. Disguised in his master's clothing, he himself went to the lady's bower, where he proceeded to ravish her.

> *He did not take the lady gay*
> *To bolster nor to bed,*
> *But down upon her chamber floor*
> *Full soon he hath her laid.*
> *He did not kiss that lady gay*
> *When he came nor when he goed.*
> *And sore mistrusted that lady gay*
> *He was of some churl's blood.*

Having taken his pleasure of the lady, Jock went home to wake his master, and Glenkindie was off to meet the lady of his heart. She was most surprised to see him.

> *O, have ye left behind with me*
> *Your hat or else your glove?*
> *Or are ye come to me again*
> *To ken more of my love?*
> *Glenkindie swore a mickle oath*
> *By oak and ash and thorn,*
> *I was never in your chamber, lady,*
> *Since the day that I was born.*
> *Then God forbid, the lady cried*
> *Such shame should e'er betide*
> *That I should first be a wild churl's thing*
> *And then a young knight's bride*
> *Then she has ta'en her wee pen knife*

That hung down by her gair
My body's kent a man this night
But it shall ken nae mair.

It worked, just as it always did. They began to sniff and wipe their eyes—and not only the ladies. It was so tragic, after all, so brave, so very *noble* of the bonny young countess, who would rather die than live despoiled.

Ronan could hardly choke out the final verses in which Glenkindie went home again to revenge himself upon his faithless servant.

Come hither now, thou Jock my boy,
Come hither thou to me.
I have not killed a man tonight,
But, Jock, thou hast killed three.
   And he pulled out his bright brown sword,
And dried it on his sleeve,
And he smote off that churl's head,
And asked no man's leave.
   He set the sword's point to his breast,
The pommel, to a stone:
Through the falseness of that serving lad
These three lives were all gone.

It was not the best Ronan had done; it was not even close. Still, silence gripped the hall when he was finished, broken by the occasional soft sob.

It was only then he dared to look at Maude. Her face was perfectly expressionless as she raised the goblet. "Well played, harper."

He stood clumsily, knocking over the stool behind him, and bowed. Maude raised the goblet to her lips and drained it in a single draught.

Eighteen

Ronan's sleep that night was troubled, filled with broken images that he could not recall on waking. By first light he was up and dressed, heading toward the kitchens, for he knew Maude's duties would carry her there first.

"Nay, master," the cook said. "She is behind her time today. But 'tis candlemaking today in the southern yard. Mayhap she went there first."

But Maude was not in the southern yard, nor in the storerooms or her bower. Ronan walked through the courtyard to the stables, thinking she might be there visiting her great brute of a horse.

The stall was empty.

"Where is Lady Maude's horse?" Ronan asked the stable lad.

"She had him saddled just now."

"Where did she go?"

The boy shrugged. "She didna say."

Ronan raced across the courtyard and up the stairs, bursting into Maude's chamber without bothering to knock. Dame Becta looked up from her sewing with a scowl.

"What d'ye mean by—"

"Where is Lady Maude?"

"Riding. Not that it is any concern of—"

"Where? Where did she go?"

Becta looked at him sharply. "What is this—"

"I have no time for questions! Just tell me."

"She's gone to the river, I would think. 'Tis her favorite path."

"What part of the river?" Ronan took the tiring woman by the wrist and pulled her toward the window. "Which way?"

"There," Becta said, pointing toward a narrow path. "She generally takes—"

Ronan did not stay to hear more. Nor did he stop for saddle or bridle, but flung himself upon his horse, clattering past the stableboy who stood openmouthed, leaning on his pitchfork.

He leaned low over the horse's neck, urging it ahead with heels and hands. He should have known last night when she asked him for that song that Maude would never make an idle threat. She had as good as told him what she was planning, but he had not believed that she would do it.

He burst upon three men-at-arms sitting by the tree line, where the path narrowed and no horse could go. They leaped up, weapons ready, as Ronan flung himself to earth.

"Where is she?"

"Walking," one answered, sheathing his dagger. "She likes to be alone down there."

Ronan ran down the narrow path until he reached the water's edge. Maude was nowhere to be seen.

He called for her, but there was no reply, only the sound of the river rushing past. The Tweed ran swift and deep just here between sharply sloping banks.

Too late, he thought, *too late!* And then he saw her.

She was knee deep in the water, walking slowly toward the center of the river.

Ronan was after her in a moment. The water was icy, the current strong. In his haste, he went down more than once, skinning knees and hands upon sharp stones. By the time he reached her, he was shaking from head to foot with cold and fear.

"Lady Maude!" he called. She turned, and he saw that her face was streaked with tears.

"Leave me!" she cried.

"No, I won't be doing that," Ronan said. "You're coming with me."

He held out his hand, bleeding from the rocks. Maude stared at it and then into his face.

"Leave me," she said again, her voice almost inaudible against the rushing of the water.

"I will *not.*"

He started toward her, and she backed away, nearly falling. Ronan froze.

"Lady, this is not the way."

"My father thought it kindness to let me live, but it was not. Seven years, Ronan, seven *years* and still I am not free of it. Whenever I begin to think I might be safe, something will remind me. A word. A scent. The angle of the sun. And then it all comes back, just as if it's happening again. And again. I cannot fight it anymore. I am tired, Ronan, so tired of being afraid and angry all the time, never knowing what I might do next or who will be hurt by it."

"Seven years is a long time for you to suffer so," Ronan said, "but you must not give up now. There is always hope."

She laughed, the first ugly sound he had heard come from her lips. "My father would have me wed Kinnon Maxwell. What hope will I have then? How could I bear for him to touch me when even you—"

Her voice broke and she turned away, starting for the

deeper water. Abandoning all caution, Ronan caught her from behind, lifted her from her feet, and bore her back to shore. Once on land, he set her down and took her hands in his.

"Lady, you must listen. Fergus swore an oath, did he not? As your father did, and you. He could not tell me why I was to come here, but it was for your sake he sent me, I am certain of it now. He sent me to you."

She tried to turn away, but he held her fast. "I swear that anything you tell me will go with me to the grave. You must think of me as you did Fergus, as someone who only wants your good."

"Why? Ronan, *look* at me, look at what I am, the things that I have done! Why would you want *my* good?"

Because I love you, he thought, but he did not speak the words. There was no healing in them, no magic, just his need to claim her as his own. But she could not belong to him or any man—not now. Perhaps not ever.

"I *am* looking at you," he said, "and what I see is a lady who has suffered more than any soul should have to bear alone. What happened to you was a terrible thing, but it does not have to rule you."

"I cannot stop it," she said thickly, her face averted. "I cannot get over it, for I have tried. I am not strong enough."

"That is not true. You are very strong; don't be telling me you're not. But you are right, you cannot get over it. Not over it or under it or around it. You must go through it."

"What does that mean?"

"The memories, lady. You must stop fighting them, for you are wearing yourself out in a battle you can never win."

She looked at him fully, her eyes wide. "Not fight them? What do you mean?"

"Remember," he said. "When the memories come, just let them happen."

"I will go mad!"

"Of course you won't," he said with a confidence he was far from feeling. "You're much too strong for that. And I'm not asking you to do this all alone. Tell the people closest to you, ask them to help you in whatever way seems best. Surely there are people you can trust."

"Becta," she said doubtfully, "she knows all and has been so good to me—but, oh, she'll think me such a coward, she will despise me—"

"Nonsense. She will want to help you, as do I. And I *can* help you, but only if you trust me."

He captured her gaze and held it, willing her to see the truth of what he said. At last she nodded.

"I do. But I cannot see what this will gain me."

He smiled and released her hands. "That," he said, "remains to be seen. Come, lady, what do you have to lose?" He nodded toward the leaden water rushing past. "As a last resort, it's always here."

Nineteen

That night Ronan paced his chamber, the last words he'd spoken by the river echoing through his mind.

"As a last resort, it's always here."

Was he a fool? A complete and total idiot? What sort of witless thing was that to say to a person who looked to him for guidance?

He turned to the shelf by the window, pulling down his scrolls, opening each one and scanning it before throwing it aside and turning to the next. The heavy book he opened carefully, his fingers moving more quickly as he flipped the heavy vellum pages until at last he slammed it shut.

He stood and stared unseeing at the fire. "I don't know what I'm doing."

There, he had said it, but he felt no better. No comforting voice spoke in his mind to deny his words. It was the simple truth. If Maude was ill, even if she had the plague, he'd have some idea how to help her. He could do his utmost, secure in the knowledge that if he failed, it would not be his fault.

But this was very different.

Lying on the floor was the wisdom of the ages, words he had copied with a careful hand, certain that if they did not contain the answers to life's questions, they held at least the method of discovering them.

But tonight they were just words upon a page.

What would Fergus do? he asked himself, feverishly pacing once again. *What would he say?*

The first thing he would say is, "For God's sweet sake, stop rushing about like a fool and use your wits." Ronan obediently sank down on a stool.

Fine, then, I'm sitting, I'm thinking, but all I can think is that I told Maude she could trust me, and it was all a lie.

No. That much, at least, was true. She *could* trust him, at least to do his best. And he could not do his best with his mind racing about in a fever of anxiety. He must calm down, take a deep breath, and think.

He cast his mind back over every person who had ever come to Fergus for help. Not one had been in Maude's position or even close. They had been ordinary people with ordinary ailments, helped by ordinary means. None of them had been sick unto the depths of their souls.

There had been that man, though, the one Fergus had mentioned once or twice. What had Fergus said? A man had come to him resolved to die, and Fergus had helped him to live. But Fergus had said it was the hardest thing he'd ever done, and more than once he had despaired. For the man—had Fergus ever said his name?—had lived through a battle in which all his companions died, and the guilt of it was more than he could bear.

Fergus had told him this to illustrate a point about the soul. Yes, Ronan remembered now, Fergus had said that when a person suffered some terrible shock, it could actually separate soul from body. Maude had said she viewed her rape from up above. Yes, it fit; that's when it had happened.

Ronan bent his head, fingers splayed through his hair and the heels of his hands pressed hard against his eyes. The soul. Its existence had been proved beyond a doubt centuries ago, though its nature was still a matter of dispute. Some said it was composed of air and others water, while a few held that it was blood. . . .

And what good did any of that do him? It wasn't facts he needed now, but wisdom.

Lifting his head, he saw the moon through the open window. It was at its full tonight. A latticework of clouds drifted across its surface, then it shone out again, serene and lofty, the undisputed mistress of the night.

Ronan took his staff and walked out into the garden. The night was mild, the air soft and damp and silent. Slowly, reluctantly, he moved deeper into the garden through a landscape grown strange and somehow threatening.

The paths were just the same, but stark black shadows sliced them into pieces between shrubs and bushes gilded with a silver light. When he left the path for the sheltered bit of lawn beside the fountain, tendrils of mist rose up from the earth to wind about his knees.

Shoulders stiff, expression one of deep wariness, he tipped his face up to the sky and regarded the moon shining high above, symbol of the ancient goddess.

Brighid, they called her in his homeland. Now she was *Saint* Brighid, safely ensconced within the confines of the church, but she had existed long centuries before Saint Patrick ever drew a breath. She had a thousand names throughout the world, most of which Ronan did not know. For all his thirst for knowledge, this was a knowledge he had never sought.

She was a mystery—*the* mystery—a deity whose existence no philosopher had ever sought to prove. She defied logic altogether. Maiden, mother, crone, she simply *was,* the earth from which all men came and to whose cold embrace all must inevitably return. She was in the laughter of every lass who ever danced around a may-pole, the groaning of the mother bringing new life into the world, the death rattle of the old woman breathing out her last.

Ronan gazed up at the silver disk, his chin tilted in aggressive challenge. "Well?" he demanded. "Here I am. What have you to say to me?"

But no, that wasn't right. Fergus had surely taught him that wisdom wasn't summoned on demand. He bent his head, though the effort felt as though it might snap the taut muscles of his neck.

"For her sake," he whispered. "Not my own."

Silence. Well, of course there would be silence, what else had he expected? He must be more weary than he thought to seek any favors here. Or more desperate.

Gritting his teeth, he knelt. Dampness seeped through the knees of his hose, cold against his skin. Just yesterday he would have laughed at the very thought of it, Ronan Fitzgerald down on his knees in the dark and mud, gazing at the sky like some moonstruck savage.

But tonight he was not amused. Resentment, anger, a thin thread of fear—all these he felt as he stared into the sky. But after a time, he was aware of something new. The first faint stir of an idea.

Twenty

"Will ye go to bed now?"

"In a moment."

Maude's voice was sharp, for this was the third time Becta had asked the same question in the same solicitous tone. Sitting through supper tonight had been enough of an ordeal. Now that she had made it to her chamber, was it too much to ask for just a bit of peace?

It wasn't as though Maude didn't *want* to sleep. She longed to lie down and let consciousness slip away. But sleep was distant as the moon tonight, and perhaps that was a good thing. She could not bear the thought that she might dream.

She combed her hair until her arms ached, but a hectic energy still ran through her body. Oh, she hated this feeling, this unnatural awareness, with every sense sharpened to the breaking point. Her mind raced, but there was no pattern to her thoughts, no way to make sense of the random impressions flitting through her mind.

"Remember," Ronan had said. "Let it all play out in your mind." Perhaps tomorrow. Not tonight. Tonight she wanted only to forget, and with an effort she forced her mind away from the scent of cowslips and the cry of the kestrel, away from the terror lurking just beneath the surface of her jumbled thoughts.

Instead she thought of Ronan, his voice, so deep and comforting, the cool, firm grip of his hand on hers, the warmth of his arms tightening around her. . . .

A light tap on the door brought her instantly to her feet, shaking as though a thunderclap had sounded through the room. *What now?* she wondered, every muscle tensed with apprehension.

Becta moved between Maude and the doorway, her solid form a welcoming shield against the world. *I don't have to worry,* Maude thought. *Whoever it is, Becta will send them away.* But Becta was stepping back, opening the door.

Maude retreated quickly to her dressing table and sat down, turning her back to her visitor.

"Good evening, my lady."

Oh, sweet God, it was him. Ronan. She couldn't look at him, couldn't speak to him, couldn't bear to see the pity on his face. She picked up her comb, then set it down again.

"I've brought you something to help you sleep," he said, setting a flagon on the table before her.

"What is it?"

"Wine, mostly, mixed with a few other things."

"I don't want it," she said, keeping her eyes fixed on the gently steaming flagon. "Take it and go."

"Oh, lady, do drink it," Becta cajoled. "Ye must sleep."

Maude cast a quick glance at Ronan and saw he had that look on his face, that stubborn look she already knew too well. She poured a bit into a cup and sipped, then set it down with a shudder. "What is in this? Worms? It tastes like worms."

"And when is the last time you tasted worms?"

Her smile died before it reached her lips, but she was able to look at him then. He looked tired, too, nearly as tired as she was herself.

Summoning every bit of her remaining strength, Maude straightened. She flicked a withering glance at the cup and then at him, dismissing them both without a word.

"Now that is very good," he said approvingly. "Did it take you long to learn?"

She shook her head, uncomprehending.

"That look." He drew himself up, glared down his nose, and was instantly transformed. Pride, disdain, and an air of fierce nobility were all stamped upon his features. *This is who he really is,* Maude thought, but the impression vanished when he relaxed and smiled faintly.

" 'Tis a fine trick, to be sure, but you see I have the way of it myself, so you may as well just drink the potion down."

He picked up the cup, and she took it from his hand.

"First tell me what is in it."

Ronan was not used to having his judgment questioned, at least in matters of healing. Most people, in his experience, wanted only to be told, "Drink this, do that, and soon you will feel better," and they needed him to speak those words with absolute conviction. The stronger the belief in the healer and his remedies, the quicker the recovery. And faith was a fragile thing, easily destroyed by whys and wherefores.

But when had Maude ever been like most people?

"Lady, you need to sleep," he began, sitting down and adopting a serious expression. "And you need to eat and take regular exercise. Would any rational soldier ride into battle without his arms? No more can you afford to let yourself grow overtired or faint from lack of food and rest."

Maude was very still now, and Ronan was pleased to see he had her complete attention.

"We strive for balance in all things," he went on, his voice dropping into a rhythmic, soothing cadence, "in blood, in bile black and yellow, and in phlegm. Each is important in its place, but none can be allowed to dominate the others. Are you following me so far?"

She nodded.

"Each of the humors has certain properties," he continued. "Black bile—or melancholy—for example, is said to be cold and dry and bitter. And so what we have here," he lifted the cup, "is warm and wet and sweet."

"And foul," Maude added.

He sipped it. "Well, I could have gone a bit heavier on the honey, but what is in here will do you good. Now will you please drink it while it is still warm?"

With a sigh, she raised the cup to her lips and drained it. "Ugh. I hope you know what you're doing."

So do I. He stood and turned from her quickly, for it would never do to let her see his doubts.

"Becta, get your lady into bed," he ordered, and the tiring woman drew back the coverlet. Maude regarded the feather mattress as though it were an instrument of torture. "Lie down, lady, and let the potion work."

Maude nodded, but she did not rise, nor would she look at him. He sat down on the window seat across from her. "What is it you fear, lady? Do you dream?"

She nodded again. "At times. And then—well . . ."

"The shadows," Becta interrupted. "They trouble her."

Maude shot her a furious look, but Becta only folded her arms across her chest. " 'Tis the truth," she retorted.

"You dream of shadows?" Ronan asked.

"No." Maude pressed her lips together as though determined not to speak another word.

"Dreams can be—" Ronan began.

"The shadows are not dreams," Maude said tightly. "They are real."

Ronan glanced at Becta. She shrugged and walked over to the bed.

"What is in the shadows?" Ronan asked gently.

"They are. All of them. They stand around my bed, watching me."

Maude's speech was slower now, not slurred but a bit more relaxed as the potion began to work.

"How long have they been there?"

"Since—" Maude sighed. "I told you, didn't I, that there had been a lad with me that day? After—when I was ill—I began to worry about him, to wonder what had happened to him. I asked my father finally, and he said . . . he said, I mustn't worry about Gavin. He said, 'Gavin won't be telling anyone, Maude, don't fear, I took care of him.' "

"Did he say how he had taken care of the lad?"

"He didn't have to," Maude said wearily. "Father doesn't do things by half measures. And that was only the beginning. He began to go hunting. That's what he called it. Every time he killed one of the Kirallens, he would tell me of it. 'There's another one for ye,' he would say, giving me their lives. Giving me their deaths," she added in a low voice. "I tried to be pleased—or, no, that is not quite true. I *was* pleased, at least a part of me was. I wanted vengeance, too."

" 'Tis only natural that you would think of vengeance," Ronan said reasonably, "that you would imagine it in detail. There is no harm in that, save to yourself if it went on too long. But to wish for something and to actually do it are two very different things. You did not kill anyone, lady, so the responsibility is hardly equal here."

"Ye can quibble if ye like, but the truth of it is that there were times I wanted him to slaughter every one of them."

"Of course you did," Ronan said at once. "But you were but a child and not mistress of yourself. What if you had asked him to stop? Would he have done it?"

"We cannot know," she argued wearily, "for I did not

ask. Whenever he—when his hunting had gone well, he would be happy. He would be like his old self again. But it never lasted long. Soon he would become restless, and he'd look at me that way—so sad, so . . . beaten. Then he would go out hunting, and . . . there would be another one."

"And they are in the shadows?"

She nodded, her gaze fixed on the floor.

"Can you see their faces?"

"Nay," she whispered. "But I ken who they are."

" 'Tis time for bed, lady," Becta said firmly. "Come, now."

"I'll sit with you awhile," Ronan offered, and Maude shot him a poignant look of gratitude.

Becta snorted, but other than a disapproving shake of her head, she made no protest as Maude lay down on the bed and she drew up the coverlet. Ronan was amused when the tiring woman planted herself solidly on a stool beside the fire and regarded him with suspicion as he took up his harp. He played for a bit, thinking hard about what he was about to say.

"Nine years ago," he began in a low voice, "I set out for the Holy Land. I started out from Donegal and took ship to France, then made my way across the Pyrenees, going from one manor to another, one village to the next, earning what I could along the way. When I reached Castile, I was sent for by the king himself, and I stayed awhile at that court."

Maude was watching him with heavy-lidded eyes, in the twilight state between waking and sleeping, the in-between place where her heart was open to his words.

"While I was there," he went on, "I saw a most marvelous thing, a bestiary that had come from Jerusalem; brought, so it was said, by one of the Knights Templar. It told of any number of wondrous creatures—gryphons and dragons and a creature that is half ant, half lion. But my favorite was the phoenix, a lovely bird with plumage all of gold and crimson."

He played for a time, letting her relax further as he chose his next words with care.

"Now, it seems that only one phoenix lives at a time, just a single bird in all the world. And when the phoenix grows old, its feathers dim and draggled and its spirit weary, it builds a nest lined with myrrh and sandalwood and jasmine. Then it lies down in the center and sets it all aflame.

"They say the fire of the phoenix burns so hot it could melt the finest steel, but at last it dwindles—as do all fires, lady, no matter how hot and bright they flame— until it disappears entirely. It is then, when all is cold and still, that the new phoenix is born, rising from its own ashes, shining new in all its glory."

He sat for a while longer, only half-awake himself, hardly knowing what he played. A run of notes began to form a half-familiar melody, dancing just beyond the edge of memory. The words rose to his mind and he sang them without thinking, his voice only a whisper yet each note clear and true.

> *Sleep a little, a little sleep,*
> *I will watch over you, uair ní heagail duit a bheg.*
> *I will watch over you.*
> *Sleep a little; you need not fear the least.*
> *I will watch over you, uair ní heagail duit a bheg.*
> *I will watch over you.*

He jerked fully awake, a strange chill around his heart. He had not meant to sing at all, let alone that song. Ill-omened, he would call it—if he were prone to fancies. Which he wasn't. He put the harp aside and stood looking down at Maude. She lay quietly at last, her hair spilled in a golden wave over the pillow, the coverlet rising and falling with her even breaths.

"Good night, Mistress Becta," he said, starting for the door.

The tiring woman stepped into his path and fixed him with a stony gaze, arms folded across her breast. "I kent your master."

"Did you?" Ronan yawned and rubbed the back of his neck.

"Aye. Oh, Fergus was a braw healer, there's no denying that, but all the same, he was no proper Christian man."

"No, I don't think one could call him that."

"And you?"

Ronan stifled another yawn. "Are you after a theological discussion, mistress? Or do you want to know if my intentions toward your lady are those of any *Christian* healer?"

"Healer?" Becta snorted. "Is *that* what ye were doing? For it seemed to me ye were trying to bedazzle a young lass wi' all your talk of courts and travel."

Ronan felt his face flush. Of course that wasn't what he had been doing. At least, he hoped it wasn't. "I was merely talking so she might fall asleep," he said with all the dignity he could muster.

"Well, I'll grant ye that it worked. Ye nearly put *me* to sleep with your blether. Next time, stick to your potions."

"Thank you for the advice, mistress. But why don't you worry about your own duties and let me tend to mine?"

"Oh, I'll tend to *my* duties."

She would, Ronan thought as he left the chamber. She would most certainly tend to her duties. And if she could, she would see him out of Aylsford before another day had passed.

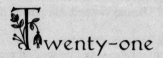

Twenty-one

"Dame Becta tells me ye were in Maude's chamber last even," Darnley said without preamble the next morning.

"I was."

Darnley grimaced as he shifted in his seat. "Is that all ye have to say?" he demanded, drawing a hissing breath as he set his foot upon a stool.

"Why, yes, my lord, it is. Would you like me to have another look at your leg? It seems to be paining you."

"It's well enough. Becta said—"

Ronan sat down across from Darnley. "I know what she said. But Dame Becta—worthy woman that she is— does not understand the first thing about Lady Maude's illness."

"Illness?" Darnley repeated sharply. "Ye said she was fine."

"Her health is fine—for now. Though I cannot promise it will stay that way. My lord, Lady Maude has suffered a terrible loss."

"D'ye think ye have to tell *me* that?" Darnley snarled. "I ken what she lost."

"Do you?" Ronan asked coolly. "For if you think I'm speaking of her virtue or her honor, you are very much mistaken. What I mean is that your daughter's *spirit* has been injured. An ordeal such as she survived damages the very soul. It is nothing to be taken lightly."

"The soul?" Darnley sighed. "Fergus went on about that, as well."

Ronan straightened. "Did he? What did he say?"

"Oh, I misremember—something about the soul leaving the body and not finding its way home again. A mortal lot of blether it all was," he added with a touch of defiance.

"Fergus never blethered," Ronan said sternly. "He was a very wise man, and you know it."

"Mayhap he was. But that was seven years ago. To keep dwelling on what's past and done is doing Maude no good. She needs to get on wi' her life."

"My lord," Ronan said carefully, "no one wants that more than Lady Maude. But she *cannot* get on with her life until she has made peace with the past. You *must* give her the chance to do that. To force her into marriage now would be disastrous."

Darnley rested his brow in his palm. "I dinna ken what to do for her."

"I do," Ronan said firmly. "Do not rush her, do not force her. Let her find her own way."

"But I *have* tried that. It has gained her nothing."

"I know. Fergus knew, as well. I'm certain now that's why he sent me here, to finish what he started."

Darnley was silent for a long moment, but at last he sighed and raised his head. "Ye didna know her . . . before. She was born on the Sabbath, ye ken, and she was all they say, bonny and blithe and fair and gay. My firstborn. The one truly fine thing that's ever happened to me." His mouth tightened. "And they took her from me. God *damn* them."

"And that's another thing," Ronan said. "If you're

thinking of starting up with the Kirallens again, 'tis the worst thing you could do for Lady Maude. If you love her, my lord, and I see you do, then start thinking of what's best for *her.*"

"*Marriage* is what's best for her. She needs a man—a strong man to look after her when I am gone. Kinnon Maxwell is what's best for her."

Ronan bit back his angry protest. "That may be true," he said mildly, "but to marry her off now, before she is ready—I think that it would drive her mad. She needs time. Surely you can give her that."

"So ye think ye can help her?"

"I do."

"Then I suppose Maxwell can cool his heels for a bit."

Ronan let out a careful breath. "You are doing the right thing."

Darnley's eyes gleamed. "Am I? Then ye can do something for me. While ye are *helping* my daughter, remind her of her duty. Convince her that she must wed Maxwell. For she will. Soon or late, she will."

Over my dead body.

"Your daughter is very much aware of her duty to you," Ronan said, his voice neutral.

"That's no answer. I want your word that ye will talk her into this match."

Ronan considered several diplomatic responses, then abandoned every one of them. "I will speak no word against it, but I would be lying if I promised more. I am a *taibhsear,* my lord, not the village matchmaker."

Darnley's face contorted, then suddenly, he laughed. "Ye have balls, lad. Just like your grandsire."

"Good God, I hope not!"

The words slipped out before Ronan stopped to think, and seemed to amuse Darnley even further.

"Oh, aye, ye are very like him. Say what ye think and the rest of us be damned. Very well, then, I'll take ye at your word. For 'tis said that the word of a Fitzgerald is unbreakable."

"I suppose my grandfather told you that."

Darnley shot him a keen glance. "Nay, lad. It wasn't him. I had *that* from the king."

Ronan bowed his head, acknowledging the thrust. "If I have your leave . . ."

"Go on, then. Ye have your time. Use it well."

Ronan hesitated at the door. "My lord, you said Lady Maude was born on the Sabbath? What day was that?"

"All Hallow's Eve. Why?"

"Birthdates can reveal a great deal," he answered vaguely. "What time was she born?"

"Hard onto midnight, mayhap a minute or two before."

Not May 11th then, at two o'clock in the afternoon, as Lady Maude had told him. All that time he had spent casting her natal chart . . . He found that he was smiling as he walked back to his chamber. *A good try, my lady,* he thought. *But not quite good enough.*

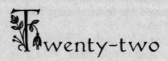

Twenty-two

"I've been thinking about the shadows," Ronan said that afternoon, sitting down beside Maude in the garden. "And—"

"The *what?*" Maude laughed lightly. "Oh, do you mean that nonsense I was spouting last night? Surely you didn't think—no, 'twas that potion—what did you say was in it?"

"—and I think," Ronan went on, ignoring her, "that I know how to send them away."

"Really? How would—" Maude caught herself. "Shouldn't you be telling me that shadows are just shadows? That they aren't real?"

"Why would I do that?" he asked, sounding honestly surprised. "Of course they're real."

That's the trouble with crying, Maude thought. Once you started, anything at all could set you off. It was weak, pathetic, utterly contemptible. But she couldn't seem to stop.

Ronan looked the other way until she composed herself.

"How?" she asked.

"Well, here's the way I'm seeing it. A violent death is a shock to the spirit, and these poor souls have gotten lost. They don't mean you any harm, lady, no more than you do them. 'Tis your grief that draws them to you and your guilt that binds them. So all you have to do is release them."

"Oh, is that all?"

"Well, and guide them home."

"Ah. I see. Tell me, Ronan, which of us is raving? At the moment, I can't be certain."

He grinned at her. "Now, lady, 'tis no simple matter, I admit, but not beyond your grasp."

"I think it might be. Why don't you do it for me?"

He considered the question seriously. "I could try, but 'twould be far more powerful if you did it yourself. That way you could bid them all farewell. I think," he added slowly, "that they would like that."

Maude touched the cool stone of the bench. It was there, just as it always was, rough beneath her fingertips. So she clearly wasn't dreaming, though it was still possible she had gone mad.

Or he had.

"They would like that?" she repeated. "I am supposed to care what they would like? A pack of shadows?"

"If you do not want to do it, say so plainly. But do not mock them."

She began to pace the garden. "I am no conjurer of spirits."

"There's no need to conjure them, is there? You only need to speed them on their way. I'll show you how. You don't have to do it by yourself. Don't eat much at supper, drink no wine, and take an hour or so to sit quietly in your chamber and remember what your father said of them. You might say a prayer, as well."

She looked at him, her face soft and young and touchingly uncertain. "You mean this?"

"I do."

"Then we will try it."

"Good. Go and rest; you want to be awake tonight."

Ronan sat on the bench and watched Maude walk into the keep. This was the right thing to do, he was certain of it. Fergus had once said that rituals were a way to reach beyond the mind, which had seemed to Ronan a peculiar thing to want to do at all. But now he thought he knew what his master had been getting at.

Whatever terrors Maude had created for herself could surely be vanquished by her will. There was nothing supernatural going on here, just a lass who had survived a terrible ordeal at great cost to herself. The words they used to describe those terrors were unimportant.

So call them spirits, call it magic, call it anything at all, so long as she believed that it would work. Wasn't magic just another word for all the mysteries of mind and heart that could not be explained? *There is no magic, really,* he reflected, half dreaming in the sunlight. *All the spells and songs are just a way of touching a part of the mind that cannot be reached by other means.*

Oh, there were spirits that roamed the earth, he supposed, though he doubted they had power over the living. Guilt, he thought, and grief were the only things hiding in those shadows, more powerful than any ghost, enough to make a body pine and sicken, even die. But tonight Maude would take a step toward freeing herself of the burden she had carried for too long.

It was all very simple, really. Not magic at all, just plain common sense. But he knew the words, he knew the songs, he knew a hundred different tricks that would give power to their ritual. They meant nothing in themselves, of course, but he would go through them just the same. The only thing that mattered was that Maude believed.

*   *   *

With that in mind, Ronan was very solemn as he prepared Maude's chamber that evening. Three candles of white beeswax burned in the center of the floor, and the scent of incense wound through the air. With Maude and Becta looking on, he went through the cleansing ritual, a handful of salt at every corner with a different prayer for each.

Two stools sat in the center of the floor. Maude was already seated on one, her lute beside her on the floor. She was dressed in a simple linen gown, hair loose and shining in the candlelight. Her face was solemn, he was pleased to see, though Becta was frankly skeptical.

"What now, *taibhsear?*" the tiring woman asked.

"You sit here." He gestured toward her place beside the hearth. "Do not interfere, mistress, no matter what you see or hear. And pray," he added solemnly. "That will help."

He sat down beside Maude and took up his harp. "Music is a bridge between this world and the next. So play, lady, a song of your own choosing, one that will make a path of light for them to follow. Hold each soul in your mind as you say farewell and wish it Godspeed on its journey. Speak the words or say them in your mind."

Maude picked up her lute.

"Take a moment to pray," Ronan advised her. "And begin when you are ready."

During the silence that followed, he watched the candles burning steadily. Shadows filled the corners of the room, but they were fixed, unmoving, behaving just as any shadow should. He sent a quick prayer into the silent air, hoping Maude would see whatever she needed to see for this to work.

She began to play a simple tune, one of her own heart-wrenching melodies. The notes wound through the incense-laden air, gathering power as she went on. Her head was bent, her face taut with concentration. Ronan repressed a smile. Not a bad job, he thought; the mood was set quite nicely. The very air seemed to stir as she played on.

In fact, the candles were not burning quite so steadily. The shadows wavered and began to writhe against the wall. He blinked and looked again, a chill winding down his back. Perhaps he'd set the mood a bit too well. It seemed they were actually moving closer, growing more solid, until one could almost imagine they were wraiths indeed, grotesque forms of men that were advancing steadily toward Maude.

Maude saw them come, just as they did every night. Her hands faltered, but she kept on with her song as Ronan had told her. *Go,* she pleaded with them silently, *be at peace, Godspeed to you all. I'm sorry that you had to die, I never meant for it to happen, but now it is time for you to go. . . .*

It wasn't working. They weren't going anywhere. But for the first time she could see their faces, young and old, stern and mournful . . . and she could feel their anger.

"Go," she said aloud, her voice wavering, "I bid you all farewell. Ronan, what is happening?"

He did not answer her. His face had gone dead white as he stared at the wraiths surrounding them.

"Ronan? Do something!"

And he did. He took up his harp and began to play as she had never heard him play before, no song that she could recognize, but a complex string of notes she could not begin to follow. It flowed through the room like a thousand strands of light, and then the strands began to weave themselves together into a melody. The shadows began to move toward the wall, and one by one they passed through the stone like smoke. The last hesitated, and Maude knew him then.

"Gavin! Oh, Gavin, ye can go, it's all right now—"

It seemed to her he lifted a hand. Then he, too, stepped into the wall and disappeared.

A rush of air passed through the chamber, extinguishing the candles. Ronan's harp fell silent.

"Ronan? Ronan, answer me—"

"I'm here." His voice was barely a whisper. "Just . . . a moment."

"Becta, light the candles."

There was no answer, just the silent darkness. Maude felt her way to the hearth and blew up the banked fire, dropping a handful of kindling on the coals. Flame sprang up, and she lit a candle. Becta was fast asleep, head leaning against the wall. Ronan was bent forward, elbows on his knees, brow resting in his hands.

"Ronan?"

"I am all right."

"You don't look all right to me!"

He straightened and dragged his fingers through his hair. "I am a fool," he said softly but very clearly. "But at least I know it now."

He rose to his feet and stood swaying. "Oh," he said. "That was a mistake. Another . . ."

She tried to catch him, but he was far too heavy for her. She only succeeded in going down as well, the two of them overturning the stools as they sprawled in a heap upon the floor. Becta sat up sharply at the sound.

"What?" she said. "Lady—oh, what's happened?"

"I'm well enough—'tis Ronan—"

Becta lit a second candle and leaned over him, touching her knuckles to his cheek, feeling for a pulse at his neck. "He'll do. What the devil went on here?"

"Did you not see?" Maude eased Ronan's head into her lap and brushed the thick, dark hair from his brow. His skin was cool to the touch, without a trace of color.

"I heard music," Becta said, "and saw the shadows cast by the candle." She shivered. "A lot of foolery, it was. Man shouldna meddle in things he doesna ken."

"You'll get no argument from me, mistress." Ronan's voice came weakly from his ashen lips.

"Here, have some wine," Maude offered. She twisted, reaching behind her, and Ronan's head hit the floor with a thump.

"Oh, I'm sorry—here, take some of this—"

She leaned forward just as he sat up, jogging her arm, spilling the wine over his face. *It isn't funny,* Maude told herself, biting her lip as he swiped a hand across his brow.

"Remind me," he said, "to keep you out of sick-rooms."

All the nervous tension burst out of her. She sat on the floor, too weak to lift herself, laughing as the tears ran down her cheeks.

"Oh, lady, my poor—" Becta began, but Ronan lifted a hand.

"Let her be," he said softly.

"I am sorry—really—" Maude gasped, wiping her eyes.

"No, it's all right, go ahead and laugh at me. It is the least that I deserve."

"Oh, but you were wonderful!"

"Hardly that, though if you want to think so, don't let me stop you."

"But it worked, didn't it? They're gone."

"Yes." He closed his eyes and sighed. "They are gone, God rest them."

"What did you do?"

"Opened the door. A curious phenomenon—not magic, of course, just a thing we don't yet understand. It was harder than I expected."

"You mean you've never done it before?"

He laughed. "No. You may be surprised, but this sort of thing doesn't happen every day."

He turned on his side and propped his head on one hand. "How are you?"

"Fine."

"Then hand me the wine, if you please."

He took the cup, but his hands were trembling so that wine splashed over the rim. She held it to his lips, steadying his head with her free hand as he drank.

"It was that bad?" she asked.

"My own fault," he answered tersely. "Don't worry, I'll be all right in the morning."

He rose stiffly to his feet. "Sleep," he ordered her. "There will be nothing to disturb you now."

Becta followed him to the door, her face stony with disapproval. "Mistress Becta," he said, making her a little bow. "You are a pearl among women, and I should take counsel of you daily."

Becta snorted. "Dinna play the fool with me!"

"Ah, but I am not playing. Good even to you. Look after your lady, now."

"What else would I be doing? Get your rest," she added, her voice grudging. "Ye look as though ye need it."

Twenty-three

Rain drummed against the walls, and wind shrieked around the corners of the keep. Maude stood at her window and stared into the wavering gray curtain.

Maude liked rainy days. Even if necessity forced her out, in her gray cloak and hood she would be all but invisible on the moor. But this day was so very wild that no one would expect her to go out at all. And no visitor would brave this storm.

She could relax. For now. Let the day be sufficient unto itself, she reminded herself, drifting over to the hearth and picking up her lute, and today should be one of the better ones. After Ronan left she had slept the night through and woken with a ravenous appetite. She had indulged herself shamelessly, lying on her pillows eating bread and honey before drifting off again.

She was well rested for the first time in memory with a long, empty day stretching out before her. There could be no reason for this nagging apprehension tugging at the corners of her mind.

Firelight flickered over the tiled hearth. Each tile was

slightly different, painted with a scene from Holy Writ. There was Noah and his ark, a good one for today, Jacob and his ladder, Samson pulling down the walls. As a child, she had loved to look at them in the hour before bed, when her father would sit with her and tell her stories.

It was a good memory, and she smiled a little as she began to play a simple tune that belonged to those far-off days. It was one Ronan would approve, for it was bright and cheerful, made entirely of those major chords he so admired.

"Summer is icumen in, sing hi, sing hey." Becta sang the words beneath her breath as she shook out Maude's gowns. Lord, but it had been a long time since the lass played anything Becta could recognize as music!

Maybe that Fitzgerald had known what he was doing after all. Or perhaps Lady Maude had come to some decision about Kinnon Maxwell. She could do better, Becta thought, but she could do considerably worse.

She could be taking up with that smooth-tongued *taibhsear*, who had somehow wormed his way into their household. He was as bad as Fergus—worse, in fact—for if Fergus had been charming as the very devil, he'd known to keep to his own place. This Fitzgerald seemed to think himself her lady's equal! Meeting her every afternoon—oh, it was all music, or so her lady said. Of course she was too innocent to see what he was after.

Becta gave the last gown a vigorous shake, glaring at it as though daring any moth to try its mischief here. The music broke off, and Becta tensed. When it did not pick up again, she walked into the inner chamber.

Lady Maude sat, one hand still forming the last chord, the other hovering above the strings. But it never moved to pluck the next note. She stared at the fire as though she was entranced.

"Lady! Why don't ye go down to the hall?"

There was no answer. Becta sighed, thinking, *Here we*

go again, but her heart moved and twisted, for it never got any easier, not even after all these years.

Maude stared into the heart of the fire, but she no longer saw the tiled hearth around it. It blazed on the open moor, the sky behind darkening to twilight. The ground was cold beneath her and the pain was every-where—she had never imagined she could hurt so much and live. The foul coppery taste of blood was in her mouth, and the man on top of her stank of sweat and ale.

But above it all was the cold, deadly will to live. It was beyond emotion, beyond thought or reason. She would not die. She could not. She would survive, she had to—and her hand moved over the heaving, stinking form atop her, fumbled at his belt, fastened on his knife. Quickly now, moving with a will of its own, her hand drew the knife, raised it high, and plunged it into his back.

"Lady!" Becta's voice cut through the memory. "Lady, stop—" and Becta's hands were on her shoulders, shaking her.

"No—no, Becta, don't—I have to remember—"

His scream was deafening—"Ye bitch—dear God, she's killed me!"—a foul gust of breath against her cheek, and she turned her head instinctively, seeking to escape the blow she knew would follow, even as she brought the knife up to slash blindly. She felt it now again, the vicious thrill of triumph when he screamed again and reeled back, blood spurting from between the fingers clapped over his face.

A new voice was speaking now, from the darkness, saying, "Christ's wounds—Carlysle, ye swiving bastard, what have ye done?" Outlined against the flames was another man, one she had not seen before, and he dragged Carlysle across the moor by the collar and threw him to the ground.

"Hinny, stop—stop now, come back—" Becta cried, but Maude could only shake her head.

The stranger was staring down at her, and she could see herself through his eyes; muddy, bleeding, sprawled half-naked on the filthy moor. His face twisted with horror and disgust.

"Christ's blood, what has he done to ye?" he whispered, and somehow his shocked pity was worse than anything that had gone before. She wasn't Maude Darnley, who loved music and hawking and dreamed of seeing far-off places; she was just a thing, ruined, pathetic, and dear God, he couldn't find out who she was, no one could know, the shame of it would kill her father.

He turned and called over his shoulder. "Ian! Ian, get over here right now!"

Maude began to scramble backwards, heels slipping on the sodden ground, pulling her skirts down, trying to find her feet. Carlysle was still screaming, and the man said, "Wait, lass—wait, don't go—" and he came after her, but it was too late; she was running into the darkness, stumbling, falling, picking herself up again.

"Oh, Becta," she said, "Becta, I remember—"

"Don't! Stop this now, ye will be ill. Lady dear, ye must forget all that, put it behind ye—"

"No!" Maude cried. "I won't. Ronan said—he said I could—I *must* remember—"

Becta drew back in outraged horror. That Fitzgerald again. Who was he to be doing this to her lady? Why, if he could see her now, shaking from head to foot, he would know the damage he had done.

"We'll see about that," she muttered. "We'll see—"

She flung the door open and shouted for a page, not caring who might hear. A few minutes later, Ronan appeared at the door.

"Look what ye have done, *taibhsear*," Becta spat, drawing him inside. "Look!"

He blanched at the sight of Maude, curled up on the settle, shaking violently. He took a step forward, hands outstretched, then stopped.

"Go to her," he said harshly. "Go—comfort her."

Becta fell to her knees beside the settle. "There, lamb," she crooned, pulling Maude's stiff and shaking form against her. "There, 'tis all right, ye are here and safe with me. Dinna greet, hinny, calm yourself—"

"No! She *should* greet—Good God, what would you have her do?"

"Forget!" Becta cried. "Why are ye bringing it all back again?"

"Because it's never left her!"

"I say—"

Maude raised her head. "Stop! Becta, don't shout at him, it isn't his fault."

"Oh, hinny, I'm sorry, 'tis only seeing ye like this—"

Maude sat up very straight. "But I remember! The man—Carlysle, that was his name—it was him, he wouldn't let any of the others touch me. But later he was drunk and he couldn't—he wasn't able—and I took the knife from his belt—and I . . . I stabbed him, I stabbed him in the back and slashed his face. . . . I couldn't believe I'd done it. He was screaming, he was so angry, he would have killed me but someone came and pulled him off. How *could* I have forgotten that?"

She looked up, her face bleached of all color. Ronan's hands clenched at his sides. "You did what you had to do," he said. "You had no choice."

But she did not seem to hear him. She was staring past him, her eyes stricken. "Oh, God," she cried, "why did I not remember?"

"You were in shock, 'tis natural that you'd forget," Ronan said quickly. "But now you—"

"You don't understand! If only I'd remembered—if my father had known—"

"Then what? What difference would that have made?"

"All the difference!" she shouted, her eyes blazing with some fierce emotion. "Don't you see? Father never knew which one it was. I could not give him a name."

Becta and Ronan exchanged lightning glances. "So he had to kill them all," Ronan said. "I understand. But you can tell him now."

"No! I won't, I can't. I killed the man, I'm sure of it. What would be the point? Father would only start it all again, and I can't bear it. Promise me—swear to me, both of you, that you will not tell him."

"It is for you to say, lady," Ronan said. "I will do nothing without your leave."

"Och, sweeting, of course I will say naught. 'Tis all right, now," Becta crooned, "dinna look back now, dinna greet."

Becta glared at Ronan over Maude's bent head. He met her gaze calmly, though she noticed his hands were trembling as he reached for the latch. "Call me if I am needed," he said, and walked out.

"I'll be right back, sweeting," Becta said, and hurried after him, catching him just outside the door.

"What are ye playing at?" she demanded.

"I am not playing, mistress, and this is exactly what I hoped for," he said with a callousness that shocked Becta to the core. "I advised your lady to share her memories with someone she can trust, and you are the one she has chosen. She is showing great courage, and if you cannot bear it, then you had better leave right now."

"Dinna use that tone on me, laddie," Becta snapped. "I can bear what I must, but *she* has borne enough already. Why bring it all up again?"

"Because her memories are locked inside, eating away at her, and they must come out. Becta," he added more gently, "do you know your lady often visits the river?"

"Aye. It has always been a favorite place of hers."

"Do you know why?"

"Why, because . . . 'tis a pretty spot," she said uncertainly.

He did not reply, just stared at her, those strange,

bright eyes boring into hers. Unexpectedly, she felt her throat tighten.

"Aye, I ken why," she whispered.

"Don't stop her from remembering or grieving, Becta. Just listen to her."

"It will make everything worse."

"It might seem to for a bit, but in the end, it will help her."

"I hope ye ken what ye are doing."

"I do. I'll be in my chamber if you want me. Just now you're the one she needs."

Becta turned back to the door, then stopped and swallowed hard. She didn't want to go in there. She didn't want to hear what Lady Maude might have to say. It had been bad enough knowing the bare facts of the tale, all that Darnley had given her at the time. Even that had been confided grudgingly, with Becta's family hostage to her silence. There was no need—she would have torn out her own tongue before speaking of her lady's shame— but she bore him no ill-will. In his place, she would have done the same.

Becta prided herself on having proved worthy of his trust, however unwillingly bestowed. It was she who had invented the tale of Maude's visit to the convent, dropping a word here, another there, until the entire keep was talking of their lady's desire to take the veil against her father's will. It was soon common knowledge that Lady Maude had never gone near Mallow at all that day, but had evaded her escort and run off to the abbey. And everyone knew that Lord Darnley had cannily ordered that she remain there for a time, with a word to the abbess to turn her from the notion.

The abbess had done her work too well, Becta had grumbled loudly on Maude's return. Surely Lord Darnley had never meant for his daughter to be treated so very harshly. Poor lamb, her health—always delicate—had quite broken beneath the strain.

Stitch by stitch Becta fashioned the lie. She had listened closely, but never a word did she hear questioning Fergus's presence at the keep. Nor was there the least surprise a few months later when Lord Darnley bundled his daughter off to court.

A neat job, Becta had congratulated herself, invisible as the finest seam. It was only later she realized that it was not so easy to mend a shattered life.

Becta did not recognize the Maude who returned from court, a cold, hard young woman it was all too easy to dislike. Many times over the past years, Becta had vowed to leave Aylsford altogether.

But she could never bring herself to go. For every so often, she could see the child looking out at her, terrified, bewildered, trapped behind a mask. And Becta knew she could never leave that child all alone, not the little lass who had spent weeks sewing her a Yule gift, though Maude hated her needle like poison. Not the lass who had ridden out on that spring day to bring gifts to the poor villagers.

It was that lass who was inside the chamber now, mourning for the life that had been stolen. *Maybe that Fitzgerald is right,* Becta thought. *Maybe she does need to tell her tale.*

But not to me. I'm too old for this. I love her too much. How can I bear to hear it? Oh, let it alone, let it be; talking about things only makes them worse.

Becta set her jaw and straightened her shoulders. Her lady had chosen her to confide in. Not her father, not that *taibhsear,* but her. She would not turn away.

Even if it tore the heart, bleeding, from her breast.

Twenty-four

Ronan paced his chamber. Five steps, turn, five more, and turn again. Back and forth, round and round, Maude's words burning themselves into his mind.

He was still shaking with the effort it had taken to hold himself in check. He had wanted to go to her, fold her in his arms, protect her from the pain she was inflicting on herself. And why was she doing such a thing? Because he had told her to. Because she believed in him; God help them all, she trusted him to know what he was doing.

And once she had done it, once she had torn open those wounds, he could do no more than stand and watch her bleed. It was Becta who had gone to her, giving her all the comfort he longed to give himself . . . and dared not. For Maude could not accept his touch, she could not respond to his embrace with anything but fear. Because of that man, that swiving, stinking bastard—

Carlysle. He had a name now, a focus. Carlysle. Was he dead? Or was he still living, walking somewhere on the earth?

It wasn't easy to kill a man. Not by stabbing him in the back. If Maude had hit a vital spot, he would have died almost at once. Of course, the wound might have been worse than it seemed. It might have festered. And Carlysle might, Ronan thought, have died slowly, in great pain.

But it wasn't a thing that could be counted on.

He sat down at the table and pulled a blank piece of parchment forward, uncapped the ink, and trimmed a quill. He stared blankly at the wall, brushing the feather back and forth across his tight-pressed lips.

Who to ask? He had to know; he must be sure the man was dead. For Maude's sake, he thought, but he knew that for a lie. It was for himself. *He* needed to know that Carlysle was rotting in cold clay.

He could not write to his foster sister Deirdre, the first name that came to mind, for she and her husband must be off to Donegal by now, just as they were every year. Not Laird Kirallen. He would want to know why Ronan sought the information, and that was a thing Ronan could never tell him.

Certainly not Lady Alyson. She was too quick by half. And whatever she knew or suspected, she would tell the laird. Ronan's mind moved quickly over all his friends at Ravenspur, dismissing every one. They were all in the laird's service. Even if he asked for silence, how could he be certain of it? He could not explain the need, and they were just men after all, only soldiers, and any one of them might let slip a careless word.

Except for Donal.

Donal had been born at Ravenspur; had served two Kirallen lairds as page and squire and knight. He knew keep and village as well as any man, yet his silence could be trusted absolutely.

The quill flew across the parchment. "I am seeking a man by the name of Carlysle, one who rode with Lord Ian Kirallen. This is a confidential matter, Donal, one of great importance. Make what inquiries are necessary, but keep my name out of it entirely. Do not write to me; I will come to you when I can."

He read over the message, then folded it in the complicated pattern he had learned at his grandfather's knee to defy any prying eyes. Taking a ring from his pouch, he dropped a thick blob of wax across the edge of the parchment and impressed it with the Fitzgerald seal.

It is not your place to judge.

Fine, then, he would not judge. He would *inquire*. It could well be that the man was dead already. Seven years was a long time, after all.

Where had he been seven years ago this spring? He could not rest until he remembered. Pamplona. That was it. Oh, how smug he had been, how arrogant, thinking of nothing beyond his own grand self.

And even as he had stood before them all, basking in their praise, Maude had ridden out to Mallow with just an old man and a green boy at her side.

Ronan sat before the fire, brooding on the hundred ways in which that day could have turned out differently. If only Maude had decided not to go . . . if her father had given her a proper escort . . .

Or if he had been there himself. He could see it so clearly, could almost feel the point of his knife against the man's throat, the spurt of hot blood as he drove it home.

> *And he pulled out his bright brown sword,*
> *And dried it on his sleeve,*
> *And he smote off that churl's head,*
> *And asked no man's leave.*

The thought brought a bitter smile to his lips. But Ronan was not Glenkindie. Not for him the mickle oath by oak and ash and thorn. He had sworn a different oath, long before he'd set eyes on Lady Maude. A *taibhsear* heals; he gives aid to any who should ask it, even if the man were Carlysle himself. It is not the *taibhsear*'s place to judge. It is not his place to kill.

Fergus had said once that it was no accident that brought Ronan to the borderlands, and Fergus had been right. Ronan had traveled half his life to get here. But he had come too late.

Seven years too late.

Don't think back. Don't brood on it. Get to your prayers; it's past time you started.

He nodded, acknowledging the truth of that. Prayer was what he needed, now more than ever. And he would get to it. Eventually. First he must finish what he'd started.

He picked up the pen. "Brother Donal, Kelso Abbey," he wrote clearly. He looked at the address, then added, "To his hand only."

That done, he capped the ink and sat staring at the sealed missive for a long time. Then he leaned his chin in his hand and went over it once more, how it would have been that day if only he were there, lingering on every detail of Carlysle's death with a mind etched sharp by hatred.

Twenty-five

Ronan lay back against the pine needles and let the late summer sunshine warm his face. Maude sat silently beside him on a fallen tree, the river at her feet. This was one of her good days. They came when they would, sudden and unexpected gifts, though he thought they came more often lately. But he could not be certain. He was not certain of anything anymore; thought and feeling were beyond him. The most he could muster was a vague sense of gratitude that they had come this far. After these past weeks, he was no longer surprised that Maude had sought the river. The wonder of it was that she had clung to life and sanity this long.

Ronan would have done anything, risked anything, if only he could shield her from her pain. But such thoughts were dangerous. They must be constantly suppressed, lest his very love should undermine her strength. Every day, every moment he must watch his lightest word and weigh his every action. Even comfort must be measured, for too much might weaken her resolve.

When he slept, his dreams were filled with Maude,

stalked by some nameless, shadowed terror. *Carlysle,* he would think in the dark hours before dawn. He is out there somewhere, not a dead man but a living threat. But in the morning he would take himself up sharply. *You're becoming an old woman, reading signs and portents into every passing dream. A little further down that road, my lad, and you'll be selling fortunes in the market square.*

"Becta tells me you are not sleeping well," he said, breaking a long silence. "The shadows have not returned, I trust?"

Maude glanced down at him. "Nay, they are gone. And Becta should learn to hold her tongue."

"Now, don't be troubling that good woman. She's only doing what is right. So tell me, why are you not sleeping well? Do you dream?"

"At times," she admitted grudgingly.

"You've never told me about your dreams," he said, sitting up. "What are they like?"

"You'll laugh."

"No, of course I won't. Oh, go on," he said. "I'm good with dreams."

She gave him a look, half-amused, half-uncertain. "You don't believe in being shy about your talents, do you?"

"Why should I when they can be of service? What do you dream about?"

She sighed. "Dragons. For years, I've had this . . . fear of dragons. There, go on, tell me 'tis ridiculous."

"But it's not," he said. "It's perfectly reasonable, not ridiculous at all. Considering their favorite fare."

"Favorite . . . ?" She frowned at him, then her eyes widened. "Oh. Their favorite fare. Well, you're right, I don't feel silly anymore. Just stupid."

"You shouldn't, lady. 'Tis difficult to interpret your *own* dreams. Even I cannot do that well."

"Well, there's a comfort. Something *you* cannot do well—the rest of us wouldn't have a hope!"

Ronan merely smiled, refusing to rise to the bait. It was impossible to get a decent argument out of him these days, Maude thought irritably.

"What sort of dragon is it?" he prompted.

"I never actually see it," Maude admitted. "But I know it's there, waiting to leap out at me. Sometimes," she continued hesitantly, "there's a child. I want to be rid of it, for I know the dragon's there, but it keeps clinging to me, and I can't run."

"What does the child look like?"

"Well . . ."

"Say the first thing you're thinking."

"Ugly. Filthy, like it's been dragged through the mud—I hate it," she added in a whisper. "I can't get away when it keeps holding on to me. . . ."

"And if you don't get away?" Ronan asked. "What will happen?"

"The dragon will get both of us."

"And then what will happen?"

She rounded on him. "What sort of witless question is that? What do you *think* would happen?"

"It doesn't matter what I think. You tell me."

"I'll die," she cried. "That's what will happen. What else would a dragon do but kill me?"

"I don't know. You're the one with all the answers here. Why do you suppose it hasn't killed you already?"

"Because it cannot catch me."

"It must not be much of a dragon," he said dismissively.

"Not much of a dragon? What do *you* know about it?"

"As much as you," he pointed out, leaning back on his elbows. "You've never even seen it."

She opened her mouth to argue, then laughed. "This is ridiculous. I cannot believe we are arguing over a dragon that doesn't even exist!"

"Ah, but it does. Dreams are very real, lady, very powerful, particularly one you have over and over again."

He broke off, frowning a little, then went on, "Not that dreams are what they seem. They speak to us in symbols, sure, yet the message is usually worth hearing. Perhaps next time you find yourself in that dream, you could stand your ground and see what the dragon looks like."

"I don't care what it looks like."

"Don't you? Strange, I thought you might have a bit of curiosity, seeing how much time you've spent on that great tapestry of yours."

Maude stared at the earth between her feet.

"And wouldn't it be interesting to hear what the child has to say, that poor child who's been dragged through the mud?" He waited a moment, then added very casually, "Does she remind you of anyone?"

"Go away," Maude said tightly.

"Have you never wondered why she's trying to hold you there?"

"I said go *away!* Leave me. I've had enough of your blether."

Ronan rose to his feet in one fluid motion. "Very well, lady, I'm going. Still, you might think about it. You might ask yourself whether the child has some reason for wanting you to meet that dragon. It might be worthwhile to know what the two of them would say to one another, and to you."

Maude watched him walking up the path, then glanced over at the river. When she looked back again, he was gone. Panic gripped her, squeezing the breath from her lungs, and when a twig broke, she turned sharply, peering into the shadows between the trees. There was nothing there. Of course there wasn't, she was quite alone, there was nothing moving in those shadows, nothing crouched between the trees, waiting to spring out with a flash of wicked teeth—

Get hold of yourself, she thought. *This is no dream; you're wide awake in daylight, and you will* not *go mad.* She wiped her sweating palms on her skirt and settled

back against the fallen log, forcing herself to breathe
deeply. There. She was all right now. Imagine being
frightened of a dragon at her age! As if there weren't
enough real terrors in the world for her to worry about.

She rose quickly and walked up the path. Her step
was firm, her chin high, and she was fine now; she was
feeling stronger by the second. Ronan was sitting by the
horses, his hands cupped before his mouth. A strange
sound was coming from his hands, and she realized he
was blowing through a blade of grass. Being Ronan, he
was actually managing to coax a tune from it. *He is such
a child,* she thought, a bit amused, a bit contemptuous,
and she was even smiling a little as he caught sight of
her and stood, the blade falling from his hands.

"Are you ready to go back?" he asked.

Maude looked up into his face, and she wanted to say,
Yes, I am fine; we should be getting back. That's what
she meant to say. Instead, she burst into tears.

Ronan felt a flutter of panic in his throat. *Another
mistake,* he thought. *I thought I was so clever, and now
look what I have done. I pushed her too hard, too fast;
her mind is breaking, and it's all my fault. . . .*

"I am going mad," she sobbed. "Soon I'll be raving."

"You are not mad," he said firmly, though his mouth
was so dry he could hardly speak. "You are . . . upset."

"Upset? *Upset?* Is that what ye call this? Ye have to
help me, Ronan, show me how to stop it. I can't think
about these things, can't talk about them. I have to lock
it up again, close the door, pretend it never happened—"

He almost agreed. He nearly told her, *Yes, you're
right, my mistake. I can show you ways to focus your
mind so you won't have to suffer like this anymore. I can
teach you how to run. And hide. And never, ever to look
back.*

"Is that how you want to live?" he demanded roughly.
"Pretending? Every day, every moment, do you want to

be pretending you're someone that you're not? Isn't that what you've been doing these seven years?"

"It was better then," she said, her voice choked. "*I* was better. Now I'm breaking into pieces. I can't control this—"

"I know it's hard. It's a terrible thing to feel you aren't in control. I know you're frightened. You're not used to these feelings, and they're powerful, they're frightening, they have sharp claws and wicked teeth—but they *will not kill you.*"

"You don't know that. You can't."

"But I do," he said, and suddenly he was certain again; he knew that he was speaking the truth. "Trust me."

"Trust you," she repeated dolefully, wiping the back of her wrist across her face. "That's all you ever say."

"'Tis what you have to do." He put his hands lightly on her shoulders and looked into her eyes, exerting all his force to reach her, to impress his words deeply on her consciousness.

"I'm not telling you that you won't feel this way again, but I promise it won't last forever. You'll remember that when you're thinking you're going mad, you'll remember what I'm saying now, and you'll know there will always be an end to it. You won't forget, no matter how you feel, you won't forget that it will always have an end. Do you understand me?"

She gazed up at him, eyes wide and dreaming, lips softly parted, so beautiful it made his heart clutch and stutter in his breast. He would have given anything, anything at all if only things could be different between them . . . everything but the way she was looking at him now.

Reluctantly, he stepped back, hands falling to his sides. "So you see, 'tis all a matter of trust," he finished lightly.

She blinked. "It is?"

"Sure and it is," he said, forcing himself to smile.

She tilted her head and looked at him curiously.

"You're not like anyone else, are you? Not like other men, I mean."

If only that were true! Once Ronan had actually believed it was, but he knew better now. He was exactly like other men, no different, no wiser, just another fool who was sick with wanting a woman he could never have. It was only Maude who could not see it. She no longer saw him as a man at all.

"No," he said, breathing carefully against the pain. "I don't suppose I am."

"Well, God be thanked for *that.*"

He helped her onto her horse, achingly aware of the light, sweet scent she wore, the brush of her cloak against his wrists. God be *thanked?* He would have laughed if only he remembered how. No, he wouldn't be thanking God just now; he'd be keeping his gratitude to himself.

Only a saint would thank any god for sending him to hell still living.

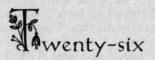

Twenty-six

"Good day, my lady," Cook said, fisting her hands on her ample hips as the light of battle glinted in her eye. "The blackberries are in, and I thought to make a junket. I'll be needing cinnamon for that."

Maude glared back at her. After hours spent inspecting linens, she had just sat down and taken up her lute when Cook's message arrived. Though she had visited the kitchen earlier, just as she did every morning, Cook had once again come up with an excuse to bring her back again.

Cook always chose her moment carefully, waiting until Maude was in the midst of some other task, usually one that took her to the far end of the keep. They'd had sharp words before, but Cook could always say—and often did—that if she no longer gave satisfaction, her lady only had to say so.

But of course Maude would not. Cook was indispensable, as well she knew, and she was far too clever to wage an open battle. Her little tricks and ploys were the only vent for the rage Maude had awakened when she

dared invade the sanctuary of the kitchen and steal away
her prize possession. The key hung in the bunch suspended from Maude's girdle, a small silver thing made
to fit an ornate lock.

Maude's key. Like all the others, it belonged without
question to the lady of the keep. It was part of Maude's
responsibility, part of the pattern, and as such it had been
as important to her as it ever was to Cook.

Impulsively, Maude unclasped it. "You'd better keep
this. You know best what you need."

Cook took the little key in her work-hardened palm,
a smile of infinite satisfaction spreading across her face.

"Keep good account of what you use," Maude added.
"I shall go over the reckoning closely."

"You'll find no cause for complaint."

"See that I do not."

With a brisk nod, Maude left the kitchens and went
out into the courtyard. She stood at the gate, smiling as
she watched the carts returning from the fields. The la-
borers were perched among the stooks, singing, for the
harvest had been good this year.

Ronan was among them. He had been out every fine
day, working like a peasant at the harvest. Even if Maude
had not known to look for him, she could never have
mistaken that voice, rising clear and true above the rest.
He jumped down from the cart and left them with a wave,
walking toward the gate where Maude stood waiting. He
was clad in a pair of threadbare braes and an old shirt,
with his jerkin slung over his shoulders, his hair coming
loose from its braid and stuck through with bits of hay.
Despite the attire, Maude doubted anyone would mistake
him for a common laborer. Not if they chanced to look
into his face.

The far-seeing look she had once noted was stronger
now, his eyes brilliant against his sunburnt skin. Or perhaps it was her own awareness that had sharpened; it
seemed an almost visible aura of magic surrounded him.

There was no one else like Ronan, no one in all the world so kind or wise or patient. Certainly no one who had ever made her laugh as he could do, even when she felt herself at the very edge of madness.

Though it had been some time since she had been to that edge. Every time she felt her world dissolving, she could hear his voice, so sure and steady, promising that what she felt would pass. For a wonder, it always did. She was beginning to believe it always would.

When he saw her, he smiled, and her heart did a giddy little skip and dip. It was a good feeling, quite different from the miserable yearning that had once kept her wakeful through the night.

"Shall we ride to Kelso Abbey?" Ronan suggested casually. "I need to see a friend. Oh, come along," he added when Maude hesitated. "Put on your oldest kirtle if you do not want to be known. We'll take Dame Becta if you like and an escort of a dozen men."

Why not? Maude thought with a recklessness she hadn't felt for years. "Becta is off at her niece's," she said, "and I think six men will do. I'll be ready in a quarter of an hour."

The ride passed quickly, for Ronan was in the mood to test his horse against Maude's, a race she was determined he would lose. They reached the outskirts of the abbey lands at a flat gallop, neck and neck. Maude reined up and tucked the windblown wisps of hair into her hood.

"Market day," Ronan observed.

Maude smiled, sniffing with pleasure as the mingled odors of roasting meat and gingerbread were carried on the breeze. She watched two white-clad nuns walk together down the path, then made a quick decision.

"You go see your friend," she said. "I'd like to visit the convent."

Ronan turned to her, brows raised. "The convent?"

"I should have done something for them long ago. They took me in, you know, and sheltered me most kindly. It was Father's idea. He and Becta put it about that I wanted to take vows. Only the abbess knew the truth, poor lady. She had Fergus to keep, too, which shocked her deeply. But she did her best, as I remember, and was always very sweet. It would be wrong not to greet her."

"Very well," Ronan said. "Have your visit, then. I'll meet you at the Abbey entrance in an hour."

Twenty-seven

Ronan walked through the cool silence of the cloister. An older monk took his name and business, then bade him wait. It wasn't long before he saw a familiar black-robed figure striding down the long passageway, his sandals beating an irregular rhythm on the stone.

"Fitzgerald! Ye worthless dog, 'tis about time ye showed your face. And here I thought this was an urgent matter."

Ronan grinned at the man before him. "Patience, my good brother. All things in their proper time."

"Whisht, ye would try the patience of a saint, which I am far from being."

Ronan wasn't so sure of that, but he only smiled and took Brother Donal's outstretched hand.

"You look well," he said, peering closely at the sunbrowned face beneath the curling red tonsure.

"I am well. This place suits me. And what of you?" He eyed Ronan critically. "Ye look as though you haven't slept or eaten in a month."

"I am fine."

Donal began to speak, then checked himself and put a hand on Ronan's shoulder, drawing him down the passageway. "And how's that brother of mine?" he asked. "He writes but tells me nothing of himself."

Donal moved well, Ronan noted, with only a slight limp. Incredible. Miraculous, one might say, if one believed in miracles. After what Donal had been through, there were more than a few at Ravenspur who did.

"The last time I saw Conal, he seemed fine," Ronan answered. "I hear he's courting Tira Nixon."

"Still?" Donal laughed. "'Tis about time he got off his—he'd best shift himself and marry the lass before she gives up on him entirely. One monk in the family is enough."

He stopped before a door where a small table held several candles in brass holders. Selecting one, he trimmed the wick and lit it from a torch before opening the door.

In the semidarkness, Ronan could just make out a table running the length of the deserted room and the tall shelves along three walls. The familiar scents of soap and beeswax, mingled very faintly with incense, made Ronan smile, taking him back to his childhood. Donal threw open the shutters and thriftily pinched the candle out.

"Sit down," he said. "We won't be disturbed here. Now what do ye want to know about Gordon Carlysle?"

Gordon. Not just Carlysle, but *Gordon* Carlysle. There was power in a name. The faceless shadow that had haunted Ronan's dreams became a little clearer, a bit more sharply focused.

"What can you tell me?"

"Weel, I didna remember the man myself. I never rode with Lord Ian's men; I was too young. And if ye recall, there aren't any of them left—save for Sir Alistair, of course, but I imagined if ye wanted to ask him, ye would have done so."

He cocked a brow in question, and Ronan nodded.

"So I wrote to Conal to see what he could find. As it happens, Carlysle wasn't a knight at all. He was an archer under Sir Alistair's command. Apparently he got into some sort of trouble on a raid and was turned off. But he—"

"What sort of trouble?" Ronan interrupted.

"Conal didna say. I don't think he knew. Does it matter?"

"No. Go on."

"Carlysle came from a good family—brewers, mostly; his uncle runs the village alehouse. Weel, it seems Gordon's father was sore angry with his son. Said as the Kirallens had no use for him, young Gordon had best be off. So Gordon went away, serving here and there and never making much of himself. He came back from time to time, trying to mend matters, but his father never did forgive him. And never will now," Donal added with a regretful shake of his head. "The old man died six months ago."

"And Gordon? What of him?"

"They say his mother has been searching high and low for him, but it seems he went off to the wars in France some years ago. 'Tis generally believed he must be dead."

He is not dead. Ronan did not stop to think; he simply knew. Gordon Carlysle was alive.

He let out a shaking breath and became aware of Donal watching him closely.

"Do ye want to tell me why ye were asking? Who is this Carlysle to ye?"

"I'm sorry, Donal, but I cannot, though I'm very grateful for the information. Listen, would you write to Conal again? If Gordon Carlysle comes home, I'd like to know about it."

Donal nodded. "Should I have Conal send to ye?"

"No. Don't use my name at all."

"All right, though I wish . . . Ronan—" He paused,

then rested a hand on Ronan's wrist. "Are ye in some sort of trouble?"

"Me? No, Donal, my word on it."

"When Darnley's man brought your message, I wondered what the devil you were up to."

"I have been at Aylsford for several months now."

"I canna say it suits ye. Ye look like holy hell."

"Fine language from a monk," Ronan said, rising. "I'm quite all right, Donal, don't worry about me. Now tell me about you. Still working in the kitchens?"

"Nay, I'm in the infirmary for the time. Would ye like to see it?"

They walked to the infirmary together and spent some time comparing remedies. Ronan felt himself relaxing; he'd missed this kind of talk, and more than that, he had missed Donal.

"What about your leg?" he asked, leaning against the long counter around the infirmary wall. "How is it healing?"

Donal held out one sandaled foot and raised his robe. "I can straighten it completely now. Brother Ambrose thinks that the limp will likely disappear in time."

Ronan bent to look at the scar, which had faded to a thin, silver line. "Incredible."

Donal had been injured in the same battle that so nearly cost Ronan his hand. Then he had been *Sir* Donal, standing at the forefront of Jemmy Kirallen's personal guard, bearing the worst of the Maxwell's surprise attack. The deep slash across his thigh had been the ugliest of his wounds.

But it was the sword thrust through the lungs that had killed him.

Ronan had seen it for himself, lying dazed on his pallet. He remembered the pain in his arm, the smell of blood and smoking candles, the sounds of weeping just beside him and the broken voice of the priest giving Donal the last rites. There were candles all around the pallet where Donal lay, pale, unmoving, silent save for the gasping breaths he drew, each one so painful that Ronan began to wish they would just stop.

And then they did.

Master Kerian, the physician, leaned forward, pressed his ear to Donal's bandaged chest, held a wetted finger to his lips, then shook his head and drew the sheet over the young knight's face.

Ronan slipped in and out of sleep that night, but he woke fully just at dawn, dragged from his dreams by the pain in his arm and the worry that Master Kerian was right, and his hand would have to go.

And so Ronan was the first one to see Donal stir beneath his winding sheet, and the first to watch in amazement as he sat up and pulled the fabric from his face.

"Where—?" Donal breathed. "Oh, God, is it a tomb?" and his voice held such terror that Ronan sat up, too, ignoring his own pain and dizziness.

"It's all right, Sir Donal, you're in the infirmary."

Donal looked at him then, dazed, and Ronan went on quickly, "I'm Ronan Fitzgerald, and you're all right, you're fine, you're only—"

Dead. You're only dead, but don't be worrying about it. He resisted the wild urge to laugh.

"Fitzgerald?" Donal sounded more confused than ever. "The harper?"

"That's right, and I think you should lie back now, wait for Lady Alyson to come—"

And see the corpse she'd laid out so carefully last night sitting up and talking. No, that would not be good for the lady, not after all she'd been through these past days. Ronan somehow got to his feet and staggered toward the door. "I'll fetch . . . someone," he said. "Master Kerian."

Donal was still looking about the chamber with dazzled eyes, but his gaze fixed suddenly on Ronan. "No," he said slowly. "I think you'd better fetch the priest."

The next days weren't easy ones for Donal. The knight was besieged with questions from the priest, his brother, his friends—there was even talk of sending for the bishop, but the laird took one look at Donal's face and put a stop to that.

For Donal had not wanted to talk about it. He had been first bewildered, then desolate, and finally angry when no explanation seemed forthcoming from God or anyone. And he had quickly grown weary of the attention he received.

"They treat me like some freak at a fair," he'd said to Ronan later, when they were both up and about again. "And the worst of it is, I'm beginning to feel like one. For two pins, I'd leave with ye tomorrow."

But Donal hadn't left, not then. It was six months later that he'd suddenly declared his intention to live among the Benedictines at Kelso Abbey for a time, and a year later that he'd taken vows.

"So you're at peace with it?" Ronan asked now.

"As much as I'll ever be. At least I'm not complaining anymore. If He wants me to ken, I will. If not," he smiled with a shrug, "I'll find out after."

"I wish I had your faith," Ronan said bitterly. "If God has this power, why are miracles not everyday occurrences?"

"But they are. Oh, not the great ones that everyone takes notice of, but a thousand little miracles happening all around us every day. The greatest part of God's work is done through his creations. I thought ye knew that, Ronan." He smiled, though his eyes were troubled as he added lightly, "Heathen though ye are."

"I did. Once. But now . . ."

"Now? What's happened to ye? What's wrong?"

"Nothing," Ronan said sharply. "Let it go, Donal. I've told you I am fine."

"Oh, aye, I can see that. Well, if ye change your mind, ye know where to find me."

"I do. And I'm sorry for my bad temper."

"So ye think ye will be at Aylsford for some time?" Donal asked as they reached the courtyard.

"I don't know. I'm not certain. . . ."

"Take care, Ronan," Donal said, and it seemed the casual farewell held a hint of warning. "I'll keep ye in my prayers."

Twenty-eight

Maude was waiting at the gate, looking like any village lass in her blue kirtle with her hair in a long plait down her back. Her attendants followed at a respectful distance as she and Ronan walked through the courtyard, which was ringed round today with stalls. At the far end a stage had been erected, and a small man was weaving through the crowd, crying out that soon the play would start.

"Shall we stay for it?" Ronan asked, and Maude nodded eagerly.

"Oh, let's. We can sit just over there." She pointed to a bench beneath the trees, beside an upturned barrel.

Her eyes were bright as they moved over the crowded market, taking it all in. Then she tensed, and Ronan followed her gaze to see a group of Kirallen men-at-arms pass through. Several were known to him, but he only stepped into the shadow of the tree and took Maude's hand in his. The Kirallens passed the Darnley men, who stood across the square, with no more than a swirl of cloaks as each side drew pointedly away.

The play began then, the tale of man's fall from paradise, with a slender lad in a yellow wig as Eve. He simpered and flirted with the serpent as Satan's attendant imps ran through the crowd, drawing shrieks of laughter as they threatened the audience with pitchforks.

The Kirallens were long gone, but Maude's hand was still in Ronan's as they laughed together at the imps and discussed how a bit of music would improve the piece. When one of the imps came by with a cap, Maude tossed him a coin. He picked it up and swept her a bow, lower and lower, until he was somersaulting across the square.

"Thank 'ee, mum," he said, gazing up at her with a grin. He leaped up, turned a handspring, and landed squarely on his feet. He began to bow, then snapped upright.

"Why, 'tis Master Fitzgerald!" he cried. "Lads, look here, 'tis Ronan Fitzgerald."

The others left the stage and crowded round. Seen close, their costumes were tawdry things, all patched and mended, and the gilt was wearing off God's crown to show the lead beneath. They were sweating in the sun, the greasepaint melting on their faces, but every one shook Ronan's hand with pleasure.

"So this is where you got to," the leader said in his ringing voice. "We all wondered what became of you."

"Some said," the lad who had played Eve put in, "that you died in Constantinople—"

"Or took holy vows in Paris," another added, pulling his mobile face into an expression of great piety and signing himself with the cross.

"*I* heard that you had married—" the dwarf chimed in.

"Married? Me?"

"—a Saracen princess!"

Ronan grinned. Maude had never seen him so animated, his face young and merry with the pleasure of the meeting. She felt a little jealous at his easy friendship with the troupe.

"Aye, well, she did ask," Ronan answered, "and wasn't it a grand kingdom altogether, the streets all paved with gold? But alas, 'twas not to be. There is no place on earth so lovely it could ever match Northumberland."

They all groaned. "A wretched place it is, all sheep dung and pissing rain! Come on, then, give us a song!"

"Not now. I'll just sit and listen."

"Oh, go on, Ronan," Maude said. "Just one."

"Only if you join me."

He spoke in jest, clearly expecting her to refuse. And of course she would; Lady Maude Darnley did not perform at market squares. The very thought was ridiculous.

But all the others looked at her with new interest. "Does she play?" the leader asked.

"Oh, aye," Ronan said. "And sings, as well, with a voice that would bring a blind man to his knees. But—"

"Come on, then, lass, let's hear what you can do."

They didn't know who she was. To them, she was simply a lass, and the only thing of interest about her was whether she could sing.

"I was only—" Ronan began, but Maude cut him off.

"Can someone lend me a lute?"

"Bob!" the leader called. "Bring the lute. We've no harp, I'm afraid," he added, shooting Ronan a grin, "but there's the old rebec if you want it."

"My lady does not—" Ronan said.

"Ooh, a lady, is she?" "Eve" made Maude a low bow, the edges of his yellow wig brushing the grass. "Pleased to make your acquaintance, Your Grace."

Maude held out her hand. *"Milady* will do," she answered haughtily, and the boy laughed and kissed her hand with an exaggerated smack, then reeled away as though overcome.

"But—" Ronan protested.

"Let's," Maude said. "Oh, Ronan, why not? Just this once."

He frowned, then smiled suddenly, a reckless grin that she answered in kind. "Why not indeed? As you will, my lady. Shall we give them 'The Blacksmith'?"

Before Maude quite knew what was happening, she was up on the makeshift stage, the lute in her hands. It was old and battered, the once fine inlay chipped away, but when she struck a few testing chords, the sound was unexpectedly good.

She looked out over the green. It was packed with people, the players standing closest to the stage, faces turned up expectantly. All at once her stomach fluttered.

"Ronan, mayhap this isn't such a good idea. . . ."

He smiled wickedly. "A bit of nerves, is it? I know the cure for that."

He began the opening bars, bow flying as he coaxed the rebec into a merry tune. Maude caught him in the middle of the verse, her fingers oddly stiff as she fumbled for the melody. Sweat gathered at her temples when she missed a chord. What was she doing up here? She was no performer. She chanced a glance at the green and saw the leader of the troupe frown and shake his head.

It was pride that kept her going, anger that stiffened her spine and made her carry on. Shake his head at her, would he? Well, she would show him. Her focus shifted, narrowed, until the green had faded to a distant memory. There was only this note, this chord, the placement of her fingers and the plucking of each string. There, that was better—no, it was more than better, it was *right*.

When Ronan looked at her, she nodded. Once more through and this was it, the moment—she leaped for it, and the first note she sang rang out clear and fine, swelling her heart until she thought that she might burst. And then there was no thought; she was flying, fingers moving effortlessly along the neck of the lute, the song pouring from her throat.

Then Ronan's voice was there, as well, entwined with hers. Oh, she had known that he was good, that he was brilliant, but it took the open air to show what he could really do. The shrill, tuneful notes of a pipe sounded from behind her, soon joined by the pounding of a tabor. Maude laughed between the verses, turning to the men behind her. They grinned back at her and bowed, playing to the crowd dancing madly on the green.

Dancing to *her* music. Feet flying, faces red, they swirled and stamped, and she was doing this, she was a part of it, they held all these people in their hands. They ended the song with a flourish, perfectly together, and the people begged for more.

What else could they do but oblige them?

When Maude stumbled from the stage, dazed and breathless, the troupe of players crowded round.

"Come with us," the leader begged, falling to his knees and holding up his hands in supplication. "Lass, we will make your fortune. Forget him," he added, rising and putting an arm about her shoulders. "Fitzgerald's all right, but he can't be trusted. Not like me. We could be rich! We could play in the finest courts—"

Ronan slipped between them, breaking the man's grasp. "You are a swine," he said, "but I've always known that. To think you'd try to steal my lady—"

"*Your* lady? Good God, lass, don't tell me you have given him your heart! Why, he's the worst rogue among us— and that's saying quite a bit. You'd do far better to cast your lot with me."

Ronan sniffed. "Cast her pearl before swine is more like it."

"For your sake, milady—and only for your sake—I'll take the both of you. There, you can't say fairer than that."

Maude laughed. "No, you cannot. Ronan, I think we should consider this man's fine offer."

"Do you?" Ronan leaned against the stage and smiled. "It would be . . . interesting."

The dwarf, still clad in horns and tail, appeared suddenly before them. He shook the cap in his hand and it jingled, a merry little sound. The leader snatched it from his hand.

"Not bad," he said, digging into the coins and holding a handful out to Maude. "Your share, milady."

"Oh, no," Maude said. "Really, I don't—"

"Take it. You earned it, didn't you?" Ronan held out his own hand, wagging his fingers. "And where is mine?"

The man poured the coins into Maude's hands and produced a smaller share. "You can have this," he said grudgingly.

"Why, thank you." Ronan bowed. "Always a pleasure doing business with you, Goddard. Try to keep out of trouble." He winked, and as he passed the dwarf, he flipped him a coin. "Take care, Samson."

"And you, too, master." The dwarf bowed. "Will we be seeing you at Windsor for the Yule feast?"

"No, I don't think so." Ronan sighed. "Not this year."

Maude stared down at the coins in her hand. Small coins, every one, amounting to far less than she carried in her purse. But these were different. Special.

Ronan laughed. "I remember that feeling," he said, bouncing his own coins in his hand. "Like fairy gold."

Maude looked back at the stage. It was no more than a collection of rough planks, looking oddly desolate now that it was empty. But standing up there, for that small space of time, she had been a queen.

"Like magic," she said, wondering.

"Oh, no, I know that look," Ronan teased, drawing her hand into the crook of his elbow. "I'd best keep hold of you or you'll be off with them."

Maude laughed. "I think I might. What shall I do with this?" she wondered aloud. "My fortune?"

"Buy a fairing," Ronan suggested.

"I shall. For you. So you will always remember today."

He looked down at her with a different smile, one that lit his eyes from within. "Do you think I could ever forget it?"

Through the rough wool of his jerkin she could feel the heat of his skin. It flowed through her in a rush, warming her to the tips of her toes, rising to her face until her cheeks were burning.

"Go on then," he said. "I'll meet you by the tree in a quarter of an hour."

Maude wandered through the stalls in a happy dream. Surely there had never been a day so fine as this one! The sky had never been such a deep blue before, the air never so delicious.

And the stallkeepers! How had she never noticed how kind they were, how witty, making little jests as they showed her all their wares. There were knives and buckles, rings and pins, some very nice but none quite right for Ronan. And then, sitting at the very bottom of a pile of hat-pins, was a harp key, an ornate piece with an ebony handle inlaid with twisting silver.

Ronan reached the meeting place first. The joy of the performance was still with him, sharpening his pleasure in the day. He poured his purchase from one hand to the other, watching gold glitter in his palm.

"Did he find you?"

Ronan looked up to see Master Goddard standing just beside him. The leader of the players held a mug in one hand and a pasty in the other.

"Who?" Ronan asked, eyeing the pasty with interest.

"The man. He was looking for a minstrel for some sort of entertainment. Or so he said." Goddard dropped a wink. "I think what he really wanted was the lass. Not that I can blame him," he added with a sigh. "Where did you find her?"

"Under a toadstool. Sure, even an ignorant sot like you

should know a fairy when you meet one. What did the man say?"

"That he wanted to hire us, at least until he found out she was not one of our company. Then he wanted to know who she was and where he might find her. I pointed him in your direction, but I suppose he changed his mind."

"Perhaps I can change it back again." Ronan smiled, his eyes moving quickly across the crowded square. "Do you see him now?"

Goddard glanced around. "No. But you can't miss him."

Ronan relaxed slightly when he saw Maude standing at a stall. "And why is that?" he asked, never taking his gaze from her.

"He lacks an eye," Goddard said, tipping the last of his ale back and belching comfortably. "And has a great long scar down one side of his face."

Maude turned from the stall. She took one step away, then halted as the stallkeeper leaned far forward, speaking earnest words that Ronan couldn't hear, though they brought a smile to Maude's lips. She composed her expression to polite disbelief before turning back again and answered something that made the stallkeeper roar with laughter.

"If you see him again today, will you tell me?"

"Are you that hard up for work?" Goddard asked. "Why don't you come with us, then?"

"It isn't that. I'd just like to speak with him." Ronan reached into the purse at his belt and offered the last of his coins.

The coins vanished as quickly as Goddard's smile. He followed Ronan's gaze and nodded. "I'll tell the lads to look sharp."

When Maude reached the oak, she found Ronan there before her, looking half asleep as he leaned against the trunk. "I thought you had run off after all," he said.

"I might yet. But first I had to give you this."

He took the harp key from her and held it up, a slow smile spreading across his face. "It is beautiful," he said. "I will keep it always."

He tucked it carefully in the purse at his belt. "There. Oh, and this is for you. Close your eyes, now, and give me your hand."

She obeyed, feeling a cool chain pool into her palm. Opening her eyes, she looked into her hand and laughed, holding the necklace up by the gold chain.

A perfect little dragon gazed back at her, worked in brilliant enamel—emerald, crimson, azure—with tiny claws of gold. She handed it to Ronan and bent her head so he could fasten it around her neck.

"My own dragon," she said. "Just what I've always wanted."

"Every lady should have one." She shivered as his fingers brushed her neck, then turned to him with a smile. "Well? How does it look?"

But he was not looking at her at all. He was staring past her with such fixed intensity that she whirled sharply to scan the crowded green.

"Ronan? What is it?"

He shook his head and smiled down at her. "Nothing. Ah, that looks very fine, lady," he went on, once again offering his arm. "Are you hungry at all? That gingerbread has been calling to me this hour past."

They sat beneath the old oak and ate meat pies and gingerbread, washing it down with tankards of warm ale. No food had ever tasted quite so good to Maude, and she finished every morsel, sitting back with a contented sigh.

"How did you find the good sisters?" Ronan asked.

"Very well. There's a new abbess now; I'd not met her before. She gave me a cup of wine and we . . . talked."

"Did you now?"

She thought of telling him, but in the end she merely

nodded without speaking. There was really nothing to tell. Not yet, at any rate. Perhaps never. In any case, she needed to know her own mind before hearing his opinion.

She brushed the gingerbread crumbs slowly from her skirt, thinking that a fortnight ago, she would not have considered making any decision so important without consulting Ronan first.

Everything is changing. I am changing. I don't need him anymore, not as I used to. But it's all happening too fast. I'm not ready—

"I wish today didn't have to end," she cried. "I wish . . ."

But she never finished the sentence, because she had no idea what she wanted so badly that every breath was like a knife thrust through her heart.

"Aye, it's been a fine day," Ronan said, his voice curiously flat. "But 'tis time we thought of going."

They walked together toward the horses, where her men already waited. The fair was closing down, the players loading their gear into a rickety old cart. Maude waved to them, but they did not see her. They looked very different without their paint and finery, ordinary men anxious for their supper.

But that was how it was. You could pretend for an hour or two, but in the end, the magic faded, and you turned back into yourself. And then you must go home. Back to real life with all its regrets and sorrows and choices to be made.

She sighed and touched the dragon at her throat. *At least I have this,* she thought. *Always now I will remember this perfect day, and how it felt to be a queen.*

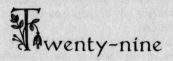wenty-nine

"Now, lads," Ronan said to their escort as they mounted their horses. "I don't know what you might have seen—or thought you saw—earlier, but . . ."

The knights grinned. They were all young men, very serious about their duty, and Ronan knew they had not taken their eyes off Lady Maude throughout the day.

"We saw some players on the stage, if that's what ye mean," one answered.

"Traveling players," another put in. "No one we could name."

"Right." Ronan flashed them a smile. "Good lads."

"But she *was* fine, was she no?" a third said, looking sideways at Lady Maude. "Whoever she might have been."

Maude sat demurely on her horse, eyes cast down. Even in the gathering twilight, Ronan could see her smile and the quick blush that stained her cheeks.

"She was indeed," Ronan answered. "Very fine."

The evening was mild, and they walked their horses, in no great hurry to get back to Aylsford Keep.

"Ronan?" Maude asked, breaking a long silence. "Do you miss it? Being on the road?"

"At times. Today—well, that was one of the better days. But there are others, too. Days when it rains or snows and you're far from where you need to be. It's a fine life when you're young and strong, but it can be hard, as well."

"You're hardly in your dotage," Maude pointed out. "Do you still plan to see Jerusalem, or have you changed your mind?"

"No, I haven't changed my mind."

When will you go? Maude wanted to ask, but she was afraid to hear the answer. Instead she said brightly, "What an adventure that will be! But it's a very long way to go . . . alone."

He was quiet for a time, then, and Maude could hear the laughing voices of the knights riding just ahead, though she could not catch their words.

"I always travel alone," Ronan said at last. "And I carry only what I must. It *is* a hard life, but it's the only one that suits me. The time I spent with Fergus was the longest I've been in any one place since I left home."

"My father says your uncle is the Earl of Desmond."

"Great-uncle," Ronan corrected absently, leaning over to adjust his horse's bridle. "My grandfather's brother. I lived at Lough Gur for some years when I was younger, after my father died."

"Is your mother still there?" Maude asked, intrigued. Somehow she had never imagined Ronan having something so ordinary as a mother. She wondered what sort of woman had borne him.

"No."

Ronan's hands clenched on the reins as he remembered the day his grandfather had taken him to Lough Gur. His mother's screams poured from the open window as Ronan was hauled, struggling and cursing, into the saddle. Warm blood dripped down his chin, and his head was reeling, both from the blow and the shock of his grandfather's unexpected arrival, coming scarce a fortnight after his father's death. His last glimpse of his mother was of her leaning out the window, hands outstretched, tears streaming down her face. Then he was jerked roughly forward, held by an iron arm across his chest.

"Pull yourself together," Grandfather said coldly. "At once."

Now Ronan carefully relaxed his grip. "My mother was not welcome at Lough Gur. She was an O'Donnell, you see, and grandfather never did approve the marriage. My father was the family disgrace."

"Where is she now?"

"Dead. She died a year after my grandfather took me."

Maude digested this in silence, trying to fit the man beside her into this noble background. "My father said," she began hesitantly, "that there *was* a grandson who ran off, but he had a different name."

Ronan nodded. "William. That was what he called me."

"But why?"

" 'Ronan?' " he said, putting on an exaggerated English accent. " 'Damned stupid name for an English lad. What's your second name? William? We'll call you that.' "

He looked at Maude and smiled, but she sensed that he was not amused. "It was the first thing he ever said to me."

"He sounds . . ." Maude groped for the word.

"English? Aye, that's Sir John—a Fitzgerald of Desmond, and don't you be forgetting it. God knows I was never allowed to. And Fitzgeralds of Desmond—at least those belonging to my grandfather—do not give their sons such heathen names.

"Not that they're all like him," he added. "Most of the Fitzgeralds are as Irish as their neighbors. But Grandfather was King Edward's man. He kept his own kin apart from the Irish—at least as far as possible, which was never far enough for him. So he waved his hand and turned me into Master William . . . for a time."

"And what was Master William like?"

"He was shaping up to be a proper little courtier," Ronan said with distaste, "saying no when he meant yes and currying favor right and left."

"So what happened to the vile creature?" Maude asked, smiling. "What turned you back into yourself?"

Ronan grinned. "The spell was broken by a lady, of course. I'd been betrothed to an Irish lass, my foster sister; a cradle match, it was, for our parents were the best of friends. Grandfather had been looking high and low for some way to break it off—damned stupid match for a Fitzgerald, don't you know—but her father refused. A brave man, he was, to stand up to Sir John. So my grandfather took himself off to London and came back again waving a new law that he and King Edward had cooked up between them."

Ronan was not smiling now. He fell silent for a time, stroking his horse's neck, the last of the sunlight limning his features with gold, accentuating the sharp lines of jaw and brow and cheekbone. When had they grown so sharp? Maude wondered suddenly. When had he lost so much flesh?

"The Statute of Kilkenny," he continued at last, "was a host of new rules, meant to bring Edward's wild Norman lords to heel. No Norman could speak Gaelic—or ride bareback, for that matter," he added with a lift of one shoulder. "One of its provisions was to outlaw marriages between the Normans and the Irish."

"So that was the end of your betrothal?"

"Aye, it was. All the rest I had choked down, but that was too much. When he started talking about the heiress he'd picked out for me, I sold everything I had to buy a harp—Grandfather smashed up my old one soon after I arrived—and passage to France."

Maude studied him curiously. "And you've never gone back?"

"I've been back to Ireland, but not Lough Gur. Grandfather would be glad to have *William* home again, but I would not be welcome there."

"How can you be certain?" Maude asked. "It has been years. He might have changed his mind."

"Not Grandfather. His heart was set on making me a knight in his service. I am no man's lackey, lady, particularly not his."

"What happened to her?" Maude asked suddenly. "The one you were betrothed to? Did you ever see her again?"

"When I left home, I went to her and asked her to run off with me. Of course she thought I was quite mad. And I thought she was heartless, for she didn't seem to care that I would surely die without her. I was only sixteen at the time," he added apologetically.

"What happened then?" Maude asked, ignoring the sharp stab of jealousy that pierced her heart.

"Oh, I sighed and drooped about, made one or two rather wretched songs lamenting her cruelty, and then—" He laughed. "Then one morning she said if I really meant to wed her, I should know she wanted children—lots of children, mayhap a dozen, just as soon as she could have them." He shuddered. "Well, that did the trick. I was halfway to France by nightfall."

Maude laughed with him. "Oh, dear, that *is* a tragic tale."

"In a way, it was. She wed—and it was a poor choice she made, a brute who treated her very badly. When he died, I thought to find her again to see if she had changed her mind. And didn't the lady refuse me yet again, *and* had the nerve to say that it was for my good as well as hers, for I didn't want a wife at all."

He smiled, looking more amused than sorrowful. "She is a good friend, a very wise lady who will have my deepest gratitude until my dying day. For the truth of it is that she was right, though it took me years to see it. I was never meant for home and hearth at all."

"You are still young," Maude said. "Later you will want to settle down and get yourself a family."

"Not I," Ronan answered firmly. "I know myself too well to ever think it. The only time I'll settle is when I'm dead."

Thirty

The next morning Ronan went to the stillroom and unpacked his market purchases. When he had first arrived, this chamber was not much used, for it stood at an inconvenient distance from the kitchens. It had been tidy—as were all the chambers at Aylsford—but very bare.

Darnley had been generous, giving Ronan leave to order whatever he thought needful and paying up with nary a complaint. Now the drying racks were filled with herbs, and the shelves held a collection of pots and flagons and folded linen strips, lancets, mortar, pestle, and scales. He set to work and soon every surface was scrubbed clean, and a mixture of horehound and honey bubbled gently on the brazier in the corner. The result was comfortable, but it was not Ronan's. He would walk away from it without a backward glance.

But this morning he was glad to be here, and the familiar work was soothing to his mind. Looking at yesterday's events more carefully, he decided it was foolish to leap to a conclusion that might easily prove false. A man had come inquiring after Maude, but what was strange in that? It would have been far stranger had something of the sort *not* happened.

Of course the scarred man might be Carlysle; one should never rule out any possibility. But Donal's observations were perhaps more to the point. Ronan knew that he had lost a stone or more since he had come to Aylsford, and he had not enjoyed a night's unbroken sleep in recent memory. It would be foolish to lend much credence to the dark fancies of an overtired mind.

By midmorning he had cleaned and salved a burn, bandaged a cut foot, and was ladling the cooled horehound mixture into small clay pots when a shadow fell across his work.

"Step in and take a seat," he said without turning. "I'll be done with this in a moment."

He sealed the pot with waxed parchment and placed it beside the others. "Now, what can I do for you?" he asked, turning, and found Maude seated on the bench, one foot tucked under her as she examined a flagon from the shelf.

It was the first time she had visited him here. Her presence seemed to change the very air, transforming the homely little chamber into something rare and special. It was not just a stillroom tucked into an inconvenient part of the manor. It was the only place Ronan wanted to be.

But that, he thought, would be the case no matter where she was.

"My father came to speak with me last night," Maude said, setting the bottle back on the shelf. "He said he wants to plan a great feast."

Ronan sat down beside her. "Does he? In honor of what?"

"My betrothal to Kinnon Maxwell."

So it had come. Ronan had known all along that their time was measured, but had put the knowledge from his mind. For a moment he didn't answer, only watched the wind blowing across the courtyard outside, sweeping everything before it.

When he was certain he could speak calmly, he asked, "And how do you feel about that?"

"I thought about it half the night, but I dinna ken how I can do it." Her voice was even, but he could tell by the thickening of her accent that she was upset.

"Can you not tell him that?"

"I did. He said I must. We went on like that for a bit, and there was nothing else to say. His mind is set and so is mine, but he is my father."

Ronan drew a deep breath. "Then can you not trust him to make the right decision?"

"I want to," she said, turning to him. "I wish I could. But I canna see—canna imagine . . . or no," she added with a harsh laugh, "the trouble is I can imagine all too well. I will not do it, how can I? I'd go mad, murder Kinnon in his bed—"

"Whisht, there's no need to talk like that," Ronan said mildly, though the very thought of Kinnon Maxwell and Maude in bed together left him sick and shaken. "Perhaps if you were to confide in Kinnon . . . ?"

"Never."

Well, that was that. Ronan had done his duty; surely there was no need to go on beating the subject to death.

"I won't do it," Maude said. "I'll just go on refusing, right up to the end. I doubt my father would have me carried kicking into the church."

"Are you sure of that?"

"Aye, I'm sure. He loves me. That's the whole trouble, really, and if I truly would not do it, he would let it go. I'd go on living here until my father died, and then Haddon would have to keep me . . . though I doubt he'd be best pleased about it," she said wryly. "Then Haddon would marry, and there I'd be, the old spinster auntie to his bairns. . . ." She dropped her head into her hands and groaned.

"That doesn't sound very appealing."

"It's awful," she said, the words muffled behind her hands. "Can ye see me? Poor old mad Aunt Maude, that's what they'd say, keep away from her, she's a bit off."

Ronan had to laugh. "You might like the children."

"I wouldn't. I don't really care for children."

"Oh, but you'd feel differently if you had your own," he said, echoing the words that had been said to him. Not that he believed it. But women were different. " 'Tis one reason to consider Kinnon Maxwell," he added, trying desperately to be fair. "If you were a mother—"

Maude raised her head and looked at him, her face curiously blank. "I will never be a mother."

"You should at least consider—"

"I could consider it from now 'til doomsday and it would make no matter. I canna. I was . . . ill," she said. The color rose to her cheeks and she looked away. "After. Fergus said—he said 'tis unlikely—probably impossible. He said I should never expect—"

"Oh." Ronan wanted to say more, but his lips seemed to have gone numb.

"And that would hardly be fair to Kinnon," Maude said.

"No," he agreed, the words coming from a great distance. "It would not be fair."

"There is another choice," she said slowly. "I could go into the convent."

"What?"

But no, that wouldn't do. He was meant to be encouraging her to make her own choices, not recoiling from any idea, no matter how ridiculous it was.

"A convent?" he added quickly. "Yes, that's true. Do you think you would be happy in that life?"

"Weel, it does have advantages. I wouldna have to marry, nor would I be counted as a failure when I canna bear a child."

As Kinnon Maxwell—or any noble she married—

would surely judge her. No one talked of barren husbands, only barren wives, and there was no worse fate that could befall a noblewoman than to fail in her most important duty to her lord. Worse, Maude would know from the beginning it was hopeless, and her marriage would be based entirely on lies.

She was right. The convent did have merit.

"There is the matter of vocation," Ronan said.

"Half the lasses forced into the nunnery have no vocation," Maude answered with a shrug. "They manage well enough."

Right again. They did manage, many of them quite happily. And given Maude's wealth, rank, and intelligence, she could rise high in the Church. Her logic was sound, her instincts good, and he should be pleased that she was looking to the future instead of dwelling in the past.

"At least I would be doing something. Helping," she added uncertainly. "Not just thinking of myself or looking after some man's comfort every moment of the day. Mayhap there are others like me, and I could . . . oh, I don't know, perhaps I could talk to them, tell them that it doesn't have to be the end of everything."

Ronan closed his eyes briefly. This was the Maude he had heard about, always quick to sympathize with those less fortunate than herself. The one whose first instinct would always be to help and comfort. Here, at last, he was seeing the lass who had ridden out to Mallow with her bags of food and clothing for the poor.

He had hoped for this. He had prayed that one day she would be able to see past her own pain to the world beyond. But he had imagined her in that world, a part of it again, not shut away from it forever.

"That must be a terribly lonely life if you aren't called to it," he heard his own voice say.

"Aye," she agreed, resting her chin in her palm. "But 'tis better than marriage to Maxwell or a life as poor old mad Aunt Maude. I want . . ." she moved restlessly in her seat, "I want to do something that matters."

"Lady Maude—" he began strongly.

"Aye?"

"I'm thinking you needn't make any decisions yet. 'Tis good that you've begun to wonder about your future, but why the rush? Surely you can put your father off for a time. You are not ready—"

Who's not ready?

"—and you need to give this all more thought when you're feeling a bit calmer."

She is calm, you fool. 'Tis you who are upset.

"What good will that do?" she asked, burying her face in her folded arms. "Nothing will ever change. The only place I'm fit for is the convent."

"You could wait. I don't mean you should sit idle. Why, there are a hundred things you could be doing here and now to help your father's tenants. I understand you wouldn't want to stay here at Aylsford forever, but that's no reason to leap into a decision you may come to regret. Give it time, lady. You're feeling now that you'll never want to marry, but that could change. If you were to fall in love—"

She made a sound, halfway between laughter and a sob. "Love?"

"It could happen. When you meet the right man, you'll be able to tell him all, and—"

She lifted her head. "And what? He'll want me anyway? Am I so sweet, then? So good, so kind? Ye ken the things I've done—to Haddon . . . and to Alyson," she added very low.

"That was before," Ronan said. "I think if you had it to do over again, you would do things very differently."

She shot him a contemptuous look, but now it was easy for him to see the uncertainty beneath.

"I'm no fit match for any man," she said harshly, "save one so desperate for my fortune he'd overlook all else. Aye, there are men like that, widowers who have their heirs already. Do ye think I have not thought of it? But even if I could find such a man and he would take me as I am, knowing all, still I could not wed him. He would want—expect—and there I'd be again."

"It might not be so bad as you think."

She lowered her head into her arms again. "It would be."

"You do not know that. Lady—"

What was he saying? Worse, what was he doing? His hand was reaching of its own accord to lightly stroke her hair. It was cool to the touch, just as he remembered, soft beneath his fingertips. She stiffened slightly but did not draw away.

"You think that lying with a man will be like—like Carlysle," he said quietly. "That every touch would bring it back again. But what he did to you—why, 'twas no more making love than a beating is a kiss. Both are ways of touching, aye, but they are so very different. . . ."

His fingers skimmed the soft skin of her neck, and he felt her shiver. "You don't know—how could you know? The way it can be between a woman and a man who love each other—"

He slid his fingers beneath her chin and lifted her face to his. "That is like—well, it isn't like anything else really. . . ."

Save for music, he thought, but the words sounded so ridiculous in his mind that he did not say them.

She smiled faintly. "I suppose *you* know all about it."

"Something," he said, pushing the bright hair back from her face, his fingers slowly tracing the outline of her ear. "Aye, I know something of it, enough to know that . . . that . . ."

What had he started out to say? Something about music—or was it love? He couldn't remember now, and it didn't seem to matter, for suddenly they had passed the point where words had any meaning. He bent to her and brushed her lips with his, then pulled back to look into her face.

She was staring at him wide-eyed, and it seemed an eternity passed as he waited for her to tell him if he had just made the most terrible mistake of his life. He had time to notice footsteps passing by the door, the faint ringing of the blacksmith's hammer, the frantic pounding of his heart.

Then she smiled.

Thank God, he thought, *thank God I did not hurt her.* And he began to speak, to apologize, explain, but she reached up and stroked his lips, and the words dissolved beneath her touch. He kissed her fingertips, and as her hand moved lightly across his face, he pressed his lips to palm and wrist, his gaze locked with hers.

At last her eyes moved downward, toward his mouth, and she swayed forward in an unconscious invitation so exciting that it took all his strength not to put his arms around her and pull her to him, crushing her soft body against his own.

But he did not. He stayed just where he was, arms at his sides. Their only contact was the touch of mouth on mouth.

Careful, he told himself. *Keep this light and easy.* He played with her, drawing just a bit away and leaving her to follow if she would. She did, one hand moving behind his head to draw him closer. Her breath was warm against his lips, her hand soft in his hair, and the light fragrance of her skin began to cloud his mind.

It was enough. He should stop now, he'd made the point, but she seemed in no hurry to be done. When he touched her lower lip with his tongue, she went very still, and then he felt her smile as she turned her head, instinctively deepening the kiss.

He was lost then, all thought of the lesson he had meant to give flying straight out of his head. He had wanted this too long and never dared to hope it would be his. He knew it was too much—too hard, too hungry—but now that he had started, he could not stop.

He closed his eyes and lost himself in her, exploring her with gentle thoroughness, every nerve alive to the pressure of her hand, the soft sound she made when he caught her lower lip between his teeth—

"Weel, look at this!"

Ronan drew back to find Celia standing in the doorway. She was smiling, but her eyes were very cold. "Maude, I am surprised at ye," she said, shaking her head. "Or come to think of it, mayhap I am not. But I daresay your poor father will be."

Ronan stood. "We shall soon find out, won't we, mistress?" he said pleasantly. "I'm sure you cannot wait to tell him."

Celia eyed him up and down. "It would be my pleasure. But I'm afraid my lord is not able to discuss the matter now."

"Why not?" Maude demanded.

"He fell from the mounting block and struck himself senseless when his leg gave out beneath him. So ye had best attend him, *taibhsear,* and be quick about it."

Ronan had already seized his pouch and was halfway out the door. As Maude followed, Celia stepped before her. "Ye are a fool, Maude."

"I gave you no leave to call me familiar," Maude answered, lifting her chin. "Get out of my way."

"If Kinnon Maxwell learns of this—"

"I do not care what Kinnon Maxwell knows or thinks. I will not marry him."

Celia seized her by the arm. "Your father has said ye shall."

"And I say that I shall not. You will release me. *Now.*"

Maude did not lift her hand. She did not even raise her voice. Still, Celia stepped back a pace and Maude pushed past her out the door.

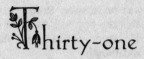

Thirty-one

There was no injury to Darnley's head. The fall was not responsible for his loss of consciousness; it was the fever that had brought him down. That, and the weakness of his leg.

Before Darnley's boots had been drawn off, Ronan knew what he would find. That sickly sweet smell was unmistakable, the scent of living flesh rotting on the bone.

Though he was prepared, he still drew a sharp breath when the damage was revealed. The sore on Darnley's leg was festering again, but that was not the worst of it. It had spread downward, and now his left foot was swollen to twice its normal size, mottled red and white and splotched with black. The right foot was little better, though the damage there was not yet so extensive.

How could he have come to such a state since Ronan last examined him? *I should have seen,* he thought, *I should have known. . . .*

But now was not the time for blame. Focusing all his concentration, he bent close and gently pressed and twisted, assessing the damage.

"Bring me hot water," he said to Darnley's squire. "And the bottle on the second shelf of the stillroom, the glass bottle standing closest to the door. I'll need all the tools in the trunk, as well, and two—no, three—strong men. Do you hear me?"

When there was no answer, Ronan looked over one shoulder to find that the boy had retreated some distance from the bed. He stood ashen-faced, hands clamped across his nose and mouth.

"Get out," Ronan snapped. "Send me someone who can take an order."

"What do you need?" Maude asked, stepping into the chamber. She glanced over at her father, and her face grew very still and white.

"Don't faint," Ronan ordered curtly, "I haven't time for that."

"I won't. Tell me what you need."

Ronan repeated his requests, and she nodded. "Why— why the men?"

"To hold him. I'll have to take off—" She swayed and put one hand against the wall. "Just do as I ask. Quickly, now, 'tis better if he does not wake."

"Yes. Yes, of course."

Ronan prepared the chamber, building up the fire, setting ewer and pitcher close to hand. Darnley he left as he was, not wanting to disturb him. With any luck, he would be insensible throughout.

When all was ready, Ronan took some time for meditation, then went over in his mind what he must do. He had performed an amputation only once before, in winter, on a village lad with a bad case of frostbite. That had been one toe, the smallest, and by springtime the boy had been running about.

Darnley would not run again. He would be lucky if he walked. The sores were but a symptom of a deeper illness. Apollonius held it was a form of dropsy; Paul of Aegina, a weakness of the kidneys, Aretaeus called it diabetes insipidus. All agreed that in the later stages, it would eat flesh from bone.

There were treatments: poultices and mandragors, exercise in moderation, restrictions of the diet. Ronan would try all of them in every combination, though he knew that even if they worked, they would do no more than purchase time.

That is not in my hands, Ronan thought. *I can do no more than I am able, but all that can be done, I will.*

He was relieved that Lady Maude did not return herself but sent all he had asked for with three large men-at-arms. Ronan laid out the ointments and tipped a portion of wine well laced with opium into a small cup, setting it aside should it be needed.

"Take hold of him," he ordered. "One at each shoulder, another at the knees."

He reached down into the box of tools and straightened, holding a small saw.

"Brighid guide my hand," he murmured.

And then he started.

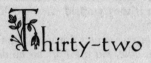

Thirty-two

Maude paced her father's antechamber, ears straining for any sounds behind the thick door. From time to time she heard a murmur of voices, too low to catch the words, then a cry and Ronan saying sharply, "Not like that! Move aside." There was nothing more.

It was hours later that Ronan himself appeared. He strode out into the chamber, drying his hands on a linen strip. There was blood on his robe.

"Find me—oh, there you are, lady. Sit down."

His voice was very cool, as though he were some hired physician and not the man who had been kissing her just hours ago. Numb, Maude sank down on the settle.

"Your father is awake. He is asking to see you. No, wait," he added as Maude started to rise.

"What d-did you do to him?" she faltered.

Ronan reached for her hand, then stopped, looking at the flecks of blood on his wrist. "I removed three toes. Perhaps I should have taken the foot, but I'm still hoping we can save it."

"He—is he—it isn't—"

"It is not leprosy. This is an illness of the blood."

"Can you cure him?

Ronan shook his head. "No. But we can control it," he added. "For a time."

"A time?" Maude repeated faintly. "How long a time?"

"Perhaps a year."

Maude knew she should feel something, but she was aware of only a great emptiness. "I see. Does he know?"

"Yes, I've told him. He asked, and I saw no point in lying."

"No," Maude agreed, "he would not want that. I—I will see him now."

Ronan walked with her to the inner chamber. She hesitated at the doorway, and he touched her shoulder briefly in a gesture of wordless comfort.

"Maude," Darnley said, looking up at her from his pillow. His eyes were dull, his grip weak as she took his hand. "Yon *taibhsear* gives me a year, but I dinna believe it will be so long as that."

"That is because you are weary, Father," Maude said, her voice lightly chiding. "Tomorrow you will—"

"I want Haddon here," Darnley interrupted. "I want my son."

Maude bit her lip. "But Father," she began.

"I ken where he is," Darnley said irritably. "But I dinna think even *they* will deny me one last look at him."

"There will be plenty of time for that."

"Nay!" Darnley struggled to sit upright.

Ronan appeared on the far side of the bed to lay a hand on Darnley's shoulder. "None of that, my lord. Lie still."

Darnley collapsed back upon his pillow, his face slick with sweat. His grip on Maude's hand tightened. "Maude, please, bring Haddon here to me."

"Yes, Father, I will," she promised recklessly. "I will bring him home."

Darnley's eyes drooped. "Ye were always a braw lass, Maude, such a bonny little thing. . . . I'm sorry that I failed ye. . . ."

"You never did," Maude said fiercely.

"Aye . . . a father's duty . . . protect . . ."

His voice trailed away to silence. Gently, Maude laid his hand upon his breast. Ronan put a finger to his lips and nodded toward the door.

"He is dazed from the medicine," he said, "and very weary. But he is not dying."

She stared at him through a shimmer of tears, and he bent to her, his mouth closing over hers in a quick, hard kiss. "Get to your rest and try not to worry. We will talk more tomorrow."

He stepped back into the chamber and closed the door.

Two days later, Maude walked into the garden. The air was cool, tinged with the coming of autumn and the scent of woodsmoke. Sunlight glinted on the hilltops, but mist still clung to the hollows. The vines on the walls of the keep were brilliant crimson against gray stone, and the Michaelmas daisies were in bloom. Maude pulled her cloak about her and moved to a patch of sunlight.

"I thought I would find you here." Ronan dropped to the seat beside her.

"How is Father?"

"Much better this morning."

"How are *you?*" she asked. "Have you slept at all?"

"I will. The worst of it is over; no sign of inflammation, and Dame Becta's sister knows just what she's about."

"Good. I'm glad."

"Has there been any word from Haddon yet?"

Maude turned from him. "No."

"That's strange. I thought by now—you did write?"

"Well . . . no. You said there was no immediate danger, so I thought . . . it seemed better . . ."

"What?"

"That I should go myself."

"You cannot go to Ravenspur!"

"Why should I not? Haven't you been saying all along how good they are, how kind? Surely such paragons of virtue won't refuse me a visit with my brother!"

"I'll go myself," Ronan said.

"Would you?" She slipped her hand into his. "You are very good to us. How would we get along without you?"

It was true, she could not begin to imagine life without Ronan. Whatever else there might be between them, he was her friend, the truest she had ever known. Here he was proving it yet again, offering to undertake this journey for her sake when he was so worn and weary.

"This is something I must do myself," she went on, "and I hardly mean to ride there unprotected. I shall be fine."

Ronan sighed. Maude was growing away from him; no more did she accept his word as Holy Writ. His time as her guide and healer was over. A kiss had marked its end—and a new beginning for them both.

During the long silent hours, Ronan had reckoned the cost of that new beginning. No wandering minstrel could hope to win the hand of Lady Maude, only a man of wealth and rank could aspire to that honor. But *Sir* Ronan Fitzgerald was as good a match as any border lord could wish for his daughter. Far better than Kinnon Maxwell, who could offer nothing to match the wealth and grandeur of Lough Gur or the patronage of the Earl of Desmond himself.

Should Maude consent to marry him, Ronan would willingly play the prodigal grandson, down on his knees if he must. His pride and independence were a small price to pay for a lifetime spent with Maude.

If she consented to marry him. Even now, he could not be certain of her heart. Nor was he sure that she knew it yet herself. Wait, he cautioned himself, you'll know the time to speak. It won't be long now. She is growing stronger by the moment.

Yet today he wished she was not *quite* so strong. He nearly spoke of Carlysle, then checked himself. What did he really *know?* The man was believed dead by all who knew him. Should he turn up again, Ronan would be informed at once. There seemed no more that he could do and no real reason to shake Maude's newfound confidence.

But still, he did not like this notion.

"It will do no good," he said. "The laird will not release Haddon. He cannot. Haddon is his one assurance of the peace."

"I will still ask," Maude insisted, "for I promised. The laird may let him come for a short visit, just long enough to set Father's mind at rest."

Ronan rubbed a hand across his face. "Your father never intended you to go yourself. He will not allow it," he said, doing his best to sound regretful.

"Then I shall not ask him," Maude said with the old imperious lift of her chin.

"Lady, I wish that you would let me go in your place."

She gazed out onto the moor, her eyes distant. "I thank you, Ronan, but you cannot do this for me. I want my brother back," she added very low. "I need to make my peace with him. Can you understand that? At least I need to try. I must go."

"Not without me," Ronan said.

She turned to him, her eyes alight. "Can you be spared?"

"The worst of it is past now, and he has as good care as I could give him. I don't suppose a day or two will do any harm. God's blood, but you're a stubborn wench."

"Stubborn? Me?" She squeezed his hand. "If that isn't the pot calling the kettle black, I don't know what is."

Thirty-three

They arrived at Ravenspur Keep just before midday. Word of their arrival had preceded them, for they had been met just over the border by a force of Kirallen men-at-arms. One had ridden back to Ravenspur and the rest had offered—in a manner that brooked no refusal—to accompany them.

Ronan sensed that Maude was frightened, though he was proud to see she gave no sign of it. He did his best to put her at her ease, greeting many of the Kirallens by name and keeping up a steady flow of conversation. When he asked after the leader's children, even that dour man allowed himself a smile.

Gradually, the atmosphere lightened, though it was still far from easy. Maude's men kept her surrounded at all times, and on both sides hands tended to stray toward weapons at any unexpected move. Ronan fell back a bit, encouraging the leader to go on about his family.

The moment Maude was out of earshot, he said casually, "Do you know Gordon Carlysle?"

"I kent his father well, poor man. Wee Gordon was

his only bairn and a sore trial to him. The last I heard, he took himself off to foreign parts. Why?"

"A matter of a debt," Ronan said vaguely.

"You, too? Weel, lad, you'll have to join the queue, much good may it do ye. I doubt we'll see him back again."

Satisfied, Ronan went ahead and caught up to Lady Maude. Side by side, they rode into the courtyard of Ravenspur.

They were greeted by Laird Kirallen himself. Jemmy waited in the courtyard, his lady on one side and his heir and nephew, Malcolm, on the other. Maude had forgotten how tall the laird was, how broad of shoulder, how very stern and proud. He was at his most imposing now, and Maude began to think that maybe Ronan had been right and this was not such a good idea after all.

"Good day, Laird, my lady," Ronan called as he dismounted. "God's greetings to you."

"Ronan." Jemmy Kirallen inclined his head slightly. "And Lady Maude. What do you here?"

If Ronan was aware of the coolness in the laird's voice, he did not show it. "Lady Maude has come to speak with her brother," he said, "on a matter that cannot wait."

"And that is . . . ?"

Ronan glanced at Maude, inviting her to take over the conversation. "My father is ill. He is asking for Haddon."

"I am sorry, Lady Maude, but—"

"My lord, our guests have come a long way and are no doubt weary," Lady Alyson put in. "Surely there is no need to keep them standing in the courtyard! Ronan, Lady Maude, will you not come inside?"

"Thank you," Ronan said at once, before Maude could refuse. "We started early, and the ride was long. Come inside, my lady," he added, taking Maude by the elbow and fairly dragging her along.

Maude scowled, but he met her gaze without flinching. "Courtesy costs you nothing," he said in her ear as they passed through the doorway. "Do not make this worse for Haddon than it need be."

She nodded, accepting the truth of that, and stepped inside. After the warmth of the morning air, the hall struck cool. An enormous hound lay on the hearth, chin resting on his paws, looking miserably resigned as two young girls tied a kerchief about his shaggy head. The long room was bright with candles, and the scents of rosemary and lavender wound through the smell of woodsmoke.

"Welcome to Ravenspur, lady."

Malcolm Kirallen made her a bow. He had grown since Maude had seen him last, though he would never have the great height of his uncle. He must be about sixteen, though he looked older, as though he had somehow skipped the awkwardness of adolescence and gone straight from a winning child to an undeniably attractive young man. A young man who was looking at her with far more interest than the child ever had.

Damned impertinent Kirallen.

"Malcolm, isn't it?" she asked coldly.

"Aye, my lady. I am honored you remember me."

He flashed her a merry smile that warmed his bright blue eyes. Could it be that this—this *boy* was *flirting* with her? He flicked a quick glance toward his uncle, then looked back at Maude, his smile growing, if possible, a little warmer.

"How *could* I forget the time I spent here?" Maude said.

There was a small, tense silence. For the time Maude had spent here had been as a prisoner, and she had escaped only by leaving Haddon in her place.

Malcolm laughed. "Not under the best of circumstances, I grant, but I hope you do not remember us unkindly."

Now that was cleverly done, Maude thought. He had

admitted no wrong, made no apology, but managed to make it all sound like a trifling disagreement between friends. For a lad of sixteen, it was an impressive show of diplomacy.

It was a pity his uncle could not match him.

Jemmy Kirallen made her no bow, nor did he waste a moment in pleasantries. He sat very straight in his great chair, and the moment the others were seated, he turned to Maude.

"Lady Maude, your father and I have an agreement. Haddon is to stay with us until his knighting, which will take place in three years. At that time, he will return home."

"Come, Laird, be reasonable," Maude said. "My father is not well, and he has not seen his only son and heir for nigh unto four years."

"Nor will he see Haddon at Aylsford until the terms of our agreement have been fulfilled. Lady, what do you expect me to say? Surely you understand that for me to rely upon your father's word is impossible."

Maude looked at Ronan. He was leaning back in his seat, watching her. There was sympathy in his gaze, but one shoulder lifted in a slight *I told you so* shrug.

"Laird," Maude began, "I understand your . . . caution. But I assure you that my father is indeed quite ill. Is that not so, Ronan?"

Ronan nodded. " 'Tis the truth, Laird."

"Will he recover from this illness?"

"Yes," Ronan said. "By God's grace, he will."

"Then at that time, Lord Darnley will be welcome to ride over here and visit with his son."

"He will never agree to that!" Maude exclaimed.

Laird Kirallen smiled, catching Maude off guard. It was startling the way his face lightened when he smiled, taking years and layers of care from his somber countenance. "No, I daresay he will not, nor can I blame him overmuch. Lady, say to your father that if we can agree upon some neutral place—mayhap the abbey—I will undertake to bring Haddon there myself."

It was fair, more than fair, and the best that Maude could hope for. She nodded. "I shall tell my father of your offer. May I see Haddon now?"

"Of course," Jemmy said at once. "I will have him sent for." He looked about the hall. "Would you like to meet him somewhere with a bit more privacy?"

"A fine idea," Ronan said, standing. "Why don't I show Lady Maude to the garden?"

They all rose. Malcolm and the laird went off, and Alyson walked with them through the hall. A small, dark-haired girl of two or three abandoned her playmates and skipped across the hall.

"Ronan!" she cried, holding up her arms. Ronan caught her up and spun her round.

"Hullo, Isobel—why, look how much you've grown! Do you have a kiss for me?"

Isobel, Maude thought, *Alyson's daughter . . . and Ronan's goddaughter.* Alyson was watching the two of them together, smiling fondly. She turned aside as a servant approached and spoke to the girl. When she turned back, she was holding a baby in her arms.

"You have a new bairn?" Maude asked, feigning an interest she was far from feeling. "I had not heard."

Alyson smiled. "Aye, wee Gawyn, born just after Yule."

What did women say in such situations? Maude searched her memory, came up with, "I trust the confinement was not too difficult."

"Oh, no, 'twas naught," Alyson said, smiling as she caressed her daughter Isobel's dark curls. "Not like this one. But the second is always easier, though Gawyn was far bigger."

"A bonny daughter and a lusty son," Maude murmured. "You must be proud."

No shrewd guess there. Alyson was clearly bursting

with pleasure in her accomplishment. *It is no great matter,* Maude told herself, *to bear a child. Any woman— even the most ignorant of peasants—can do it.*

Any woman save for me.

Alyson stood, her son in her arms and her daughter at her knee, the heavy folds of her moss green gown falling softly about her feet. The fiery mass of her hair was confined in golden cauls, but a few strands escaped to curl about a face that glowed with health and happiness. Beside her, Maude felt as faded and brittle as last year's heather.

"Lady Maude?"

It was Ronan's voice, but Maude could not look at him just now.

"Your brother will be waiting," he said.

"Yes. Of course."

"We'll see you at supper, then," Alyson said. "You'll stay the night, of course."

"Thank you," Ronan answered for her. "That is very kind."

"Oh, 'tis no bother. You'll have your old chamber, Ronan, and Maude, send someone to find me when you're finished with Haddon."

She swept off, and Ronan held out his arm. "Shall we?"

They walked together through the courtyard. Maude was thinking of how easy Ronan had been with the child—Alyson's child—and how natural he had looked holding her. No matter what he might say now, he would want children of his own. Any man would.

Ronan was her friend, and he might enjoy a kiss or two, but he had never claimed to love her. Indeed, she thought, all he had ever wanted was to prove to her that she was still capable of desire, a point he had made well and truly.

The trouble was, she could not imagine feeling such a thing for anyone but him: a homeless, rootless wanderer whose sole ambition was to get back on the road again.

Ronan did not speak as they left the courtyard and passed through the edges of an apple orchard. He thought he could guess the reason for Maude's silence, for he had seen the look in her eyes as she gazed at the babe in Lady Alyson's arms. If he had known what words might comfort her, he would have spoken them. As it was, he judged silence was the kindest course.

The path narrowed as it led into the garden, and Ronan stepped aside to allow Maude to precede him. They had gone only a few steps when a couple, arm in arm despite the narrow path, came around the corner. Maude stopped so suddenly that Ronan walked straight into her.

"Ronan!" the woman cried. "Oh, Ronan, I didn't know that you were here! When did you arrive?"

"Just this moment," Ronan answered, stepping past Maude to take Deirdre Kirallen's outstretched hand.

"Why have you not written?" Deirdre demanded. "I have been so worried. Are you well, *mo deartháir?*" she asked, peering into his face. "Have you been ill?"

Mo deartháir. My brother. Deirdre had taken to calling Ronan that just after she was married, underscoring their long friendship and ignoring all the rest. Once he had resented it, but now it made him smile.

"I'm fine, Dee, never better. Hello, Alistair."

Sir Alistair Kirallen did not return his greeting, nor did he seem aware that Ronan had spoken at all. The knight's cool gray eyes were fixed on Maude. Turning, Ronan saw that she was standing very straight, her chin lifted at a defiant angle as she gave the knight back stare for stare.

"There, I've forgotten my manners altogether," Ronan said easily. "Lady Maude, may I present Sir Alistair and Lady Kirallen."

"Good day, Lady Maude," Deirdre said, dropping Maude a quick reverence as she shot a startled glance at Ronan. "I trust you had a pleasant journey."

Her words fell into the well of silence between Maude and Alistair. With a none-too-subtle gesture, Deirdre elbowed her husband in the ribs. Still he did not bow nor did he speak.

"Sir Alistair and I have met before," Maude said evenly. "And I have seen him since in London."

Alistair nodded briefly. "Aye."

"Though I am surprised to see him here," Maude went on, "as I was present when the old laird banished him."

"Weel, the new laird had second thoughts about that," Alistair said.

"Did he?" Maude said coldly. "What a pity."

Without another word, she walked away.

"What—?" Deirdre began, turning to her husband, but Ronan didn't stay to hear Alistair's explanation. He caught up to Maude at a turning in the path.

"Wait, lady, stop. I said *wait,*" he ordered, taking her by the arm. "What was that about?"

"If I had known—if I had ever thought that man would be here, I never would have come! Why did you not tell me?"

"Tell you? Why would I? How was I to know you knew him?"

"Oh, I know him. Four years ago he swore a blood oath against my father. He followed us to London; there was no escaping him; he was always there, lurking in some corner with one hand on his dagger. He never said a word, Ronan, not a word. He would just stand there, watching us, smiling. . . ."

"That sounds like Alistair," Ronan said. "But you needn't worry about him now. You know how the laird feels about this peace; he's absolutely determined to make it work. I'm sure he's keeping Alistair on a tight lead."

"But that is not all," Maude said. "He was there. That night. I remember now. He—he pulled Carlysle away—it was him, looking down at me. From the moment I saw him—years later, when they brought me here as prisoner—I was terrified of Sir Alistair, even before the blood oath, before he ever spoke a word to me. Now I know why. He was *there,* Ronan, he *saw* me, he *knows*—"

"Whisht, now." Ronan grasped her by the shoulders and shook her gently. "He does not know. Nay, lady, sure and he does not, or he would have said something long since—"

"Would he?" she cried. "Why? When?"

"When the old laird wanted his son to marry you— was Sir Alistair not against it? Is that not what started all his troubles, that he would not accept the marriage? If he had known anything he could twist to your discredit, do you think he would not have used it then?"

"I don't know! How can I know what he would do or why?"

"Lady," Ronan said, "did he hurt you? Did he even so much as touch you that night?"

"No. No, he—he came after me when I ran, but I think he meant to help me—or mayhap he only wanted to find me to be certain who I was—"

"He does not know. I swear to you that he does not."

"I could not bear it," she whispered. "Not that. Even if he does not know now, what if he remembers—as I did? What if he—"

"He will *not.* He has no reason to think of that night at all. It was seven years ago, lady, and so much has happened since. If he was going to remember, he would have done so long ago. You are safe, I swear it."

"I will never be safe," she said. "I was a fool to think I ever could be."

"Hush, now, that is nonsense. I'm here, aren't I? Of course you're safe. Your hands are freezing—" he said, chafing them between his own. "I *knew* this was a mistake. You should have listened to me."

"You were right, I admit it. There, does that make you happy?"

"Well, yes," he said. "It does."

She looked up at him and laughed through her tears. "You are insufferable!"

"I know," he admitted, pleased to see some color come back into her cheeks. "But there, we can't all be right, can we? Now, this is what I think we should do next. Speak to Haddon and then we will be off. There is no need to linger."

"But the men . . . the horses . . ."

"The horses will be fine, and if the men can't ride as hard as their mistress, they've no business calling themselves knights. Now don't move—just let me find Haddon."

The moment Ronan was gone, Maude began to pace the garden. She wanted to go now, this moment, but Ronan was right, she had come this far to see Haddon, and it would be cowardly to leave without finishing her errand.

"Maude?"

It was Haddon's voice behind her; she knew it at once, though it had deepened since she heard it last. Bracing herself, she turned to face him.

Oh, he had grown! The last time she had seen him, he had been smaller than she, but now she had to tilt her head to look into a face that was beginning to lose its boyish roundness. His jaw and cheeks had firmed, his nose gone from a little upturned button to one that was high-arched, exactly like their father's. Yet he was still Haddon, with his bright red curls and blue green eyes. *Oh, he is a handsome lad,* she thought with a rush of pride, *a Darnley through and through.*

"Maude, what are ye doing here?"

His voice was hard, and he made no move to take her outstretched hands.

"Haddon," she began, her hands falling awkwardly to

her sides. "Father is ill. Very ill. I wanted to—"

"Why did ye really come?"

"I wanted to tell you myself. And—and I wanted to see you."

"To *see* me? Ye expect me to believe that? Four years, Maude, and ye never saw fit to send me a single greeting, or even to inquire if I lived or died!"

"I wanted to write. I did begin to, but . . ."

"Well, it doesna matter now. I don't care anymore."

"Haddon, listen to me," she began in a low, rapid voice. "Father isn't well. He hasn't been well for a long time now. He has asked for you, but he did not send me, he does not even know that I am here. I had to see you. I had to say—"

"I don't want to hear it," he said, his jaw, so like their father's, set in a stubborn line. "Belike 'tis all lies, anyway. Father doesn't care about me. He only wants to use me to start things up again. I hate him!" Haddon cried, his voice cracking. "I ken now what he did to Alyson's mother. I was so ashamed when I found out," he said, brushing a sleeve across his eyes. "I wish I wasn't a Darnley at all."

"Well, you are," Maude said. "There is no help for it. And you are my brother, no matter how you feel about that, either. I swear to you, Haddon, I only wanted to see you again, to say I'm sorry for what happened before and ask if we—if perhaps you could forgive me."

"For what? Riding off to London and leaving me here alone? Or for sending Alyson away—our *sister*—though she could have died?"

"But—but Haddon, that was not my idea. It was Uncle Robert who said—"

"Uncle Robert is sorry for his part, he told me so, and he told Alyson, as well. But you—you laughed about it! I was there, I remember—and that I will *not* forgive. I despise you, Maude, and I want nothing more to do with you, not now or ever. *Nothing.* Just go home and don't bother coming back, for I don't want ye here, no one does, 'tis only for my sake they put up with ye at all. Even Uncle Robert said—"

"Haddon."

The boy whirled sharply, and there was Ronan, standing in the entrance of the alcove. How long had he been there? Maude wondered. How much had he heard?

"Apologize to your sister."

"I will not. Why should I?"

"I hope to God that when you have grown up a little, you will find that answer for yourself. For now, you can do it because I told you to."

"But she—"

"Beg her pardon. *Now.*"

"Very well," Haddon said stiffly, his face flaming. "I beg your pardon, Maude."

Shooting her one last contemptuous glance, he turned and walked away.

When he was gone, the garden was very quiet. Maude picked a dead leaf from the wall and crumbled it between her fingers.

"Thank you," she said. "He was . . . upset."

"He was unkind," Ronan answered tightly. "He hurt you."

She shrugged. "It doesn't matter."

"It does to me."

The leaf wavered before Maude's eyes, then fell to the ground as she put her hands over her face.

"I shouldn't have come," she sobbed. "You were right, it was all a mistake—"

"Seeing your brother was *not* a mistake. What you tried to do was right, it needed to be done, and you were very brave to say the things you did. 'Tis no fault of yours that Haddon is too thick-headed to hear you."

Footsteps passed down the gravel pathway, and Maude turned away, her hands still covering her face.

"Come, lady, let us leave here."

Ronan put an arm around her shoulder and guided her from the garden. Maude leaned against him, too grateful to question when he turned off the path and led her through an apple orchard. Bees buzzed among the trees, and the air was scented with ripe fruit. They reached a willow tree, and he ducked, held back a trailing branch, and she stepped through into a small space, bordered on three sides by a high, crumbling wall. When Ronan let the branch drop, it fell like a curtain to the ground.

Ronan put his hands on her waist and lifted her to a thick, low-hanging branch, then leaned back beside her on his elbows.

"I wanted you to see this. I come here when I visit, when all the noise and bustle gets to be too much. I doubt anyone knows of it but me."

They did not speak for a time, but the silence was a comfortable one. Maude had never met anyone so untroubled by silence as Ronan; he never rushed to fill it with words as other people did. Once again, she was grateful, for she needed time to think about what had just happened, yet the last thing she wanted was to be alone.

"It was true," she said at last, "everything that Haddon said. I did send Alyson here."

"But what you said was true, as well. I'll wager the idea was Sir Robert's from the first. Take some peasant lass and train her up, then see if his handiwork would pass the test. Oh, I can just hear him wondering if he could make a ballad out of it."

Maude laughed shakily. "He did say that."

"There, you see? It isn't fair that you take all the blame."

"I went along with it. I—I wanted to do it."

"Why?"

He was standing just beside her now, his shoulder brushing hers, but she could not bring herself to look at him.

"I hated Alyson. She was so . . . strong. So brave.

Everyone liked her," Maude said rapidly, "all the servants—even Becta was fond of her. Uncle Robert would go on and on about how clever she was—how brave—and she is, she is all that, and beautiful and kind. 'Tis only right that she's so happy now. She deserves to be happy."

"And you do not?"

Maude shook her head. "It won't happen now," she whispered. "It's too late."

He put a finger beneath her chin and tipped her face to his. "That is nonsense. Do you think you're the only person in this world who has done things they regret?"

"What have you done? The worst thing?"

He looked at her, his lips twisted in a mirthless smile. "Where do I begin? Well, for one thing, I helped bring an innocent man to death for a crime he never did. I stole what belonged to him and handed it over to his enemies so he might be taken for a murderer. And when he was taken, I stayed silent."

Maude blinked. "You did that? *You?* But why?"

"Because he wanted the woman I loved, and I could not bear to lose her. I lied and I stole and I allowed myself to be used by evil men to evil purposes."

This was not easy for him. His face was twisted with pain, and without thinking, she took his hand and squeezed it hard.

"Did he—was he—"

"No. When it came to the point, I could not do it. By then, though, it was nearly too late. He could have died—and the laird and his family were nearly murdered—"

"And the woman?"

"I lost her . . . again."

Again? She remembered him telling her about the lass he was betrothed to from the cradle. His foster sister, he had said. And now she thought of the woman she had met earlier, the one who spoke with a faint Irish accent and addressed Ronan as her brother. "Was it—?"

"Aye, it was Deirdre, and the man was Sir Alistair."

Maude had hardly noticed Sir Alistair's lady earlier, but now she saw her clearly, a slender woman perhaps a few years older than herself. She had been fairly attractive, Maude supposed. If one admired the combination of raven hair, skin as pale as cream, deep red lips, and eyes the color of sapphires, one might call her . . .

Ravishing.

" 'Tis a strange thing," he said slowly, tucking a strand of hair behind Maude's ear. "Alistair has always been decent enough to me—more than decent, considering. But I cannot stand the sight of him. Sometimes I think it is a good deal easier to forgive those who harm us than those we have done wrong."

"Perhaps," Maude said slowly, "it is not *them* we cannot forgive."

He drew back and looked at her, brows raised. "No, perhaps it isn't."

"Deirdre," Maude said, "is a fool."

"Well, she was in love, and love makes fools of all of us," Ronan answered lightly. "Though in her case, it made her wise."

"You love her still, don't you?"

"She is very dear to me and always will be, but I don't regret the way things went. Everything I said to you was true. We would never have been happy together. She's best off with Sir Alistair, and I . . ."

"And you?"

"I told you, lady, that I was never meant for marriage."

How had he come to be standing so close? Maude hadn't been aware of either of them moving, yet she could feel the heat of his body against hers.

"No more am I," she said.

"Then we are well matched, aren't we?" he asked and, even as she nodded in agreement, he bent to her.

It began exactly where they had left off in the stillroom, as if all the time between had never happened. Then his arms went around her, and she stiffened, not meaning to, but before the fear could register, he released his hold. His fingers played lightly on her neck, along her jaw, one thumb touching the corner of her mouth as he deepened the kiss, then ended it, only to begin all over again.

Maude was not aware of any one moment when the distance between them dwindled into nothing. He stood before her, her arms wound around his neck, his circling her waist, bodies pressed so close that there was no telling anymore where he began and she left off. He lifted her from the branch and set her down before him, but she was trembling so hard that she could barely stand. She could feel him shaking, too, hear his breath come harshly as he kissed her cheeks, her eyes.

Her hands fumbled at the fastening of his cloak, and he tried to help her, but his own hands were shaking so that he could scarce unpin the clasp. Maude began to laugh, and then he was laughing, too, and his cloak fell in a swirl of green to settle on the grass.

The leaves fluttered in a sudden breeze, falling in a bright shower. Maude brushed them from his hair, his shoulders, her eyes locked with his. It was only the two of them now, alone in an enchanted chamber curtained in living green and gold. Moving slowly, without haste, she removed her gown and stood before him in her shift.

He drew a sharp breath. "Lady . . . acushla, are you—"

"Don't," she cried in sudden fear, putting her hand against his mouth. "Do not ask, for I would have to answer no, I am not certain—and yet—oh, I do not have the words. . . ."

He ran the tip of his tongue over her fingers, and she drew a sharp breath. "Asked and answered, lady." He drew her close, his fingers trailing down her spine. "You cannot help but tell me all that I would know," he said, his breath soft in her ear, "though you do not speak a single word. . . ."

She turned her head, blindly seeking, and his mouth found hers. There were no words then, only the sound of her own heartbeat in her ears, her breath coming more quickly as his thumbs moved from waist to breast, the low sound, between a purr and a growl that he made when she arched against his hand. His hand moved against her breasts, her belly, then downward. She gasped as he reached the juncture of her thighs, instinctively tightening her legs.

He did not press her, but his fingers stroked her lightly, and he turned her in his arm, his mouth firm and sweet on hers. Now it was his tunic in her hands, and she tugged at it, until he released her long enough to pull it over his head and cast it aside.

The flowing robes he usually wore concealed his body, but now she saw that his chest was broad and strong, his belly hard with muscle. Her eyes traveled lower, then she looked up quickly at his face.

"Now you," he said. She removed her shift and stood before him naked. He looked at her for a long moment, then he reached out, drawing his hands slowly from her shoulders to her breasts, down the curve of her belly, leaving a trail of fire in his wake.

"You are so beautiful," he said. He drew her against him very softly, the heat of his skin against her, and she pressed closer to his warmth. She felt his manhood, hard and straining, and drew away, shaking, hating herself but unable to stop the fear. He knelt, taking her hands in his, a knight before his lady, a supplicant before an altar. His lips were feather light upon her palms, her wrists, the soft skin of her inner arm. Her hands were in his hair now, and she moaned, her eyes falling shut, when his tongue teased the peaks of her breasts, then moved downward, her gasp of shock lost in the sweet tide of pleasure rippling through her.

She opened her eyes to see sun and shadow playing over the fair skin of his shoulders, the thick black hair spilling down his back. She heard her own breath, coming quick and harsh, and the music of the wind in the boughs above. She felt his hair, soft beneath her hands, the roughness of his cheek against the tender skin of her inner thigh . . . and then it was all one, the light, the warmth, and she was melting, dissolving, and she heard herself cry out his name.

He stood then, to take her in his arms, holding her as the tremors slowly faded. And then he bore her back, laid her down upon his cloak. His face, when he bent to her, was drawn as if in pain.

"If you would—you want—*mo rún,* you must help me now—it is for you to say—"

"I would." She pulled him down to her. "I want."

"Brave lass," he murmured. "Come, lay your head on me—aye, like that—oh, sweet Maude, you're trembling." His fingertips were light against her back, his palm firm as he drew her closer to his warmth. "Don't be afraid. *Mo mhúirnín bán.* There is no need to fear me, not ever . . ."

She buried her face in the hollow between his neck and shoulder.

"It is not fear," she whispered. "I am not afraid."

He drew back to look into her face, smiling as he read the truth in her eyes. She stroked his cheeks, his lips, her hands moving over his shoulders, the taut muscles of his arms. His mouth found hers again in a kiss that was no question but a demand, fierce and wild, and her heart rose to it with a joyful leap as she answered with all she had to give.

When he entered her, she cried out, her voice lost in the pounding of her heart. Slowly, almost lazily, as though time had ceased to be, he began to move inside her, gently at first until she arched to meet him.

She wrapped her arms around his neck and held him,

his breath soft against her cheek as he whispered in a language she did not know. A secret spell, a prayer, a blessing . . . or was it just her name he spoke, over and over until it ceased to be a word at all. It was music, welling up from his soul and passing into hers until she was altogether lost, drawn deep into the living heart of magic.

She swam up through fathoms of soft darkness and opened her eyes to see the deep blue autumn sky through shivering gold green leaves. Ronan lay beside her, his head resting on her breast, one arm lying across her belly. She smiled, fingers playing in his hair, tracing the soft skin of his neck.

"Ronan."

"Mmm?"

"Nothing. I just wanted to say your name."

He smiled, watching her through half-closed eyes. "I like to hear you say it."

He turned and pulled Maude against him so her head rested on his chest and the beat of his heart was strong beneath her cheek. His lips moved in her hair, and she smiled as she twined her legs with his.

She drifted then, perfectly content and utterly secure, waking fully with a start at the sound of Ronan's voice. Raising herself, she saw that he was sleeping, though not happily. His head turned restlessly from side to side, and he muttered something she could not catch.

"Ronan?" she whispered. "Ronan, wake up now."

"No!" He bolted upright, staring wildly about.

"You were dreaming," she said. "That's all it was."

"A dream . . ." He lay back again. "Just a dream. Holy Mother," he muttered, running shaking hands across his eyes.

Maude looked down into his face, her lips swollen with kisses and her eyes still soft with sleep. She was his now, just as he had always known she was. His to cherish, his to protect . . . but even as he smiled at her, a dark thread of fear wound through his joy.

"Marry me," he said.

"What?" Her smile vanished and her eyes were suddenly very wide-awake. "Don't say that because you think you must. I am no maid you have despoiled, Ronan. I knew just what I was doing."

"Did I say you didn't? Now I'm hoping that you might want to marry me." He sat up and took her hand. "We'll go to Ireland. You'll like it there, I'm certain, 'tis very beautiful. I can go to my grandfather, and he will take me back."

She pushed the tangled hair from her face. "Ireland? You said you would not go back there."

"I never had a wife to keep. I never wanted one. But Maude, I love you. Do you have any idea how long I've loved you?"

"No. Tell me."

Ronan had imagined this moment a thousand times, carefully selecting each word he would use when he revealed his heart to her. Poetic words, poignant phrases; he had never thought of laughter, or that she would look at him as she was doing now, her eyes glowing and her cheeks tinted with vivid rose.

"Well, let me think," he said, relaxing back on his elbows. "Could it have been . . . no, not then. Oh, yes, that's it, I have it now. It was the very moment I laid eyes upon you."

"Don't be ridiculous! Things like that don't happen."

"Of course they don't," he agreed, "I know that. And yet it did."

"Oh, Ronan—"

"Though by the time you'd finished calling me—what was it now?" He bent and nipped her shoulder. "A peasant?"

"I never did!" But her impish grin told him that she remembered the occasion as well as he did.

"Aye, a peasant, that was what you said, along with several other things that made me doubt my senses. But it seems I was right all along; I'd lost my heart to you, and there is nothing to be done about it. I love you, Maude. And if you love me . . ."

"I do. You know I do."

There it was, as plain a declaration as ever had been spoken. It seemed impossible; how could such a thing be true? She knew him as no one else had ever done, yet still she said the words with a sincerity he could not doubt.

"Then marry me," he said. "We'll go far away from here, and the past will never worry you again. Say you will."

"I would go anywhere, so long as you were with me. If you are certain . . ."

"I have never been more certain of anything."

"Then, yes. Yes, Ronan, I will marry you."

Even as he bent to kiss her, he shivered as though a cold finger had been drawn across his neck.

Reluctantly, he drew away and began to gather their clothing from the ground, moving with an urgency he did not understand. "We must go. The hour grows late."

Maude looked at him a little strangely but quickly dressed and braided her tumbled hair. Ronan held back the branch for her to pass.

The dream was gone, vanished beyond recall, but the memory of fear still tugged at the edges of his mind. The more he tried to dismiss it, the deeper grew his feeling that something was very wrong. As they passed through the garden, his head began to ache and a strange pressure built behind his eyes.

"But Ronan, I must at least say farewell!" Maude protested as he drew her quickly along. "Alyson is expecting us to stay."

"No. We must leave now. You can write to her—or I will, it does not matter—" He stopped and caught

Maude's hand as she stepped out into the courtyard.

"Don't!" he said sharply. "I'll get the men and horses. Wait for me in the garden—not where we just were, 'tis far too isolated. Go to the place you spoke with Haddon."

"Can I not see Alyson for a moment?"

"No," Ronan said at once. "Just wait for me." He forced himself to smile. "I'm being foolish, love, but will you just do as I ask? Please?"

"Yes," she said, bewildered.

Turning so his back was to the courtyard, he kissed her quickly. "Speak with no one. Just wait for me. I'll be back for you in no time."

He strode quickly to the stables and cursed beneath his breath when he found only half the Darnley men inside. "Where are the rest of the men?" he demanded of the captain.

"I gave them leave to go to the alehouse. Why?"

"We're leaving. Now. Send someone—no, never mind, I'll go myself. Just get the horses ready."

He started down the long stone stairway leading to the village square. By the time he reached the bottom, he was running.

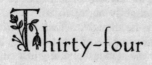

Thirty-four

The alehouse was a poor place, small and dim and stinking of stale ale and sweat. At this hour, only a handful of villagers sat at the plank trestles, muttering darkly into their mugs. The Darnley men had claimed a table in the corner. They sat with their backs against the wall and their eyes fixed warily upon the villagers.

"Master Fitzgerald!" one cried out as he walked inside. "What do ye here? Have ye come to drink with us?"

"No," Ronan said. "Not now. We're off to Aylsford."

"But I thought we were meant to stay the night," one man protested, though the others had already risen with obvious relief.

"A change of plans. Get moving now, we don't want to be riding through the dark."

With no more than a few token grumbles, the men finished their ale. "I'll just settle up," one said, but Ronan waved him outside.

"I'll do it. Go on to the stables."

He flung some coins at the barman and hurried after them, nearly running straight into a man in the doorway.

With a murmured apology, Ronan brushed past him, took three running steps and stopped dead, staring back the way he'd come.

The pressure behind his eyes increased. The rough stone building, the cat seated just outside the door were strangely dim, slightly out of focus.

I must hurry, he thought. *Maude is waiting for me.*

Slowly, hardly aware of what he did, he turned and walked back to the alehouse, halting just outside the door. *I don't have to go in there,* he thought. *I can still go back.*

And then he stepped inside.

The man stood at the long plank running across one side of the taproom, talking to the barman.

"—a fortune," he was saying earnestly. "If you could only see your way to—"

"I've heard it all before, and not a brass farthing will you have from me, not on my life," the barman answered sharply. "Go ask your poor mother if ye—yes?" He broke off and turned to Ronan. "How may I serve ye?"

"Ale," Ronan said.

He watched the other man from the corner of his eye. A tall, good-looking man, with curling cinnamon hair and hazel eyes.

Or no, Ronan saw when the man turned his head. He hadn't been mistaken. There was only one eye. The other was covered by a patch, and a long scar ran from brow to jaw.

The man stared hard at Ronan, as if trying to place him. Then his face cleared and he shrugged, turning back to his mug.

"You were at the abbey fair the other day?" Ronan said.

"I might have been."

Ronan felt the world slip a little further out of focus. He handed a coin to the barman and turned back to the scarred man.

"I sang there. Do you remember? My friends said you came asking after me. They said you might have work."

"They were wrong. I have no work for ye."

"Was it the woman you were looking for?" Ronan insisted. "I might be able to get a message to her."

"Who, *milady?*" He smiled down into his mug. "Somehow I doubt that. Gammoned ye all, she did. I need no errand boy in any case. I'll carry my own message." He tossed back his ale and headed for the door.

Ronan drew a deep breath. "Gordon Carlysle."

The man turned back. "What?"

Be careful, Ronan told himself, easing his hand slowly from his knife. *It is Maude that matters now and our future that's hanging in the balance here. One slip and you could lose it all.*

He forced himself to speak calmly. "Any message you might have for the lady goes through me."

"The lady?" Carlysle laughed. "Do ye ken who ye are speaking of?"

"I do."

"Oh, so ye were in on it, were ye? Weel, then, ye may carry my greetings to your mistress. Say to her that we met some time ago, just outside the village of Mallow. She was singing then as well. A pretty sound, eh, boy? Not easily forgotten. We were no properly introduced, but I think she will remember me."

Oh, yes, Maude remembered. The pain, the shame, the helpless terror—they were a part of her forever now. Because of *him.* The man that was standing here before him, stroking his scarred cheek.

"I've often thought on *her,*" Carlysle went on. "I would have sent to her long since, had she but given me her name. But 'tis no matter, I ken it now. Can ye remember all that, boy? Say to your *lady* that she'll be hearing from me soon."

He grinned, pleased at his own cleverness, and flipped Ronan a coin. Ronan watched it arc slowly through the air and fall into the filthy rushes at his feet.

Never. Maude must never hear from him, it would destroy her. *Careful,* Ronan told himself again, *don't think of yourself, remember Maude. She is waiting for you now, waiting to begin our life together.*

He glanced up to see Carlysle at the door. In two steps, Ronan was across the floor, grasping his shoulder and spinning him around.

"Listen to me and listen well, for I'll say this only once. You keep away from her."

Carlysle shrugged free of his hand. "Who the devil do ye think ye are?"

"I am Ronan Fitzgerald and the lady is—"

Carlysle shouldered him aside. "Get out of my way."

Ronan did not plan to draw his knife. The first he knew of it was the feeling of the hilt, cool and solid in his palm, and the hard glint of the blade as he swept it from its sheath.

He stared down at it, stunned that he had so nearly made such a terrible mistake. This was no matter for an alehouse; he must have been mad to start this here. He began to lower his arm when a voice cried out behind him.

" 'Ware, Gordon! He has a knife!"

Carlysle turned back, his one eye narrowing. "Why, ye swiving little churl."

"All right, laddie, that's enough, just put the knife down."

The barman's hand closed around Ronan's wrist. In the moment his attention was distracted, Carlysle drew and came for him. Ronan leaped back, narrowly avoiding the blade, and they went down together in a crash of benches and spilled ale. The other men drew back against the wall, watching silently as Ronan fell beneath the larger man, the knife spinning from his hand.

His other hand shot up to grasp Carlysle's wrist, halting the dagger inches from his face. Carlysle's knee was planted firmly in his belly, pinning him to the floor. Ale dripped down his face, stinging his eyes, and he could not catch his breath.

He twisted, trying to reach his knife, but it lay just beyond his grasp. The movement brought the dagger a little closer to his throat, and he twisted, using both hands to force it back.

Carlysle bent down, his breath warm in Ronan's ear. "Have ye had the bitch? Is that it?"

Don't listen to him, Ronan told himself, desperately trying to force back the red tide that began to cloud his vision. *He is sick—mad—it doesn't matter which. His words mean nothing.*

"Does she play the whore to all her serving men?"

The red tide receded with a rush, and all at once the world was bright and very sharp. Time itself seemed to alter to a crawl.

"Do not call her that. For your life, do not—"

Carlysle's face contorted, and he drove his knee a little deeper into Ronan's belly. "I'll call her what I like. No man has a better right. Ye see, lad, I had her first, back when she was young and fresh. That's the only way I'll take them, before they turn to whores."

Ronan did not even try to answer. He had moved past speech, beyond all thought into an icy calm that crept slowly through each limb.

"But in her case, I might just break my rule." Carlysle laughed. "And this time I mean to—"

Ronan never heard what Carlysle meant to do. The ice swept over him, searing like a flame, and he ceased to think at all.

It seemed but a moment later that he stepped back from Carlysle's lifeless body. He turned, the breath rasping in his throat, and found the men standing like a wall between him and the door. He looked down at his hands, still holding the knife. They were covered in blood, his cuffs drenched, his tunic blotched with red. Warm moisture dripped down his cheek.

He plunged his knife point down into the wooden board and faced them, hands outstretched, palms facing outward. He made no protest as he was seized from either side. He went without a fight, without a word, into the back room of the alehouse. They threw him in and bolted the door behind him.

Thirty-five

Maude drifted back through the garden, hardly aware of where she was going until she reached the alcove where she had spoken with Haddon. She walked to the low stone wall and sighed, picking a late-blooming rose and holding it to her nose, smiling as she inhaled its fragrance.

Poor Haddon, she thought, *he does not understand. All he said to me was true . . . yet it was false, as well. I am not the same person I was four years ago, and all his blame and my regret accomplish nothing but to chain us to the past.*

The past was gone. It could not be altered now, no matter how much Maude might wish that it could be. All she had was now, this moment . . . and the future.

The garden glowed in sunlight. The moss on the stone wall, the grass beneath her feet—everything was clean, washed fresh and new, as though it had just this moment been created. Beyond the low wall encircling the alcove she could see the distant hills, deep brown and purple in the sunlight.

Soon she would be leaving the borderlands forever. She had heard that Ireland was lovely, an enchanted land of shimmering green and silver. As a child, Maude had always longed to travel, a dream that had been lost to her for years. Now it all rushed back again, but she was not a child any longer, and it was not a dream. A wellspring of joy bubbled up in her until she wanted to sing or laugh or shout.

She was going to marry Ronan. He had asked—he had actually asked her to marry him, and she had accepted. Father would agree, Maude was certain of it. It wasn't as though Ronan were a beggar after all. His family was an old one, a powerful one, a good connection. Such things held weight with Father, though she would not have cared a whit if Ronan had been no more than a wandering minstrel.

She frowned a little, remembering what he had once said. "I am no man's lackey . . . the only time I'll settle is when I'm dead."

But that was all before, she thought with an uprush of optimism. Everything was different now. Ronan would be happy. She would make him so happy that he would never regret his decision to go home. The thought of the form their joy would take sent a wave of warmth tingling through her body.

It seemed long since he had left her. She needed to see him again, for his absence was an ache in her heart. Already she was starved for the sound of his voice, his touch. She leaned her elbows against the wall and sighed and blushed, remembering the things they had said and done, imagining the things that they would say and do the next time they were alone.

"Lady Maude?"

She turned, still smiling, and found two men standing at the entrance to the alcove. Tall men, stern of face, dressed in the Kirallen livery. A tiny thrill of uneasiness pricked the soft skin of her neck.

"Yes?"

"The laird would like to speak with ye."

"For what purpose?"

"I canna say," the taller, a red-haired man, answered stolidly. "If ye would come this way . . . ?"

Maude retreated a step, casting a quick look about the garden. It was deserted now, the shadows growing long. Where was Ronan? Surely he should have been back long ago.

"I am engaged at the moment. Say to the laird that I shall wait upon him presently."

"Now, my lady. If ye would . . ."

Maude took another step back, her uneasiness sharpening to fear.

"I said I shall come presently."

Her voice was shaking, and the edge of the wall was sharp against her back. *Be calm,* she told herself, *there is no danger here; they are but servants on an errand.*

Yet they continued to advance.

There is some mistake, she told herself, *some explanation for their disobedience. Surely they mean me no harm.*

"Lady," the second knight said impatiently, "ye must come with us now. The laird has ordered it."

They stepped forward, the sun behind them casting their features into shadow.

Wait, Maude thought, *this is not right. Surely what I fear cannot be happening, not now, not to me.* But she knew too well that it *could* happen. Here. Now. To her.

"Leave me," she ordered, her voice shrill in her own ears. "I—I order you to go. I have said I am engaged."

For a moment she stood helpless, watching the Kirallens come for her. Oh, she knew this feeling, the deadness of panic creeping over her until even when she tried to scream, it came out as a whisper. She remembered how it felt to be too numb with fear to run . . . to run . . .

But not this time. Not again.

She was over the wall in an instant. The ground below sloped sharply, and she tumbled down the hill, then picked herself up and bolted like a hunted animal, no thought in her mind but to escape.

"Lady, stop, wait!"

She cast a quick look over her shoulder, and her steps faltered when she saw how close they were. It was useless to run, hopeless to resist.

Rage flowed through her, lending her new strength. She sped up the slope, across the courtyard, shrieking aloud when a hand fastened on her elbow.

"What is going on here?" a voice demanded from inside the stable. "You, there, take your hands off Lady Maude. Lads! To me! Our lady is attacked!"

"Holy Mother," the Kirallen muttered, holding both his hands in the air and stepping back from Maude. "I am no touching her," he said, backing up, as half a dozen of Darnley's men spilled from the stable, weapons drawn.

Maude heard the voices, but the sense of the words could not break through her terror. She saw her chance and took it.

"Hi! Lady, wait!"

But Maude was already gone, fleeing toward the village far below. She reached the long stone stairway and started down. Three steps she took before a hand touched her shoulder.

She wrenched away and tried desperately to find her footing. A voice cried out—fingers brushed her arm— she was falling, falling. . . . She heard shouting voices, the sound of steel on steel, then sharp pain exploded through her head, and she was swallowed by the darkness.

Sir Conal stood, hand still outstretched, his last cry ringing in his ears.

"He pushed her!" a Darnley cried. "The swiving Kirallen has murdered our lady!"

"No!" Conal whirled to face them. "No, I tried to stop her! I swear it by—"

His words were lost in the sounding of a horn. Sir Rupert leaped to the mounting block, blowing for all that he was worth. The call to arms split the air and was answered almost instantly. Then Rupert dropped the horn and drew as the Darnley men came after him. The courtyard erupted into battle when the Kirallen knights arrived.

Conal bolted up the stairs to meet them, shouting, "Don't kill them! For God's sake, lads, don't kill them! Just disarm them!"

But it was too late. There was nothing he could do but watch in frozen horror as first one of Darnley's men and then another fell beneath the bright Kirallen swords.

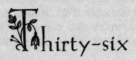

Thirty-six

The laird's antechamber was packed with people. Knights diced beside the fire, and the long benches were filled with tradesmen in their robes and fathers looking for appointments for their sons or to make a marriage for their daughters. A squire stood with his back to the door, waiting to announce each new arrival. Conal and Sir Rupert went through the press and gave their names to the lad. He slipped inside, then reappeared a moment later, holding the door open for them.

Jemmy Kirallen looked up from his writing table as the knights walked into his presence chamber. The laird stood, looking past the knights, then raised his brows. When he looked at them more closely, his expression darkened. Conal swallowed hard.

"Where is Lady Maude?"

"Laird, I dinna ken what happened. We brought her your message, just as ye asked, and she broke and ran. We followed—and—and some of her men came from the stables—they thought we were attacking her."

"What happened then?"

"They came after us, and then some of our lads came—"

"How many dead?" Jemmy interrupted.

"Two, Laird, both theirs. I told our men not to kill them—disarm them, I said, and they obeyed, they did, Laird, as soon as they understood."

"Where is Lady Maude?"

Conal flinched and stared down at his boots. "She fell. Down the south stairway. I tried to stop her. I nearly had her. . . ." He looked at his outstretched hand and let it fall slowly to his side. "There was a mortal lot of blood," he whispered. "Lady Alyson is with her now."

Jemmy sank down into his seat. "Send for Sir Alistair."

"I'm here, Laird."

The two knights sagged with relief when Sir Alistair walked into the chamber. No one could handle the laird like their captain, and you could always count on him to stand up for his men. He dismissed them with a nod, and they went at once.

"Did you hear?" Jemmy asked.

"Aye. Everyone has by this time."

"Do you know what this could mean?"

"I do."

"Why did she run?" Jemmy struck his fist against the table. "Was it because of Ronan?"

"Fitzgerald? What's this to do with him?"

"You haven't heard, then. He is down at the alehouse under lock and key. There was a fight, and a man named Gordon Carlysle is dead."

"Carlysle? What is he doing back? I thought that we were rid of him for good. But surely ye don't mean Fitzgerald killed him? Nay, Jemmy, that I don't believe."

"Oh, he killed the man, there's no question about that. But Alistair, there's more. Carlysle wrote to me and said he had information to sell, something that would work to Darnley's discredit and our advantage. The whole thing reeked of gutter intrigue, but still, I thought it might be best to find out what he wanted. I was to see him tomorrow."

"And now he's dead. And Fitzgerald—are ye certain?"

"There were at least a dozen witnesses."

Alistair took a flagon and a goblet from a small table by the hearth. He poured and set the goblet down in front of Jemmy. "Drink that," he said, "and let me think."

Jemmy sipped his wine as Alistair sank into a seat and stared into the fire. "Darnley," Alistair said at last, "and Carlysle have both been off to France. They come back at roughly the same time, and the next thing ye ken, here is Carlysle peddling some bit of information to Darnley's enemy. Did he say what it was about?"

"He only hinted. Apparently Darnley is considering an alliance with Maxwell."

"Lady Maude and Kinnon Maxwell?" Alistair whistled softly. "Weel, there's a match made in hell, if ye happen to be us. So Carlysle writes to ye and says . . . ?"

"That he has information that will break the alliance."

"That could be worth something," Alistair said thoughtfully, "if it is true. But Carlysle is a liar—among other things—and canna be trusted worth a damn. Then we have Fitzgerald, living for some months in Darnley's household."

"At Fergus's request," Jemmy put in.

"So he says. But we have no way of knowing, do we? It wouldna be the first time he's bent the truth to suit his own devices. And before Carlysle can tell ye what he knows, Fitzgerald and Lady Maude just happen to visit. And Fitzgerald kills Carlysle in an alehouse."

"It sounds bad, doesn't it? If it were anyone else . . . but it is Ronan! I don't believe it."

"D'ye think I *want* to? Christ's blood, he's Dee's foster brother! This will break her heart."

"I'd forgotten about Deirdre. Look, Alistair, you'd best keep out of this. I can handle Ronan."

"And Lady Maude?"

Jemmy muttered a curse. "God grant she recovers. And if God is feeling exceptionally generous, perhaps she won't remember anything."

Alistair nodded. "As ye say, Laird. But . . . Christ, Jemmy, this is bad."

"I am well aware of that. Does Haddon know yet?"

"If he doesna now, he will soon enough. And," Alistair added glumly, "it won't be long before Darnley does as well."

Jemmy nodded. "I'm certain someone is on his way to Aylsford this very moment. Have you considered, too, that someone else is on his way to Cranston Keep?"

"To Maxwell? Christ. I'd best strengthen the watch."

"Go ahead if you think it will help."

Alistair stood. "Should Lady Maude die, I doubt anything will help. We'll have Darnley from the south and Maxwell from the east . . . and we'll have no allies rushing to defend us when it gets about the lady was murdered while our guest."

"Do you think anyone who knows me would believe—"

"Ye are a Kirallen, are ye no? She is a Darnley. Aye, Jemmy, they'll believe it."

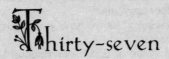

Thirty-seven

The storeroom was dim and cold, lit only by a few shafts of sunlight falling through the chinks in the roughly timbered wall. Ronan sat on an upturned cask, elbows on his knees and fingers splayed through his hair.

In the great silence he could see his entire life leading to the moment in the alehouse. Fate, he thought, or destiny, call it what you would, but he no longer doubted its existence. He had not wanted to love Maude. He had never planned to fall in love at all. But words like *want* or *plan* were meaningless; he could no more help loving Maude than he could help but breathe.

And loving her as he did, killing Carlysle had been necessary.

As the hours dragged past, he went over every memory of Maude, from the first moment he had seen her, sitting in her bower in her ivory gown, to the last touch of her lips.

The last? Everything that was alive and vital rose in violent protest at the thought. They had barely begun to love. Could it really end like this? Surely it was impossible that soon he would be dead, most likely hanged.

He stood and paced the storeroom. Hanged. Ronan had seen hangings before, in the village squares where he had once plied his trade. He remembered now the jostling crowds, the laughter of the lads and squealing of the maidens, peeking eagerly between spread fingers, and the cries of "Who will buy?"

If the neck was not broken on the drop, hanging was an ugly death. The crowd would shout as the poor bastard twisted, legs kicking, tongue protruding, face slowly turning purple. They would laugh and jeer as bowel and bladder let loose. . . .

Ronan stopped, staring into the dimness, the scent of old ale sharp in his nostrils. *Dear God, give me a clean death,* he prayed, then wondered how many men had sent up that prayer before. All of them, he imagined. Every one. But only a few were granted it.

"Wait," he said aloud, "just wait."

Because this could not be happening. Not to him. He was no common murderer, he was Ronan Fitzgerald, and he had basked in the applause of kings. His life simply could not end on the gallows in some forgotten corner of the world while a group of Scottish peasants looked on, laughing.

Of course, there was one simple remedy. All he need do was speak the truth, and he would be set free. With that thought came the memory of Darnley speaking of Stephen Kirallen. "I would have let him go. I told him he only had to ask. *Properly.* But he would not. God *damn* him, he would not."

Now Ronan understood Darnley's anger, his need to belittle Stephen even after all these years. Such courage was almost an affront; a mirror in which all one's fears and weakness were magnified a hundredfold. If one could not smash the mirror, shatter the man, the instinct was to make of him a villain . . . or a hero. Either way, he was not quite human anymore.

But Stephen *had* been human; Ronan knew that now. Not a hero, surely not a wise man to risk all that he had risked. Just a man who loved a woman. A man of honor.

He looked up as the lock was drawn. *Saint Brighid, help me to get through this. Can you do that much for me? All I ask is the strength to see it through.*

"The laird has sent for ye," the barman said.

Ronan drew a deep breath.

"Of course he did," he answered with a scornful glance as he flicked the man a coin. "Did you think he would be leaving me in this place?"

Thirty-eight

Jemmy had sent an escort to the alehouse. Ronan knew them all, but they did not greet him, nor did he speak to them. With a feeling of disbelief, he held out his hands and watched as they were bound before him.

When they reached the hall at Ravenspur, Ronan found Jemmy was already seated at the high table, and the long room held perhaps a dozen men. Some had been in the alehouse earlier; the rest were tradesmen, prosperous, to judge from their attire. Carlysle's family, Ronan thought. Jemmy was wasting no time.

Nor did he waste a word on Ronan. One measured look was all he got, lasting half a moment. Ronan had expected nothing more. He knew the laird too well to hope for leniency. They had greeted many a dawn together, yawning over their wine, having spent the night trading stories of their travels. The laird was a man of many parts, but Ronan knew the greatest part was devoted to his clan. And to justice.

It was the laird's passion, the thing that made him not only admired but revered among his people. Sitting up there now, Jemmy was most definitely the laird: cool, impartial, absolutely and forever neutral.

Ronan tensed as the first witness was called. The alehouse owner, Gordon Carlysle's uncle.

"Master Carlysle, can you tell us what happened?"

"Weel, I didna see the start of it. The two of them—Gordon and the Irishman—"

"Fitzgerald," the laird supplied.

"—they were talking for a time, but I paid them little mind, until someone cried out that Fitzgerald had a knife. I tried to calm them down, but then Gordon drew as well. We didna dare to meddle then, not with steel flying about."

Jemmy Kirallen nodded. "Go on."

"Gordon was a big man and a braw fighter. He took Fitzgerald down at once, pinned him to the floor, and it seemed it would be over in a moment."

"Over? What do you mean?" the laird asked.

"Weel, Fitzgerald had lost his knife and as near as I could tell, Gordon was doing his damn-all to cut his throat."

Carlysle looked about the hall, and several men nodded in agreement. The laird relaxed slightly in his seat. Ronan could almost hear him thinking, *Self-defense. Not murder after all.* But though Ronan still could not remember the details of the fight, he knew how it had ended. And he knew that Jemmy's relief would be short-lived.

"Words passed between them," Carlysle went on, "too low for me to hear, but Gordon must've said *something,* for up jumps Fitzgerald like a flash and gets his knife again. They went at it hammer and tongs then, back and forth, until Fitzgerald kicked the dagger clean out of Gordon's hand. And it was then that things turned ugly."

A general murmur of agreement filled the air, and the laird held up a hand. "You will all have your chance to speak. What do you mean, ugly?"

"Well, I've seen my share of fights," Carlysle said. "A bellyful of ale can give a man a hasty temper. But him—" He nodded toward Ronan. "I never saw his like before. First he went after Gordon with his fists—hit him only once and broke his nose. He took his time about it, too, cool as anything, like he knew just what he meant to do."

Yes, Ronan thought, *that's right. I did know.* It had seemed only justice at the time, that Gordon Carlysle should suffer as fully as possible what Maude had suffered at his hands.

"Then he got Gordon up against the wall and—weel, I'm not sure what he was about. Pricked him on the neck once, I remember that, and it seemed for a moment he meant to slice him into pieces—either that or frighten him to death. And Gordon—" He looked at the other men and sighed. "Weel, there's no getting around it. He was screaming like stuck grumphie by that time, begging for mercy and I don't know what else."

"So at this point he was unarmed?" the laird asked.

"Aye. He'd lost his dagger long ago."

"Did he yield? Did he say those very words?"

"Say them? Laird, he yelled them fit to wake the dead."

"What did Fitzgerald do then?"

Ronan found that he was gripping the table hard enough to numb his fingers. He remembered now what he had done—what he had said—oh, God, how near had Gordon's uncle been? How much had he heard?

"He leaned real close and spoke to Gordon," Carlysle said, and Ronan felt his heart leap to his throat. Then Carlysle shook his head and added, "but I couldna make it out at all."

Relief rushed through Ronan, so intense it left him sick and shaking. "Lady Maude is my betrothed," he had breathed in Gordon's ear. "And she has told me *everything.*"

"Whatever it was," Gordon's uncle went on, "it shut

Gordon up right sharp. And then it was all over. One thrust, straight to the heart it must have been, and Gordon dead before he hit the ground."

The story was repeated half a dozen times with the details varying only slightly. The only thing that mattered to Ronan was that none of the men had heard anything of importance. A few made guesses at the words he and Carlysle had spoken, but none were near the mark.

At last the laird turned to him.

"Ronan Fitzgerald," he said, "you stand accused of murder. What have you to say in your defense?"

Ronan straightened to his full height and swept the hall with a haughty glance. "It started a week or so ago at Kelso Abbey market," he began, "when I met a few friends—players of my acquaintance—and joined them on the stage. Apparently the man—what was his name?"

"Carlysle," Jemmy said.

"This Carlysle was in the audience and did not think much of my abilities. When I met him again down in the alehouse, he accosted me in the most insolent way imaginable. 'Twas clear he had no idea who I was, but even when I told him, he went on. When he had insulted me one time too many, I took him to task for it."

Ronan looked up at Jemmy with a half-smile and a shrug, inviting him to agree that he'd had no other choice.

There was no answering smile. But then, Ronan hadn't expected one.

"So you killed him?" the laird asked, a hint of incredulity shading his measured tone.

"He drew on me—"

"That's a damned lie!" one of the Carlysles shouted. "They all say that ye drew first."

"Well, perhaps I did at that," Ronan answered with a shrug.

"Let me be certain I understand you," Jemmy said

evenly. "You are telling us you killed a man because he insulted your singing?"

"No, I killed him because he was an impertinent churl."

"And that is *all?*" Jemmy Kirallen demanded.

Ronan drew himself a little straighter. "Yes."

Before the laird could answer, Ronan turned to the Carlysles. "Now, masters, that's done, and you can name your price. Whatever it is, my great-uncle—the Earl of Desmond, that is—will pay it."

He brought out the words with utter confidence, for they were true enough. The Fitzgeralds looked after their own. But he knew the request would not be made. There were many places where a man of Ronan's breeding could kill a commoner and walk away unscathed, but Ravenspur was not one of them. Not while Jemmy Kirallen ruled.

"A life for a life, Laird," the eldest of the Carlysles said. "That is the price we're asking."

"Yes, of course you have to start with that," Ronan said impatiently, "but—"

"Ronan, if you did this thing, you cannot be allowed to walk free in my demesne."

"Then I shall leave your *demesne,*" Ronan said, bringing out the word with a sneer. "I shall leave Scotland altogether and return to Ireland. Now have them name the price so we can have this over with."

Jemmy leaned back in his seat. "If you had only killed the man, that would be one thing, for he was armed as well. But he had yielded already, he had no weapon. . . . Do you really think that there will be no consequences?"

"Oh, I know there will be. But don't worry, my kinsmen will pay. And then I will pay when I get home," he added with a rueful smile. "But I'm prepared to deal with that."

Jemmy was pale with anger as he rose to his full height. "You have murdered a man on my lands, and the penalty is death. If you could give me one reason—one good reason—"

"I have *given* you a reason," Ronan said. "He insulted me. What more is there to say?"

"I do not understand you, Ronan."

"Then understand this: I am a Fitzgerald of Desmond, ·Laird, and I do not suffer insults from any man. Release me now, or you'll be sorry for it."

Jemmy leaned across the table. "Was that a threat?"

"It was a warning. If I were you, I would not take it lightly."

"I don't take any of this lightly. Would that I could say the same of *you*. It seems I have been much mistaken in you, Ronan."

"It seems you are very much mistaken about a good many things!" Ronan snapped. "Now stop this ridiculous charade before it is too late."

"It is already too late."

Thank God, it was over. Ronan stood, straight-backed, expressionless, as the verdict was delivered. He started slightly when Jemmy named the time and place: tomorrow at dawn.

"Laird, hanging is too good for him!" the oldest of the Carlysles growled. "He should be drawn and quartered."

Ronan clenched his fingers around the table's edge. He had not considered this. Hanged, cut down still living, slit from end to end, and hacked to pieces, and the measure of an executioner was how long he could make his victim suffer.

"Not on my lands," the laird said sternly.

Ronan had never thought to be grateful to the man who sentenced him to hang, but he was. Hanging sounded good to him just now, a mere trifling inconvenience compared to what might have been.

Jemmy turned to leave, and the Carlysles filtered out the door, still muttering but generally appeased. Ronan drew the first proper breath he had allowed himself for what seemed like hours. He released it slowly, every muscle in his body unclenching.

And then Jemmy stopped in the doorway. "Bring him to me," he ordered the guards. "I would speak with him alone."

It wasn't over then. Not at all. In fact, Ronan feared that his ordeal was only just beginning.

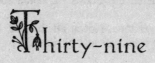

Thirty-nine

The first thing Maude was aware of was the pain. Her head throbbed, her body ached, and her mouth was parched with the memory of terror.

"Fergus?" she whispered. "Fergus, are ye there?"

"Quiet now," a voice answered.

Maude forced her eyes open, though the light was a new shaft of pain that threatened to split her skull. A man sat beside her bed, but he was not Fergus. He held a dripping linen in his hand. Water splashed on her face as he leaned over her.

"Get away!" she cried. "What are ye doing?"

"I am Master Kerian, the laird's physician. Just lie back, lady."

"Don't touch me," Maude said hoarsely, twisting away. "Don't put your hands on me!"

"Maude, it is all right." Alyson stood beside the bed. "You took a fall. Let Master Kerian see—"

"No!" Maude scrambled back. Her head struck the wall, sending a bolt of pain lancing through her skull. "Where is Ronan?"

"Lady Maude," the physician said firmly, "stop this. You will do yourself an injury."

"Don't touch me!" Maude cried. "Stay away!"

She struck out at him, her hand catching the edge of the small table to send it crashing to the floor.

"Bring two men to hold her," the physician ordered.

The room began to blur before Maude's eyes. "No," she whispered, "no, don't . . . please, Alyson, please . . ."

"Don't fear, Maude," Alyson said gently. "We will not. You are quite safe, no one will hold you."

"That wound needs looking at. If she will not be still—"

"She will," Alyson said. "Don't worry, Maude, I'm going to bring Ronan."

"Fitzgerald? But he—"

"I'll bring him," Alyson repeated firmly. "Try to rest, Maude. Master Kerian, please come with me."

"The laird will not—" the physician began, but again, Alyson cut him off.

"That is not your concern, master," she said, and Maude could hear no more, for the door shut behind them, leaving her alone.

Forty

It was a chamber Ronan was taken to, not a prison cell. This was no compliment to him, for Jemmy, in his first years as laird, had ordered the dungeons turned to store-rooms. Ronan knew this decision stemmed from Jemmy's own horror of enclosed spaces, which he had confided during one of their midnight talks.

Ronan had never cared to be closed in himself. It made little difference that his prison had a window, stoutly barred, and a small straw mattress instead of a stone shelf to sleep on. There was a table as well, complete with candle, pitcher and ewer, two stools, and a leather bucket tucked discreetly into a corner. For all the attempt at comfort, it was still a prison, and there was only one way out.

Don't think about that now, he ordered himself. *You'll have plenty of time later to imagine how you'll leave.*

Jemmy sat down and gestured Ronan to the second stool. "There is more to this than you are saying. What did Darnley offer you?"

"Darnley? What has any of this to do with him?"

"Carlysle had offered to sell me information, Ronan."

"About what?"

"I'll never know now, will I? He hinted of an alliance between Darnley and the Maxwells."

"Oh, I could have told you that," Ronan said. "Kinnon Maxwell has offered for Lady Maude, and Darnley is all in favor of the match."

Jemmy nodded. "But Carlysle said, as well, that he had something to tell me that would break the alliance."

The *bastard*. Ronan knew very well what information he'd been selling. As if what he'd done to Maude hadn't been enough, he had wanted to destroy the last bit of her pride, along with any thought she might have had of making a decent marriage.

But Carlysle wouldn't do it now. He was dead, the worthless churl, and Ronan's one regret was that he hadn't made him suffer more.

"Really?" he said, all innocent astonishment. "And what could that have been?"

"Why don't *you* tell *me?*"

"I? Why, I can tell you nothing, Laird. I haven't the first idea what information Carlysle was peddling."

"Why did Darnley send you and Lady Maude here just now?"

"Lord Darnley did not send us. He is ill, just as we told you, and was asking for Haddon. The business with Carlysle had naught to do with him."

Jemmy rested a hand on Ronan's shoulder. "Does Darnley have some sort of hold over you? Is that it? For God's sake, Ronan, just tell me what it is, and I swear that I will help you."

Ronan suddenly remembered the day of Deirdre's wedding. Jemmy had sat with him throughout the feast, refusing to let him slink off and nurse his misery. Ronan had been grateful later, for he would never have forgiven himself for casting a shadow over Deirdre's happiness. It was Jemmy who had done that for him, holding him to his place, asking him a hundred questions while plying him with ale. They had both ended too drunk to stand, and Lady Alyson had been furious.

It was a good memory, one from which the bitterness had faded long ago. Which made it all the harder to hold Jemmy's gaze when he answered.

"Laird, you are mistaken. It was a private quarrel I had with Carlysle, and it just got out of hand. It was . . . well, what can I say? An impulse. Had I known he had value to you, I would have spared his life."

Jemmy's hand fell from his shoulder. "So this had naught to do with Darnley?"

"Of course not! The whole idea is absurd."

He kept his gaze straight, knowing if he hesitated he would be lost. For of course it had everything to do with Darnley . . . and with Maude.

Where was Maude now? How long had she waited for him, wondering why he did not come?

"Is Lady Maude on her way home?" Ronan asked casually.

"Lady Maude will be staying the night."

"I trust you won't be troubling her with these sorts of questions."

Jemmy looked at him for a long moment without speaking. "No," he said at last. "We will not."

Jemmy stood and walked toward the door. Was it enough? Ronan wondered. Had he convinced him entirely?

Better to be certain. Have it all done now, for Ronan doubted he could go through this again. And having come this far, what would the last step matter?

It did matter, though; it mattered very much, but Ronan steeled himself against all feeling as he shouted, "Wait! You're not leaving yet! Jemmy, you said you would help me! It was only a mistake—anyone can make a mistake—"

"Not this kind. I'm sorry, Ronan, but there is nothing I can do for you."

"You don't mean that! I've sat at your table—stood godfather to your daughter—Jemmy, you wouldn't, you can't. . . . Please—"

Jemmy turned to him with a look that froze Ronan to his soul. He would not forget that look, not for whatever time was left to him would he be free of the memory of Jemmy's scorn.

But I can bear it, he told himself. *I must.*

"Take hold of yourself," Jemmy said with cold distaste.

"But—but—Jemmy, wait, don't go, don't leave me here—"

Jemmy stepped out and closed the door behind him.

Ronan continued to cry out for him, his ear pressed to the door. Jemmy wasn't moving. Damn him, what was he waiting for? At last, at last Ronan heard footsteps passing down the hallway, hesitating on the stairway and then going on. Only when Jemmy had reached the bottom of the stairs did Ronan stop shouting and sink down on the floor, resting his forehead on his bent knees.

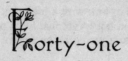

Forty-one

"Jemmy," Lady Alyson said as she strode into his presence chamber, "you must let me send for Ronan. I don't know what to do; Maude is out of her senses."

Jemmy sat at his writing table, an empty sheet of vellum spread before him and a goblet at his elbow.

"Christ's wounds," he muttered, throwing down his quill. "How bad is it?"

"I don't know, she won't let any of us near her. What did Sir Conal do to frighten her so badly?"

"Nothing. He merely asked her to come to me. God knows why she broke and ran from him. Alyson, you know Conal, he's not the man to go about terrorizing helpless women."

Alyson frowned. "No, he isn't. What Maude did makes no sense. But I'm afraid she will do herself a worse injury if we cannot calm her. Ronan will know what to do—and she asks for him every time she's in her senses. Can we not bring him to her?"

"Very well," Jemmy said. "Just be sure he is well guarded."

"You think he will attempt escape?"

"Why ask me? 'Tis clear I never knew him at all. Nothing he might do would surprise me now."

"Jemmy, are you certain . . . ?"

He stood and looked down at her, his eyes dark with pain. "Alyson, I tried. I told him he only had to speak the truth and I would help him. And what does he say? 'Sure and I did it, Laird, the man annoyed me. Now, you won't be holding that against me, will you?' "

He turned and hurled his goblet against the wall. "What was he *thinking?*"

"I don't know," Alyson said sadly. "I don't understand. Why would he lie? Unless . . . Unless he has a reason—something he can't say—"

"That is exactly what I'm afraid of. If Darnley put him up to this—"

"Oh, no! I don't believe that—I won't believe it!"

"I wish I could be so certain. But whatever his reasons, he has been tried and condemned by his own confession. So if you will excuse me, I must go make sure that the gallows are in working order."

He stalked out of the chamber and slammed the door behind him.

Forty-two

Despite Maude's best efforts, once she was alone she could not keep her eyes from closing. She sank deeper into darkness, and then it lifted, and all at once she found herself on a barren hillside, trying to run but unable to move a step.

A child held her by the hand, a lass with a torn gown and face smeared with dirt. "Don't run! You mustn't!"

A cloud of steam rose from behind the jagged rocks and a tongue of flame licked the stone. "Let me go!" Maude cried. "Don't hold me!"

She heard Ronan's voice, calling to her from very far away.

"Let me go." She pleaded with the child, but the girl only shook her head and held her more tightly.

"Have you given her any of this?"

"No. She refuses all."

The voices wound through her dream, dissolving the hillside, the flame, the girl staring up at her with pleading eyes. They swirled together and vanished into mist.

"Ronan—" That was Alyson's voice. Maude knew it

now, but for some reason it sounded oddly choked.

"I will need hot water," Ronan interrupted curtly, "and vinegar."

"Very well," Alyson said and sighed heavily. "I'll get them."

A hand touched Maude's brow, another grasped her hand, but it was all right, it was Ronan's hand, Ronan's touch.

"Maude," he said urgently, "Maude, you must wake now."

She forced her eyes open and saw him bending over her. His hair was loose and tangled, and a long scratch ran the length of his cheek.

"Ronan? Oh, Ronan, where have you been?"

"Maude, I—"

"I waited for you in the garden, but you didn't come. I was so frightened," she whispered, turning her cheek against his hand.

"I know you were, acushla, and I am sorry for it. But, Maude, you must listen to me."

Tears trailed from the corners of her eyes and ran into her hair. "It was the dragon," she said weakly, "it was there behind the rock, but I did not stand. I wanted to, but I was too . . . too . . ."

She felt him sit beside her on the bed. "Open your eyes, Maude, and watch the candle. Can you follow the light? That's it. Close your eyes . . . just wait a moment . . . now open them. Once more, can you do that for me? Perfect."

He turned and set the candle on the table. "Now turn your head and let's have a look at this. . . ."

She drew a sharp breath as he pushed her hair aside and touched a damp cloth to her head. "Head wounds always bleed," he said, "but this one does not look so bad; it won't even need a stitch. You will be fine."

"Can we go now?"

"Not yet," he answered, "you are not well enough."

"I will . . . be well now. Now that you are here."

His face twisted strangely, but his voice was gentle when he spoke.

"I know you had a fright, but 'tis all over now. They did not mean you any harm. Why, I know Sir Conal well. I saw his brother not long ago; he is one of the brothers at Kelso Abbey. Do you remember when we rode there, Maude? I know how Conal frightened you, I understand what happened, but it was all an accident. Do you understand that? An accident."

"I . . . could not think. It was all . . . it was like . . ."

He took her hands in his and raised them to his lips. "I know. Do you think I'm blaming you? Oh, no, acushla, not a bit of it! They should not have come after you that way, that was very wrong, and of course you ran, what else would you be doing? But 'tis all over now. You are here and you are safe, and once you drink this, you can sleep again."

"What is it?"

The corners of his mouth turned up in a half-smile. "Worms. I remembered how you like them."

He slid a careful hand beneath her head and lifted her so she might drink. When she had finished, she lay back against the pillow with a sigh.

"Why did you not come, Ronan? Where have you been?"

He looked down at her for a long moment without answering. She tried to keep her eyes open, but it was so hard, the lids so heavy. . . .

"Maude. Maude, look at me."

Ronan bent closer to her, his eyes very bright as they stared into hers. "You will be well soon. You are very strong, Maude, very brave. You—" His voice faltered and he swallowed hard. "You will be stronger still to-morrow, and I need you to be strong, sweet lady. You mustn't worry if I'm not here when you wake. Do you hear me? Everything is well with me, exactly as I want it. Do you understand?"

"But—"

"Now, no arguments. I need to know that you have heard. I am well content," he said clearly. "Do you understand?"

"Content," she repeated drowsily. "Aye, Ronan, I hear ye."

"Promise me you won't forget."

"I promise. But where . . . have you been?"

"Don't worry about that. Don't worry about anything tonight. Just rest, and when you wake, you will be better. You will be strong, Maude. You must be," he whispered. "For me."

"Stay," she murmured, "don't go."

He sat down beside her and traced a finger down her cheek. "I will stay . . . awhile. You have made me so happy, Maude, happier than I ever thought to be. I never knew—never imagined that I could feel what I felt today. All for you, my love."

He smiled down at her, but there was something in his face she had never seen before, a tenderness that made her heart constrict with something close to pain.

"Ronan . . . what is it? You look so . . ."

"Nothing. Nothing but . . . Tell me that you love me. I want to hear you say it."

"Ronan, I have loved you . . . not from the first, but . . ."

"When? When did you know?"

She turned and kissed his hand. "I did not want to love you at all," she said, concentrating on each word. "I tried so hard . . . but . . . I cannot say when, only that I do. I will always love you . . . always . . ."

He looked away, his jaw clenching briefly, but when he turned back, he was smiling. "Maude, there have been other women in my life, but I knew nothing about love until I found you. And today—you are my heart, and all my joy, and you have made me the happiest of men."

"Mmm . . ." she sighed, feeling herself sinking into the soft mattress. "Don't leave."

He passed his hand from brow to lips, his palm feathering her lashes.

"Sleep a little, a little sleep," he sang softly.

I will watch over you, uair ní heagail duit a bheg.
I will watch over you.
   Sleep a little; you need not fear the least.
I will watch over you, uair ní heagail duit a bheg.
I will watch over you.
   Far away a linnet sings;
her fear makes her loathe to sleep.
Listen, a stag in the east is calling;
his thoughts will not turn to sleep.
   Parting the two of us is as the parting of children
from one home.
   Parting the two of us—"

His voice faltered, and he swallowed hard, then finished in a whisper, "Parting the two of us is as the parting of the body from the soul." He looked down at her for a long moment, tracing every feature, then bent and kissed her brow.

When the door opened, he was on his feet, staring into the fire.

"She will be fine," he said to Alyson. "Keep her quiet for a day or two—no visitors, lady, nothing that might upset her. Do you understand me?"

"Why did she run?" Alyson asked. "Ronan, what is happening? Why did you—"

Before she could finish her question, Ronan stepped past her and threw open the door. "Sean!" he called. "I'm finished here. You can take me back."

The guard stationed in the passageway rose to his feet. "Come along, then."

"Farewell, lady," Ronan said. "God keep you."

"Wait—" Alyson began, but Ronan was already out the door. He went so quickly down the corridor that his guards took several running steps to catch him.

"What's the rush?" one asked as they reached his chamber.

"I need to get my sleep," Ronan replied gravely. "No doubt they mean to have me up at some ungodly hour."

It took the man a moment to see the jest. For of course they would have him up at dawn . . . up on the gallows. Before he could answer, Ronan had stepped into the chamber and closed the door behind him.

Forty-three

The hammering came in short bursts, interspersed by voices shouting orders. Malcolm Kirallen followed the sounds across the courtyard and back behind the stables. A fine mist blurred the torchlight, encircling each flame with a halo that softened the stark lines of the gallows.

The boy stood at the edges of the darkness, watching as a sandbag was lifted onto the platform. One man, perched on the high arm, called down to another. Malcolm could not catch the words, but he could hear the laughter that greeted them. He shivered and wished he had thought to bring his cloak.

"It is cold."

Malcolm jumped and whirled to see a tall form leaning against the wall of the stable.

"Uncle Jemmy," he said, a little ashamed of his reaction. "We missed ye at supper. But I suppose ye wanted to see to . . . things."

The lever squeaked as it was drawn back, and the sandbag fell through the trapdoor, hitting the ground beneath with a muffled thud.

"It—it seems to be in working order," Malcolm said.

Jemmy did not answer. Malcolm shivered again as the men oiled the hinges of the lever and hauled the sandbag up for a second trial.

"Did you want something?" Jemmy asked.

"Yes. Weel, no, not really. Or—"

"Which is it?"

The question was rapped out so suddenly that Malcolm could not repress a nervous start. Uncle Jemmy never lost his temper; it was rare for him to even raise his voice. But then, he seldom had to. Uncle Jemmy had a way of giving orders that ensured they were obeyed.

Malcolm swallowed hard. "I was thinking—that is, wondering . . ."

He trailed to a stop. Now that his eyes had adjusted to the night, he could make out Jemmy's face. What he read there made him want to turn and run.

"Why I sentenced Ronan to die?"

"No, I ken the why of it. 'Tis the *how* I canna understand. He—I always thought—or at least it seemed to me he was—"

"My friend? He was."

Malcolm scuffed his toe across the cobbles. "My father always said that there was nothing more important than a friend."

"Your father was right."

"Then how—"

"But your father was not laird."

"I don't see what difference that makes," Malcolm argued, troubled. "Either a thing is true or it is not."

"A few years ago, I would have said the same. In fact, I think I did, or something very like it. Here," Jemmy said, unpinning his cloak and offering it to Malcolm. "You're shivering."

Malcolm wrapped the cloak around himself, grateful for its warmth, but when Jemmy began to drape an arm across his shoulders, he drew away.

"Malcolm, Ronan killed a man."

"I know. Gordon Carlysle. I remember him a little from before, when my father turned him off. His mother came to the hall and made a fuss, said as how he'd been injured in Kirallen's service and should get some sort of compensation. My father was very angry, though, and said he was lucky to get off as lightly as he did."

"What did Carlysle do?" Jemmy asked.

"I dinna ken—but I think it was something bad. Even Alistair says he was a waste of a man, and the only wonder is that no one killed him long ago."

Jemmy was silent for a time, then he sighed and ran a hand through his hair.

"Alistair is welcome to his opinion. But the Carlysles have a right to justice, and I have a duty to see it done."

"Ronan saved Aunt Alyson's life!"

"He did."

"And that time when I was so ill—he never slept for a week, you know he didn't."

"Ronan was—is—a gifted healer," Jemmy said evenly. "You don't have to tell me that. He has been a good friend to all of us. But he killed a man who had done him no wrong, a man who was disarmed and had already yielded. The law says—"

"My father used to say the laird *was* the law."

Jemmy turned on him with sudden passion. "God knows I loved my brother, but at times he was—" He stopped and drew a deep breath, then went on more calmly. "If Ian said that, he was wrong. No man is the law and no man is above it, least of all the laird."

"Ye can do as ye like," Malcolm said stubbornly, "no one can say ye nay."

"That is true. But if once I start down that road, bending the law to suit my whim, soon it will mean nothing."

The law. It was always the law with Uncle Jemmy. He talked about justice with the same reverence other men gave God. But God at least would forgive a man his sins, while the law was a cold and lifeless thing that made no allowances at all.

"Malcolm, a laird must do what is best for all the clan; he cannot set one man above the rest. That is not justice."

"Justice," Malcolm said with cold contempt. "When *I* am laird, I will not be ruled by words upon a page. I ken the meaning of friendship—aye, and loyalty."

The men had finished their work upon the scaffold. It was empty now, the rope twisting slightly in the breeze. Malcolm took the cloak from his shoulders and flung it at Jemmy. It fell to the ground between them.

"I wish I was laird now," he cried. His voice, which he'd thought was finished changing, betrayed him on the last word. He knew his blush was invisible in the shadows, but his face was burning and quick tears stung his eyes. He didn't understand—not Uncle Jemmy or himself or the sudden chasm that had sprung up between them.

Jemmy bent to retrieve his cloak. He stared down at it, brushing bits of hay from the thick wool. "Well, you are not. Not yet. Now go inside, it is late."

Stiff-backed, Malcolm walked past the silent scaffold toward the courtyard. When he reached the corner, he glanced back, but at first he did not see his uncle. Then he saw Jemmy up on the gallows, torchlight etching shadows on the bold contours of his face. Head tilted back, he stared up at the rope, then put out a hand and tugged it, testing its strength. But that was Jemmy; every detail had to be in place, everything done precisely to his order.

Jemmy laid a hand on the lever and pulled it forward. A section of the planking fell away with a thud. He stared into the opening for a long time, so long that Malcolm began to wonder what he was seeing down there.

Just as Malcolm began to think of calling out, Jemmy straightened and walked to the edge of the platform, dropping lightly to the cobbles beneath. He went back to his place by the stable wall, the darkness closing over him.

Did he mean to stand there all night, then? Maybe he was afraid to go inside, afraid to face them all.

But no, that was not fair. Jemmy was no coward. And he did not give a tinker's dam for what anyone might say; he was too stubborn to admit he might be wrong. And yet he *was* wrong. Malcolm was certain of it. Ronan might mean little to Jemmy, but he was Malcolm's friend. It would be cowardly indeed to let the matter end this easily.

He was halfway to the stables when he froze, listening hard, eyes straining to peer into the darkness. After a moment he turned and went back the way he'd come, careful not to make a sound.

"Did you see him?" Deirdre asked as Malcolm entered the hall.

"I talked to him," Malcolm said heavily, holding his hands out to the fire. "It didna help."

"What did he say?"

"The same as he said to you, I would think, that the law is the law. Now he has said it to the both of us—and likely to my aunt, as well."

"Well, he can say it all again, for I won't—"

"Don't go out there, Deirdre," a voice said from behind Malcolm. "My lord has made his decision, and we must accept it."

Malcolm turned to see his aunt Alyson standing with her back against the door. Her face was ashen, her eyes steely.

"Of course *you* would say that," Deirdre cried. "Everything he does is perfect in your eyes. But in case you haven't noticed, he isn't God. He's just the laird. He can make mistakes the same as any other man."

"Aye, you're right, he's just the laird," Alyson answered fiercely. "Just the one who's walking the knife's edge between war and peace, just the man who holds the lives of all the clan in his two hands. Of course he makes mistakes. Do you think I don't know that? I watch him suffer for them every day."

Malcolm stared into the heart of the fire. He wanted to hold onto the clear, bright anger that had carried him out behind the stables. He wanted to go on believing that he was right and Jemmy was a heartless, stubborn bastard who did not understand the first thing about loyalty or friendship.

But he could not do it. Not when he knew that his uncle was already suffering, out there all alone mourning his lost friend. Why, Malcolm thought, is he doing this— not only to Ronan but to himself? Why is he tearing himself to pieces when he could just take the easy way?

Alyson and Deirdre were sitting together now, and both of them were crying. Malcolm wished he could cry, too, but that would not change anything. For he was terribly afraid he knew the answers to his questions.

When I am laird . . .

Despite the heat of the fire, Malcolm shivered. Earlier he had said those words with pride and confidence, but suddenly he didn't like the sound of them so much.

In fact, he did not like the sound of them at all.

Forty-four

Maude opened her eyes and stared at the canopy of the bed. It was not the familiar roses she expected, but plain blue wool. She sat up and put a hand to her aching head. Where was she? Something was wrong, she knew that much, but what exactly it was she could not quite remember.

A woman sat slumped in a chair beside the bed, cheek resting on her palm.

"Becta?"

Maude's voice sounded strange to her own ears, as though it came from very far away. She blinked, trying to focus on the chamber around her. The sleeping woman—a stranger—woke with a little start and turned to her. She had a broad face, highly colored, and kind eyes.

"Lady, how are ye feeling?"

"Well enough," Maude answered, "though my head aches."

"Aye, of course it does. Ye took quite a fall yesterday."

"A fall?" Maude frowned, trying to remember. "Where? What is this place?"

The woman bit her lip. "Ravenspur Keep."

Ravenspur? Yes, of course, she and Haddon had been taken when they rode out . . . or no, she thought, her confusion deepening, surely that had happened long ago.

"How did I come here?"

"Ye came to visit wi' your brother, lady," the woman answered cautiously.

Yes, that sounded right. She had wanted to see Haddon for a long time.

"Where *is* my brother? I—I would like to see him."

The woman nodded. "I will find him. Do ye lie back again and rest. Can ye eat?"

"Not now. Perhaps later, after I've seen Haddon . . . or could we eat together? What time is it?"

The woman looked toward the window. "An hour until dawn. I'll wake him."

Maude lay back among the pillows. She could not have been so badly hurt. Else Haddon would be with her now. Unless . . . unless he was angry with her. She was suddenly quite sure that Haddon was angry, though she could not remember why. *"I want nothing more to do with ye. . . . No one wants you here, 'tis only for my sake that they put up with you at all. Even Uncle Robert said . . ."*

What had Uncle Robert said? Maude tried to remember, but it was a maddening blank. She and Haddon had quarreled, and then someone had interrupted them.

Apologize to your sister.

Ronan. It was Ronan who had stopped it. Where was Ronan? He had been here last night . . . or had that been a dream?

She sat up, the movement sending pain lancing through her temples. Something was wrong. Very, very wrong. She remembered the ring of swords, voices shouting. And running. The memory of terror urged her to her feet.

She stood swaying, clutching the bed-curtains for support. She had to leave this place right now, this very moment. But first she must find Ronan. He would explain it all to her, fill in the gaps, make sense of the terrifying impressions flitting through her mind. Where was he? If she had been hurt, why was he not with her? How *could* he have left her all alone?

The door opened, and a woman walked inside. She was dark-haired, young, not a servant by her dress.

"You are awake, then? Good."

Maude stared at her. "I know you," she said. "But I know not your name."

"Deirdre Kirallen."

"Deirdre? Aye, I remember now, you're Ronan's foster sister. He loves you very much. But you married someone else. . . ."

"You should sit down, Lady Maude. You're not looking very well."

"Oh, I'm all right. I'm fine. Only . . . only I do need to see Ronan. Where is he?"

Deirdre's eyes filled with tears. They spilled over her black lashes, winding down her pale cheeks.

"What is it?" Maude whispered, pushing back the panic that threatened to overwhelm her. "What is wrong?"

You will be strong . . . you must be.

Ronan had said that. . . . Was it last night? And there had been more, something about him being content. . . .

"Where is Ronan? I want to see him. I—I need—"

"You won't be seeing him. Not today. Not ever again."

"What? You're lying," Maude cried, her voice trembling. "Ronan said—he promised—"

That they would go to Ireland. That he would take her

away from here and marry her and keep her safe in Ireland.

"What did Ronan promise you, Lady Maude?"

"I—I cannot say. He said I must not . . ."

"Oh, but you can tell me," Deirdre said. "Am I not his own foster sister? Ronan and I have no secrets."

"Then why do you not ask him yourself?"

"Because he is in prison, Lady Maude, and the laird will not allow him any visitors."

"Prison?" Maude repeated blankly. "Nay, that isna true. Why would Ronan be in prison?"

"Why, for murder, lady. Do you truly not remember?"

Maude sat down on the edge of the bed. Prison? Murder? The room had steadied, but there was still something wrong with her mind. Deirdre's words made no more sense than a fever dream.

"Ronan murdered someone? Who?"

"A man named Carlysle."

Maude pressed her palms to her temples. "This is not happening," she said clearly.

"But it is." Deirdre sat down beside her. "I've told you nothing but the truth. Ronan has killed Gordon Carlysle. The name means something to you, doesn't it? Why did Ronan do this thing?"

Everything is well with me, exactly as I want it. . . . I am well content.

"What did he say?" Maude managed to whisper.

"That Carlysle insulted his singing."

You must be very brave, Maude, very strong.

"How did he kill him?"

"He stabbed him to the heart, though Carlysle had been disarmed and was begging for mercy. Who was he?" Deirdre added sharply. "Who was this man?"

Maude shook her head blindly. Carlysle. He had been alive then; all this time he had been alive. How had Ronan found him? What had been said between them?

Come hither now, thou Jock my boy,
Come hither now to me,
I have not killed a man tonight,
But Jock, thou hast killed three.

The old songs never lied, Maude thought with deadly calm. The tale must be told in full, the circle finished. She had known long ago what she must do, but in her cowardice she had believed she could escape her fate. Now she had dragged Ronan down with her ... or had she ever really had a choice? Had Ronan? Had it not been fated long ago?

You will be strong, he had said. *For me.*

Aye, she would be strong. It would be simple, really, for there wasn't much time left, and without false hope to blind her, she could see the truth at last.

"Lady Maude," Deirdre said sharply. "Tell me what you know of this."

Maude looked at Deirdre, Ronan's first love, and felt pity stir in her breast. Deirdre could not understand. No one could. But she offered what comfort she had to give. "What has happened is what was meant to be."

Deirdre drew a sharp breath. *"Meant* to—? Did you ever care for him at all?"

Care for him? But no, she dared not think of Ronan. If she did, she would begin to weep, and that she would not do, for it would only weaken her. If she left now, she could be at the river by midafternoon. By sunset it would all be over.

She let the rushing of the water fill her mind, deadening the pain.

"When can I leave?" she asked.

Deirdre gave a choked cry. "You—" Words seemed to fail her. She drew back her hand and slapped Maude hard across the face.

"Leave? Is that all you can talk about? When Ronan is to hang?"

Maude blinked hard, dizzy from the blow. "But there is nothing I can do to change it," she said, "nothing anyone can do."

She mustn't weep. She must keep her mind on the river . . . the river . . . not Ronan in his prison or walking up the steps to the gallows. . . . *Don't think, don't feel, just end it. . . .*

"Do you think I wanted this?" she cried, and then the tears began to come, burning as they slipped down her cheeks.

"I don't know," Deirdre said coldly. "Did you?"

You will be strong.

She tried to remember how Ronan had looked when he said that, but all she could see was him smiling that day in the garden, holding out a rose, saying, "Look around you, lady, sure and the world is full of flowers. It is for you to choose."

"He was wrong!" she cried, brushing the tears from her cheeks. "It isn't ours to choose. I never chose anything, it all just happened—and there's no escaping it, the circle, it's always three lives . . . three . . ."

There were tears on Deirdre's face. Maude could feel them on her neck as the other woman put her arms around her and drew her close. "Choose what?" she asked gently. "Lady Maude, stop now; calm yourself. Don't make me hit you again!"

"I will. I am."

"What did he say? Tell me, lady, what did Ronan say to you? Choose *what?*"

"Our fates. He said—he said we could make our own future, but how? *How?* All the choices have been made already!"

Deirdre drew back and looked into her face. "What are you talking about? What choices?"

Life. That was the choice he had been speaking of. And even now, she suddenly realized, that choice remained to her.

Life or death.

"It doesn't have to happen," she said aloud. "I can still decide."

Deirdre took her by the shoulders and shook her. "Then for God's sake, lady, do it! Do *something!*"

Maude's mind focused with a snap. "Aye, you're right, I—please, I must speak to the laird—or no, not him, your husband. Sir Alistair will know."

"Oh, but he will not see you," Deirdre said.

"He must. Tell him—" Maude pressed her hands to her temples, wincing as she touched the bruise. "God help me, where can I begin?"

"Alistair has sworn to keep out of this matter altogether, and everything pertaining to Darnley," Deirdre said, rising. "Let me send word to the laird."

"No!" Maude grasped her by the wrist. "Not the laird. He will not understand. Say to Sir Alistair . . ." Oh, dear God, what could she say? What would make him listen? "Say that I know why his foster brother died. For Lord Ian's sake, ask him to come to me."

"But what does that have to do with Ronan?"

"Everything. It's all the same, all twisted together. . . ."

"Very well, lady," Deirdre said, "but we must go quickly. They mustn't find us here."

She led Maude through the silent hall and across into the courtyard, moving swiftly through the predawn light. "Here," she said, throwing open the door to the armory. "No one will think to look here. I'll be back soon with my husband."

"He will come?"

"Oh, he'll come," Deirdre said grimly, "if I have to drag him here myself."

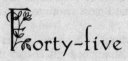

Forty-five

Deirdre found Alistair in their chamber, standing by the window. He was already dressed, she noted with relief, and armed with sword and dagger.

"Where have you *been?*" he demanded tightly. "I've been all over the keep looking for you."

"I have been with Lady Maude," Deirdre said. "I've hidden her away in the armory, and she is waiting there to speak with you."

"What?"

Alistair Kirallen raked his fingers through his hair, staring at his wife in disbelief. "Dee, what have ye done? Did ye no hear me when I said—"

"I heard you. But you were wrong."

"Nay, Dee, *you* are wrong. I'm sorry about Fitzgerald, I really am, though I know ye don't believe it. But there is naught that we can do. Now get Lady Maude back to her chamber before she runs off again."

"You have to come." Deirdre took hold of Alistair's wrist and tried to pull him toward the door. It was like trying to uproot a tree. "Alistair!" she cried, "you must! She wants to speak with you."

"I do not want to speak with *her*. I *will* not. I ken ye are no thinking straight just now, but there is something strange going on here, Dee, some madness in the air."

Absently, he rubbed a spot just above his neck, where Deirdre knew a knot of scar tissue was hidden by his hair. "You ken that I have sworn to keep out of the Darnley matter."

"When? To whom? You would never speak of it."

His gray eyes sharpened. "It doesna matter. The oath is sworn and I willna break it."

"But Alistair—"

"I am sorry, sweeting, truly, but I cannot. I dare not. Not even for you." He bent and splashed cold water on his face. "If Lady Maude has aught to tell, 'tis best told to the laird."

"She said," Deirdre insisted, "that it must be you. She said that she would tell you why your foster brother died."

Alistair looked up sharply. "Ian? This has naught to do with him."

"Lady Maude said that it does."

"What were her words, Dee? Exactly."

"She said, 'Say that I know why his foster brother died. For Lord Ian's sake, ask him to come to me.' "

Alistair straightened slowly, his hand once again rubbing restlessly at the spot above his neck. He stared past Deirdre, a strange light in his eyes, one she had not seen there for years. It was the way he used to look when he told her of his dreams and visions, all of which had mercifully stopped after their marriage.

"Keep out of the Darnley matter," he said softly. "Unless a woman comes to ye and asks something in my name. . . ."

"What are you talking about?" Deirdre demanded. "Who said that?"

"Ian. That day, when ye found me on the moor, do ye no remember?"

Deirdre repressed a shudder. Of course she remembered. How could she forget? Alistair half dead in her arms as they rode back to Ravenspur, and all the while he had been raving, carrying on a conversation with the air. He had insisted it was the shade of his foster brother walking beside them that day, though once he had recovered from his injuries, he never spoke of it again.

"Are ye certain, Dee? Is that what she said?"

"Yes."

"Where is she?"

"In the armory. Let me go with—"

"No. I dinna ken what is going on here, but I want ye out of it. Wait for me here."

Before she could argue, he was gone.

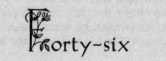

Forty-six

"Well, Lady?" Alistair Kirallen demanded as he stepped into the armory, a lantern in his hand. "What is it ye want with me?"

By the lantern's light, Maude could see the room where she had been waiting for a quarter of an hour. The walls were hung with hauberks, greaves, and helms. Spears and pikes stood upright in their cases, sharp points glittering wickedly in the lantern light.

Though he was of but middling height, Sir Alistair's presence filled the room. Maude stared at the sword hanging at his hip, the sword she had heard so much about over the years. They said he was the best, the finest swordsman on the borderlands. Perhaps the finest who had ever lived. And now she was shut up in this tiny space with him. Alone.

Maude felt herself begin to shake as he closed the door behind him.

"Sir Alistair."

"Out with it, lady. I'll give ye but a moment."

What the *devil* had Deirdre been thinking to drag the

Darnley wench from bed? Lady Maude looked too weak to stand alone and was as pale as twice-skimmed milk. She closed her eyes briefly, and Alistair bit back a curse, hoping she was not about to faint—or worse—here at his very feet.

But when she opened her eyes, her gaze was steady. "Do you remember riding over to my father's demesne, seven years ago last spring? Your men burned a village, Mallow 'tis the name, about four miles on the English side."

"*What?* Sweet Christ, lady, did ye drag me here at this hour to take me to task for a thing I canna even remember? Whatever was done, 'twas no more nor less than your father has done many times."

"Do you remember," Lady Maude said steadily, "that the man Carlysle rode with you?"

"He did not ride with *me.*"

"But he did. That day, he did. Think back, Sir Alistair."

"Aye," he said slowly. "He did ride with me the once."

"And now do you remember the raid on Mallow?"

Alistair sat down on the bench. "I do."

"And what Carlysle did that day?"

"But how do ye—she lived, then?"

"Yes."

"And was known to ye?"

The lady did not answer. She stood, back pressed against the door, face bleached of all color. Alistair stared at her, a terrible suspicion forming in his mind, only to be discounted in a moment.

"I'm glad to hear she lived," he said. "But I dinna understand what that has to do with Fitzgerald. Or Lord Ian, for that matter."

Still Maude didn't speak, though he saw her throat work as she swallowed hard. The suspicion came back again, tinged with horror now, and not so easily set aside.

He saw again the glint of golden hair in the firelight as he pulled Carlysle off the lass. He had not seen much more of her than that, for her face was bruised and swollen, smeared with blood and mud.

"Lady, why do ye ask me about this now?" he asked hoarsely.

"You stopped him."

"Aye, but how—how could ye know that? Unless . . ."

His words trailed into a silence that seemed to last a long, long time. Alistair did not break it. He dared not. He could only sit in frozen silence, waiting for her answer.

"I thought I killed him," she said, her voice almost inaudible.

Then Alistair saw her as she had been that night, when he was certain she must die, so cruelly had she been used.

"No," he said at last. "He lived. It was a near thing," he added, "and in truth, I hoped he *would* die, for there was naught that I could do to touch him. But he never rode with me again. I lost sight of him for years, until . . ."

But no, if Lady Maude did not already know, he would not tell her that Carlysle had run hotfoot to Ravenspur, peddling some damning bit of information that would ruin the marriage Lord Darnley was planning for his daughter. Could Carlysle really have thought that Jemmy would ever sink so low as to reward him for his shameful crime, let alone use it to his own advantage? Even to the end, Carlysle had been a fool.

Lady Maude wrapped her arms about herself, trembling so hard that she looked near to falling.

"Lady, please, sit down," he said, but she shook her head.

"No. I wanted to say—to tell you—it was for that Lord Ian died. All these years I could not remember what had happened or who—who had—and so my father swore to kill every one of you."

Darnley had stabbed Ian in the back. Even after all the years the families had spent fighting, Alistair had been shocked at such cold treachery. But now, thinking of his own daughters, he felt an unwelcome flash of understanding.

"It all came back to me just recently," Lady Maude went on. "When Ronan . . ." She drew a long sobbing breath.

"Fitzgerald knew?" Alistair asked, speaking more to himself than her. "Aye, of course he knew."

"I told him. Fergus sent him—Fergus was a *taibhsear,* a healer—"

"I know who Fergus was."

"He promised to come back, but then he died, and Ronan came instead. He was so kind," she whispered. "I cannot say how kind he was, how good to me. I did not think—never imagined that he would . . . he would . . ."

Alistair looked away, his heart wrung with shame and pity, for she had told him far more than she meant to. Even now, after all this time, she had not believed that Fitzgerald could love her, she who was so young and fair. *And she loves him, as well,* Alistair thought. *Nothing else could have driven her to me, surely the last man she would have chosen to confide in.*

Alistair stood.

"Lady, we must move swiftly. Fitzgerald killed the man before a dozen witnesses, and Carlysle's family is crying out for justice. I canna do this alone. Will ye no tell this to the laird?"

She went a shade paler, and he knew she had nearly reached the limit of her strength.

"Have I your leave to tell him?" he asked gently.

"Yes. Tell him—tell him what you must—"

"*Only* what I must."

"Will he let Ronan go?"

"I canna promise anything, lady. But I think he might."

"Thank you. That night—you tried to help me. I remember that, though for a long time I did not."

"But I didna help you, did I? Carlysle was under my orders. I should have kent what sort of man he was."

"It doesn't matter now," she said, and her voice was stronger now that it was finished.

"Not to you, perhaps. But it matters verra much to me. Come, lady, we must hurry. I only hope 'tis not too late."

Forty-seven

Ronan stepped into the courtyard and shivered as the cool air hit his skin, for he was clad only in a thin tunic and no one had bothered to offer him a cloak. *But then,* he thought, *the cold won't be troubling me for long.*

The gallows rose before him with startling suddenness. Everything was rushing by, moments slipping one into the other with terrifying speed. He began to shake as he climbed the steps. The hangman was waiting for him, a burly fellow in a buff tunic. He nodded, his face expressionless. Ronan nodded back.

"Anything ye'd like to say?"

There weren't many people present; a mere handful had risen at this hour to watch him die. There were no laughing maidens, no vendors crying out their wares. Only a few knights—Conal was among them, standing very stiff and straight, his eyes fixed on some point in the distance—and perhaps half a dozen men-at-arms. The laird was there, as well, just at the foot of the gallows. He was staring straight at Ronan.

"No," he said, his eyes locked with Jemmy's. "I think I've said too much already."

He managed a brief smile and was both surprised and relieved when Jemmy smiled in return.

The hangman held out a piece of dark cloth with a questioning lift of his brow. A hood. Yes, Ronan nodded, he would take it. He held out his hand, unclenching his fingers. Sunlight glinted off the silver in his palm. The hangman took the coin and slipped it in his purse.

As his hands were bound behind him, Ronan looked around once more, past the crowd, over the walls and out onto the open fields beyond. There had been a frost last night, and the moor was rimed with silver. The rising sun struck brilliant sparks from every tree and bush and bit of heather. It seemed the whole earth was glowing with life, etched in crystalline clarity. He drew a long breath of sharp autumn air.

Then he turned to the hangman and bowed his head. The hood was soft and heavy as it slipped over his ears, his eyes, encasing him in muffled darkness. It smelled of tansy, a scent that called forth an image of his old nurse, a woman he had not thought about for years. But now he could see her face quite clearly.

His heart was beating in his ears, quick and light, and all at once he could not catch his breath.

" 'Tis a good long rope," the hangman said. "Ye willna feel a thing."

Not much longer. Just a few more moments, and it would all be over. He had spent the night playing every song he had ever known, concentrating fiercely on the music. But now, at last, the time had come when he could safely think of Maude.

He summoned her image, but for one panicked moment there was nothing, no picture in his mind. Then it was all right, he could see her, laughing as he held her in his arms. He fixed his mind on her, blocking out all else, hardly noticing—yet a part of him was very much aware—as the rope was placed around his neck. The good long rope.

Don't think of that. Think of Maude, and pray that she does not take this so very hard. *God help her to get past it,* he thought, *God help her. . . .*

All at once he was not alone. Warm light filled his mind and he knew, he *knew* that Maude would be well, was already well, that strange as it might seem, everything was exactly as it should be.

Do it, he thought. *Do it now, I am ready.*

He closed his eyes and waited for the drop.

Jemmy watched as the hood was drawn over Ronan's face. The house priest was at his elbow, lips moving in a scarcely audible prayer, but Jemmy was only dimly aware of him. There were others here, but they could not touch him. He had never been more alone in his life than he was at this moment. The hangman stood impassively beside Ronan, watching for Jemmy's signal. All he need do was raise his hand, bring it down again, and Ronan would be dead.

He tried to summon his anger against Ronan, but it was gone. Strange, but the only thing he felt just now was pride. Ronan had done so well. He should have expected that, but he had worried that Ronan's nerve might break. Perhaps, he thought, he should have worried less about Ronan's nerve and a bit more about his own.

His arm felt as though it were weighted with lead, but his mind was flying, searching vainly for some way out. There was none. The prisoner had been fairly tried and justly condemned. Now it was for the laird to order the sentence carried out. For three years Jemmy had been lucky; not a single man had died by his command. But today his luck—and Ronan's—had run out.

It was wrong to draw this out, certainly no kindness to Ronan. That thought alone gave him the strength to lift his arm. The hangman put his own hand on the lever, his eyes fixed on Jemmy. Then he broke the gaze, his eyes opening wide, moving to Jemmy's right, and Jemmy's wrist was seized in a hard grip.

"Wait."

Alistair was breathing hard, as though he had been running. "Wait," he said again.

"God *damn* you," Jemmy said between clenched teeth. "Do you *dare* to—"

"Laird." Alistair released him immediately and dropped to one knee on the cobbles. "Forgive me. But ye must *listen.*"

"Whatever you have to say should have been said before. This is not the time."

Alistair stood. "It *is* the time, for 'tis the only time I have. Jemmy, ye must," he began, then broke off and took a step back. "Laird, I beg of ye to wait a moment."

"Very well. But I warn you, Alistair, that I am not inclined to grant you any favors. Not when asked like this. Do you have any idea what you are doing to *him?*" He jerked his head toward Ronan. "I cannot think of anything more cruel."

"Oh, for Christ's sake," Alistair said, "do ye think I dinna know that? I *know* who Carlysle was to him, and ye should know it, too. Jemmy, ye would not thank me for keeping silent."

Jemmy turned to the hangman. "Stand by until I return."

He whirled back to face Alistair. "Out with it."

The hangman, known to his family as Old Angus, shook his head in disgust. The old laird must be turning in his grave to see the hash his son was making of a simple hanging.

"Sorry, lad," he muttered to the prisoner. "Ye will have to bide a bit."

The prisoner—Angus made a point not to learn their names until after—began to shake, choked sounds com-

ing from behind the hood. And who could blame him?
It took all a man's courage to stand up here without
breaking into pieces. Until the laird mucked everything
up, this lad had been doing very well indeed.

"Don't give way," he said encouragingly. "It won't be
long."

"Thank you." The voice was shaking but surprisingly
strong. Angus realized the sounds he'd heard were laughter. "I never botched a performance in my life. Wouldn't
you know this would happen at the last?"

"Steady on. There, the laird's come back again. Are
ye ready?" Angus added, surprising himself. He'd never
asked that question before, holding to the firm belief that
if a man wasn't ready by the time he climbed the steps,
he never would be. But the man who could laugh at his
own hanging deserved a bit more than the ordinary.

"Ready enough."

"Oh, bugger it," Angus muttered. "What now?"

For the laird was climbing the steps himself, which
was so very much against propriety that Angus was momentarily speechless.

"Get that off him," the laird ordered curtly. "Turn him
loose."

"But he has been condemned!"

"Now he has been pardoned. Surely you have heard
of a pardon," the laird added caustically.

"Ye left it a bit late," Angus muttered, taking the rope
from around the prisoner's neck. "Your father—"

"My father *what?*"

Angus took one look at the laird's face and decided
this was not the time for a lecture. "Nothing. Here he is."

He whipped off the hood and stepped back. The lad
looked more dead than alive already, his lips dead white
and his skin the pale gray of ashes. He stared dazedly
around, his gaze passing over the laird and Sir Alistair
to fasten upon Angus.

"Thank you," he said, and bowed. "Ronan Fitzgerald at your service."

"Angus Kirallen at yours." Angus dug in his pouch and produced the silver coin.

"Oh, keep it," Fitzgerald said. "With my thanks."

Nicely spoken, Angus thought, returning the coin to his belt. *At least* someone *here knows how to manage things!* Irritated with the whole business, he stamped off down the stairs.

"You have ruined his day," Ronan remarked, hearing his own voice coming from very far away. "And he really is a decent fellow, very good at what he does. I don't imagine anyone has ever been in the position to tell you, Laird, but you can take it from me that he knows just the right thing to say."

He looked up at the rope and swayed, reaching out blindly with one hand. It fastened on the lever and he stumbled, putting all his weight on it. The trapdoor opened at his feet.

"Holy Saint Brighid," he breathed, staring downward.

"Catch him," Alistair said. "He's going to—"

"I am *not.*" Ronan drew himself up, but the effort was almost too much. He was shaking with such bitter cold that it seemed he surely must have died and this was some strange dream.

Then Alistair's hand fastened on his arm, guiding him firmly across the planks.

"I don't understand," he whispered.

"Aye, I know," Alistair said, leading him toward the stairway, "you've had a bit of a shock, but you'll be fine."

Ronan took the first step, then laughed. "Two go up, but only one goes down. That's what they say, you know."

"Aye, they do, Ronan, that's just what they say," Alistair said, his grip tightening a bit. "But this time they were wrong."

Why was Alistair being so kind to him? Never once, in all the years Ronan had known him, had the knight addressed him by his given name. Ronan wanted to ask, but he had to use all his concentration to keep walking. The stairs were behaving very oddly, first rushing toward him then drawing far away. It seemed a long time until he was on solid ground.

The cobbles were wet from last night's frost, glistening beneath his feet. How odd, he thought, that he should be standing on the earth again. How very strange. He glanced back toward the gallows, half-expecting to see himself there, twisting on the good long rope, feet dangling far above the ground.

"Ronan," Alistair bellowed, his mouth close to Ronan's ear. "Can ye hear me?"

Ronan heard, but he did not answer. He was staring wide-eyed about the courtyard, which was beginning to fill with people. The sound of many voices rose and fell in waves, though the words were indistinguishable.

"Laird!" a high voice cried, cutting through the rest, even as the slender figure of a squire slipped through the press. "Laird!"

Ronan turned, following the boy's progress toward the laird with distant interest. And then he saw Maude standing just inside the doorway.

Forty-eight

Maude's hood was drawn forward to shadow her face, but Ronan knew her at once. He found himself walking forward. He could not feel his feet, but they must have been connecting with the earth, because he was making steady progress. At last he reached her.

"My lady."

He went down on both knees and took her hands, raised them to his lips, and kissed each one, but even Maude's touch could not pierce the frozen shell encasing every thought and feeling. He was so cold, as cold as death, and nothing seemed quite real.

Then her hands pulled from his, fastened on his shoulders and tugged him to his feet. He went unresisting, looking down into the shadow of her hood, not quite sure what was happening but grateful just to see her once again.

The pale oval of her face was even more perfect than he'd remembered. *Like an angel,* he thought, and nodded to himself, thinking that at last *something* made sense. If an angel had Maude's form, he wasn't about to start complaining. Her lips, those sinfully full lips, parted, and he waited patiently for her to speak, certain that her words would make everything clear.

"You *idiot.*"

He blinked, thinking he had not heard her properly. But then she hurtled forward, nearly knocking him from his feet. He staggered back a pace, instinctively bringing up his arms to hold her.

"How could you!" Her voice was muffled against his chest and her hands were fisted in his tunic. "Did you think—did you really think that I could—that I would ever—that anything mattered to me more than you?"

Oh, God, she was warm, so warm, and when she raised her face, he kissed her, hardly daring to believe that she was real. Her mouth tasted of salt and of herself, a taste he could never mistake for it was hers, it was Maude, and then he knew this was no dream, he wasn't dead at all, he was alive. *Alive.*

Her body was pressed close to his, breast and hip and thigh snugged close against his own. He pushed the hood back and wound his fingers through her hair, deepening the kiss, wanting nothing but to dissolve into the heat of her.

He was dimly aware of voices, small and unimportant, nagging at the edges of his mind.

"Oh, for Christ's sake, Jemmy, give them a moment."

"There is no time."

Go away, Ronan thought, *just go away.* But they did not. Slowly, reluctantly, he broke the kiss, though he had no thought for anything but Maude, looking up at him with brilliant blue green eyes through lashes spiked with tears.

"I never thought to see you again," he said.

"You nearly didn't."

She burrowed against his chest, and he held her close, feeling life and strength return. With life came questions, and he pushed Maude gently away from him, holding her by the shoulders.

"Why am I here?" he demanded. "Maude, what have you done?"

"I did what was needed," she answered curtly.

"You should *not*—" he began, and Maude stepped away, shrugging off his hands.

"I do not want to quarrel, Ronan, so just let it be."

"Quarrel? With *me?* But why?"

"You should have told me," she whispered fiercely.

"Told you? When, last night? You were hardly in any condition—"

"No, I wasn't. Nor was I much better a few hours later—but that did not stop your foster sister. I had to hear of this from her, not you, and God be thanked she did not have your scruples. We could have helped each other, Ronan, but no, you decided everything without so much as asking."

Ronan stared at her. "But—but it was for you I did it, Maude. It was for you."

Her face twisted. "I have heard that before. 'Tis what my father always said, as well. Do you think I wanted another death—*your* death—laid at the holy shrine of my honor? Did you really think I would *thank* you for it?"

"No," Ronan began, but it was a lie. He *had* thought she would thank him. He had imagined she would be grateful that he had taken the decision from her hands.

"Aye, ye did, ye great fool. But this time *I* chose. Now they know, Ronan, they know it all. And I'm still standing here. I haven't expired from the shame."

She faced him defiantly, but her bravado was a mask. Say what she would, he knew what it had cost her to cast aside seven years of silence.

"Forgive me, Maude. I should have told you."

"Hmph," she sniffed, though he could see that she was very close to tears. "That's something, anyway. Now the laird has something to say, and we have kept him waiting long enough."

She took a few steps toward the door. "You wanted to speak with us?"

"I do. Lady Maude," Jemmy said, "your father is on his way."

Maude drew herself up to her full height and looked Jemmy Kirallen in the eye. "That is hardly to be wondered at. We both know that you have men at Aylsford, just as he has here. No doubt he has heard of my . . . accident and seeks to learn if I am still alive. Would you refuse him?"

"No," Jemmy answered, "I would not. It is not your father that concerns me, lady. It is the army at his back."

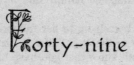

Forty-nine

It is scarce an hour past dawn, Ronan thought, the day barely begun. Where would they all be when it ended?

"We had best—" Maude began, when another voice spoke over hers, the words tumbling over themselves in haste and anger.

"I knew it! Laird, did I no tell ye so? She isn't to be trusted for a moment! Maude, what have ye—"

Maude turned to her brother. "Haddon, you can help or you can stand aside. In either case, be silent. Laird, Ronan and I will go at once. Once my father sees I am unharmed, he will turn back."

"Lady," Jemmy answered, "I shall ride with you."

Maude slanted him a measured look. "With how many men?"

"All of them."

"Laird," Ronan put in mildly, "you should listen to Lady Maude."

"No, don't!" Haddon cried. "Ye canna trust—"

"That is enough, Haddon," Jemmy said. "I am speaking with your sister."

The words were mild, as was his tone, but the effect was instantaneous. Haddon stepped back and bowed his head. "I am sorry, Laird."

"Lady Maude," Jemmy said, "are you ready?"

"Aye. But you must let me ride ahead."

"With me," Ronan said.

Maude took his hand. "Of course with you," she said, and Ronan squeezed her hand hard.

Alistair appeared beside them suddenly. "Welladay," he said, "what next?"

Maude glanced at him, then looked away. "You have my thanks, Sir Alistair," she said stiffly.

Alistair bowed to her. "At your service, lady."

When he straightened, Ronan tensed, watching him closely. But there was no mockery in Alistair's gaze, no pitying averting of the eyes or knowing glance. The knight looked full at Maude and smiled. And for the first time Ronan saw the warmth and charm that had captured Deirdre's heart.

"Please thank your lady for me, as well," Maude added more naturally. "I am very grateful to her."

"Dee is a most . . . determined lady, is she no? Aye, I'll give her your thanks." Alistair turned to Ronan. "Are ye all right now?"

"I was."

"You'll do." He grinned and clouted Ronan on the shoulder, a gesture usually reserved for one of his knights who had performed beyond his expectations. "Good fortune to ye both."

With that he was gone, heading for the stables and shouting for his men.

Maude and Ronan followed him. "Can my father truly be with them?" she asked doubtfully.

" 'Tis unlikely he could even mount a horse. But don't be worrying about that. I know the captain. He will listen to us." *I will make him listen,* Ronan thought. *I will force him to turn back.* Though precisely how he was to accomplish that miracle, he wasn't sure.

Fifty

After the threat of last night's frost, the weather turned again. The day was warm and overcast; the sun, when it appeared, blazed in a burst of light and heat before vanishing again. So mild was the air that it could have been springtime instead of autumn. Ronan watched Maude closely, fearing the same thought must be in her mind. If it was, she did not speak it. She rode in silence, her hood drawn up despite the heat. Ronan stayed close and left her to the privacy of her reflections.

The laird rode on Maude's other side, as silent as the lady was herself. Behind them ranged the Kirallen knights and men-at-arms, as large a force as could be mustered in the time. Only Sir Alistair was not with them. He had gone with a small number of men to watch the eastern border, though, as he admitted privately to Ronan, if Kinnon Maxwell came in force, there would be damn-all he could do to stop him.

It was just past midday when Ronan shaded his eyes and peered ahead. Tiny points of light . . . sunlight glancing off the tips of pikes and spears.

"There they are," he said. "Lady, are you ready?"

"Aye."

"I will ride with you," Jemmy said. "I must have speech with Lord Darnley." He turned and spoke to one of his men, who handed him a pike to which had been affixed a white standard unadorned by crest or badge.

Maude drew back her hood and loosened her cloak. With only a nod, she clapped her heels to her stallion and cantered across the distance between the armies, her hair streaming behind her. It took Ronan and Jemmy some time to catch her, for her stallion was easily the fastest.

As they drew nearer, two riders came forward to meet them.

"Father!" Maude cried. "Father, do not fear, I am well!"

It *was* Darnley. He sat erect in the saddle, though his face was dangerously flushed and bathed in sweat. Ronan could not imagine what it had taken to force his mutilated foot into a boot, let alone put weight upon it. His captain rode at his side.

"My lord!" Jemmy cried. "I bring your daughter back to you."

"Maude?" Darnley shook his head as though to clear it. "Maude, is it you? They said that ye were dead."

"I'm sorry, Father, I never meant to worry you. I was certain I could be back before you missed me. I only wanted to bring Haddon home."

"That is true, my lord," Jemmy said. "Lady Maude came to parley for her brother's release."

Darnley passed a hand across his eyes, swaying slightly in the saddle. Ronan nudged his horse close enough to take his wrist and after a moment looked up sharply. "You must get back to bed, my lord. Let us go at once."

"Aye," Darnley said. "Aye, *taibhsear,* all right. My head aches something fierce. The light . . ." He blinked hard, turning to his captain. "We're going back."

The knight let out a long breath of relief. "As you say, my lord." He rode off to give the order.

"Not a bad muster, Kirallen," Darnley said, pulling himself upright with an obvious effort. "I wonder how it would have gone."

Jemmy turned to glance back at his men. "Hard to say, my lord." He looked Darnley in the eye. "I'm hoping we need never find out."

"We won't today, at any rate. But—"

Darnley jerked in his saddle, an expression of incredulous surprise on his face.

"My lord!" Ronan was off his horse in time to catch Darnley as he fell. He eased him to the ground, and Maude knelt beside them. "Father! What has happened? Ronan, what is it? What is wrong with him?"

Darnley's face twisted; he tried to speak, but the words were only garbled sounds.

"Don't talk, Father, it's all right, we'll soon have you home."

Darnley's eyes turned to Maude, fixed on her face as the breath rasped in his throat. She clasped his hand in both of hers, but there was no answering pressure. "It's all right," she said again, knowing that it wasn't. "We'll get you home, and you'll be fine, you'll be well in no time. . . ."

Ronan passed a hand across Darnley's face and closed the staring eyes. "Now is the soul set free," he said softly. "Christ and Saint Michael prepare your path."

Maude stared at her father, lying still and silent on the moor. She looked up at Ronan. "No."

"Maude, I am sorry. The ride—the heat—he should never have attempted it."

"Ronan," Jemmy said, "take Lady Maude and go. Lady, I am sorry, but you must go with Ronan now. Do you hear me? Ronan, get her up. I must get back to my men."

A few of the Darnleys rode forward to see what was happening. The moment they broke the line, the Kirallens began to advance. Then both forces began to move, slowly but inevitably, two waves gathering to break upon the ground between.

Maude stared first north, then south, measuring the distance. Ronan started for the horses, looking from the Darnleys to the Kirallens, no doubt seeing what Maude had seen herself. He went very still, a frown creasing his brow.

"Ronan!" Jemmy shouted. "What are you doing?"

Ronan did not answer. He closed his eyes and raised his arms, his cloak snapping in a sudden breeze. The sound of hooft_ats grew louder; Maude thought she could feel the ground trembling beneath her feet.

"Lady, get on your horse," Jemmy Kirallen ordered, pulling Maude upright and giving her a hard push toward the horses. "Ronan! To me!"

The last words were torn from his mouth by the rushing of the wind. Maude stopped, one foot in the stirrup, as Ronan called her name.

"Maude! Give me your father's cloak."

She obeyed without question, shaking Jemmy's restraining hand from her arm. She unfastened the brooch at her father's shoulder and gently turned him, trying not to look into his face as she tugged the fabric from beneath his lifeless form.

"And his helm," Ronan called.

This was harder; it was impossible not to look at her father now, to see the slackness of his features, the pallor of his skin. She bit her lip hard to keep from weeping as she eased the helm from his head.

She handed helm and cloak to Ronan, casting a quick look over her shoulder. What she saw chilled her to the bone.

"Ronan—" she began.

He dropped to his knees before her. "Lady, give me your blessing."

His face was so taut, his voice so urgent that she did not question even such a strange request. She rested both hands on his head and did as he had asked.

He stood, holding the cloak and helm before him.

"Ronan, are you mad?" Jemmy shouted. "Get Lady Maude to safety!"

Ronan began to speak, his words barely more than a whisper.

"Am gaeth tar na bhfarraige, am tuil os chinn maighe, am dord na daithbe. . . ."

He tipped his head back to the sky. "I am the wind across the sea, I am the flood across the plain, I am the roar of the tides. . . ." His voice rose and fell with the rushing wind. "I am the shield over every head, I am the spear of battle. . . . *I am the word of knowledge.*"

He swung the cloak over his shoulders and donned the helm, then mounted Darnley's charger with a leap.

"Wait!" Jemmy shouted. "Where are you—"

He stopped, his mouth still open, as Ronan turned the horse so sharply that it reared. A ray of sunlight caught the helm in a blinding flash, and he was gone, galloping toward Darnley's men.

"Sweet *Christ,*" Jemmy breathed, signing himself with the cross. As one, he and Maude turned to stare at Lord Darnley and then at each other.

A voice cried out, a deep rough voice that was part of Maude's earliest memories.

She looked at her father, still and silent on the moor, and a cold shiver wound down her spine. "Fall back! I said turn about! To me, to me, all of ye, at once! Can ye no follow a simple order?"

A horn cut through the battle cries and pounding hoof-beats, caught the wind and flew across the moor. It was Darnley's horn, sounding his own call, and Darnley's soldiers responded as a single man.

"Fall back! Fall back!"

And they were gone, leaving only a cloud of dust behind as they galloped headlong toward Aylsford.

Jemmy looked as dazed as Maude felt herself. "I'd always heard—dear God, but they are something to behold. Let us hope my men can match them! Lady, come."

"No," Maude said. "Ronan will be back for me."

Jemmy started toward her, then stopped. "I cannot stay to argue it."

Then he was gone as well, heading off at a flat gallop toward his men, winding his horn for all that he was worth. His doubts had been groundless, Maude thought as she watched the Kirallens turn back neatly at his command. She sank down beside her father and took his cold hand in hers as the sounds of horns and hoofbeats faded slowly into silence.

Fifty-one

"It was an illusion," Ronan said. "They saw the cloak and the helm and heard what sounded like your father's voice."

"I was there," Maude protested. "I know what I saw. Tell me the truth."

He looked down at their hands, clasped between them. "Acushla, if I could, I would. But even now I am not certain what was real and what was an illusion."

"It was magic," she breathed.

After a moment, he nodded. "It was. I don't understand it, but . . . Well, I've come to see that there isn't much I *do* understand."

They sat hand in hand on a settle, watching the sun set over the moors from Maude's bower window. Her ladies had long since gone down to the hall, and she and Ronan were enjoying the first privacy they'd had since their return to Ayslford. The chamber was dim, but neither had suggested lighting candles. There was peace here, a thing that Maude had not experienced in the past ten days, which had rushed by like a dream.

There had been Haddon's return, followed by arrangements for the funeral feast, which Maude had planned as a quiet affair attended only by the family and Lord Darnley's tenants. But Haddon had other plans, which he did not see fit to confide to her. Maude had been as shocked as the rest of Aylsford by the sudden appearance of Malcolm Kirallen at the chapel.

Shocked, aye, and angry, and hurt that Haddon had not warned her. During the next days she had found herself entertaining half the manor in her chamber and had reassured everyone from the captain of the guard to Cook herself that Haddon had her full support in all he did. Still, she could not help but feel he had made a bad start that promised to get worse.

But she had reckoned without Malcolm Kirallen. When he set out to make himself agreeable to all and sundry, there were few who could resist. Then there was Haddon himself, who had inherited a good measure of his father's steel, honed by four years of Jemmy Kirallen's tutelage.

When Haddon declared that Malcolm was a welcome guest, no one quite dared to contradict him. And last night, when he stood up in the hall and bade his household drink to the prosperity of the Kirallens, his foster family and his allies, only a handful had the courage to refuse.

Maude suspected that handful had been seen and noted. And unless she missed her guess, they would either reconsider their position or be seen no more at Aylsford.

It is finished, she thought, gazing out upon the twilit moor. *The long feud is finally over. And I am free.*

It was a heady thought. She wasn't certain yet exactly what it meant, but she was ready to find out.

With the trick he had of following her thoughts, Ronan said, "Maude, is this the time to be talking about the future? Is it too soon for you?"

"No, it is the perfect time."

"I wrote to my grandfather. I told him all about you and said I'd like to bring you to Lough Gur so he can see you for himself."

"Ronan, are you sure? Is this really what you want?"

"I can hardly wait for it. He's a proud old man, and stubborn with it, and far too used to having his own way." He grinned and raised her hand to his lips. "Sure, the two of you will get on famously."

"That wasn't what I meant—" Maude began, then broke off as a squire tapped upon the open door.

"Lord Darnley," he announced, stepping back. And Haddon walked into the room.

Maude rose and made a reverence to her brother. "Good evening, Haddon."

She smiled as she spoke, for this was the first time he had sought her out since his return.

"What are ye doing, sitting here in the dark?" he said. "Do ye no care what people might say? Ellis, bring a light at once."

The light was brought, and the chamber glowed in candlelight. Maude kept her silence while the squire was in the room, though every muscle was tensed with anger. Ronan put a hand on her arm.

"Shall I . . . ?" he murmured and Maude shook her head, sitting up a little straighter. He smiled and took up his harp as the squire retreated to his place outside the door.

"No, Haddon," Maude said when they were alone, "I do not care what anyone might say, if they should say anything at all."

"Well, I do," Haddon said, taking a seat. "Already I've heard rumors—"

"Rumors? About me? And pray, what might they be?"

Before he could answer, the door opened, and her uncle Robert walked in. "Haddon, forgive me, the steward kept me longer than—oh, hullo, Maude," he said, smiling at her with such genuine concern that tears started to her eyes. "How are you, my dear? I've hardly had the chance to speak to you at all."

"I'm well enough, uncle," Maude answered.

"You've had a hellish time of it, haven't you? But now things should settle down again. What say you we go hawking tomorrow? I have brought Robin Bowden back with me. You remember him, I'm sure, such a lad with the hawks and a great admirer of yours. He brings you the loveliest little tiercel that he took with his own hand and swears he would not trust to anyone but you. She is just ready to try her wings, and—"

"That was very kind of Robin," Maude said, breaking into the flow of words, "but I fear the journey to Ireland might prove too unsettling for such a young bird."

Sir Robert raised his brows. "Ireland? I did not know you proposed a visit so far from home. And in all truth, Maude, I cannot recommend it, not at present. You need to be here with your family."

"Lady Maude *will* be with her family," Ronan said. "For we wish to wed as soon as ever we can."

"My father gave you no leave to wed," Haddon protested.

Ronan stilled his fingers on the harp strings. "Maude, it might be best if I speak to Lord Darnley and Sir Robert privately."

"Why?"

He smiled at her. " 'Tis how the thing is generally done."

"Yes, but—" She looked from brother to uncle and back to Ronan. "This concerns me, as well."

"Sure, it does," Ronan agreed, "and if you'd like to stay, of course you must. Lord Darnley, Sir Robert," he went on, "please forgive us for not having spoken of this earlier. What with one thing and another, there has been no time at all. But as you've no doubt understood, Maude and I wish to marry."

He sat back, noting their appalled expressions with some amusement. Looking at it through their eyes, he *was* an unlikely match for the daughter of an earl. They knew him only as a common minstrel who had, moreover, been convicted of a murder—even if he had been inexplicably pardoned by the laird.

"I should have said, we *mean* to marry," he added. "For that is the truth of it."

"*Mean* to?" Haddon repeated. "Well, Fitzgerald, you'll need our leave for that. And if you think—"

"Now, Haddon," Sir Robert put in quickly, "let us not be hasty here. If Maude wishes to marry, we must consider the matter. We must consider it very carefully indeed. But in the meantime," he said to Maude, "there are some things you should think about, as well."

He took Maude's hand and looked earnestly into her face. "My dear, forgive me if I speak plainly. I understand that you and Haddon have not been the best of friends of late. And I have not always shown you the consideration you have every right to expect from your uncle—and your guardian as well, now. But you mustn't feel you are not wanted here."

There was no doubt in Ronan's mind that Sir Robert meant every word he said. The knight might be doing his level best to destroy Ronan's own hope of happiness, but Ronan could not help but like him for it.

"Give it time," Sir Robert went on. "I think you will find that things will be very different now. Please, Maude, you must let us prove that you can be happy here."

"Thank you, Uncle," Maude said. "You are very kind. But please do not think that either you or Haddon are the cause of my decision. Ronan and I reached an understanding some time ago." She put her hand into Ronan's and smiled. "I love him," she said simply, "and I mean to marry him."

Robert drew a long breath, preparing, Ronan suspected, to launch a new attack.

"We will be going to Ireland," Ronan put in, "to the household of the Earl of Desmond. My kinsman, Sir Robert," he added gently, "who is awaiting my return."

He drew a parchment from his belt and unfolded it. "My grandfather has written to welcome us to Lough Gur. If you wish, we shall wed there."

Sir Robert raised his brows. "I had no idea you were one of *those* Fitzgeralds! Maude, why did you not say so?"

"I did not think it was important, Uncle. Nor do I now."

"I will take good care of your sister, my lord," Ronan said. "You can be sure of that. She will want for nothing."

Robert studied the two of them for a long moment. "Very well," he said at last, throwing up his hands in surrender. "Haddon, lad, we can both see there is no stopping them, so why not give in with good grace? Of course you must marry here," he added to Maude. "This is your home."

"But Uncle Robert—" Haddon argued.

Robert's face was alight with excitement. "We'll have a feast—aye, a great feast, one everyone will talk about for years."

"Uncle Robert," Maude began, but the knight was off, already running through the guests.

"Haddon, what about Maxwell? A bit awkward, that, but it might look odd if we do not invite him, given that he and John were . . ."

Maude tugged Ronan's hand and led him toward the door. "Let him have his way," she said with a shrug. "What difference does it make so long as we are married?"

They walked together through the passageway. When they reached Maude's chamber, Ronan stooped to kiss her brow. "A strange sort of a betrothal," he said.

"Aye," she agreed, smiling. "But strange or not, I'll hold you to it. What did your grandfather say?" she added, looking down at the parchment Ronan was still holding.

"Here, read it for yourself," he said, offering it to her. "Until tomorrow, lady."

Once inside her chamber, Maude sat at her dressing table and tipped the parchment toward the candle. It was as Ronan said. Sir John Fitzgerald had written that he was pleased to hear of the upcoming nuptials and anxious to welcome his grandson and new granddaughter to Lough Gur, adding that he remembered Lord Darnley, and it was a match that had his full approval. He went on to say that he hoped for a Yule knighting "if you can manage to couch a lance without disgracing the family." The letter ended with the mention of some money he had sent for the purchase of a wedding suit.

Maude laid the parchment on the table and rested her chin in her palm. It was a kind message. Oh, the tone was gruff, almost curt at times, but even that could not disguise John Fitzgerald's pleasure and excitement at the prospect of Ronan's return.

There was only one trouble with the letter. In his bold, clear hand, Sir John had addressed it to "my grandson, William."

Fifty-two

Maude yawned and stretched, feeling every muscle relax as she lay back among the pillows. Two days more. Just two days more and she would be wed, and the next day she would be riding off for Ireland.

God be thanked for an uncle wise in the ways of diplomacy. Only he could have convinced Father Aidan to cry all the banns on a single Sunday, but even that dour man could not withstand Sir Robert once his mind was set.

She closed her eyes and let her thoughts drift. Uncle Robert's unexpected kindness . . . Haddon's continuing hostility . . . she must speak to Haddon, try once more before she left . . . Ireland, so green . . . Lough Gur . . . Sir John's letter. Ronan . . . William . . . he said he did not care, so long as Maude remembered his name it made no difference what anyone else might say. *Does it matter?* she wondered as she slipped into sleep. *It is just a name . . . only who he is . . .*

The next thing Maude knew she was standing on a hillside. The slope was deserted, just as it always was, and bare stone rose sharply to a jagged peak. She knew this place; she had been here many times before. The dragon was close by; she could hear it breathing, but it was hidden in the sharp rocks that ringed her round.

A hand tugged her sleeve. "There," the child said, her filthy face solemn as she raised her hand and pointed. "There it is. Hurry, you must go to it before it is too late."

Maude gazed down at the child. "I will not run. Not this time."

She walked in the direction that the child had indicated. "Are you coming?" she asked over her shoulder, but the slope was empty now.

"It doesn't matter," she told herself. "I will do it. Then I can tell Ronan."

She turned the corner boldly, then stopped and stared.

It was much like the dragon of her tapestry, she thought; she'd gotten the shape of it precisely. And the size. Though it was lying down, she had to tilt her head far back to look into its face. The only difference was the color. Her dragon had been emerald and gold, with markings of brilliant crimson. This one was a dull greenish brown.

There was another difference, Maude realized. Her dragon had been fierce, with cruel sharp eyes and wicked fangs. This one gazed down at her with liquid eyes, filled with such gentle sorrow that her throat constricted. Even as she stood unmoving, its scales began to fall, landing with little clinks against the stone. It let out a great sigh and rested its head on its forepaws, a thin wisp of smoke rising from its nostrils.

"What is it?" she asked. "What is wrong with you? Are you—you can't be dying!"

It sighed again, and a tear fell from one eye to vanish in a puff of steam upon the stone.

"No," Maude said. "No, you cannot be—"

She broke off and stepped back, shielding her face

against a burst of heat and light as the dragon burst into flame.

It burned for what seemed like hours as she stood watching, her heart aching with wild sorrow. At last the flames died away to show a heap of gray ash that began to scatter in the wind.

Maude bent and picked up a scale. "I will bring this back and show it to Ronan. Then he will believe me."

The ashes stirred from within. Maude stared in amazement as a tiny dragon, hardly bigger than a cat, crawled out of the ashes. Even as she watched, it grew, shaking itself and spreading its wings, its scales glowing green and gold and crimson. It turned to her, jaws agape in what looked like a grin. Then it stretched its wings and rose, circled the bare peak once, and flew off into the distance, growing ever smaller until it disappeared. *It's gone,* she thought. *It will never come back.*

She remembered the scale she had taken. "At least I have this," she thought, and was comforted. But when she looked down at her hand, it was not the dragon's scale she held. It was her lute.

Fifty-three

Maude woke with tears on her face, her hand still clenched into a fist. She scrambled out of bed and flew down the corridor, bursting into Ronan's chamber without knocking. He was awake already, standing by the window, his back to her as he twisted his long black hair into a braid.

"Ronan!" she cried. "Oh, Ronan, I had such a dream!"

He turned, smiling, and knotted a thong about the braid. "Did you? You must tell me all about it."

"I saw it!" she began, but he shook his head.

"Later. I've kept your uncle waiting an hour already. He wants to go over the marriage settlement." He grimaced. "Again."

Maude knew that Uncle Robert was worried about her dowry. It was ridiculously large, and the knight had said—with justice—that to pay all her father had promised in a single stroke would beggar Aylsford for years. Not that Ronan cared about her dowry, Maude thought, and yet the matter must be settled.

"Ronan—" she began.

"Why don't we go riding this afternoon?"

"Yes," she said, brightening, and then she sighed. "The guests are coming today."

Ronan blew out an exasperated breath. "That's right, I'd forgotten. Well, we'll just have to steal time, won't we?"

He bent to kiss her. "You are beautiful in the morning, acushla. I wish I could stay."

"But you cannot."

"No. But I will find you later."

When he was gone, Maude sat down on his bed with a sigh, remembering the days when Ronan cared more for dreams than gold. Though she tried to push her melancholy aside, she could not help but wonder if what had just happened was to be the pattern of all their days together.

Maude went restlessly through her morning duties, filled with the sort of hectic energy she had not felt for weeks. Finally, she pulled the last of the Michaelmas daisies from the garden and walked through the chapel and down the steps leading to the tombs.

Her father's was still bare, for his effigy would not be completed for months. She removed the drooping flowers from the holder and set the fresh ones in their place.

"I wish I could pray," she said aloud. "But you understand, don't you?"

She smiled wryly, running her hand lightly across the cool marble. Strange how one began to attribute all manner of wisdom to the dead. When he was alive, her father had never understood anything about her. He had been too busy giving her what he thought she needed to ever ask what she might want for herself.

Like Ronan.

She pushed the thought aside with guilty haste. The two men were nothing alike! How *could* she be so ungrateful? Ronan was only doing what he must to make a life for both of them. He loved her and she loved him and that was all that mattered.

Wasn't it?

The sound of footsteps on the stair saved her from pursuing that line of thought. It must be Haddon, she thought, come at last to mourn with her. She straightened, smiling, waiting to receive her brother.

But it was Alyson who stepped into the chamber.

"Oh!" Alyson started back, her face mirroring Maude's shock. "I thought—they said you were—forgive me, Maude, I had no wish to intrude. I'll come back another time."

"No! Wait!"

Alyson turned back.

"Why are you here?" Maude said. "I never thought *you* would want to see him! Even Haddon has not been down once."

Alyson stepped into the chamber and gazed at the tomb. "I am not certain why I came," she confessed. "Only that I had to."

She brushed her fingertips across the marble, just as Maude had done. "God knows he never cared for me," she said.

"Count yourself lucky, sister."

Alyson lifted her head. "Sister? Now that's a word I never thought to hear from you."

"I never thought to say it," Maude admitted. "It slipped out when I wasn't watching."

Alyson laughed, then put her hand across her mouth, glancing guiltily at the tomb.

"Oh, go ahead," Maude said. "Why should you not laugh? I would think you would be glad that he is dead."

"I thought I would be," Alyson said slowly. "And yet . . ."

"And yet *what?*"

"I used to have this dream—oh, it was very silly, really—that one day there would be peace, and he would acknowledge me."

"Really?" Maude said, intrigued. "What would you have done if he did?"

Alyson smiled. "Spit in his eye and thrown him out the door. But I had such fun imagining it! When one of the babies was wakeful or I had naught to do but sit and sew, I would go over it all, what he would say, what I would do. . . ." She shook her head. "Such foolish fancies. It was only you he loved."

Maude was silenced by the words. She stared down at her hands folded on the tomb through a veil of tears. "He did love me. But . . ."

"But what?"

"He did such terrible things."

"Aye, he did."

"For me," Maude whispered. "He did them for me."

"Maude, your father—*our* father—had done many terrible things before either of us was born. Whatever he did later may have been done in your name, but never think you made him what he was."

Maude lifted her head. "He was an evil man, wasn't he?"

"Weel, evil is a word that's easy to use, but what does it really mean? He did many evil deeds *and* he truly loved you. You loved the part of him that was the good father, and that part was just as real as the other."

Her words were brisk and so sensible that Maude felt some of the dark confusion lift from her heart.

"He was not a good father to you," she said.

"No, he was not. He was a very bad father. And yet he gave me life. Whatever he was, he is a part of me. And you. And Haddon."

Maude thought about that for a time. "Haddon loves you," she said at last.

"And so he should, for blood ties are the strongest. He loves you, as well, though he's forgotten it just now.

I think," she added quietly, "that he should hear the truth."

Maude felt her face flame. "The laird told you, then."

"Jemmy told me nothing." Alyson reached across the tomb and covered Maude's hands with hers. "He did not have to. But I have the use of my senses, God be thanked. There's no need for me to know more, but Haddon . . . think about speaking your heart to him, Maude. He deserves that much, and he is old enough to keep your confidence."

"I cannot. I dare not. Look at what it did to Father—and to Ronan—"

"But that's all over, isn't it? Ronan saw to that."

Maude lifted her head sharply, but Alyson was not looking at her. She was staring down at the tomb, her expression pensive. "Ronan is a fine man, far better than he knows. I've been very worried for him." She looked at Maude and smiled. "But he'll be all right now. He has you to help him find his way."

It is no wonder everyone loves her, Maude thought, turning her hands and giving Alyson's a squeeze. She was tempted to speak of the new trouble in her heart, but that would not be right. That was a private matter between her and Ronan.

"Have you rested yet at all?" she asked. "Or eaten?"

"No, I came straight here. I'm glad I did," Alyson said, "but I would welcome something warm to drink. Does Cook still make that mulled wine with all the cinnamon?"

"She does. Now that she is mistress of the box again, she tosses the spices about with mad abandon."

"Again?" Alyson's brows rose. "Don't tell me you dared take the sacred key?"

They walked up the steps together, laughing. The sound lingered behind them long after they were gone, echoing and reechoing against the cold and silent tomb.

Fifty-four

Maude meant to leave Alyson, for she had far too much to do to linger in conversation. But one thing led to another, and when Alyson asked what she would be wearing for her wedding, they ended in Maude's chamber, a flagon of mulled wine between them on the table.

"Let me see what you have," Alyson said.

"Becta!" Maude called, but when there was no answer, she went to the garderobe herself and pulled several gowns from their hooks. She heard the outer door open and Becta's startled voice as she greeted Lady Alyson. Becta had always been fond of her, Maude remembered, though now the thought held no rancor.

She stopped inside the doorway, shaking her head as she heard Alyson say earnestly, "—have known him for years, and truly, Becta, there is no need to worry. But you will see for yourself. You are going with them, aren't you?"

"She is not," Maude said, stepping inside. "Becta is abandoning me for her family." She dropped the gowns on the settle and rested a hand on Becta's shoulder.

"Though how I'll find anyone else to put up with me is more than I can answer for!"

"Oh, lady—"

"No tears now, Becta, you know that I won't have them. I'll scrape along somehow, and you know your niece can't get along without you, not with the new baby coming. Now sit down and have some wine and help me choose a gown."

Becta wiped her eyes and sniffed. "And leave Lady Alyson and the laird to a bare bed and cold hearth? The two of ye can fribble the day away, but some of us have work to do."

Alyson sat down. "Well, she put us in our place, didn't she? Let me see what you brought."

"Perhaps this?"

Maude held up her saffron gown, and Alyson shook her head. "Too . . . yellow. Have ye naught in green?"

"Well, I do have this, but 'tis very plain."

"Oh, no, that is perfect! It only needs a bit of—"

The door flew open, and Deirdre Kirallen burst in, laughing. "Holy Saint Brighid, either I've just seen a miracle or else I'm going mad! Here—" She ran to the window and beckoned the others to join her. "Tell me what you see. Is that our Ronan in the tiltyard?"

"It is," Maude said. "He has been out there every day."

Deirdre signed herself with the cross. "God be thanked, I thought I'd lost my senses. Is it true, then? Are you really going to Ireland?"

"Yes. It is true."

Deirdre turned to her, eyes wide. "Lady Maude, you have done the impossible. I didn't think he ever would go home, and I'm so happy for him—and you—"

She threw her arms around Maude's neck and kissed her cheek. "Not that I'm not a bit put out about it," she added with a sniff. "He never offered such a thing to *me!*

And doesn't that just show he's found the right woman after all?"

Maude blinked, not used to such plain speaking, but Deirdre only laughed and slipped an arm about her waist.

"You've made a man of our Ronan," she said, gesturing toward the window. "He looks older already!"

"He said once," Maude admitted, "that I was aging him quickly."

"He needed it. And now look at him. Why, I can hardly imagine what the old man will say!"

"His grandfather is already talking about a Yule knighting at Lough Gur."

Maude spoke cheerfully, but a small sigh escaped her. Even as Deirdre laughed, Maude was aware of Alyson watching her.

" 'Tis only natural he'd want to give you a proper place in the world. In his family," Alyson said thoughtfully.

"I know. But . . ."

"Will you be going back to Donegal?" Deirdre asked eagerly.

"I think so."

"Then we will see you there next spring! Alistair and I had talked of sending our daughter Maeve to my father in a few years. Oh, it would be grand to know that you were there to look after her!"

"I'm not sure we will be staying," Maude said. "Ronan doesn't like to be in one place too long, you know."

"Oh, that will all change now," Deirdre said, waving her hand. "He'll settle down in Donegal. Once the babies come, you won't want to be traveling about."

Maude stiffened, then forced herself to smile. It was natural enough for Deirdre to talk of children; weren't they the point of marriage, after all? But there would be no babies, not for her and Ronan. In that moment, all her vague misgivings came together into a piercing vision of their future.

She saw Ronan, busy all the day, working at a hundred tasks that he would not enjoy but just endure. She saw herself, trapped in the old familiar pattern, seeing to the meals and linen, settling disputes between the village and the manor, sitting in the bower for hours upon end, listening to her women chatter about nothing. The only difference was that the Irish women would be forever with their eyes upon her waistline, wondering what ailed their lady that she did not quicken.

"Be damned to that," she said aloud.

"Be damned to what?" Deirdre asked, turning to her in surprise.

"Maude," Alyson said, "I don't like the look in your eye. What are you planning?"

"I don't know. I need to think."

"Are you certain you don't need to *talk?*" Alyson asked.

Maude was tempted, but she shook her head. " 'Tis between me and Ronan."

"You aren't thinking of—well, of doing anything rash?" Deirdre asked.

"Rash?" Maude repeated the word with relish. "Aye, Deirdre, I'm afraid I am." She put an arm about each woman's shoulders and guided them firmly toward the door.

"But—" Deirdre began.

"Maude kens exactly what she's doing," Alyson said. "Come along, Dee, and let her be. 'Tis past time we greeted Haddon."

Fifty-five

Ronan walked into the hall that night in a foul temper. He had spent the morning with Sir Robert, who dragged him over half the manor, proving once again that Maude's dowry could not be paid in a single stroke without bringing ruin upon the Darnleys.

"Sod her dowry," Ronan wanted to say, but he could not. His grandfather would go over the marriage settlement in every detail, quick to spot the smallest flaw in its execution. And Maude's gold would make all the difference between a life spent at Lough Gur and the relative freedom to be found in Donegal.

"Sir Robert," he said at last, "we will have plenty of time to settle this. Once Maude and I reach Lough Gur, I'll send a clerk to work it all out fairly."

Even then he could not see Maude, for it was time for his daily practice in the tiltyard. Ronan went at it with grim determination, for he had no intention of shaming either himself or his family by his inability to couch a lance with style. But God help him, how he hated it, the whole false ritual involved.

It was close to dusk by the time he reached his chamber, and by then Maude had gone already to the hall. He washed and changed his clothes, staring at the outfit with distaste. The tunic was cut in the latest fashion, ridiculously short and dyed in garish gold and crimson. Ronan would never have chosen such a thing, but in a moment of pure madness he had accepted Sir Robert's offer to see to his new wardrobe. The result was deplorable, but once again he had no time to think about it, for he was already late.

So it was that he strode into the hall in a foul humor, only to find Maude seated in the center of the floor, strumming on her lute.

Ronan leaned against the wall, watching her, listening with half an ear to the questioning murmurs all around him, interspersed with the occasional disapproving sniff. For of course it was not done for a lady to perform in her own hall like a common minstrel. Maude would have to learn to curb such headstrong impulses when they reached Ireland, for his grandfather would be appalled.

Almost as appalled as Ronan was himself for even having such a thought. Maude would always do exactly as she liked, he vowed, no matter what his grandfather or any of his legion of aunts and uncles and cousins might have to say about it.

He suspected they would have a great deal to say about him and Maude no matter what they did, and none of it would make pleasant hearing. Even before he had run off, the half-Irish stranger in their midst had not been welcomed by any of them—save for his grandfather, which made the rest of them resent him all the more. But Grandfather's favorite had never been Ronan. It had been William.

But of course there was no need to trouble Maude with any of that yet.

She was nervous, Ronan saw, though he doubted anyone else would mark it. When she began to sing he glanced about the hall, measuring the reaction with a minstrel's eye. She had them. Even the ladies were leaning forward, caught up in the song. Pride swelled in him, mingled with a touch of envy. It felt very odd to be part of the audience now, nevermore to be a performer.

The song ended, and Maude inclined her head, her cheeks pink with pleasure. Oh, he remembered that feeling. There was nothing like it. With unerring instinct she began her next song while the applause was at its height, forcing them to be suddenly silent to hear her. Where had she learned that trick? He had not taught her. She played the opening, then turned to him.

"Ronan!" she called. "Will you sing with me?"

"You are doing well enough on your own," he called back. "Sure you don't need me."

"No," she agreed, lifting her chin proudly. "But I *want* you."

Laughter greeted her words, and she smiled, but her eyes were grave as they held his.

Shrugging, he came to join her, sinking to the floor at her feet. "Lady, I am yours to command."

"Are you?" she asked softly.

Before he could answer, she began to sing. He joined her on the chorus, and at the first note his bad mood vanished. They finished the song together, their voices blending into a single sound of such beauty that he felt the hair stir on his neck. He would have willingly sung more, but Maude rose and held out her hands to him, drawing him to his feet.

"Oh, that was wonderful," Alyson said as they reached the high table. "Just think, Ronan, if only you'd had Maude with you on the road!"

Maude smiled as they took their seats. "Aye, Ronan, just think of it."

"That is no life for a woman. You'd have to be mad to even dream of it."

"Then I am mad," Maude said, looking at him directly. "The only question is, are you?"

Ronan laughed, but the sound held no amusement. "You are jesting. You cannot mean—"

"I am not jesting," she said, and now her eyes flashed with anger. "I am making you an offer. Accept it or refuse it, but do not laugh at me."

"And if I refuse?"

"Then you refuse." She shrugged. "And you shall go to Ireland and at Yule become Sir William, that staid, responsible fellow with all his lands to tend. He sounds like a great bore to me, and I must confess I rather dread to meet him, let alone be married to the vile creature."

Ronan rose so abruptly that his chair crashed to the dais behind him. The table fell silent as Maude stood and faced him.

"Well?" she said, her voice lightly challenging.

He grabbed her hand. "Excuse us, my lord," he said to Haddon, and pulled her from the hall.

"What is this, Maude?" he demanded. "Why are you saying these things now?"

"Because it is time someone spoke the truth. Ronan, if that is the life you want, then you should have it. Go ahead, take back your lands and fortune, and God give you joy in them. But surely you must see that I am the wrong woman for Sir William."

"You are talking nonsense."

"Am I? You say you want to make a future for us, and don't think I am ungrateful. But Ronan," she took his hand and looked into his eyes, "that is the kind of future a man builds for his children."

He drew a sharp breath. "I *never* said—"

"No, you did not," she said gently. "But your silence does not make it any less the truth."

"What are you saying?" he demanded. "Are you trying to tell me that you have changed your mind? Will you come with me to Ireland or not?"

She released his hand. "Yes. Even knowing it is a mistake, I will go, for I love you too much to part from you. But—oh, Ronan, would you not rather come with me to Jerusalem? Just think of it, the two of us together— what a grand adventure!"

Jerusalem. His heart lifted at the thought, then thumped down again as he looked at Maude. She was wearing white tonight and looked insubstantial as a flower in the simple gown and veil. She had no idea of the hardships of the road, the poor food and rough lodgings, never knowing at the start of any day where you would find yourself at the end of it.

"You do not know what it is like," he began.

"Did you? When you first set out, did you know what it would be like? No, of course you didn't, you couldn't know, but that never stopped you. Because you wanted to see it for yourself. And so do I, Ronan. I want to see it for myself. With you."

Maude held her breath, waiting for his answer. He glared at her for a long moment, then his lips twitched in a ghost of his old reckless grin.

"And I'll wager," she went on, "that in a year, we'll be playing before royalty."

He sighed, running a hand through his hair, dislodging the gold and crimson cap. He took it off and turned it in his hands, frowning. "Six months," he said. "Or I'll eat my harp."

"Strings and all?" Maude laughed, taking the cap from his hands and flinging it aside. "Do you mean it?"

"About eating my harp? Well, no—oh, the other? Maude, are you really certain that this is what you want? It *is* a hard life, and it has its dangers."

"Any life can be hard," she said, "and nothing is certain. Danger can be anywhere, Ronan, anywhere at all. Of course I am afraid, but that's a poor reason to chain both of us to a future that neither of us wants. After all," she added with a smile, "a wise man once told me that the whole purpose of life is to live it."

Ronan smiled, leaning against the wall. "A wise man, was he?"

"Very wise. So long as he remembers to listen to his wife, I don't doubt he will grow wiser still."

"I will listen," he said softly. "Always."

"We must still go to Ireland," she said quickly. "Your grandfather is expecting us."

"We'll go. For a visit. A very *short* visit."

"No Sir William?"

"*Definitely* no Sir William," Ronan agreed, slipping an arm around her waist and drawing her back toward the hall. "What will your brother say?" he asked suddenly. "And your uncle?"

"I spoke with Haddon earlier. We had a long talk, and I'm certain he will wish us well. As for Uncle Robert," she added with a grin, "he'll be too busy gasping with relief at not having to pay my dowry to care *what* we do."

"That's right." Ronan drew a hand across his brow. "God be thanked, no more marriage settlement. But Maude, you mustn't let your uncle cheat you out of what is yours."

"I don't want it. If it's my fortune you're after . . ."

"Sod your dowry." Ronan laughed, the last lines of care vanishing from his face. "God, but I've been wanting to say that all day. You're right. We won't be needing it. We'll make our own fortune."

Just inside the door, he stopped and set his hands on her shoulders, gazing deep into her eyes.

"Maude, if I refuse my grandfather this time, I doubt he'll give me another chance. Lough Gur is beautiful, and rich, and you would live in wealth and comfort there."

Maude touched the dragon at her throat and smiled. "Wealth? Comfort? Now, why would I settle for so little when I could be a queen?"

Fifty-six

The last of the wedding guests were departing when Alyson found Jemmy in the courtyard, bowing right and left and calling out farewells. He greeted her with some relief.

"I think the point's been made, don't you?" he said.

Alyson smiled and waved to Brother Donal, who was mounting one of the Abbey's spirited little donkeys.

"If they haven't fathomed the peace by now, they're too dim to bother about," she agreed, taking Jemmy's arm.

Jemmy lifted his free hand, returning the wave of a rider going toward the gate.

"Who—?" Alyson began. "Oh, Kinnon Maxwell. I can't imagine why Haddon insisted on having him here."

"Why, isn't he Haddon's friend and ally, just as he is ours?"

Alyson sniffed. "A strange sort of ally."

"Oh, Kinnon's not so bad. I wouldn't turn my back on him, but—"

"Who is that with him?" Alyson interrupted.

Jemmy squinted. "That lass—what's her name, the one who came with you to Ravenspur?"

"Celia?" Alyson stood on tiptoe, peering toward the gate. "So it is! Did Haddon not say she was working in the dairy?"

"Not anymore," Jemmy remarked.

"Well, that's fast work, even for Celia! And here I thought Kinnon was meant to be courting Maude!"

"Weel, it seems the maid was more willing than the mistress."

Alyson began to answer but was halted by a voice behind her.

"So here you are," Ronan said. "We couldn't leave without saying farewell."

Yesterday's wedding finery was but a memory this morning. Ronan and Maude were both dressed for travel, he in his old green cloak and she in one of plain gray wool.

"You're not going now!" Alyson exclaimed.

"No time to waste," Ronan answered. "We've much to do."

Maude smiled up at him, her eyes shining. "And to see."

"Farewell, lady," Ronan said, taking Alyson's hand. "God and Saint Brighid keep you until we meet again."

"And you, Ronan. Maude—"

Maude leaned forward to kiss Alyson's cheek. "Thank you," she whispered, pressing a bag into Alyson's hand. "For you—and Isobel—no, don't look now, it's nothing, really, just some things I won't be needing."

"I'll keep them to remember you. But you will be back again, won't you?"

"Of course we will," Ronan said, then grinned, "when you least expect us."

There was a small silence, then Ronan squared his shoulders and turned to Jemmy. "Well, Laird? Will you wish us Godspeed, too?"

Jemmy shook his head. "One would think I'd be glad to see the back of you. Yes, Ronan, I wish you Godspeed and a pleasant journey." He smiled suddenly and caught Ronan in a hard embrace. "Just try to stay out of trouble."

"We will. Try, that is. Whether we'll succeed . . ."

"Lady Maude, you have my sympathy," Jemmy said. "I trust you know what you have undertaken."

"Oh, I do. And I will keep him out of trouble, Laird."

Jemmy's face softened as he smiled down at her. "Aye," he said, "I do believe you will."

Two grooms led their horses forward. Alyson's eyes widened as Maude mounted an enormous stallion, black as the devil and dancing on the cobbles. Maude smiled as she gathered up the reins and nudged the beast into a walk beside Ronan's brown gelding. She did not look back, Alyson noticed, not even once.

Jemmy and Alyson followed them more slowly to the gate and watched them ride down the ribbon of road stretching across the open moor. The sky was clouding over, and a few drops of rain spattered the cobbles at their feet.

"They are mad," Jemmy said.

"Are they? Off to see new lands, their journey just beginning and everything before them. Are you not the least bit jealous?"

"No. Well, not much, anyway." Jemmy bent and kissed her lightly. "Are you coming in, or do you mean to stand here in the rain?"

"I'll be in presently."

Alone, she opened the bag Maude had given her, her breath catching at the jumble of diamonds, emeralds, rubies, and sapphires within. She stirred them with one finger, now and again lifting a bright strand to look at it more closely. A few were familiar, for she had worn them long ago. Most she had not seen before.

Alyson was no judge of jewels, but even she could see it was a fortune she was holding. A legacy. The acknowledgement her father never would have given her. The bright colors blurred before her eyes.

"No, you won't need them, will you?" she said softly.

The rain came then, sweeping in a sheet across the courtyard. Alyson darted halfway to the door and stopped, looking back toward the gate. A gust of wind drove the rain into her face and yet she smiled, for it also carried the sound of voices from the moor.

Maude's voice. And Ronan's.

And they were singing.

Turn the page for a sneak peek
at the new fantasy romance by
Elizabeth English writing as Elizabeth Minogue,
coming in November 2004
from Berkley Sensation.

Rose twisted through the crowd, sweating in her heavy kirtle as the relentless sun beat down upon her uncovered head. Safe within the press, she dared cast a quick look over her shoulder. As far as she could tell, she had not been followed.

Yet.

Two weeks on shipboard had left her legs uncommonly stiff. The wooden planks rose to meet her, jarring her off-balance. *Clap clap, clapclap.* Heel and toe of her wooden pattens hit the planks more quickly as she found her land legs. She hurried on, breathing through her mouth against the oily smell of fish, thick as fog on the unmoving air. She kept to the most crowded places, head down, meeting no man's eye. Yet still the sailors noticed her.

"Slow down, Jenny—sweeting—*chevra*," they called after her. "What can be the rush? Stay a moment, let me show you—"

Despite the paralyzing heat, she wished desperately for cloak and hood. The past year of silent solitude had stripped her of defenses. Even before that, she had never been the focus of so many eyes. On the few occasions she was permitted to appear in public, her cousins were always present. The two of them rendered her as invisible as any magic cloak could ever do.

But today Melisande and Berengaria were far away. She was alone in a place where no respectable woman would be seen. No woman at all just now, not in this unrelenting heat. Even the dockside whores had retreated to some shady chamber to wait for evening's cool.

But she could not afford to wait. She must go now, and swiftly, before her absence had been noticed. Eyes fixed on the wooden planks beneath her feet, she concentrated on her destination.

I must be calm, she told herself. *Or,* she amended, wincing as a sailor trod upon her toe, *I must* look *calm*. But that should present no problem. She was good at looking calm; so good, in fact, that those who knew her best would swear she was half-witted.

But *he* must not think that. He must believe her story, strange as it might seem. She would be bold. Bold and firm . . . yet not overbearing. After all, she was a suppliant. Or would be, if she ever got there.

Almost running, she crashed into a bearded sailor no taller than her chest with a broad basket balanced on his head.

"Forgive me—please, sir, could you tell me—"

"Piss off," he snarled, shoving her away.

She took a few stumbling steps toward the edge of the dock, but was halted on the edge by a hand fastened on her wrist.

The moment she regained her balance, her plump dark rescuer released her and turned away, wiping his palm fastidiously upon his flowing crimson robe.

"Wait!" she cried, hurrying after him. "Pardon, sir, but could you tell me—"

"Channa zayra," he snapped, not slowing his pace.

"Alet amia," she answered sharply.

He stopped instantly and turned, one hand moving to his brow. "Forgive me, *serra*. How may I serve you?"

"Can you tell me where the Prince of Venya may be found?"

He shut one eye in the Jexlan manner, a courteous gesture denoting careful thought.

"I have not seen him," he said at last. "And had I done so, I would not tell you."

"But I must find him! Please, *serrin*, it is a matter of life and death."

He sighed. "Daughter, whatever this matter is, you should take it to your family. The . . . one you speak of cannot help you." He clicked his tongue, a *tsk tsk* of disapproval. "To so much as speak his name is to sully your honor."

Perhaps in Jexal; if it were so in Valinor, every maiden in the country was already sullied beyond redemption, for the Prince of Venya's name was shouted out constantly in every market square. Despite a dozen edicts, half the troubadours in the country made their living courtesy of his adventures.

"But I must speak to him," she insisted. "My family is dead; they cannot help me, and I haven't a moment to waste."

He studied her face for a long moment, then gestured toward the row of stalls. "If the Venyans are here at all, that is where you will find them."

He touched his brow again, this time with one finger only. *Why, the man thinks I am a whore,* she realized with a shock as he turned away without the customary bow. *Jehan help me, will he think the same?*

I must behave with dignity, she thought, turning toward the stalls. *Dignified, bold, calm, and spirited—*

"Good day, master," she said to the man behind the counter. "Are there any Venyans here?"

"Oh, thou dost not want those sly sorcerers," the man

said with an ingratiating smile. "Whatever they have, 'tis no match for what I can offer you. See, here is—"

"I thank you, but only Venyan will do."

His smile vanished. "I cannot help thee."

She tried the next stall.

"Venyans!" A burly man spat at her feet. "I have no truck with their kind. Move off, you're blocking the way."

An hour later she was soaked with sweat and so thirsty she could barely rasp out another question. But all that was nothing to the anxiety gnawing at the pit of her stomach. She started at each footstep behind her, heart leaping to her parched throat. What if he was not here? What if she had misheard or Captain Jennet had been mistaken?

She had no food, no water, not a single coin with which to buy the most basic necessities, let alone passage on a ship. And soon, if not already, she would be hunted.

She dragged shaking hands across her eyes. *I'm not giving up. Not yet. Not while there is still the slightest hope.*

She reached the end of the row of booths and turned the corner. A single stall stood in the deserted stretch of dock. She held her breath as she approached it.

The shelf was not crowded, but what was there drew and held the eye. A knife with a plain silver hilt, two rings, a glittering crystal on a stand of twisted strands of gold and silver. A tiny bejeweled windmill whirred and chirped a merry tune without a breath of air to stir it.

The man who stood above these offerings was no less exotic. He was immensely old, his eyes lost within a network of wrinkles. Hair the pale silver of *carna* blossoms fell nearly to his waist.

"The blessing of the day upon you," she said cautiously in Venyan. The man's eyes lit and he smiled.

"And upon you, *acelina*," he replied in the same tongue, his weathered face creasing in a smile. "How may I serve you?"

He is a mage, she thought, giddy with relief. A Venyan mage. So they *do* exist.

"A *sheeral* ring, perhaps?" he offered. "One for you and one for your . . ." he used a Venyan word that could mean either husband or lover. "It will burn with Leander's fire should he ever be unfaithful, recalling him his vows."

"No," she said, "Not that. I—"

"Then perhaps this knife. Have him wear it for a moonspan. When he journeys forth, it will be a comfort to you. So long as it stays bright, you can rest easily, knowing he is well. Should it rust . . ." He ran a finger across the shining edge. "Is it not better to know than sit and wonder?"

She shook her head. "No—though they are very fine. I am searching for your prince."

The mage carefully replaced the knife in its sheathe. "*My* prince? Lady, I am but a simple wanderer without home or country."

"But you are Venyan."

"Ah, you seek Prince Rico? Then I fear you have gone far astray. You would do better to look in Valinor, perhaps at Larken Castle."

She shook her head. "Not him. Your *true* prince."

"I am sorry, but I do not know of whom you speak."

"Of course you do! Everyone knows of him! And he is here somewhere, I'm certain of it. Please, can you not take me to him?"

"I am sorry," he repeated, reaching upward. "I cannot help you."

A wooden shutter rolled down across the opening. She caught it before it latched and lifted it an inch. "He who will return upon the flood tide with all who have been lost," she said rapidly in Venyan. "His cause is just, his followers true, and you shall know them when they speak his name."

She shoved the shutter up another few inches. "Well? I spoke his name, didn't I?"

"You did."

"And I know the words. By right of custom, you must answer me!"

The shutter began to fall.

"I am Rose of Valinor."

It halted.

"And I demand—no, I entreat you to take me to your prince."

The sorcerer bent to peer through the opening, regarding her with hooded eyes. "Venya *has* no prince."

"Until the true prince is restored," she answered promptly. "When Leander's heir returns, the stones will sing and the land rejoice."

When he did not answer, she tried again, raising her voice a trifle. "I *said*, when Leander's heir—"

"I heard you. My silence was an indication of surprise, not failing hearing."

"I know a half a dozen more but I really haven't time. So if you don't mind, I'd like to see him now."

"Wait. I will see what I can find."

Not another round of questions, Rose thought, *I cannot bear it.* Her last inquisitor, an elderly man with a tired face and piercing eyes, had taken far too long to accept that she would give him nothing but her name. Now she followed him into an alehouse and down a tiny passageway, halfway between fury and despair. She wanted to rage at him, to insist that she be taken to the prince, yet she knew she was utterly dependent on his good will.

"Please," she said, "I have told you all I can and time presses."

"You shall have your audience," he said. He opened

a door, stepped back, and with a stiff little bow gestured for her to enter.

The squalid little chamber was stifling and the stench of it made her empty stomach twist uncomfortably. It took her a moment to realize she was not alone. A clerk sat at a tiny writing table in the corner, quill scratching frantically. He looked up briefly when she entered, then lowered his head over his work.

She sat down on a stool, folded her hands, stiffened her spine, and lifted her chin. After several minutes her neck began to ache and her stomach grumbled noisily. She cast a quick, embarrassed glance at the clerk, but he was oblivious to everything but his work.

You'd think a prince's clerk would have offered me at least a cup of water, she thought with an inward sniff, *let alone a crust of bread.*

Standing, she paced the chamber. It only took a moment to go from end to end. A single glance was enough to show her four bare walls of rough planks, a bare floor, and a straw mattress on a wooden frame. Her silent companion still wrote on. He was youngish, perhaps a year or two older than her own twenty-four, dressed in sober black, light hair combed neatly back.

She sidled closer, peering sideways at the page he was writing. A black sleeve moved to block her view.

"Good day," he said, though he did not look up again and the quill did not so much as pause.

"And to you," she answered with a sigh, retreating to her seat again and fixing her eyes expectantly on the door.

Any moment now it would open and the Prince of Venya would stand before her in the flesh. Her heart gave a nervous lurch. He was the hero of a hundred songs and stories, the sorcerer pirate whose name struck terror into every captain on the nine seas. Bold and dashing, wily and clever, the Prince of Venya was as deadly to his foes as he was loyal to his followers. It was widely sung that a single smile had the power to melt a woman's bones within her flesh.

Not that Rose wanted her bones melted, if such a thing were even possible. All she wanted was one small favor. Surely that was not too much to ask of the Prince of Venya, the living embodiment of every chivalric ideal!

"Your Highness," she would say firmly, "you must help me."

No, that wouldn't do. She had a feeling that a pirate— let alone a prince—did not take orders well.

"Venya and Valinor were once allies. Now I offer you a new alliance, one that will work to your advantage."

She nibbled at her thumbnail. That sounded well. The only trouble was, it was a lie. The moment he asked *how* it would work to his advantage, all would be lost. Perhaps something a bit more spirited would catch his interest.

"What ho, Your Highness, Rose of Valinor here. Damned if I'm not in a bit of a spot. Long story—uncle hates me—think he wants me dead. What say you play the hero and get me to Sorlain?"

She groaned, starting on another nail. Spirited, yes. But she doubted idiotic would appeal to him.

"I am Rose of Valinor and I am fleeing for my life. Venya and Valinor were allies for many years and the breaking of that alliance is something I regret with all my heart. Venyans have ever acted with honor toward my people; for that I dare appeal to you to help me to Sorlain."

Yes. That was it. Calm, dignified, yet spirited—if only she could remember it. She drew a breath and closed her eyes.

"Your Highness," she murmured. "I am Rose of Valinor and—and—oh, bloody hell, I've forgotten it already. Where in blazes is he?"

"I'm sorry?"

Her head whipped toward the clerk. "Listen, can you possibly hurry things up a bit? I haven't got all day."

"Nor have I. Your pardon, lady, but the letter could not wait."

For a clerk, his voice was oddly cultured, the words tinged with an accent she could not quite define.

He stood and stepped from behind the writing table. He was clad entirely in black, but now that she saw him fully, she could not call it sober. His flowing shirt was unlaced halfway down his chest and tucked into a pair of sable breeches that clung to the hard muscles of his thighs. Bare feet were silent on the wooden floor as he approached.

This is no mere clerk, she thought uneasily. He must be one of the prince's men. She swallowed hard and sat a little straighter. The Prince of Venya might commit acts of piracy, but he had been driven to such desperate measures by cruel necessity. At heart, he was no pirate, but a nobleman. What she had not considered was that his crew—even his clerk—would be the real thing.

A thin white scar, very prominent against his sun-bronzed skin, ran down one cheek; another through an eyebrow. A gold ring glittered in his ear. Looking into that hard young face, Rose sensed instinctively that this man knew more about survival than she could ever hope to learn.

Or wanted to.

She swallowed hard and stood, taking a step back as he continued to advance. The stool overturned with a small clatter that she barely noticed. Another step and her back was to the wall.

"I suppose an introduction is in order," he said, sweeping her a bow that no courtier could have bettered for its grace. There was nothing of the humble clerk about him now. How could she have ever been so blind as to mistake this man for a servant?

Stupid, credulous fool, she raged at herself, *they never meant for me to see the prince at all. I have been tricked, trapped . . . and sold? Oh, Jehan, not that, not sold. Not me!* But why not her? It happened every day, women carried off by pirates and never seen again. *At least now I'll know what becomes of them,* she thought. She almost laughed, but the sound tangled in her throat and came out as a gasping sob.

She shot a desperate glance toward the door, praying that even now the prince would walk in and rescue her. But that hope died when the pirate spoke again.

"Florian of Venya at your service."

Elizabeth English is a technical writer and editor. She has penned several short stories. She is also the author of *The Border Bride* and *Laird of the Mist*. She lives in Pennsylvania.

> *I love to hear from my readers.*
> *Please write to me at*
> *P.O. Box 539*
> *Kimberton, PA 19442*

Berkley Books proudly presents

Berkley Sensation

a brand-new romance line
featuring today's best-loved authors—
and tomorrow's hottest up-and-comers!

Every month…
Four sensational writers.

Every month…
Four sensational new romances
from historical to contemporary,
suspense to cozy.

To sign up for the romance newsletter,
visit www.penguin.com